Praise for *334:*

"Disch is a phenomenal young writer in that he
is totally in control of what he is writing. His
prose has a hard glittering surface that covers
immense depths of perception and of imagery
. . . 334 is one of the best Science Fiction
novels ever."

—D. G. Hartwell in *Crawdaddy*.

334

THOMAS M. DISCH
334

Carroll & Graf Publishers, Inc.
New York

Published by arrangement with The Karpfinger Agency

First Carroll & Graf edition 1987

Carroll & Graf Publishers, Inc.
260 Fifth Avenue
New York, NY 10001

ISBN: 0-88184-340-7

Manufactured in the United States of America

For Jerry Mundis,
who lived here.

CONTENTS

334

PART I: LIES

PART II: TALK

PART III: MRS. HANSON

PART IV: LOTTIE

PART V: SHRIMP

PART VI: 2026

THE DEATH OF SOCRATES

1.

There was a dull ache, a kind of hollowness, in the general area of his liver—the seat of the intelligence according to the Psychology of Aristotle—a feeling that there was someone inside his chest blowing up a balloon or that his body was that balloon. Stuck here at this desk, it tethered him. It was a swollen gum he must again and again be probing with his tongue or his finger. Yet it wasn't, exactly, the same as being sick. There was no name for it.

Professor Ohrengold was telling them about Dante. Blah, blah, blah, born in 1265. *1265* he wrote in his notebook.

His legs ached from sitting forever on this bench—there was something definite.

And Milly—that was about as definite as you could get. *I may die,* he thought (though it wasn't exactly thinking). *I may die of a broken heart.*

Professor Ohrengold became a messy painting. Birdie stretched his legs out into the aisle, locking his knees tight and firming the thighs. He yawned. Pocahontas gave him a dirty look. He smiled.

And Professor Ohrengold was back again with "Gibble-gabble Rauschenberg and blah, blah, the hell that Dante describes is time-less. It is the hell that each of us holds inside his own most secret soul."

Shit, Birdie thought to himself, with great precision.

It was all a pile of shit. He wrote *Shit* in his notebook, then made the letters look three-dimensional and shaded their sides carefully. It wasn't as though this were really education. General Studies Annexe was a joke for the regular Barnard students. Milly'd said so. Sugar on the bitter pill of something-or-other. Chocolate-covered shit.

Now Ohrengold was telling them about Florence and the Popes and such, and then he disappeared. "Okay, what is simony?" the proctor asked. No one volunteered. The proctor shrugged and turned the lecture on again. There was a picture of someone's feet burning.

He was listening but it didn't make any sense. Actually he wasn't listening. He was trying to draw Milly's face in his notebook, only he couldn't draw very well. Except skulls. He could draw very convincing skulls, snakes, eagles, Nazi airplanes. Maybe he should have gone to art school. He turned Milly's face into a skull with long blond hair. He felt sick.

He felt sick to his stomach. Maybe it was the candy bar he'd had in place of hot lunch. He didn't eat a balanced diet. A mistake. Half his life he'd been eating in cafeterias and sleeping in dorms. It was a hell of a way to live. He needed a home life, regularity. He needed a good solid fuck. When he married Milly they'd have twin beds, a two-room apartment all their own and one of the rooms with just those two beds. He imagined Milly in her spiffy little hostess uniform. Then with his eyes closed he began undressing her in his head. First the little blue jacket with the PanAm monogram over the right breast. Then he popped the snap at the waist and unzipped the zipper. The skirt slithered down over the smooth Antron of the slip. Pink. No—*black,* with lace along the hem. Her blouse was an old-fashioned kind, with lots of buttons. He tried to imagine unbuttoning the buttons one by one, but Ohrengold chose just then to crack one of his dumb jokes. Ha, ha. He looked and there was Liz Taylor from his course last year in History of the Cinema, huge pink boobs and hair that was blue string.

"Cleopatra," said Ohrengold, "and Francesca da Rimini are here because their sin was least."

Rimini was a town somewhere in Italy, so here once again was the map of Italy.

Italy, Shitaly.

What the hell was he supposed to care about this kind of crap? Who *cares* when Dante was born? Maybe he was *never* born. What difference did it make to *him,* to Birdie Ludd?

None.

He should come right out and ask Ohrengold *that* question, lay it on the line to him, straight. But you can't talk to a teevee screen and that's what Ohrengold was—flickering dots. He wasn't even alive anymore, the proctor had said. Another goddamn dead expert on another goddamn cassette.

It was ridiculous: Dante, Florence, "symbolic punishments" (which was what trusty old Pocahontas was writing down that moment in her trusty old notebook). This wasn't the fucking Middle Ages. This was the fucking 21st Century, and he was Birdie Ludd and he was in love and he was lonely and he was unemployed (and probably unemployable, too) and there wasn't a thing he could do, not a goddamn thing, or a single place to turn to in the whole goddamn stinking country.

What if Milly didn't *need* him any more?

The hollow feeling in his chest swelled. He tried easing it away by thinking of the buttons on the imaginary blouse, the warm body beneath, his Milly. He did feel sick. He ripped the sheet with the skull out of his notebook. He folded it in half, tore it neatly along the crease. He repeated this process until the pieces were too small to tear any further, then put them in his shirt pocket.

Pocahontas was watching him with a dirty smile that said what the poster said on the wall: Paper is valuable. Don't waste it! Pocahontas's button was Ecology and Birdie had pushed it. He counted on her notebook for the finals, so he smiled a soft pardon-me at her. He had a very nice smile. Everyone was always pointing out what a bright, warm smile he had. His only real problem was his nose, which was short.

Ohrengold was replaced by the logo for the course—a naked man trapped inside a square and a circle—and the proctor, who could have cared less, asked if there were any questions. Much to everyone's suprise Pocahontas got to her feet and sputtered something about what? About Jews, Birdie gathered. He disliked Jews.

"Could you repeat your questions?" the proctor said. "Some of those in back couldn't hear."

"Well, if I understood Dr. Ohrengold, it said that the first circle was for people who weren't baptised. They hadn't *done* anything wrong—they just were born too *soon.*"

"That's right."

"Well, it doesn't seem *fair* to me."

"Yes?"

"I mean, *I* wasn't baptised."

"Nor was I," said the proctor.

"Then according to Dante we'd both go to hell."

"Yes, that's so."

"It doesn't seem fair." Her whine had risen to a squeak.

Some people were laughing, some people were getting up. The proctor raised her hand. "There'll be a test."

Birdie groaned, the very first.

"What I mean is," she persisted, "that if it's anyone's *fault* that they're born one way and not another it should be *God's.*"

"That's a good point," the proctor said. "I don't know if there's any answer to it. Sit down, please. We'll have a short comprehension test now."

Two old monitors began distributing markers and answer sheets.

Birdie's bad feelings became particular, and it helped to have a reason for his misery that he could share with everyone else.

The lights dimmed and the first multiple choice appeared on the screen: 1. Dante Alighieri was born in (a) 1300 (b) 1265 (c) 1625 (d) Date unknown.

Pocahontas was covering up her answers, the dog. So, when was fucking Dante born? He remembered writing the date in his notebook but he didn't remember what it had been. He looked back at the four choices but the second question was already on the screen. He scratched a mark in the (c) space, then erased it, feeling an obscure sense of unluckiness in the choice, but finally he checked that space anyhow.

The fourth question was on the screen. The answers he had to choose from were all names he'd never seen and the question didn't make any sense. Disgusted, he marked (c) for every question and carried his paper up to the monitor guarding the door, who wouldn't let him out anyhow until the test was over. He stood there scowling at all the other dumb assholes scratching their wrong answers on the answer sheets.

The bell rang. Everyone breathed a sigh of relief.

334 East 11th Street was one of twenty units, none identical and all alike, built in the pre-Squeeze affluent '80's under the first federal MODICUM program. An aluminum flagpole and a concrete bas-relief representing the address decorated the main entrance just off 1st Avenue. Otherwise the building was plain. One night many years ago the Tenants' Council, as a kind of protest, had managed to knock off a segment of the monolithic "4," but by and large (assuming that the trees and prosperous shopfronts had been no more than polite fictions to begin with) the original renderings published in the *Times* were still a good likeness. Architecturally 334 was on a par with the pyramids—it had dated very little and it hadn't aged at all.

Inside its skin of glass and yellow brick a population of three thousand, plus or minus (but excluding temps), occupied the 812 apartments (40 to a floor, plus 12 at street level, behind the shops), which was not much more than 30 per cent above the Agency's original optimum of 2,250. So, realistically, it could be regarded as a fair success in this respect as well. Certainly there were worse places people were willing to live in especially if you were, and Birdie Ludd was, temporary.

Right now, at half past seven of a Thursday night, Birdie was temporary on the sixteenth-floor landing, two floors down from the Holt apartment. Milly's father wasn't home, but he hadn't been asked in anyway, so here he was freezing his ass and listening to someone yelling at someone else about money or sex. ("Money or sex" was a running gag on some comedy show Milly was always playing back to him. "Money or sex—that's what it all boils down to." Yuck, yuck.) Meanwhile someone else again was telling them to shut up, far off and nonstop, like an airplane circling the park, a baby was being murdered. HERE'S MY LOVE, a radio sang. HERE'S MY LOVE. IF YOU TAKE IT APART, I MAY DIE. I MAY DIE OF A BROKEN HEART. Number Three in the nation. It had been going through Birdie's head all day, all week.

Before Milly he'd never believed that love was anything more complicated or awful than just getting goodies. Even the first couple months with her had only been the usual goodies with a topping. But now any damned dumb song on the radio, even the ads sometimes, could tear him to pieces.

The song snapped off and the people stopped yelling and Birdie heard, below, slow footsteps mounting toward him. It had to be Milly—the feet touched each step with the crisp whack of a woman's low-heeled shoe—and a lump began to form in his throat—of love, of fear, of pain, of everything but happiness. If it were Milly, what would he say to her? But, oh, if it weren't. . . .

He opened his textbook and pretended to be reading, smearing the page with the muck he'd got on his hand when he'd tried to open the window onto the utility shaft. He wiped the rest off on his pants.

It wasn't Milly. Some old lady lugging a bag of groceries. She stopped half a flight below him on the landing, leaning against the handrail, and set down her bag with an "oof." A stick of Oraline was stuck in the corner of her mouth with a premium button on it, a trick mandala that seemed to spin as she moved, like a runaway clock. She looked at Birdie, and Birdie scowled down at the bad reproduction of David's *Death of Socrates* in his book. The flaccid lips formed themselves into a smile.

"Studying?" the woman asked.

"Yeah, that's what I'm doing all right. I'm studying."

"That's good." She took the pale-green stick out of her mouth, holding it like a thermometer, to study what was gone and what was left of her ten metered minutes. Her smile tightened, as though she were elaborating some joke, honing it to an edge. "It's good," she said at last, with almost a chuckle, "for a young man to study."

The radio returned with the new Ford commercial. It was one of Birdie's favorites, so lighthearted but at the same time solid. He wished the old witch would shut up so he could hear it.

"You can't get anywhere these days without studying." Birdie made no reply.

She took a different tack. "These stairs," she said.

Birdie looked up from his book, peeved. "What about them?"

"What about them! The elevators have been out of commission for weeks. That's what about them. Weeks!"

"So?"

"So, why don't they fix the elevators? But just try to talk to the area office and get an answer to a question like that and see what happens. Nothing, that's what happens."

He wanted to tell her to rinse her hair. She talked like she'd spent all her life in a coop or something instead of the crummy subsidized slum tattooed all over her face. According to Milly it had been years, not weeks, since the elevators in any of these buildings had been working.

With a look of disgust he slid over toward the wall so the old lady could get past him. She walked up three steps till her face was just level with his. She smelled of beer and spearmint and old age. He hated old people. He hated their wrinkled faces and the touch of their cold dry flesh. It was because there were so many *old* people that Birdie Ludd couldn't get married to the girl he loved and have a family of his own. It was a goddamned injustice.

"What are you studying about?"

Birdie glanced down at the painting. He read the caption, which he had not read before. "That's Socrates," he said, remembering dimly something his Civilization teacher last year had said about Socrates. "It's a painting," he explained. "A Greek painting."

"You going to be an artist? Or what?"

"What," Birdie shot back.

"You're Milly Holt's fellow, aren't you?" He didn't reply. "You waiting down here for her to come home?"

"Is there any law against waiting for someone?"

The old lady laughed right in his face, and it was like sticking your nose inside a dead cunt. Then she made her way from step to step up to the next landing. Birdie tried not to turn around to look after her but he couldn't help himself. Their eyes clinched, and she laughed again. Finally he had to ask her what she was laughing about. "Is there a law against laughing?" she asked right back. Then her laughing disintegrated into a cough right out of some old Health Education movie about the dangers of smoking. He wondered if maybe she was an addict. She was old enough. Birdie's father, who had to be ten years younger than her, smoked tobacco whenever he could get any. Birdie thought it was a waste of money but only slightly disgusting. Milly, on the other hand, loathed it, especially in women.

Somewhere glass shattered, and somewhere children shot at each other—Acka! Ackitta! Ack!—and fell down screaming in a game of gorilla warfare. Birdie peered down into the abyss of the stairwell. A hand touched a railing far below, paused, lifted, touched the railing, approaching him. The fingers were slim (as Milly's would be) and the nails seemed to be painted gold. In the dim light, at this distance, it was hard to tell. A sudden surge of unbelieving hope made him forget the old woman's laughter, the stench, the screaming; the stairwell became a scene of romance, a mist of slow motion. The hand lifted and paused and touched the railing.

The first time he'd come to Milly's apartment he'd walked up these stairs behind her, watching her tight little ass shift to the right, to the left, to the right, and the tinsel fringes on her street shorts shivering and sparkling like a liquor-store display. All the way to the top she hadn't looked back once.

At the eleventh or the twelfth floor the hand left the railing and didn't reappear. So it hadn't been Milly after all.

He had a hard-on just from remembering. He unzipped and reached in to give it a couple half-hearted strokes but it was gone before he could get started.

He looked at his guaranteed Timex watch. Eight, on the dot. He could afford to wait two more hours. Then, if he didn't want to pay a full fare on the subway, it was a forty-minute walk back to his dorm. If he hadn't been on probation because of his grades, he might have waited all night long.

He sat down to study the History of Art. He stared at the picture of Socrates in the bad light. With one hand he was holding a big cup, with the other he was giving somebody the finger. He didn't seem to be dying at all. The midterm was going to be tomorrow afternoon at two o'clock. He really had to study. He stared at the picture more intently. Why did people paint pictures anyhow? He stared until his eyes hurt.

The baby started up again, zeroing in on Central Park. Some Burmese nationals came barreling down the stairs, gibbering, and a minute later another gang of kids in black masks—U.S. gorillas—came after them, screaming obscenities.

He began to cry. He was certain, though he wouldn't admit it yet in so many words, that Milly was cheating on him. He loved her so much and she was so beautiful. The last time he'd seen her she'd called him stupid. "You're so stupid, Birdie Ludd," she said, "sometimes you make me sick." But she *was* so beautiful. And he loved her.

A tear fell into Socrates's cup and was absorbed by the cheap paper. He realized that he was crying. He hadn't cried before in all his adult life. His heart had broken.

2.

Birdie had not always been such a droop. Quite the opposite—he'd been friendly as a flower, easygoing, uncomplaining, and a lot of fun. He didn't start a contest going the minute he met you, and when contests were unavoidable he knew how to be a graceful loser. The competitive factor had received little emphasis at P.S. 141 and even less at the center he was moved to after his parents' divorce. A nice guy who got along, that was Birdie.

Then in the summer after his high school graduation, just when the thing with Milly was developing towards total seriousness, he'd been called in to Mr. Mack's office and the bottom had dropped out of his life. Norman Mack was a thin, balding, middle-aged man with a paunch and a Jewish nose, though whether or not he *was* Jewish Birdie could only guess. His chief reason, aside from the nose, for thinking so was that at all of their counseling sessions Birdie got the feeling, which he also got with Jews, that Mr. Mack was toying with him, that his bland, professional good will was a disguise for an unbounded contempt, that all his sound advice was a snare. The pity was that Birdie could not in his very nature help but be caught in it. It was Mr. Mack's game and had to be played by his rules.

"Sit down, Birdie." The first rule.

Birdie had sat down, and Mr. Mack had explained that he'd received a letter from the upstate Regents Office. He handed Birdie a large gray envelope from which Birdie took out a bonanza of papers and forms, and the gist of it was—Birdie tucked the papers back inside—that Birdie had been reclassified.

"But I've taken the tests, Mr. Mack! Four years ago. And I *passed*."

"I've called Albany to make certain this wasn't the result of a crossed wire somewhere. And it wasn't. The letter—"

"Look!" He reached for his wallet, took out his card. "Look, it says there, right in black and white—twenty-seven."

Mr. Mack took the frayed card with a sympathetic sucking of his cheeks. "Well, Birdie, I'm sorry to say that your *new* card says twenty-four."

"One point? For one point you're going to—" He couldn't bring himself even to think of what it was they were going to do. "Oh, Mr. Mack!"

"I know, Birdie. Believe me, I'm as sorry as you are."

"I took their goddamn tests and I *passed* them."

"As you know, Birdie, there are other factors to be weighed besides the test scores, and one of those *has* changed. Your father, it seems, has come down with diabetes."

"That's the first I've heard of it."

"It's possible that your father doesn't know himself yet. The hospitals have an automatic data link with the Regents system, which in turn mailed you that letter automatically."

"But what does my father have to do with anything?"

Over the years Birdie's relationship with his father had been whittled down to a voice on the phone on holidays and a perfunctory visit to the federal flophouse on 16th Street an average of four times a year, on which occasions Mr. Ludd would be issued meal vouchers for an outside restaurant. Family life was the single greatest cohesive force in any society, and so, willy-nilly, the MODICUM people tried to keep families together, even families as tenuous as one father and one son eating lasagna at twelve-week intervals at The Sicilian Vespers. His father? Birdie almost had to laugh.

Mr. Mack explained first of all that there was nothing to be ashamed of. A full 2½ % of the population scored under 25, or over twelve million people. A low score didn't make Birdie a freak, it didn't debar him from any of his civil rights, it only meant, as of course he knew, that he would not be allowed to father children, either directly, through marriage, or indirectly, by artificial insemination. He wanted to make certain that Birdie understood this. *Did* Birdie understand this?

Yes. He did.

Brightening, Mr. Mack pointed out that it was still quite possible—probable even, considering he was right on the borderline—to be reclassified again: up. Patiently, point by point, he went over with Birdie the components of his Regents score, indicating the ways he could hope to add to his score as well as the ways he couldn't.

Diabetes was a hereditary disease. Treatment was costly and could continue for years. The original proposers of the Act had wanted to put diabetes on a par with hemophilia and the XYY gene. That was rather Draconian but surely Birdie could understand why a genetic drift towards diabetes had to be discouraged.

Surely. He could.

Then there was the other unfortunate matter concerning his father—that, during the past decade, he had been actively employed less than 50 per cent of the time. At first sight it might seem unfair to penalize Birdie for his father's carefree life-style, but statistics showed this trait tended to be quite as heritable as, say, intelligence.

The old antithesis of heredity versus environment! But before Birdie protested too strongly he should look at the next item on his sheet. Mr. Mack tapped it with his pencil. Now here was a curious illustration of history at work. The Revised Genetics Testing Act had finally gone through the Senate in 2011 as a result of the so-called Jim Crow Compromise, and here was that compromise virtually breathing down Birdie's neck, for the five points he'd lost through his father's unemployment pattern he'd gained back by being a Negro!

On the physical scale Birdie had scored 9, which placed

him at the modal point, or peak, of the normal curve. Mr. Mack made a little joke at his own expense concerning the score *he* would probably have got on the physical scale. Birdie could ask for a new physical but it was rare that anyone's score on this scale went up, while only too often it sank. For instance, in Birdie's case, the least tendency towards hypoglycemia might now, in view of his father's diabetes, drop him altogether out of reach of the cutoff point. Didn't it seem best, then, to leave well enough alone?

It did seem best.

Mr. Mack could feel more hopeful about the other two tests, the Stanford-Binet (Short Form) and the Skinner-Waxman Scale. Birdie had not done badly on these (7 and 6), but he had not done very well either. People often improved dramatically a second time around. A headache, anxiety, even indifference—there are so many things that can get in the way of a top mental performance. Four years was a long time, but did Birdie have any reason to believe he *hadn't* done as well as he might have?

He did! He remembered wanting to complain about it at the time, but since he'd passed the tests he hadn't bothered. The day of the test a sparrow had got into the auditorium. It kept flying witlessly back and forth, back and forth, from one sealed window to the other. Who could concentrate with that going on?

They decided that Birdie would apply to be retested on both the Stanford-Binet and the Skinner-Waxman. If for any reason he wasn't feeing confident on the date the Regents office slotted him into, he could take a rain check. Mr. Mack thought that Birdie would find everyone ready to bend over backward.

The problem appeared to be solved and Birdie was ready to go, but Mr. Mack was obliged, for form's sake, to go over one or two more details. Beyond hereditary factors and the Regents tests, both of which measured potentiality, there was another group of components for accomplishment. Any exceptional service for the country or the economy was an automatic twenty-five points but this was hardly anything to count on. Similarly, a demonstration of physical, intellectual, or creative abilities markedly above the levels indicated by et cetera, et cetera.

Birdie thought they could skip that too.

But here, beneath the eraser, here *was* something to consider—the educational component. Already Birdie had five points for finishing high school. If he were to go on to college—

Out of the question. Birdie wasn't the college type. He wasn't anybody's fool, but on the other hand he wasn't anybody's Isaac Einstein.

In general Mr. Mack would have applauded the realism of such a decision, but in the present circumstances it was better not to burn bridges. Any New York City resident had a right to attend any of the colleges in the city, either as a regular student or, lacking certain prerequisites, in a General Studies Annexe. It was something for Birdie to bear in mind.

Mr. Mack felt terrible. He hoped Birdie would learn to look at his reclassification as a setback rather than a permanent defeat. Failure was only a point of view.

Birdie agreed, but even this wasn't enough to obtain his release. Mr. Mack urged Birdie to consider the question of contraception and genetics in the broadest possible light. Already there were too many people for the available resources. Without some system of voluntary limitation there would be more, more, disastrously more. Mr. Mack hoped that eventually Birdie would come to see that the Regents system, for all its obvious drawbacks, was both desirable and necessary.

Birdie promised to try and look at it this way, and then he could go.

Among the papers in the gray envelope was a pamphlet, "Your Regents," put out by the National Educational Council, who said that the only effective way to prepare for his reexamination was to develop a confident, lively frame of mind. A month later Birdie kept his appointment on Centre Street in a confident, lively frame of mind. Only afterward, sitting by the fountain in the plaza discussing the tests with his fellow martyrs, did he realize that this had been Friday, July 13th. Jinxed! He didn't have to wait for the special delivery letter to know his score was a cherry, an apple, and a banana. Even so, the letter was a mind-staggerer. He'd gone down one point on the I.Q. test; on the Skinner-Waxman Creativity

Scale he'd sunk to a moron-level score of 4. His new total: 21.

The 4 riled him. The first part of the Skinner-Waxman test had involved picking the funniest punch line from four multiple choices, and ditto the best endings to stories. This much he remembered from before but then they took him into a weird empty room. Two pieces of rope were hanging from the ceiling and Birdie was given a pliers and told to tie the two ropes together. You weren't allowed to pull the ropes off their hooks.

It was impossible. If you held the very end of one rope in your hand, you couldn't possibly get hold of the other rope, even by fishing for it with your toe. The extra few inches advantage you got from the pliers was no help at all. He was about ready to scream by the end of the ten minutes. There were three more impossible problems but by then he was only going through the motions.

At the fountain some jerkoff boy genius explained what they all could have done: tie the pliers to the end of one string and set it swinging like a pendulum; then go and get—

"Do you know what I'd like to see," Birdie said, interrupting the boy genius, "tied up and swinging from that ceiling? Huh, schmuck? *You!*"

Which the others agreed was a better joke than any of their multiple choices.

Only after he'd lucked out on the tests did he tell Milly about his reclassification. A coolness had come into their love affair about then, just a cloud across the sun, but Birdie had been afraid all the same what her reaction might be, the names he might be called. As it turned out, Milly was heroic, all tenderness, concern, and stouthearted resolve. She hadn't realized before, she cried, how much she did love, and need, Birdie. She loved him *more* now, because— But she didn't have to explain: it was in their faces, in their eyes, Birdie's brown and glistening, Milly's hazel flecked with gold. She promised to stand by him through the whole ordeal. Diabetes! And not even his own diabetes! The more she thought about it the angrier she got, the more determined never to let some Moloch of a bureaucracy play God with her and Birdie. (Moloch?)

If Birdie was willing to go to Barnard G.S.A., Milly was willing to wait for him as long as need be.

Four years, as it turned out. The point system was gimmicked so that each year only counted half a point until graduation, but that was worth 4. Had Birdie been content with his old Regents scores, he could have worked his way back up to 25 in two years. Now he'd actually have to go for a degree.

But he did love Milly, and he did want to marry Milly, and let them say what they like, a marriage isn't a marriage unless you can have children.

He went to Barnard. What choice had there been?

3.

On the morning of the day of his Art History test Birdie lay in bed in the empty Annexe dorm, drowsing and thinking about love. He couldn't get back to sleep, but he didn't want to get up yet either. His body was bursting with energy, full to the top and flowing over, but it wasn't energy for getting up to brush his teeth or going down to breakfast. Anyhow it was too late for breakfast and he was happy where he was.

Sunlight spilled in through the south window. A breeze rustled outdated announcements pinned to the bulletin board, spun round a shirt that hung on a curtain rail, touched the down on the back of Birdie's hand, where her name was now just a faded smudge inside a ballpoint heart. Birdie laughed with a sense of his own fullness and the promise of good weather. He turned over on his left side, letting the blanket slide to the floor. The window framed a perfect blue rectangle of sky. Beautiful! It was March but it might have been April or May. It was going to be a wonderful day, a wonderful spring. He could feel it in the muscles of his chest and the muscles of his stomach when he took a breath of air.

Spring! Then summer. Breezes. No shirts.

Last summer out at Great Kills Harbor, the hot sand, the sea breeze in Milly's hair. Again and again her hand would lift to push it back, like a veil. What had they talked about all that day? Everything. About the future. About her rotten father. Milly was desperate to get away from 334 and live her own life. Now, with her airline job, she had the option of a dorm, though, not being as used to a communal life as Birdie was, it was hard for her. But soon, soon. . . .

Summer. Walking with her, a snake dance through the other bodies spread out across the sand, lawns of flesh. Rubbing the lotion into her. Summer Magic. His hand slithering. Nothing definite and then it *would* be definite, as daylight. As though the whole world were having sex, the sea and the sky and everyone. They'd be puppies and they'd be pigs. The air would fill up with the sound of songs, a hundred at a time. At such moments he knew what it must be like to be a composer or a great musician. He became a giant, swollen with greatness. A time bomb.

The clock on the wall said 11:07. *This is my lucky day:* he made it a promise. He threw himself out of bed and did ten push-ups on the tile floor, still damp from its morning mopping. Then ten more. After the last push-up Birdie rested on the floor, his lips pressed against the cool, moist tile. He had a hard-on.

He grabbed it, closing his eyes. Milly! Your eyes. O Milly, I love you. Milly, O Milly, O Milly. So much! Milly's arms. The small of her back. Bending back. Milly, don't leave me! Milly? Love me? I!

He came in a smooth, spread-open flow till his fingers were covered with semen, and the back of his hand, and the blue heart, and "Milly."

11:35. The Art History test was at two. He'd already missed a ten o'clock field trip for Consumership. Tough.

He wrapped his toothbrush, his Crest, his razor, and foam in a towel and went to what had been, in the days when the Annexe was an office building, the executive washroom of the actuarial division of New York Life. The music started when he opened the door: SLAM, BANG! WHY AM I SO HAPPY?

> Slam, Bang!
> Why am I so happy?
> God Damn,
> I don't really know.

He decided to wear his white sweater with white Levis and white sneakers. He brushed a whitening agent into his hair, which was natural again. He looked at himself in front of the bathroom mirror. He smiled. The sound system started in on his favorite Ford commercial. Alone in the empty space before the urinals he danced with himself, singing the words of the commercial.

It was a fifteen-minute ride to the South Ferry stop. In the ferry building was a PanAm restaurant where the waitresses wore uniforms just like Milly's. Though he couldn't afford it, he ate lunch there, just the lunch that Milly might be serving that very moment at an altitude of seven thousand feet. He tipped a quarter. Now, except for the token to take him back to the dorm, he was broke. Freedom Now.

He walked along the rows of benches where the old people came to sit every day to look out at the sea while they waited to die. Birdie didn't feel the same hatred for old people this morning that he'd felt last night. Lined up in helpless rows, in the glare of the afternoon sun, they seemed remote, they posed no threats, they didn't matter.

The breeze coming in off the Hudson smelled of salt, oil, and rot. It wasn't a bad smell at all. Invigorating. Maybe if he had lived centuries ago instead of now, he'd have been a sailor. Moments from movies about ships flitted by. He kicked an empty Fun container out through the railing and watched it bob up and down in the green and the black.

The sky roared with jets. Jets heading in every direction. She could have been on any of them. A week ago what had she said. "I'll love you forever." A week ago?

"I'll love you forever." If he'd had a knife he could have carved that on something.

He felt just great. Absolutely.

An old man in an old suit shuffled along the walk, holding on to the sea railing. His face was covered with a thick, curly, white beard, though his head was as bare as a police helmet. Birdie backed from the rail to let him go by.

He stuck his hand in Birdie's face and said, "How about it, Jack?"

Birdie crinkled his nose. "Sorry."

"I need a quarter." A foreign accent. Spanish? No. He reminded Birdie of something, someone.

"So do I."

The bearded man gave him the finger and then Birdie remembered who he looked like. Socrates!

He glanced at his wrist but he'd left his watch in the locker as it hadn't fit in with today's all-white color scheme. He spun round. The gigantic advertising clock on the face of First National Citibank said 2:15. That wasn't possible. Birdie asked two of the old people on the benches if that was the right time. Their watches agreed.

There was no use trying to get to the test now. Without quite knowing why, Birdie smiled. He breathed a sigh of relief and sat down to watch the ocean.

In June there was the usual family reunion at The Sicilian Vespers. Birdie polished off his tray without paying too much attention to either the food or the story his dad was dawdling over, something about someone at 16th Street who'd opted for Room 7, after which it was discovered that he had been a Catholic priest. Mr. Ludd seemed upset. Birdie couldn't tell if it was the idea of Room 7 or the idea of having to cut down his intake because of the diabetes. Finally, to give the old guy a chance at his noodles, Birdie told him about the essay project Mr. Mack had arranged, even though (as Mr. Mack had pointed out and pointed out) Birdie's problems and his papers belonged to Barnard G.S.A., not to P.S. 141. In other words, this would be Birdie's *last chance*, but that could be, if Birdie would let it, a source of motivation. And he let it.

"And you're going to write a book?"

"Goddamn, Dad, will you *listen?*"

Mr. Ludd shrugged, wound the food on his fork, and listened.

What Birdie had to do to climb back to 25 was demonstrate abilities markedly above the abilities he'd demonstrated back on that Friday the 13th. Mr. Mack had gone over the various components of his profile, and since he'd scored most on Verbal Skills they decided that his best bet would be to write something. When Birdie asked what, Mr. Mack had given him, to keep, a copy of *By Their Bootstraps*.

Birdie reached under the bench where he'd set it down when they came in. He held it up for his dad to see: *By Their Bootstraps*. Edited and with an Introduction (encouraging but not too clear) by Lucille Mortimer Randolph-Clapp. Lucille Mortimer Randolph-Clapp was the architect of the Regents system.

The last string of spaghetti was wound and eaten. Reverently Mr. Ludd touched his spoontip to the skin of the spumoni. Holding back from that first taste, he asked, "And so they're paying you money just to . . . ?"

"Five hundred dollars. Ain't it a bitch. They call it a stipend. It's supposed to last me three months but I don't know about that. My rent at Mott Street isn't so bad, but other things."

"They're crazy."

"It's the system they have. You see, I need time to develop my ideas."

"The whole system's crazy. Writing! You can't write a book."

"Not a *book*. Just a story, an essay, something like that. It doesn't have to be more than a page or two. It says in the book that the best stuff usually is very . . . I forget the exact word but it means short. You should read some of the crap that got past. Poetry and stuff where every other word is something foul. I mean, *really* foul. But there's some okay things, too. One guy that didn't finish eighth grade wrote a story about working on an alligator preserve. In Florida. And philosophy. There was this one girl who was blind *and* crippled. I'll show you." Birdie found the place where'd he left off: "My Philosophy" by Delia Hunt. He read the first paragraph aloud:

"Sometimes I'd like to be a huge philosophy, and sometimes I'd like to come along with a big axe and chop myself down. If I heard somebody calling out Help, Help! I could just sit there on the trunk and think, I guess *somebody's* in trouble. But not me, because I'm sitting here looking at the rabbits and so on running and jumping. I guess *they're* trying to get away from the smoke. But I would just sit there on my philosophy and think, Well, I guess the forest is really on fire now."

Mr. Ludd, involved in his spumoni, only nodded pleasantly. He refused to be bewildered by anything he heard
or make protests or try to understand why things never
worked out the way he planned. If people wanted him to
do one thing he'd do it. If they wanted him to do something else he'd do that. No questions asked. *La vida,* as
Delia Hunt also observed, *es un sueño.*

Later, walking back to 16th Street, his father said, "You
know what you should do, don't you?"

"What?"

"Use some of that money they gave you and get somebody really smart to write the thing for you."

"Can't. They got computers that can tell if you do that."

"They do?" Mr. Ludd sighed.

A couple blocks further on he asked to borrow ten
dollars for some Fadeout. It was a traditional part of
their reunions and traditionally Birdie would have said no,
but having just been bragging about his stipend? He had
to.

"I hope you're able to be a better father than I've
been," Mr. Ludd said, putting the folded-up bill into his
card-carrier.

"Yeah. Well, I hope so, too."

They both got a chuckle out of that.

Next morning, following the single piece of advice he'd
been able to get out of the advisor he'd paid twenty-five
dollars for, Birdie made his first solo visit (years ago he'd
been marched through the uptown branch with a few
dozen other fourth graders) to the National Library. The
Nassau branch was housed in an old wrapped-glass building a little to the west of the central Wall Street area.
The place was a honeycomb of research booths, except
for the top floor, 28, which was given over to the cables
connecting Nassau to the uptown branch and then, by
relays, to every other major library outside of France,
Japan, and South America. A page who couldn't have
been much older than Birdie showed him how to use the
dial-and-punch system. When the page was gone Birdie
stared glumly at the blank viewing screen. The only thought
in his head was how he'd like to smash in the screen
with his fist: dial and *punch!*

After a hot lunch in the basement of the library he felt better. He recalled Socrates waving his arms in the air and the blind girl's essay on philosophy. He put out a call for the five best books on Socrates written at a senior high school level and began reading from them at random.

Later that night Birdie finished reading the chapter in Plato's *Republic* that contains the famous parable of the cave. Dazedly, dazzled, he wandered through the varied brightnesses of Wall Street's third shift. Even after twelve o'clock the streets and plazas were teeming. He wound up in a corridor full of vending machines, sipping a hot Koffee, staring at the faces around him, wondering did any of them—the woman glued to the *Times,* the old messengers chattering—suspect the truth? Or were they, like the poor prisoners in the cave, turned to the rockface, watching shadows, never imagining that somewhere outside there was a sun, a sky, a whole world of crushing beauty?

He'd never understood before about beauty—that it was more than a breeze coming in through the window or the curve of Milly's breasts. It wasn't a matter of how he, Birdie Ludd, felt or what he wanted. It was there inside of things, glowing. Even the dumb vending machines. Even the blind faces.

He remembered the vote of the Athenian Senate to put Socrates to death. Corrupting the youth, ha! He hated the Athenian Senate but it was a different sort of hate from the kind he was used to. He hated them for a reason: Justice!

Beauty. Justice. Truth. Love, too, probably. Somewhere there was an explanation for everything. A meaning. It all made sense. It wasn't just a lot of words.

He went outside. New emotions kept passing over him faster than he could take account of them, like huge speeded-up clouds. One moment, looking at his face reflected in the darkened window of a specialty food shop, he wanted to laugh out loud. The next moment, remembering the young prostitute in the room downstairs from where he lived now, lying on her shabby bed in a peekaboo dress, he wanted to cry. It seemed to Birdie that he could see the pain and hopelessness of her whole life as clearly as if her past and future were a physical object in front of him, a statue in the park.

He stood alone beside the sea-railing in Battery Park. Dark waves lapped at the concrete shore. Signal lights blinked on and off, red and green, white and white, as they moved past the stars toward Central Park.

Beauty? The idea seemed too slight now. Something beyond beauty was involved in all of this. Something that chilled him in ways he couldn't explain. And yet he was exhilarated, too. His newly-awakened soul battled against letting this feeling, this principle, slip away from him unnamed. Each time, just as he thought he had it, it eluded him. Finally, towards dawn, he went home, temporarily defeated.

Just as he was climbing the stairs to his own room, a gorilla, out of uniform but still recognizably a gorilla, with stars and stripes tattooed across his forehead, came out of Frances Schaap's room. Birdie felt a brief impulse of hatred for him, followed by a wave of compassion for the girl. But tonight he didn't have the time to try and help her, assuming she wanted his help.

He slept fitfully, like a dead body sinking into the water and floating up to the surface. At noon he woke from a dream that stopped just short of being a nightmare. He'd been inside a room with a beamed ceiling. Two ropes hung from the beams. He stood between them, trying to grasp one or the other, but just as he thought he had caught hold of a rope, it would swing away wildly, like a berserk pendulum.

He knew what the dream meant. The ropes were a test of his *creativeness*. That was the principle he'd tried to define last night standing by the water. Creativeness was the key to all his problems. If he would only learn about it, analyze it, he'd be able to solve his problems.

The idea was still hazy in his mind but he knew he was on the right track. He made some cultured eggs and a cup of Koffee for breakfast, then went straight to his booth at the library to study. The tremendous excitement of last night had leaked out of things. Buildings were just buildings. People seemed to move a little faster than usual, but that was all. Even so, he felt terrific. In his whole life he'd never felt as good as he did today. He was free. Or was it something else? One thing he knew for sure: nothing in the past was worth shit, but the future, Ah! the future was blazing with promise.

4.

From:

PROBLEMS OF CREATIVENESS

By Berthold Anthony Ludd

Summary
From ancient times to today we have seen that there is more than one criteria by which the critic analyzes the products of Creativeness. Can we know which of these measures to use? Shall we deal directly with the subject? Or indirectly.

There is another source to study Creativeness in the great drama of the philosopher Wolfgang Gothe, called "The Faust". No one can deny this the undisputed literary pinnacle of "Masterpiece". Yet what motivation can have drawn him to describe Heaven and Hell in this strange way? Who is the Faust if not ourselves. Does this not show a genuine need to achieve communication? Our only answer can be yes.

Thus once more we are led to the problem of Creativeness. All beauty has three conditions: 1, The subject shall be of literary format. 2, All parts are contained within the whole. And 3, The meaning is radiantly clear. True Creativeness is only present when it can be observed in the work of art. This too is the Philosophy of Aristotle that is valid for today.

No, the criteria of Creativeness is not alone sought in the area of "language". Does not the scientist, the prophet, the painter offer his own criteria of judgement toward the same general purpose. Which road shall we choose if this is so? Or is it true, that "All roads lead to Rome". We are more then ever living in a time when it is important to define every citizen's responsibilities.

Another criteria of Creativeness was made by Socrates,

*so cruelly put to death by his own people, and I quote,
"To know nothing is the first condition of all knowledge."
From the wisdom of that great Greek Philosopher may we
not draw our own conclusions concerning these problems?
Creativeness is the ability to see relationships where none
exist.*

5.

While Birdie stayed in bed digging at his toenails,
Frances went down for the mail. Except when she was
at work Birdie more or less lived in her room, his own
having got out of hand during the period when he was
writing his essay. It was not a sexual relationship, though
a couple of times, just to be friendly, Frances had offered and Birdie'd accepted a blow-job, but it had been a
chore for both of them.

What did bring them together, besides sharing a bathroom, was the sad, immovable fact that Frances's Regents score was an absolute 20. Because of some disease
she had. Aside from one kid at P.S. 141 who'd been a kind
of dwarf and almost an idiot, Frances was Birdie's first
personal acquaintance who'd scored lower than he had.
Her own 20 didn't bother her, or she knew enough not
to let it, but for the whole two months Birdie was working
on "Problems of Creativeness" she'd listened to every
draft of every paragraph. If it hadn't been for her constant praise and her getting behind him and pushing
whenever he got depressed and hopeless, he'd never have
seen his way out the other end. It seemed unfair in a
way that, now that he was through, he'd be going back
to Milly. But Frances had said she didn't mind about that
either. Birdie had never known anyone so completely un-
selfish, but she said no, it wasn't that. Helping him had
been her way of fighting the system.

"Well?" he asked, when she came back.

"Nope. Just this." She tossed a postcard onto the
bed. A sunset somewhere with palm trees. For her.

"I didn't think they could write, these guys."

"Jock? Oh, he's always sending me stuff. This—" she

grabbed a handful of her heavy, glittering bathrobe "—came from Japan."

Birdie snorted. He'd meant to buy Frances a present himself, as a token of his appreciation, but his money was gone. He was living, till his letter came, on what he could borrow from her. "He doesn't have much to say for himself."

"No, I suppose not." She sounded down. Before she'd gone to get the mail, she'd been happy as an ad. The postcard must have meant more than she'd let on. Maybe she was in love with this Jock. Though back in June, on the night of their first heart-to-heart drunk, after he'd told her about Milly, she'd said that she was still waiting for the real thing to come along.

Whatever it was, he decided, he wasn't going to let it bring him down too. He plugged himself into the idea of getting dressed. He'd get out his sky-blues and a green scarf and then he'd stroll in his clean bare feet to the river. Then uptown. Not as far as 11th Street, no. In any case it was Thursday, and Milly wouldn't be home on a Thursday afternoon. In any case he wasn't going to see her until he could rub her pretty nose in the story of his success.

"It's bound to come tomorrow."

"I suppose so." Frances was sitting cross-legged on the floor, combing her wispy, dull-brown hair down across her face.

"It's been two weeks. Almost."

"Birdie?"

"That's my name."

"Yesterday when I was in Stuyvesant Town, the market, you know?" She found her part and pulled half the veil to one side. "I bought two pills."

"Great."

"Not that kind. The pills you take for . . . you know, so you can have babies again? They change the stuff that's in the water. I thought maybe if we each took one. . . ."

"You can't just go and do it like that, Frances. For Christ's sake! They'd make you have an abortion before you could say Lucille Mortimer Randolph-Clapp."

It was her pet joke that she'd made up herself, but

Frances not so much as smiled. "Why would they have to know? I mean, until it was too late."

"You know what they do, don't you, to people who try and pull that kind of stunt? To the man as well as the woman?"

"I don't care."

"Well, I do." Then, to close the discussion: "Jesus Christ."

She gathered all the hair at the back of her head and fumbled a knot into her strand of yellow yarn. She tried to make the next suggestion sound spontaneous. "We could go to Mexico."

"Mexico! Goddamn, don't you read anything but comic books?" Birdie's indignation was all the more fierce for the fact that not that long ago he'd made essentially the same proposition to Milly. "Mexico! Boy oh boy!"

Frances, her feelings hurt, went over to the mirror and started in with the lotion. Birdie had known her to spend half a day scraping and rubbing and puttying. The result was always the same scaly, middle-aged face. Frances was seventeen.

Their eyes met for a moment in the mirror. Frances's skittered off. He realized that his letter had come. That she'd read it. That she knew.

He went up behind her and took hold of the spindly arms inside the bulky sleeves of the robe. "Where is it, Frances?"

"Where is what?" But she knew, she knew.

He bent the two arms together like a spring exerciser.

"I—I threw it away."

"You threw it away! My private letter?"

"I'm sorry. I shouldn't have. I wanted you to be—I wanted just another day like the last couple."

"What did it say?"

"Birdie, stop!"

"What did it fucking say?"

"Three points. You got three points."

He let go of her. "That's all? That's all it said?"

She rubbed her arms where he'd held her. "It said you had every reason to be proud of what you'd written. Three points is a good score. The team who scored you didn't know how much you needed. If you don't believe me, read it yourself. It's right here." She opened a drawer, and there was the yellow envelope with its Albany post-mark and the burning torch of knowledge in the other corner.

"Aren't you going to read it?"

"I believe you."

"It said if you wanted that one extra point you could get it by enlisting in the service."

"Like your old friend Jock, huh?"

"I'm sorry, Birdie."

"So am I."

"Now maybe you'll reconsider."

"About what?"

"The pills I bought."

"Will you leave me alone with those pills? Will you?"

"I'll never say who the father is. I promise. Birdie, look at me. I *promise*."

He looked at the black, bleary eyes, the greasy, flaking skin, the hard little lips that never smiled far enough to betray the fact of her teeth. "I'd as soon jerk off into the toilet as give it to you. Do you know what you are? You're a moron."

"I don't care what you call me, Birdie."

"You're a goddamned subnormal."

"I love you."

He knew what he had to do. He'd seen the thing last week when he'd gone through her drawers. Not a whip, but he didn't know what else to call it. He found it again at the bottom of the underwear.

"What was that you just said?" He thrust the thing into her face.

"I love you, Birdie. I really do. And I guess I'm about the only one who does."

"Well, this is how I feel for *you*."

He grabbed the collar of her robe and pulled it down off her shoulders. She'd never let him see her naked before and now he understood why. Welts and bruises covered her body. Her ass was like one big open wound from being whipped. This was what she got paid for, not being fucked. This.

He laid into her with his whole strength. He kept going until it didn't matter anymore, until he had no feelings left.

The same afternoon, without even bothering to get

drunk, he went to Times Square and enlisted in the U.S. Marines to go and defend democracy in Burma. Eight other guys were sworn in at the same time. They raised their right arms and took one step forward and rattled off the Pledge of Allegiance or whatever. Then the sergeant came up and slipped the black Marine Corps mask over Birdie's sullen face. His new ID number was stenciled across the forehead in big white letters: USMC 100–7011–D07. And that was it, they were gorillas.

BODIES

1.

"Take a factory," Ab said. "It's the same sort of thing exactly."

What kind of factory Chapel wanted to know.

Ab tipped his chair back, settling into the theory as if it were a warm whirlpool bath in Hydrotherapy. He'd eaten two lunches that Chapel had brought down and felt friendly, reasonable, in control. "Any kind. You ever worked in a factory?"

Of course he hadn't. Chapel? Chapel was lucky to be pushing a cart. So Ab went right on. "For instance— take an electronics-type factory. I worked in one once, an assembler."

"And you *made* something, right?"

"Wrong! I put things together. There's a difference if you'd use your ears for one minute instead of that big mouth of yours. See, first off this *box* comes down the line, and I'd stick in this red board sort of thing, then tighten some other mother on top of that. Same thing all day, simple as A-B-C. Even you could have done it, Chapel." He laughed.

Chapel laughed.

"Now what was I really doing? I *moved* things, from here to there. . . ." He pantomimed here and there. The little finger of the left hand, ended at the first knuckle. He'd done it himself at his initiation into the K of C twenty years ago (twenty-five actually), a single chop of the old chopper, but when people asked he said it was an industrial accident and that was how the goddamned system destroyed you. But mostly people knew better than to ask.

"But I didn't *make* anything at all, you see? And it's the same in any other factory—you move things or you put them together, same difference."

Chapel could feel he was losing. Ab talked faster and louder, and his own words came out stumbling. He hadn't wanted to argue in the first place, but Ab had tangled him in it without his knowing how. "But something, I don't know, what you say is. . . . But what I mean is— you've got to have common sense, too."

"No, this is *science.*"

Which brought such a look of abject defeat to the old man's eyes it was as if Ab had dropped a bomb, boff, right in the middle of his black, unhappy head. For who can argue against science, Not Chapel, sure as hell.

And yet he struggled up out of the rubble still championing common sense. "But things get made—how do you explain that?"

"Things get made, things get made," Ab mimicked in a falsetto voice, though of the two men's voices Chapel's was deeper. "What things?"

Chapel looked round the morgue for an example. It was all so familiar as to be invisible—the slab, the carts, the stacks of sheets, the cabinet with its stock of fillers and fluids, the desk. . . . He lifted a blank Identi-Band from the clutter on the desk. "Like plastic."

"Plastic?" Ab said in a tone of disgust. "That just shows how much you know, Chapel. Plastic." Ab shook his head.

"Plastic," Chapel insisted. "Why not?"

"Plastic is just putting *chemicals* together, you illiterate."

"Yeah, but." He closed one eye, squeezing the thought into focus. "But to make the plastic they've got to—heat it. Or something."

"Right! And what's heat?" he asked, folding his hands across his gut, victorious, full. "Heat is kinetic energy."

"Shit," Chapel maintained. He massaged his stubbly brown scalp. Another argument lost. He never understood how it happened.

"Molecules," Ab summed up, "moving. Everything

breaks down to that. It's all physics, a law." He let loose a large fart and pointed his finger, just in time, at Chapel's groin.

Chapel made a smile acknowledging Ab's triumph. It was science all right. Science battered everyone into submission if it was given its way. It was like trying to argue with the atmosphere of Jupiter, or electric sockets, or the steroid tablets he had to take now—things that happened every day and never made sense, never would, never.

Dumb nigger, Ab thought, feeling friendlier in proportion to Chapel's perplexity. He wished he could have kept him arguing a while longer. There was still religion, psychosis, teaching, lots of possibilities. Ab had arguments to prove that even these jobs, which looked so mental and abstract on the surface, were actually all forms of kinetic energy.

Kinetic energy: once you understood the meaning of kinetic energy all kinds of other things started becoming clear.

"You should read the book," Ab insisted.

"Mm," Chapel said.

"He explains it in more detail." Ab hadn't read the entire book himself, only parts of the condensation, but he'd gotten the gist of it.

But Chapel had no time for books. Chapel, Chapel pointed out, was not one of your intellectuals.

Was Ab? Intellectual? He had to think about that one for a while. It was like wearing some fruity color transparency and seeing himself in a changing booth mirror, knowing he would never buy it, not daring even to walk out on the sales floor, but enjoying the way it fitted him anyhow: an intellectual. Yes, possibly in some other reincarnation Ab had been an intellectual, but it was a goofy idea all the same.

Right on the button, at 1:02, they rang down from 'A' Surgery. A body.

He took down the name in the logbook. He'd neglected to start a new page and the messenger hadn't come by yet for yesterday's, so he entered Time of Death as 11:58 and printed the name in neat block letters: NEWMAN, BOBBI.

"When can you get her?" asked the nurse, for whom a body still possessed sex.

"I'm there already," Ab promised.

He wondered what age it would be. "Bobbi" was an older type name but there were always exceptions.

He booted Chapel out, locked up, and set off with the cart to 'A' Surgery. At the bend of the corridor, right before the ramp, he told the new kid at the desk to take his calls. The kid wiggled his skimpy ass and made some dumb joke. Ab laughed. He was feeling in top shape, and it was going to be a good night. He could tell.

Chapel was the only one on and Mrs. Steinberg, who was in charge tonight, though not actually his boss, said, "Chapel, 'B' Recovery," and handed him the slip.

"And move," she added off-handedly, as another woman might have said, "God bless you," or "Take care."

Chapel, however, had one speed. Difficulties didn't slow him down; anxieties made him go no faster. If somewhere there were cameras perpetually trained on him, viewers who studied his slightest actions, then Chapel would give them nothing to interpret. Loaded or empty, he wheeled his cart along the corridors at the same pace he took walking home after work to his hotel on 65th. Regular? As a clock.

Outside 'M' Ward, on 4, by the elevators, a blond young man was pressing a urinal against himself, trying to make himself piss by groaning at his steel pot. His robe hung open, and Chapel noticed that his pubic hair had been shaved off. That usually meant hemorrhoids.

"How's it going?" Chapel asked. His interest in the patients' stories was quite sincere, especially those in Surgery or ENT wards.

The blond young man made an anguished face and asked Chapel if he had any money.

"Sorry."

"Or a cigarette?"

"I don't smoke. And it's against the rules, you know."

The young man rocked from one leg to the other, coddling his pain and humiliation, trying to blot out every other sensation in order to go the whole way. Only the older patients tried, for a while at least, to hide their pain. The young ones gloried in it from the moment they gave their first samples to the aide in Admissions.

While the substitute in 'B' Recovery completed the

transfer forms Chapel went over to the other occupied unit. It held, still unconscious, the boy he'd taken up earlier from Emergency. His face had been a regular beef stew; now it was a tidy volleyball of bandages. From the boy's clothes and the tanned and muscly trimness of his bare arms (on one biceps two blurry blue hands testified to an eternal friendship with "Larry") Chapel inferred that he would have had a good-looking face as well. But now? No. If he'd been registered with one of the private health plans, perhaps. But at Bellevue there was neither staff nor equipment for full-scale cosmetic work. He'd have eyes, nose, mouth, etc., all the right size and sitting about where they ought to, but the whole lot together would be a plastic approximation.

So young—Chapel lifted his limp left wrist and checked the age on the Identi-Band—and handicapped for life. Ah, there was a lesson in it.

"The poor man," said the substitute, meaning not the boy but the transfer. She handed Chapel the transfer form.

"Oh?" said Chapel, unlocking the wheels.

She went round to the head of the cart. "A subtotal," she explained. *"And. . . ."*

The cart bumped gently into the door frame. The bottle swayed at the top of the intravenous pole. The old man tried to lift his hands but they were strapped to the sides. His fingers clenched.

"And?"

"It's gone to the liver," she explained in a stage whisper.

Chapel nodded somberly. He'd known it must have been something as drastic as that since he was routed up to heaven, the 18th floor. Sometimes it seemed to Chapel that he could have saved Bellevue a lot of needless trouble if he'd just take all of these to Ab Holt's office straightaway instead of bothering with the 18th floor.

In the elevator Chapel paged through the man's file. WANDTKE, JWRZY. The routing slip, the transfer form, the papers in the folder, and the Identi-Band all agreed: JWRZY. He tried sounding it out, letter by letter.

The doors opened. Wandtke's eyes opened.

"How are you?" Chapel asked. "Do you feel okay? Hm?"

Wandtke began laughing, very softly. His ribs fluttered beneath the green electric sheet.

"We're going to your new ward now," Chapel explained. "It's going to be a lot nicer there. You'll see. Everything is going to be all right, uh. . . ." He remembered that it was not possible to pronounce his name. Could it be, despite all the forms, a mistake?

Anyhow there wasn't much point trying to communicate with this one. Coming up from surgery they were always loaded so full of whatever it was that there was no sense to anything they said. They just giggled and rolled their eyes around, like this Wandtke. And in two weeks, cinders in a furnace. Wandtke wasn't singing at least. Lots of them sang.

Chapel's shoulder started in, a twinge. The twinge became an ache and the ache thickened and enveloped him in a cloud of pain. Then the cloud scattered into wisps, the wisps vanished. All in the distance of a hundred yards in 'K' wing, and without his slowing, without a wink.

It wasn't bursitis, that much seemed certain. It came and went, not in flashes, but like music, a swelling up and then a welling away. The doctors didn't understand it, so they said. Eventually it went away, and so (Chapel told himself) he had nothing to complain about. That things could have been a lot worse was demonstrated to him all the time. The kid tonight, for instance, with the false face that would always ache in cold weather, or this Wandtke, giggling like he'd come from some damned birthday party, and with his liver changing itself all the while into some huge, horrible growth. Those were the people to feel sorry for, and Chapel felt sorry for them with some gusto. By comparison to such wretched, doomed creatures, he, Chapel, was pretty lucky. He handled dozens every shift, men and women, old and young, carting them here and there, up and down, and there wasn't one of them, once the doctors had done their job, who wouldn't have been happy to change places with the short, thin, brittle, old black man who wheeled them through these miles of scabby corridors, not one.

Miss Mackey was on duty in the men's ward. She signed for Wandtke. Chapel asked her how he was supposed to pronounce a name like that, Jwrzy, and Miss

Mackey said she certainly didn't know. It was probably a Polish name anyhow. Wandtke—didn't it look Polish?

Together they steered Wandtke to his unit. Chapel connected the cart, and the unit, purring softly, scooped up the old body, lifted, and stuck. The unit shut itself off. It was a moment before either Chapel or Miss Mackey realized what was wrong. Then they unstrapped the withered wrists from the aluminum bars of the cart. The unit, this time, experienced no difficulty.

"Well," said Miss Mackey, "I know two people who need a day's rest."

5:45. This close to clocking out, Chapel didn't want to return to the duty room and risk a last-minute assignment. "Any dinners left?" he asked the nurse.

"Too late here, they've all been taken. Try the women's ward."

In the women's ward, Havelock, the elderly aide, dug up a tray that had been meant for a patient who had terminated earlier that evening. Chapel got it for a quarter, after pointing out the low-residue sticker Havelock had tried to conceal under his thumb.

NEWMAN, B, the sticker read.

Ab would have her now. Chapel tried to remember what unit she'd been in. The blonde girl in the corner who couldn't stand sunlight? Or the colostomy who was always telling jokes? No, her name was Harrison.

Chapel pulled one of the visitors' chairs over to the window ledge. He opened the tray and waited for the food to warm. He ate from one compartment at a time, chewing at his single stolid speed, though the whole dinner was the consistency of a bowl of Breakfast. First, the potatoes; then, some steamy, soft meat cubes; then, dutifully, a mulch of spinach. He left the cake but drank the Koffee, which contained the miracle ingredient that (aside from the fact that no one ever returned) gave heaven its name. When he was done he shot the tray downstairs himself.

Havelock was inside, on the phone.

The ward was a maze of blue curtains, layers of translucence overlapping layers of shadows. A triangle of sunlight spread across the red tile floor at the far end of the room: dawn.

Unit 7 was open. At one time or another Chapel must

have carted its occupant to and from every division of
the hospital: SCHAAP, FRANCES, 3/3/04. Which made
her eighteen, barely. Her face and neck were speckled
with innumerable scarlet spider nevi, but Chapel remembered when it had been a pretty face. Lupus.

A small gray machine beside the bed performed, approximately, the functions of her inflamed liver. At irregular intervals a red light would blink on and, quickly,
off, infinitesimal warnings which no one heeded.

Chapel smiled. The little miracles were starting to unfold themselves in his blood stream, but that was almost
beside the point. The point was simple:

They were dying: he was alive. He had survived and
they were bodies. The spring sunlight added its own additional touch of good cheer to the here of heaven and
the now of six A.M.

In an hour he would be home. He'd rest a while, and
then he'd watch his box. He thought he could look forward to that.

Heading home down First, Ab whistled a piece of trash
that had stuck in his head four days running, about some
new pill called Yes, that made you feel better, and he
did.

The fifty dollars he'd got for the Newman body brought
his take for the week up to a handsome $115. Once he'd
seen what Ab was offering, White hadn't even haggled.
Without being necrophile himself (to Ab a body was just
a job to be done, something he carted down from the
wards and burned or—if there was money to burn instead—shipped off to a freezing concern) Ab understood
the market well enough to have recognized in Bobbi Newman a certain ideal quality of deathliness. Lupus had
taken a fulminant course with her, rapidly destroying one
internal system after another without, for a wonder, mar-
ring the fine texture of the skin. True, the disease had
whittled face and limbs down to bone thinness, but then
what else was necrophilia about? To Ab, who liked them
big, soft, and lively, all of this fuss over corpses was pretty
alien, yet basically his motto was *"Chacun à son goût,"*
though not in so many words. There were limits, of course.
For example, he would willingly have assisted at the cas-
tration of any Republican in the city, and he felt nearly

as passionate a distaste for political extremists. But he possessed the basic urban tolerance for any human peculiarity from which he stood a good chance of making money.

Ab considered his commissions from the procurers to be gifts of fate, to be spent in the same free spirit that fortune had shown showering them on him. In fact, when you totted up the various MODICUM benefits the Holts were disbarred from by virtue of Ab's salary, his real income wasn't much more (without these occasional windfalls) than the government would have paid him for being alive. Ab usually managed to sidestep the logical conclusion: that the windfalls were his essential wage, the money that made him, in his own consciousness, a free agent, the equal of any engineer, expert, or criminal in the city. Ab was a man, with a man's competence to buy whatever, within bounds, he wanted.

At this particular April moment, with the traffic so light on the Avenue you could drink the air like a 7-Up, with the sun shining, with nowhere in particular to be until ten that night, and with $115 of discretionary income, Ab felt like an old movie, full of songs and violence and fast editing. Boff, smack, pow, that's how Ab was feeling now, and as the opposite sex approached him from the other direction, he could feel their eyes fastening on him, measuring, estimating, admiring, imagining.

One, very young, very black, in silvery street shorts, stared at Ab's left hand and stared at it, as though it were a tarantula getting ready to crawl right up her leg. (Ab was everywhere quite hairy.) She could feel it tickling her knee, her thigh, her fancy. Milly, when she was little, had been the same way about her father's missing finger, all silly and giddy. Mutilations were supposed to be passé now, but Ab knew better. Girls still wet themselves feeling a stump, but guys today were just too chickenshit to chop their fingers off. The macho thing now was a gold earring, for Christ's sake—as though there had never been a 20th century.

Ab winked at her, and she looked away, but with a smile. How about that?

If there were one thing missing from a feeling of pure content it was that the wad in his pocket (two twenties, seven tens, and one five) was so puny it almost wasn't there. Before revaluation a three-body week like this would have put a bulge in his front pocket as big as another cock, a comparison he had often at that time drawn. Once Ab had actually been a millionaire—for five days running in July of 2008, the single most incredible streak of luck he'd ever had. Today that would have meant five, six thousand—nothing. Some of the faro tables in the neighborhood still used the old dollars, but it was like a marriage that's lost its romance: you said the words but the meaning had gone out of them. You looked at the picture of Benjamin Franklin and thought, this is a picture of Benjamin Franklin. Whereas with the new bills $100 stood for beauty, truth, power, and love.

As though his bankroll were a kind of magnet dragging him there, Ab turned left on 18th into Stuyvesant Town. The four playgrounds at the center of the complex were the chief black market in New York. In the facs and on TV they used euphemisms like "flea market" or "street fair," since to come right out and call it a black market was equivalent to saying the place was an annex of the police department and the courts, which it was.

The black market was as much a part of New York (or any other city), as basic to its existence, as the numbers from one to ten. Where else could you buy something without the purchase being fed into the federal income-and-purchase computers? Nowhere was where, which meant that Ab, when he was flush, had three options open to him: the playgrounds, the clubs, and the baths.

Used clothing fluttered limply from rack after rack, as far as the fountain. Ab could never pass these stalls without feeling that Leda was somehow close at hand, hidden among these tattered banners of the great defeated army of the second-rate and second-hand, still silently resisting him, still trying to stare him down, still insisting, though so quietly now that only he could hear her: "Goddamn it, Ab, can't you get it through that thick skull of yours, we're poor, we're poor, we're *poor!*" It had been the biggest argument of their life together and the decisive one. He could remember the exact spot, under a plane tree, just here, where they had stood and raged at each other, Leda hissing and spitting like a kettle, out of her mind. It was right after the twins had arrived and Leda was saying there was no help for it, they'd have to wear what they could get. Ab said fuckshit, no, no, no kid of his was going to wear other people's rags, they'd stay in the house naked first. Ab was louder and stronger and less afraid, and he won, but Leda revenged herself by turning her defeat into a martyrdom. She never held out against him again. Instead she became an invalid, weepy and sniveling and resolutely helpless.

Ab heard someone calling his name. He looked around, but who would be here this early in the day but the people from the buildings, old folks plugged into their radios, kids screaming at other kids, babies screaming at mothers, mothers screaming. Half the vendors weren't even spread out yet.

"Ab Holt—over here!" It was old Mrs. Galban. She patted the space beside her on the green bench.

He didn't have much choice. "Hey, Viola, how's it going? You're looking great!"

Mrs. Galban smiled a sweet, rickety smile. Yes, she said complacently, she did feel well, she thanked God every day. She observed that even for April this was beautiful weather. Ab didn't look so bad himself (a little heavier maybe), though it was how many years now?

"Twelve years," said Ab, at a venture.

"Twelve years? It seems longer. And how is that good-looking Dr. Mencken in Dermatology?"

"He's fine. He's the head of the department now, you know."

"Yes, I heard that."

"He asked after you the other day when I ran into him outside the clinic. He said, have you seen old Gabby lately." A polite lie.

She nodded her head, politely believing him. Then, cautiously, she started homing in on what was, for her, the issue. "And Leda, how is she, poor thing?"

"Leda is fine, Viola."

"She's getting out of the house, then?"

"Well no, not often. Sometimes we take her up to the roof for a bit of air. It's closer than the street."

"Ah, the pain!" Mrs. Galban murmured with swift, professional sympathy that the years had not been able to blunt. Indeed, it was probably better exercised now than when she'd been an aide at Bellevue. "You don't have to explain—I know it can be so awful, can't it, pain like that, and there's so little any of us can do. *But . . .*" she added, before Ab could turn aside the final thrust, ". . . we must do that little if we can."

"It's not as bad as it used to be," Ab insisted.

Mrs. Galban's look was meant to be understood as reproachful in a sad, helpless way, but even Ab could sense the calculations going on behind the brown, cataracted eyes. Was this, she asked herself, worth pursuing? Would Ab bite?

In the first years of Leda's invalidism Ab had picked up extra Dilaudin suppositories from Mrs. Galban, who specialized in analgesics. Most of her clients were other old women whom she met in the out-patient waiting room at the hospital. Ab had bought the Dilaudin more as a favor to the old pusher than from any real need, since he got all the morphine that Leda needed from the interns for next to nothing.

"It's a terrible thing," Mrs. Galban lamented quietly, staring into her seventy-eight-year-old lap. "A terrible thing."

What the hell, Ab thought. It wasn't as if he were broke.

"Hey, Gabby, you wouldn't have any of those things I used to get for Leda, would you? Those what-you-call-ums?"

"Well, Ab, since you ask. . . ."

Ab got a package of five suppositories for nine dollars, which was twice the going price, even here on the playground. Mrs. Galban evidently thought Ab a fool.

As soon as he'd given her the money, he felt comfortably unobligated. Walking off he could curse her with buoyant resentment. The old bitch would have to live a damned long time before he ever bought any more plugs off her.

Usually Ab never made the connection between the two worlds he inhabited, this one out here and the Bellevue morgue, but now, having actively wished Viola Galban dead, it struck him that the odds were strong that he'd be the one who'd shove her in the oven. The death of anyone (anyone, that is, whom Ab had known alive) was a depressing idea, and he shrugged it away. At the far edge of his shrug, for the barest instant, he saw the young, pretty face of Bobbi Newman.

The need to buy something was suddenly a physical

necessity, as though his wad of bills had become that cock
and had to be jerked off after a week-long abstinence.

He bought a lemon ice, his first ice of the year, and
strolled among the stalls, touching the goods with thick,
sticky fingers, asking prices, making jokes. Everywhere
the vendors hailed him by his name when they saw him
approach. There was nothing, so rumor would have it,
that Ab Holt couldn't be talked into buying.

2.

Ab looked at his two hundred and fourteen pounds of
wife from the doorway. Wrinkled blue sheets were wound
round her legs and stomach, but her breasts hung loose.
"They're prizewinners to this day," Ab thought affection-
ately. Any feelings he still had for Leda were focused
there, just as any pleasure she got when he was on top of
her came from the squeezing of his hands, the biting of
his teeth. Where the sheets were wrapped round her, however, she could feel nothing—except, sometimes, pain.

After a while Ab's attention woke Leda up, the way a
magnifying glass, focusing on a dry leaf, will start it
smoldering.

He threw the package of suppositories onto the bed.
"That's for you."

"Oh." Leda opened the package, sniffed at one of the
wax cylinders suspiciously. "Oh?"

"It's Dilaudin. I ran into that Mrs. Galban at the market, and she wouldn't get off my back till I'd bought something."

"I was afraid for a moment you might have got it on
my account. Thanks. What's in the other bag, an enema
bottle for our anniversary?"

Ab showed her the wig he'd bought for Beth. It was
a silly, four-times-removed imitation of the Egyptian
style made popular by a now-defunct TV series. To Leda
it looked like something you'd find at the bottom of a
box of Xmas wrapping, and she was certain it would look
the same way to her daughter.

"My God," she said.

"Well, it's what the kids are wearing now," Ab said doubtfully. It no longer looked the same to him. He brought it over to the wedge of sunlight by the bedroom's open window and tried to shake a bit more glitter into it. The metallic strings, rubbing against each other, made soft squeaking sounds.

"My God," she said again. Her annoyance had almost betrayed her into asking him what he'd paid for it. Since the epochal argument beneath the plane tree she never discussed money matters with Ab. She didn't want to hear how he spent his money or how he earned it. She especially didn't want to know how he earned it, since she had, anyhow, a fair idea.

She contented herself with an insult. "You've got the discrimination of a garbage truck, and if you think Beth will let herself be seen in that ridiculous, obscene piece of junk, well. . . !" She pushed at the mattress until she was sitting almost upright. Both Leda and the bed breathed heavily.

"How would you know what people are wearing outside this apartment? There were hundreds of these fucking things all over the playground. It's what the kids are wearing now. What the fuck."

"It's ugly. You bought your daughter an ugly wig. You have every right to, I suppose."

"Ugly—isn't that what you used to say about everything Milly wore? All those things with buttons. And the hats! It's a stage they go through. You were probably just the same, if you could remember that long ago."

"Oh, Milly! You're always holding Milly up as though she were some kind of *example!* Milly never had any idea how—" Leda gave a gasp. Her pain. She pressed her hand flat against the roll of flesh to the side of her right breast, where she thought her liver might be. She closed her eyes trying to locate the pain, which had vanished.

Ab waited till Leda was paying attention to him again. Then, very deliberately, he threw the tinselly wig out the open window. Thirty dollars, he thought, just like that.

The manufacturer's tag fluttered to the floor. A pink oval with italic letters: Nephertiti Creations.

With an inarticulate cry Leda swiveled sideways in bed till she'd made both feet touch the floor. She stood up.

She took two steps and reached out for the window frame to steady herself.

The wig lay in the middle of the street eighteen floors below. Against the gray concrete it looked dazzlingly bright. A Tastee Bread truck backed up over it.

Since there was no reproach she might have made that didn't boil down to a charge of his throwing away money, she said nothing. The unspoken words whirled round inside her, a plague-bearing wind that ruffled the wasted muscles of her legs and back like so many tattered flags. The wind died and the flags went limp.

Ab was ready behind her. He caught her as she fell and laid her back on the bed, wasting not a motion, smooth as a tango dip. It seemed almost accidental that his hands should be under her breasts. Her mouth opened and he put his own mouth across it, sucking the breath from her lungs.

Anger was their aphrodisiac. Over the years the interval between fighting and fucking had grown shorter and shorter. They scarcely bothered any longer to differentiate the two processes. Already his cock was stiff. Already she'd begun to moan her rhythmic protest against the pleasure or the pain, whichever it was. As his left hand kneaded the warm dough of her breasts, his right hand pulled off his shoes and pants. The years of invalidism had given her lax flesh a peculiar virginal quality, as though each time he went into her he were awakening her from an enchanted, innocent sleep. There was a kind of sourness about her too, a smell that seeped from her pores only at these times, the way maples yield sap only at the depth of the winter. Eventually he'd learned to like it.

A good sweat built up on the interface of their bodies, and his movements produced a steady salvo of smacking and slapping and farting sounds. This, to Leda, was the worst part of these sexual assaults, especially when she knew the children were at home. She imagined Beno, her youngest, her favorite, standing on the other side of the door, unable to keep from thinking of what was happening to her despite the horror it must have caused him. Sometimes it was only by concentrating on the thought of Beno that she could keep from crying out.

Ab's body began to move faster. Leda's, crossing the threshold between self-control and automatism, struggled upward away from the thrusts of his cock. His hands grabbed her hips, forcing her to take him. Tears burst from her eyes, and Ab came.

He rolled off, and the mattress gave one last exhausted whoosh.

"Dad?"

It was Beno, who certainly should have been in school. The bedroom door was halfway open. Never, Leda thought, in an ecstasy of humiliation, never had she known a moment to match this. Bright new pains leapt through her viscera like tribes of antelope.

"Dad," Beno insisted. "Are you asleep?"

"I would be if you'd shut up and let me."

"There's someone on the phone downstairs, from the hospital. That Juan. He said it's urgent, and to wake you if we had to."

"Tell Martinez to fuck himself."

"He *said*," Beno went on, in a tone of martyred patience that was a good replica of his mother's, "it didn't make any difference what you said and that once he explained it to you you'd thank him. That's what he said."

"Did he say what it was about?"

"Some guy they're looking for. Bob Someone."

"I don't know who they want, and in any case. . . ." Then it began to dawn: the possibility; the awful, impossible lightning bolt he'd known he would never escape. "Bobbi Newman, was that the name of the guy they're looking for?"

"Yeah. Can I come in?"

"Yes, yes." Ab swept the damp sheet over Leda's body, which hadn't stirred since he'd got off. He pulled his pants on. "Who took the call, Beno?"

"Williken did." Beno stepped into the bedroom. He had sensed the importance of the message he'd been given and he was determined to milk it for a maximum of suspense. It was as though he knew what was at stake.

"Listen, run downstairs and tell Williken to hold Juan on the line until. . . ."

One of his shoes was missing.

"He left, Dad. I told him you couldn't be interrupted. He seemed sort of angry and he said he wished you wouldn't give people his number any more."

"Shit on Williken then."

His shoe was way the hell under the bed. How had he. . . ?

"What was the message he gave you exactly? Did they say who's looking for this Newman fellow?"

"Williken wrote it down, but I can't read his writing. Margy it looks like."

That was it then, the end of the world. Somehow Admissions had made a mistake in slotting Bobbi Newman for a routine cremation. She had a policy with Macy's.

And if Ab didn't get back the body he'd sold to White. . . . "Oh Jesus," he whispered to the dust under the bed.

"Anyhow you're supposed to call them right back. But Williken says not from his phone 'cause he's gone out."

There might be time, barely and with the best luck. White hadn't left the morgue till after 3 A.M. It was still short of noon. He'd buy the body back, even if it meant paying White something extra for his disappointment. After all, in the long run White needed him as much as he needed White.

"Bye, Dad," Beno said, without raising his voice, though by then Ab was already out in the hall and down one landing.

Beno walked over to the foot of the bed. His mother still hadn't moved a muscle. He'd been watching her the whole time and it was as though she were dead. She was always like that after his father had fucked her, but usually not for such a long time. At school they said that fucking was supposed to be very healthful but somehow it never seemed to do *her* much good. He touched the sole of her right foot. It was soft and pink, like the foot of a baby, because she never walked anywhere.

Leda pulled her foot away. She opened her eyes.

White's establishment was way the hell downtown, around the corner from the Democratic National Convention (formerly, Pier 19) which was to the world of contemporary pleasure what Radio City Music Hall had been to the world of entertainment—the largest, the mildest, and the most amazing. Ab, being a born New Yorker, had never stepped through the glowing neon vulva (seventy feet high and forty feet wide, a landmark) of the entrance. For those like Ab who refused to be grossed out by the conscious too-muchness of the major piers, the same basic styles were available on the sidestreets ("Boston" they called this area) in a variety of cooler colors, and here, in the midst of all that was allowed, some five or six illegal businesses eked out their unnatural and anachronistic lives.

After much knocking a young girl came to the door, the same probably who had answered the phone, though now she pretended to be mute. She could not have been much older than Beno, twelve at most, but she moved with the listless, enforced manner of a despairing housewife.

Ab stepped into the dim foyer and closed the door against the girl's scarcely perceptible resistance. He'd never been inside White's place before and he would not even have known what address to come to if he hadn't once had to take over the delivery van for White, who'd arrived at the morgue too zonked out to function. So this was the market to which he'd been exporting his goods. It was less than elegant.

"I want to see Mr. White," Ab told the girl. He wondered if she were another sideline.

She lifted one small, unhappy hand toward her mouth.

There was a clattering and banging above their heads, and a single flimsy facs-sheet drifted down through the half-light of the stairwell. White's voice drifted down after it: "Is that you, Holt?"

"Damn right!" Ab started up the stairs but White, light in his head and heavy on his feet, was already crashing down to meet him.

White placed a hand on Ab's shoulder, establishing the fact of the other man's presence and at the same time holding himself erect. He had said yes to Yes once too often, or twice, and was not at this moment altogether corporeal.

"I've got to take it back," Ab said. "I told the kid on the phone. I don't care how much you stand to lose, I've got to have it."

White removed his hand carefully and placed it on the bannister. "Yes. Well. It can't be done. No."

"I've got to."

"Melissa," White said. "It would be. . . . If you would please. . . . And I'll see you later, darling."

The girl mounted the steps reluctantly, as though her

certain future were waiting for her at the top. "My daughter," White explained with a sad smile as she came alongside. He reached out to rumple her hair but missed by a few inches.

"We'll discuss this, shall we, in my office?"

Ab helped him to the bottom. White went to the door at the far end of the foyer. "Is it locked?" he wondered aloud.

Ab tried it. It was not locked.

"I was meditating," White said meditatively, still standing before the unlocked door, in Ab's way, "when you called before. In all the uproar and whirl, a man has to take a moment aside to. . . ."

White's office looked like a lawyer's that Ab had broken into at the tag-end of a riot, years and years before. He'd been taken aback to find that the ordinary processes of indigence and desuetude had accomplished much more than any amount of his own adolescent smashing about might have.

"Here's the story," Ab said, standing close to White and speaking in a loud voice so there could be no misunderstanding. "It turns out that the one you came for last night was actually insured by her parents, out in Arizona, without her knowing. The hospital records didn't say anything about it, but what happened is the various clinics have a computer that cross-checks against the obits. They caught it this morning and called the morgue around noon."

White tugged sullenly on a strand of his sparse, mousy hair. "Well, tell them, you know, tell them it went in the oven."

"I can't. Officially we've got to hold them for twenty-four hours, just in case something like this should happen. Only it never does. Who would have thought, I mean it's so unlikely, isn't it? Anyhow the point is, I've got to take the body back. Now."

"It can't be done."

"Has somebody already . . . ?"

White nodded.

"But could we fix it up again somehow? I mean, how, uh, badly . . ."

"No. No, I don't think so. Out of the question."

"Listen, White, if I get busted over this, I won't let myself be the only one to get hurt. You understand. There are going to be questions."

White nodded vaguely. He seemed to go away and return. "Well then, take a look yourself." He handed Ab an old-fashioned brass key. There was a plastic Yin and Yang symbol on the keychain. He pointed to a four-tier metal file on the far side of the office. "Through there."

The file wouldn't roll aside from the doorway until, having thought about it, Ab bent down and found the release for the wheels. There was no knob on the door, just a tarnished disc of lock with a word "Chicago" on it. The key fit loosely and the locks had to be coaxed.

The body was scattered all over the patchy linoleum. A heavy roselike scent masked the stench of the decaying organs. No, it was not something you could have passed off as the result of surgery, and in any case the head seemed to be missing.

He'd wasted an hour to see this.

White stood in the doorway, ignoring, in sympathy to Ab's feelings, the existence of the dismembered and disemboweled corpse. "He was waiting here, you see, when I went to the hospital. An out-of-towner, and one of my very . . . I always let them take away whatever they want. Sorry."

As White was locking up the room again, Ab recollected the one thing he would need irrespective of the body. He hoped it hadn't gone off with the head.

They found her left arm in the coffin of simulated pine with the Identi-Band still on it. He tried to persuade himself that as long as he had this name there was still half a chance that he'd find something to hang it on.

White sensed Ab's renascent optimism, and, without sharing it, encouraged him: "Things could be worse."

Ab frowned. His hope was still too fragile to bear expression.

But White began to float away in his own mild breeze. "Say, Ab, have you ever studied yoga?"

Ab laughed. "Shit no."

"You should. You'd be amazed what it can do for you. I don't stick with it like I should, it's my own fault, I suppose, but it puts you in touch with. . . . Well, it's hard to explain."

White discovered that he was alone in the office. "Where are you going?" he asked.

420 East 65th came into the world as a "luxury" coop, but like most such it had been subdivided by the turn of the century into a number of little hotels, two or three to a floor. These hotels rented rooms or portions of rooms on a weekly basis to singles who either preferred hotel life or who, as aliens, didn't qualify for a MODICUM dorm. Chapel shared his room at the Colton (named after the actress reputed to have owned the entire twelve rooms of the hotel in the 80's and 90's) with another ex-convict, but since Lucey left for his job at a retrieval center early in the morning and spent his afterhours cruising for free meat around the piers the two men rarely encountered each other, which was how they liked it. It wasn't cheap, but where else could they have found accommodations so reassuringly like those they'd known at Sing-Sing: so small, so spare, so dark?

The room had a false floor in the reductionist style of the 90's. Lucey never went out without first scrupulously tucking everything away and rolling the floor into place. When Chapel got home from the hospital he would be greeted by a splendid absence: the walls, one window covered by a paper screen, the ceiling with its single recessed light, the waxed wood of the floor. The single decoration was a strip of molding tacked to the walls at what was now, due to the raised floor, eye-level.

He was home, and here, beside the door, bolted to the wall, quietly, wonderfully waiting for him, was his twenty-eight-inch Yamaha of America, none better at any price, nor any cheaper. (Chapel paid all the rental and cable charges himself, since Lucey didn't like TV.)

Chapel did not watch just anything. He saved himself for the programs he felt really strongly about. As the first of these did not come on till 10:30, he spent the intervening hour or two dusting, sanding, waxing, polishing, and generally being good to the floor, just as for nineteen years he had scoured the concrete of his cell every morning and evening. He worked with the mindless and blessed dutifulness of a priest reading his office. Afterwards, calmed, he would roll back the gleaming floorboards from his bed and lie back with conscious worthiness, ready to receive. His body seemed to disappear.

Once the box was on, Chapel became another person. At 10:30 he became Eric Laver, the idealistic young lawyer, with his idealistic young notions of right and wrong, which no amount of painful experience, including two disastrous marriages (and the possibility now of a third) ever seemed to dispel. Though lately, since he'd taken on the Forrest case . . . This was *The Whole Truth.*

At 11:30 Chapel would have his bowel movement during an intermission of news, sports, and weather.

Then: *As The World Turns,* which, being more epic in scope, offered its audience different identities on different days. Today, as Bill Harper, Chapel was worried about Moira, his fourteen-year-old problem stepdaughter, who only last Wednesday during a stormy encounter at breakfast had announced to him that she was a lesbian. As if this wasn't enough, his wife, when he told her what Moira had told him, insisted that many years ago *she* had loved another woman. Who that other woman might have been he feared he already knew.

It was not the stories that engaged him so, it was the faces of the actors, their voices, their gestures, the smooth, wide-open, whole-bodied way they moved. So long as they themselves seemed stirred by their imaginary problems, Chapel was satisfied. What he needed was the spectacle of authentic emotion—eyes that cried, chests that heaved, lips that kissed or frowned or tightened with anxiety, voices tremulous with concern.

He would sit on the mattress, propped on cushions, four feet back from the screen, breathing quick, shallow breaths, wholly given over to the flickerings and noises of the machine, which were, more than any of his own actions, his life, the central fact of his consciousness, the single source of any happiness Chapel knew or could remember.

A TV had taught Chapel to read. It had taught him to laugh. It had instructed the very muscles of his face how to express pain, fear, anger, and joy. From it he had learned the words to use in all the confusing circumstances of his other, external life. And though he never read, or laughed, or frowned, or spoke, or walked, or did anything as well as his avatars on the screen, yet they'd seen him through well enough, after all, or he would not have been here now, renewing himself at the source.

What he sought here, and what he found, was much more than art, which he had sampled during prime evening hours and for which he had little use. It was the experience of returning, after the exertions of the day, to a face he could recognize and love, his own or someone else's. Or if not love, then some feeling as strong. To know, with certainty, that he would feel these same feelings tomorrow, and the next day. In other ages religion had performed this service, telling people the story of their lives, and after a certain lapse of time telling it to them again.

Once a show that Chapel followed on CBS had pulled down such disastrous ratings for six months running that it had been canceled. A pagan forcibly converted to a new religion would have felt the same loss and longing (until the new god has been taught to inhabit the forms abandoned by the god who died) that Chapel felt then, looking at the strange faces inhabiting the screen of his Yamaha for an hour every afternoon. It was as though he'd looked into a mirror and failed to find his reflection. For the first month the pain in his shoulder had become so magnificently more awful that he had almost been unable to do his work at Bellevue. Then, slowly, in the person of young Dr. Landry, he began to rediscover the elements of his own identity.

It was at 2:45, during a commercial for Carnation Eggies, that Ab came pounding and hollering at Chapel's door. Maud had just come to visit her sister-in-law's child at the observation center to which the court had committed him. She didn't know yet that Dr. Landry was in charge of the boy's case.

"Chapel," Ab screamed, "I know you're in there, so open up, goddammit. I'll knock this door down."

The next scene opened in Landry's office. He was trying to make Mrs. Hanson, from last week, understand how a large part of her daughter's problem sprang from her own selfish attitudes. But Mrs. Hanson was black, and Chapel's sympathy was qualified for blacks, whose special dramatic function was to remind the audience of the other world, the one that they inhabited and were unhappy in.

Maud knocked on Landry's door: a closeup of gloved fingers thrumming on the paper panel.

Chapel got up and let Ab in. By three o'clock Chapel had agreed, albeit sullenly, to help Ab find a replacement for the body he had lost.

3.

Martinez had been at the desk when the call came from Macy's saying to hold the Newman body till their driver got there. Though he knew that the vaults contained nothing but three male geriatric numbers, he made mild yes-sounds and started filling out both forms. He left a message for Ab at his emergency number, then (on the principle that if there was going to be shit it should be Ab who either cleaned it up or ate it, as God willed) got word to his cousin to call in sick for the second (two to ten) shift. When Ab phoned back, Martinez was brief and ominous: "Get here and bring you know what. Or you know what."

Macy's driver arrived before Ab. Martinez was feeling almost off-balance enough to tell him there was nothing in storage by the name of Newman, Bobbi. But it was not like Martinez to be honest when a lie might serve, especially in a case like this, where his own livelihood, and his cousin's, were jeopardized. So, making a mental sign of the cross, he'd wheeled one of the geriatric numbers out from the vaults, and the driver, with a healthy indifference to bureaucratic good form, carted it out to his van without looking under the sheet or checking the name on the file: NORRIS, THOMAS.

It was an inspired improvisation. Since their driver had been as culpable as the morgue, Macy's wasn't likely to make a stink about the resulting delay. Fast post mortem freezing was the rule in the cryonic industry and it didn't pay to advertise the exceptions.

Ab arrived a bit before four. First off he checked out the log book. The page for April 14 was blank. A miracle of bad luck, but he wasn't surprised.

"Anything waiting?"

"Nothing."

"That's incredible," Ab said, wishing it were.

The phone rang. "That'll be Macy's," Martinez said equably, stripping down to street clothes.

"Aren't you going to answer it?"

"It's your baby now." Martinez flashed a big winner's smile. They'd both gambled but Ab had lost. He explained, as the phone rang on, the stopgap by which he'd saved Ab's life.

When Ab picked it up, it was the director, no less, of Macy's Clinic, and so high in the sky of his just wrath it would have been impossible for Ab to have made out what he was screaming if he hadn't already known. Ab was suitably abject and incredulous, explaining that the attendant who had made the mistake (and how it could have happened he still did not understand) was gone for the day. He assured the director that the man would not get off lightly, would probably be canned or worse. On the other hand, he saw no reason to call the matter to the attention of Administration, who might try to shift some of the blame onto Macy's and their driver. The director agreed that that was uncalled for.

"And the minute your driver gets here Miss Newman will be waiting. I'll be personally responsible. And we can forget that the whole thing happened. Yes?"

Yes.

Leaving the office, Ab drew in a deep breath and squared his shoulders. He tried to get himself into the I-can-do-it spirit of a Sousa march. He had a problem. There's only one way to solve a problem: by coping with it. By whatever means were available.

For Ab, at this point, there was only one means left.

Chapel was waiting where Ab had left him on the ramp spanning 29th Street.

"It has to be done," Ab said.

Chapel, reluctant as he was to risk Ab's anger again (he'd nearly been strangled to death once), felt obliged to enter a last symbolic protest. "I'll do it," he whispered, "but it's murder."

"Oh no," Ab replied confidently, for he felt quite at ease on this score. "Burking isn't murder."

On April 2, 1956, Bellevue Hospital did not record a

single death, a statistic so rare it was thought worthy of remark in all the city's newspapers, and there were then quite a few. In the sixty-six years since, there had not been such another deathless day, though twice it had seemed a near thing.

At five o'clock on the afternoon of April 14, 2022, the city desk computer at the *Times* issued a stand-by slip noting that as of that moment their Bellevue tie-line had not dispatched a single obit to the central board. A printoff of the old story accompanied the slip.

Joel Beck laid down her copy of *Tender Buttons,* which was no longer making sense, and considered the human-interest possibilities of this nonevent. She'd been on standby for hours and this was the first thing to come up. By midnight, very likely, someone would have died and spoiled any story she might have written. Still, in a choice between Gertrude Stein (illusion) and the Bellevue morgue (reality) Joel opted for the latter.

She notified Darling where she'd be. He thought it was a sleeping idea and told her to enjoy it.

By the first decade of the 21st century systematic lupus erythematosis (SLE) had displaced cancer as the principle cause of death among women aged twenty to fifty-five. This disease attacks every major system of the body, sequentially or in combination. Pathologically it is a virtual anthology of what can go wrong with the human body. Until the Morgan-Imamura test was perfected in 2007, cases of lupus had been diagnosed as meningitis, as epilepsy, as brucellosis, as nephritis, as syphillis, as colitis . . . The list goes on.

The etiology of lupus is infinitely complex and has been endlessly debated, but all students agree with the contention of Muller and Imamura in the study for which they won their first Nobel prize, *SLE—the Ecological Disease*: lupus represents the auto-intoxication of the human race in an environment ever more hostile to the existence of life. A minority of specialists went on to say that the chief cause of the disease's proliferation had been the collateral growth of modern pharmacology. Lupus, by this theory, was the price mankind was paying for the cure of its other ills.

Among the leading proponents of the so-called "doomsday" theory was Dr. E. Kitaj, director of Bellevue Hospital's Metabolic Research unit, who now (while Chapel bided his time in the television room) was pointing out to the resident and interns of heaven certain unique features of the case of the patient in Unit 7. While all clinical tests confirmed a diagnosis of SLE, the degeneration of liver functions had progressed in a fashion more typical of lupoid hepatitis. Because of the unique properties of her case, Dr. Kitaj had ordered a liver machine upstairs for Miss Schaap, though ordinarily this was a temporary expedient before transplantation. Her life was now as much a mechanical as a biologic process. In Alabama, New Mexico, and Utah, Frances Schaap would have been considered dead in any court of law.

Chapel was falling asleep. The afternoon art movie, a drama of circus life, was no help in keeping awake, since he could never concentrate on a program unless he knew the characters. Only by thinking of Ab, the threats he'd made, the blood glowing in his angry face, was he able to keep from nodding off.

In the ward the doctors had moved on to Unit 6 and were listening with tolerant smiles to Mrs. Harrison's jokes about her colostomy.

The new Ford commercial came on, like an old friend calling Chapel by name. A girl in an Empire coupe drove through endless fields of grain. Ab had said, who said so many things just for their shock value, that the commercials were often better than the programs.

At last they trooped off together to the men's ward, leaving the curtains drawn around Unit 7. Frances Schaap was asleep. The little red light on the machine winked on and off, on and off, like a jet flying over the city at night.

Using the diagram Ab had scrawled on the back of a transfer form, Chapel found the pressure adjustment for the portal vein. He turned it left till it stopped. The arrow on the scale below, marked P/P, moved slowly from 35, to 40, to 50. To 60.

To 65.

He turned the dial back to where it had been. The arrow shivered: the portal vein had hemorrhaged.

Frances Schaap woke up. She lifted one thin, astonished hand toward her lips: they were smiling! "Doctor,"

she said pleasantly. "Oh, I feel . . ." The hand fell back
to the sheet.

Chapel looked away from her eyes. He readjusted the
dial, which was no different, essentially, from the controls
of his own Yamaha. The arrow moved right, along the
scale: 50. 55.

" . . . so much better now."

60. 65.

"Thanks."

70.

"I hope, Mr. Holt, that you won't let me keep you from
your work," Joel Beck said, with candid insincerity. "I
fear I have already."

Ab thought twice before agreeing to this. At first he'd
been convinced she was actually an investigator Macy's
had hired to nail him, but her story about the computer
checking out the obits and sending her here was not the
sort of thing anyone could have made up. It was bad
enough, her being from the *Times*, and worse perhaps.

"Am I?" she insisted.

If he said yes, he had work to do, she'd ask to tag along
and watch. If he said no, then she'd go on with her
damned questions. If it hadn't been that she'd have reported him (he could recognize the type), he'd have told
her to fuck off.

"Oh, I don't know," he answered carefully. "Isn't it me
who's keeping you from your work?"

"How so?"

"Like I explained, there's a woman up on 18 who's sure
to terminate any minute now. I'm just waiting for them to
call."

"Half an hour ago you said it wouldn't take fifteen minutes, and you're still waiting. Possibly the doctors have
pulled her through. Wouldn't that be wonderful?"

"*Someone* is bound to die by twelve o'clock."

"By the same logic someone was bound to have died by
now—and they haven't."

Ab could not support the strain of diplomacy any
longer. "Look, lady, you're wasting your time—it's as
simple as that."

"It won't be the first time," Joel Beck replied complacently. "You might almost say that that's what I'm paid to

do." She unslung her recorder. "If you'd just answer one or two more questions, give me a few more details of what you actually do, possibly we'll come up with a handle for a more general story. Then even if that call does come I could go up with you and look over your shoulder."

"Who would be interested?" With growing astonishment Ab realized that she did not so much resist his arguments as simply ignore them.

While Joel Beck was explaining the intrinsic fascination of death to the readers of the *Times* (not a morbid fascination but the universal human response to a universal human fact), the call came from Chapel.

He had done what Ab asked him to.

"Yeah, and?"

It had gone off okay.

"Is it official yet?"

It wasn't. There was no one in the ward.

"Couldn't you, uh, mention the matter to someone who can make it official?"

The *Times* woman was poking about the morgue, fingering things, pretending not to eavesdrop. Ab felt she could decipher his generalities. His first confession had been the same kind of nightmare, with Ab certain all his classmates lined up outside the confessional had overheard the sins the priest had pried out of him. If she hadn't been listening he could have tried to bully Chapel into . . .

He'd hung up. It was just as well.

"Was that the call?" she asked.

"No. Something else, a private matter."

So she kept at him with more questions about the ovens, and whether relatives ever came in to watch, and how long it took, until the desk called to say there was a driver from Macy's trying to bring a body into the hospital and should they let him?

"Hold him right there. I'm on my way."

"*That* was the call," Joel Beck said, genuinely disappointed.

"Mm. I'll be right back."

The driver, flustered, started in with some story why he was late.

"It's skin off your ass, not mine. Never mind that anyhow. There's a reporter in my office from the *Times*—"

"I knew," the driver said. "It's not enough I'm going to be fired, now you've found a way—"

"Listen to me, asshole. This isn't about the Newman fuckup, and if you don't panic she never has to know." He explained about the city desk computer. "So we just won't let her get any strange ideas, right? Like she might if she saw you hauling one corpse into the morgue and going off with another."

"Yeah, but. . . ." The driver clutched for his purpose as for a hat that a great wind were lifting from his head. "But they'll crucify me at Macy's if I don't come back with the Newman body! I'm so late already because of the damned—"

"You'll *get* the body. You'll take back *both*. You can return with the other one later, but the important thing now—"

He felt her hand on his shoulder, bland as a smile.

"I thought you couldn't have gone too far away. There's a call for you and I'm afraid you were right: Miss Schaap has died. That is whom you were speaking of?"

Whom! Ab thought with a sudden passion of hatred for the *Times* and its band of psuedo-intellectuals. *Whom!*

The Macy's driver was disappearing toward his cart.

It came to Ab then, the plan of his salvation, whole and entire, the way a masterpiece must come to a great artist, its edges glowing.

"Bob!" Ab called out. "Wait a minute."

The driver turned halfway round, head bent sideways, an eyebrow raised: who, me?

"Bob, I want you to meet, uh. . . ."

"Joel Beck."

"Right. Joel, this is Bob, uh, Bob Newman." It was, in fact, Samuel Blake. Ab was bad at remembering names.

Samuel Blake and Joel Beck shook hands.

"Bob drives for Macy's Clinic, the Steven Jay Mandell Memorial Clinic." He laid one hand on Blake's shoulder, the other hand on Beck's. She seemed to become aware of his stump for the first time and flinched. "Do you know anything about cryonics, Miss uh?"

"Beck. No, very little."

"Mandell was the very first New Yorker to go to the freezers. Bob could tell you all about him, a fantastic story." He steered them back down the corridor toward the morgue.

"Bob is here right now because of the body they just. . . . Uh." He remembered too late that you didn't call them bodies in front of outsiders. "Because of Miss Schaap, that is. *Whom*," he added with malicious emphasis, "was insured with Bob's clinic." Ab squeezed the driver's shoulder in lieu of winking.

"Whenever possible, you see, we notify the Clinic people, so that they can be here the minute one of their clients terminates. That way there's not a minute lost. Right, Bob?"

The driver nodded, thinking his way slowly toward the idea Ab had prepared for him.

He opened the door to his office, waited for them to go in. "So while I'm upstairs why don't you and Bob have a talk, Miss Peck. Bob has dozens of incredible stories he can tell you, but you'll have to be quick. Cause once I've got his body down here . . ." Ab gave the driver a significant look. ". . . Bob will have to leave."

It was done as neatly as that. The two people whose curiosity or impatience might still have spoiled the substitution were now clamped to each other like a pair of steel traps, jaw to jaw to jaw to jaw.

He hadn't considered the elevator situation. During his own shift there were seldom logjams. When there were, carts routed for the morgue were last in line. At 6:15, when the Schaap was finally signed over to him, every elevator arriving on 18 was full of people who'd ridden to the top in order to get a ride to the bottom. It might be an hour before Ab and his cart could find space and the Macy's driver would certainly not sit still that much longer.

He waited till the hallway was empty, then scooped up the body from the cart. It weighed no more than his own Beno, but even so by the time he'd reached the landing of 12, he was breathing heavy. Halfway down from 5 his knees gave out. (They'd given fair warning but he'd refused to believe he could have gone so soft.) He collapsed with the body still cradled in his arms.

He was helped to his feet by a blond young man in a striped bathrobe many sizes too small. Once Ab was sitting up, the young man tried to assist Frances Schaap to her feet. Ab, gathering his wits, explained that it was just a body.

"Hoo-wee, for a minute there, I thought. . . ." He laughed uncertainly at what he'd thought.

Ab felt the body here and there and moved its limbs this way and that, trying to estimate what damage had been done. Without undressing it, this was difficult.

"How about you?" the young man asked, retrieving the cigarette he'd left smoking on a lower step.

"I'm fine." He rearranged the sheet, lifted the body and started off again. On the third floor landing he remembered to shout up a thank-you at the young man who'd helped him.

Later, during visiting hours in the ward, Ray said to his friend Charlie, who'd brought in new cassettes from the shop where he worked: "It's incredible some of the things you see in this hospital."

"Such as?"

"Well, if I told you you wouldn't believe." Then he spoiled his whole build-up by twisting round sideways in bed. He'd forgotten he couldn't do that.

"How are you feeling?" Charlie asked, after Ray had stopped groaning and making a display. "I mean, in general."

"Better, the doctor says, but I still can't piss by myself." He described the operation of the catheter, and his self-pity made him forget Ab Holt, but later, alone and unable to sleep (for the man in the next bed made bubbling sounds) he couldn't stop thinking of the dead girl, of how he'd picked her up off the steps, her ruined face and frail, limp hands, and how the fat attendant from the morgue had tested, one by one, her arms and legs, to see what he'd broken.

There was nothing for her in the morgue, Joel had decided, now that the day had yielded its one obit to nullify the nonevent. She phoned back to the desk but neither Darling nor the computer had any suggestions.

She wondered how long it would be before they fired her. Perhaps they thought she would become so demoralized if they kept her on stand-by that she'd leave without a confrontation scene.

Human interest: surely somewhere among the tiers of this labyrinth there was a story for her to bear witness to. Yet wherever she looked she came up against flat, intractable surfaces: Six identical wheelchairs all in a row. A doctor's name penciled on a door. The shoddiness, the smells. At the better sort of hospitals, where her family would have gone, the raw fact of human frangibility was prettied over with a veneer of cash. Whenever she was confronted, like this, with the undisguised bleeding thing, her first impulse was to avert her eyes, never—like a true journalist—to bend a little closer and even stick a finger in it. Really, they had every reason to give her the sack.

Along one stretch of the labyrinth iron curlicues projected from the walls at intervals. Gas brackets? Yes, for their tips, obscured by layer upon layer of white paint, were nozzle-shaped. They must have dated back to the nineteenth century. She felt the slightest mental tingle.

But no, this was too slim a thread to hang a story from. It was the sort of precious detail one notices when one's eyes *are* averted.

She came to a door with the stenciled letters: "Volunteers." As this had a rather hopeful ring to it, human-interest-wise, she knocked. There was no answer and the door was unlocked. She entered a small unhappy room whose only furniture was a metal filing cabinet. In it was a rag-tag of yellowing mimeographed forms and equipment for making Koffee.

She pulled the cord of the blinds. The dusty louvres opened unwillingly. A dozen yards away cars sped past on the upper level of the East Side Highway. Immediately the whooshing noise of their passage detached itself from the indiscriminate, perpetual humming in her ears. Below the highway a slice of oily river darkened with the darkening of the spring sky, and below this a second stream of traffic moved south.

She got the blinds up and tried the window. It opened smoothly. A breeze touched the ends of the scarf knotted into her braids as she leaned forward.

There, not twenty feet below, was her story, the absolutely right thing: in a triangle formed by a feeder ramp to the highway and the building she was in and a newer building in the bony style of the 70's was the loveliest vacant lot she'd ever seen, a perfect little garden of knee-high weeds. It was a symbol: of Life struggling up out of the wasteland of the modern world, of Hope . . .

No, that was too easy. But some meaning, a whisper, did gleam up to her from this patch of weeds (she wondered what their names were; at the library there would probably be a book . . .), as sometimes in *Tender Buttons* the odd pairing of two ordinary words would generate similar flickerings poised at the very threshold of the intelligible. Like:

An elegant use of foliage and grace and a little piece of white cloth and oil.

Or, more forcibly: *A blind agitation is manly and uttermost.*

4.

The usual cirrus at the horizon of pain had thickened to a thunderhead. Sleepless inside a broken unit in the annex to Emergency, he stared at the red bulb above the door, trying to think the pain away. It persisted and grew, not only in his shoulder but in his fingers sometimes, or his knees, less a pain than an awareness that pain were possible, a far-off insistent jingling like phone calls traveling up to his head from some incredible lost continent, a South America full of dreadful news.

It was the lack of sleep, he decided, since having an explanation helped. Even this wakefulness would have been tolerable if he could have filled his head with something besides his own thoughts—a program, checkers, talk, the job . . .

The job? It was almost time to clock in. With a goal established he had only to whip himself toward it. Stand: he could do that. Walk to the door: and this was possible though he distrusted his arhythmic legs. Open it: he did.

The glare of Emergency edged every commonplace with a sudden, awful crispness, as though he were seeing it all raw and naked with the skin peeled back to show the veins and muscles. He wanted to return to the darkness and come out through the door again into the average everydayness he remembered.

Halfway across the distance to the next door he had to detour about a pair of DOA's, anonymous and neuter beneath their sheets. Emergency, of course, received more bodies than actual patients, all the great city's gore. Memories of the dead lasted about as long as a good shirt, the kind he'd bought back before prison.

A pain formed at the base of his back, rode up the elevator of his spine, and stepped off. Braced in the doorframe (sweat collected into drops on his shaved scalp and zigzagged down to his neck), he waited for the pain to return but there was nothing left but the faraway jingle jingle jingle that he would not answer.

He hurried to the duty room before anything else could happen. Once he was clocked in he felt protected. He even swung his left arm round in its socket as a kind of invocation to the demon of his usual pain.

Steinberg looked up from her crossword puzzle. "You all right?"

Chapel froze. Beyond the daily rudenesses that a position of authority demands, Steinberg never talked to those under her. Her shyness, she called it. "You don't look well."

Chapel studied the wordless crossword of the tiled floor, repeated, though not aloud, his explanation: that he had not slept. Inside him a tiny gnat of anger hatched and buzzed against this woman staring at him, though she had no right to, she was not actually his boss. Was she still staring? He would not look up.

His feet sat side by side on the tiles, cramped and prisoned in six-dollar shoes, deformed, inert. He'd gone to the beach with a woman once and walked shoeless in the heated, glittering dust. Her feet had been as ugly as his, but . . .

He clamped his knees together and covered them with his hands, trying to blot out the memory of . . .

But it seeped back from places inside in tiny premonitory droplets of pain.

Steinberg gave him a slip. Someone from 'M' was routed to a Surgery on 5. "And move," she called out after him.

Behind his cart he had no sense of his speed, whether fast or slow. It distressed him how this muscle, then that muscle, jerked and yanked, the way the right thigh heaved up and then the left thigh, the way the feet, in their heavy shoes, came down against the hard floors with no more flexion than the blades of skates.

He'd wanted to chop her head off. He'd often seen this done, on programs. He would lie beside her night after night, both of them insomniac but never talking, and think of the giant steel blade swooping down from its superb height and separating head and body, until the sound of this incessantly imagined flight blended into the repeated zoom zim zoom of the cars passing on the expressway below, and he slept.

The boy in 'M' Ward didn't need help sliding over onto the cart. He was the dunnest shade of black, all muscles and bounce and nervous, talky terror. Chapel had standard routines worked out for his type.

"You're a tall one," it began.

"No, you got it backwards—it's your wagon that's too short."

"How tall are you anyhow? Six two?"

"Six four."

Reaching his punch line, Chapel made a laugh. "Ha, ha, I could use those four inches for myself!" (Chapel stood 5' 7" in his shoes.)

Usually they laughed with him, but this one had a comeback. "Well, you tell them that upstairs and maybe they'll accommodate you."

"What?"

"The surgeons—they're the boys that can do it." The boy laughed at what was now *his* joke, while Chapel sank back into a wounded silence.

"Arnold Chapel," a voice over the PA said. "Please return along 'K' corridor to 'K' elevator bank. Arnold Chapel, please return along 'K' corridor to 'K' elevator bank."

Obediently he reversed the cart and returned to 'K' elevator bank. His identification badge had cued the traffic control system. It had been years since the computer had had to correct him out loud.

He rolled the cart into the elevator. Inside, the boy repeated his joke about the four inches to a student nurse.

The elevator said, "Five."

Chapel rolled the cart out. Now, right or left? He couldn't remember.

He couldn't breathe.

"Hey, what's wrong?" the boy said.

"I need. . . ." He lifted his left hand towards his lips. Everything he looked at seemed to be at right angles to everything else, like the inside of a gigantic machine. He backed away from the cart.

"Are you all right?" He was swinging his legs down over the side.

Chapel ran down the corridor. Since he was going in the direction of the Surgery to which the cart had been routed the traffic control system did not correct him. Each time he inhaled he felt hundreds of tiny hypodermic darts penetrate his chest and puncture his lungs.

"Hey!" a doctor yelled. "Hey!"

Into another corridor, and there, as providentially as if he'd been programmed right to its door, was a staff toilet. The room was flooded with a calm blue light.

He entered one of the stalls and pulled the door, an old door made of dark wood, shut behind him. He knelt down beside the white basin, in which a skin of water quivered with eager, electric designs. He dipped his cupped fingers into the bowl and dabbled his forehead with cool water. Everything fell away—anger, pain, pity, every possible feeling he'd ever heard of or seen enacted. He'd always expected, and been braced against, some eventual retribution, a shotgun blast at the end of the long, white corridor of being alive. It was such a relief to know he had been wrong.

The doctor, or was it the boy routed to surgery, had come into the toilet and was knocking on the wooden door. Neatly and as though on cue, he vomited. Long strings of blood came out with the pulped food.

He stood up, zipped, and pushed open the door. It was the boy, not the doctor. "I'm better now," he said.

"You're sure?"

"I'm feeling fine."

The boy climbed back onto the cart, which he'd wheeled himself all this way, and Chapel pushed him around the corner and down the hall to Surgery.

Ab had felt it in his arms and his hands, a power of luck, as though when he leaned forward to flip over each card his fingers could read through the plastic to know whether it was, whether it wasn't the diamond he needed to make his flush.

It wasn't.

It wasn't.

It wasn't.

As it turned out, he needn't have bothered. Martinez got the pot with a full house.

He had lost as much blood as he comfortably could, so he sat out the next hands munching Nibblies and gassing with the bar decoration, who was also the croupier. It was said she had a third interest in the club, but so dumb, could she? She was a yesser and yessed everything Ab cared to say. Nice breasts though, always damp and sticking to her blouses.

Martinez folded after only his third card and joined Ab at the bar. "How'd you do it, Lucky?" he jeered.

"Fuck off. I started out lucky enough."

"A familiar story."

"What are you worried—I won't pay you back?"

"I'm not worried, I'm not worried." He dropped a five on the bar and ordered sangria, one for the big winner, one for the big loser, and one for the most beautiful, the most successful businesswoman on West Houston, and so out into the heat and the stink.

"Some ass?" Martinez asked.

What with, Ab wanted to know.

"Be my guest. If I'd lost what you lost, you'd do as much for me."

This was doubly irking, one, because Martinez, who played a dull careful game with sudden flashes of insane bluffing, never did worse than break even, and two, because it wasn't true—Ab would not have done as much for him or anyone. On the other hand, he was hungry for something more than what he'd find at home in the ice-box.

"Sure. Okay."

"Shall we walk there?"

Seven o'clock, the last Wednesday in May. It was Martinez's day off, while Ab was just sandwiching his excitement in between clock-out and clock-in with the assistance of some kind green pills.

Each time they passed one of the crosstown streets (which were named down here instead of numbered) the round red eye of the sun had sunk a fraction nearer the blur of Jersey. In the subway gallery below Canal they stopped for a beer. The sting of the day's losses faded, and the moon of next-time rose in the sky. When they came up again it was the violet before night, and the real moon was there waving at them. A population of how many now? Seventy-five?

A jet went past, coming in low for the Park, winking a jittery rhythm of red, red, green, red, from tail and wing tips. Ab wondered whether Milly might be on it. Was she due in tonight?

"Look at it this way, Ab," Martinez said. "You're still paying for last month's luck."

He had to think, and then he had to ask, "What luck last month?"

"The switch. Jesus, I didn't think any of us were going to climb out from under that without getting burnt."

"Oh, that." He approached the memory tentatively, not sure the scar tissue was firm yet. "It was tight, all right." A laugh, which rang half-true. The scar had healed, he went on. "There was one moment though at the end when I thought I'd flushed the whole thing down the toilet. See, I had the Identi-Band from the first body, what's-her-name's. It was the only thing I got from that asshole White. . . ."

"That fucking White," Martinez agreed.

"Yeah. But I was so panicked after that spill on the stairs that I forgot, see, to change them, the two bands, so I sent off the Schaap body like it was."

"Oh Mary Mother, that *would* have done it!"

"I remembered before the driver got away. So I got out there with the Newman band and made up some story about how we print up different bands when we send them out to the freezers than when one goes to the oven."

"Did he believe that?"

Ab shrugged. "He didn't argue."

"You don't think he ever figured out what happened that day?"

"That guy? He's as dim as Chapel."

"Yeah, what *about* Chapel?" There if anywhere, Martinez had thought, Ab had laid himself open.

"What about him?"

"You told me you were going to pay him off. Did you?"

Ab tried to find some spit in his mouth. "I paid him off all right." Then, lacking the spit: "Jesus Christ."

Martinez waited.

"I offered him a hundred dollars. One hundred smackers. You know what that dumb bastard wanted?"

"Five hundred?"

"Nothing! Nothing at all. He even argued about it. Didn't want to get his hands dirty, I suppose. My money wasn't good enough for him."

"So?"

"So we reached a compromise. He took fifty." He made a comic face.

Martinez laughed. "It was a damned lucky thing, that's all I'll say, Ab. *Damned* lucky."

They were quiet along the length of the old police station. Despite the green pills Ab felt himself coming down, but ever so gently down. He entered pink cloudbanks of philosophy.

"Hey, Martinez, you ever think about that stuff? The freezing business and all that."

"I've thought about it, sure. I've thought it's a lot of bullshit."

"You don't think there's a chance then that any of them ever will be brought back to life?"

"Of course not. Didn't you see that documentary they were making all the uproar over, and suing NBC? No, that freezing doesn't stop anything, it just slows it down. They'll all just be so many little ice cubes eventually. Might as well try bringing them back from the smoke in the stacks."

"But if science could find a way to . . . Oh, I don't know. It's complicated by lots of things."

"Are you thinking of putting money into one of those damned policies, Ab? For Christ's sake, I would have thought that you had more brains than that. The other day my wife . . ." He took a step backwards. "My ex-wife got on to me about that, and the money they want . . ." He rolled his eyes blackamoor-style. "It's not in our league, believe me."

"That's not what I was thinking at all."

"So? Then? I'm no mind-reader."

"I was wondering, if they ever do find a way to bring

them back, and if they find a cure for lupus and all that, well, what if they brought her back?"

"The Schaap?"

"Yeah. Wouldn't that be crazy? What would she think anyhow?"

"Yeah, what a joke."

"No, seriously."

"I don't get the point, seriously."

Ab tried to explain but he didn't see the point now himself. He could picture the scene in his mind so clearly: the girl, her skin made smooth again, lying on a table of white stone, breathing, but so faintly that only the doctor standing over her could be sure. His hand would touch her face and her eyes would open and there would be such a look of astonishment.

"As far as I'm concerned," Martinez said, in a half-angry tone, for he didn't like to see anyone believing in something he couldn't believe in, "it's just a kind of religion."

Since Ab could recall having said almost the same thing to Leda, he was able to agree. They were only a couple blocks from the baths by then, so there were better uses for the imagination. But before the last of the cloudbank had quite vanished, he got in one last word for philosophy. "One way or another, Martinez, life goes on. Say what you like, it goes on."

EVERYDAY LIFE IN THE LATER ROMAN EMPIRE

1.

The three of them were sitting in the arbor watching the sun go down over her damp melon fields—Alexa herself, her neighbor Arcadius, and the pretty Hebrew bride he'd brought back from Thebes. Arcadius, once again, was describing his recent mysterious experience in Egypt, where in some shattered temple the immortal Plato had addressed the old man, not in Latin but a kind of Greek, and shown him various cheap-jack signs and wonders—a phoenix, of course; then a crew of blind children who had prophecied, in perfect strophe and antistrophe, the holocaust of earth; finally (Arcadius drew this miracle from his pocket and placed it on the dial) a piece of wood that had metamorphosed to stone.

Alexa picked it up: a like but much larger hunk of petrified wood dignified G.'s work table at the Center: russet striations giving way to nebular sworls of mauve, yellow, cinnabar. It had come from a sad and long-since-deleted curio shop on East 8th. Their first anniversary.

She dropped the stone into the old man's proffered palm. "It's beautiful." No more than that.

His fingers curled round it. Dark veins squirmed across white flesh. She looked away (the lowest clouds were now the color flesh should be), but not before she had imagined Arcadius dead, and swarming.

81

No, the historical Alexa would have dreamt up nothing so patently medieval. Ashes? At most.

He flung the stone out into the steaming field.

Merriam rose to her feet, one arm extended in a gesture of protest. Who was this strange girl, this wisp of a wife? Was she, as Alexa might have wished, just a new mirror image of herself? Or did she represent something more abstract? Their eyes met. In Merriam's, reproach; in Alexa's an answering guilt contested against her everyday skepticism. It came down to this, that Arcadius, and Merriam too in a subtler way, wanted her to accept this scrap of rock as proof that lunatics in Syria have died and then risen from their graves.

An impossible situation.

"It's growing chilly," she announced, though this was as patent a fiction as any Arcadius had brought back from the Nile.

The path back home dipped down almost to touch the unfinished pool. A small brown toad squatted on the rib cage of the handsome wrestler that Gargilius had shipped up from the south. He had waited two years so, in mud and dust, for the pool to be done and his pedestal to be raised. Now the marble was discolored.

Merriam said, "Oh look!" The toad got off. (Have I ever seen a toad alive, or only pictures of toads in *Nature World*? Had there been toads that summer in Augusta? or in Bermuda? in Spain?) Out of the long grass, a deep burp. And again the burp.

The timer on the oven?

No, there was still—she checked her watch—a quarter-hour before Willa's pies came out and her own daube went in.

Merriam faded to a gape. Worn strips of maple replaced the damp, elaborate grass, and the toad—

It was the garbage bell. Had she remembered? She rose and rounded the bend of corridor into the kitchen just as the platform inside the shaft dropped. Bags from 7 and 8 came down the chute, rattling, and far below, muffled, it all smashed together into the smasher. But her own garbage was still waiting in the pail, unsorted and unwrapped.

Let it, she thought. She tried to return to the villa, closing her eyes and clutching for the talismanic image that would place her there: a wedge of sunlight, a window, sky, and the slight sway of the pine.

Alexa was reclining on the double bed. Timarchus knelt before her, head bowed (he was a new boy, Sarmatian, and rather shy), offering his mistress, on a scalloped tray, a small cake covered with pineae. (She *was* hungry.)

"But I won't touch it," she told herself.

To Timarchus she said: "This afternoon when the bailiff can spare you, my boy, go down by the pool with a rag and rub the statue where it's stained. Ever so gently, you know, just as though the stone were skin. It will take days, but—"

She sensed that there was something wrong with the boy.

A smile. "Timarchus?"

He raised his head in answer: the olive skin formed two small, smooth hollows where eyes would have been.

It wouldn't do. She ought to have known better by now than to try to bull her way through once she'd lost contact. The result was inevitably nightmares and silliness.

She set to work. It was, anyhow, nearly three o'clock. She spread a page of the *Times* across the counter and emptied the pail over it. A story in the second column caught her attention: a plane had been stolen from the Military Fair at Highland Falls. Apparently it had been flown away. But why? To have found out she would have had to brush aside a skum of eggshell, peelings, paper, sweepings, and a week's worth of shit and husks from Emily's cage. Actually, she was not that curious. She made a tidy bundle, over and under, around and under once more, the only skill surviving from her flirtation with origami twenty years before. Her Japanese instructor, with whom she had also conducted a flirtation, had had to agree to a vasectomy as a condition of entering the U.S. It left the tiniest scar. His name was Sebastian . . . Sebastian. . . . His last name escaped her.

She put the bundle on the platform.

She stopped in the doorway to untie, strand by strand, the knot of muscle from her forehead down to her shoulders. Then four deep breaths. Noises seeped into this brief stillness: the icebox, the higher-pitched purr of the filter, and, intermittently, a grinding whine that she had never understood. It seemed to come from the apartment overhead but she never remembered to ask what it might be.

Was there somewhere she was supposed to have gone?

This time it was the timer. Willa's pies had a fine glaze. Alexa had used one of her own (real) eggs to brush the crust, a courtesy that would probably be invisible to Willa, who was capable of only the broadest gastronomic distinctions, as between beef and ice cream. The casserole squeezed in beside the rice pudding she was doing for Larry and Tom, who, lacking an oven of their own, paid for their time in Alexa's with tickets to the opera from their subscription series, an informal, inflexible contract of many years' standing. She closed the door, reset the timer, rewound and unplugged the instruction cassette.

And that, except for the mail, was that.

The key was in the penny dish, and the elevator, god bless it, was alive and well and only one floor off. Plotting how in coming up she would escape them by reading her mail, she read the graffiti going down: obscenities, the names of politicians, and everywhere (even the ceiling) "love," which some patient cynic edited, each time it was scratched into the paint, to "Glove." The super's endearing theory was that this was all the work of lumpenprole delivery men, the residents themselves being too well-bred and status-conscious to muck up their own walls. Alexa had her doubts about this, since she'd added her own tiny "shit" coming home drunk last year from her section's Xmas party. There it was, just below the cloudy plastic cover of the Inspection Certificate, as humorless now, as ineloquent as all the rest. The doors opened, stuck, strained, and opened all the way.

The mailman was just beginning to stuff the boxes, so she said "Hello, Mr. Phillips," and asked the polite question or two from her standard casework repertoire of family, weather, teevee. Then she went out to the street and tested the air. It was palatable, but beyond that something suddenly seemed wonderfully right.

A sky of curdled cloud, a bit of breeze that flapped the fringe of the canopy. As it moves from a smaller to a larger space, an answering expansion of the spirit. The concrete swept clean. And?

She only realized what the wonder had been when it was taken from her: out of the third brownstone in the row across the street a woman wheeled a baby buggy. She had been alone.

The buggy descended to the pavement at a controlled jounce and was steered inexorably toward Alexa.

The woman (whose hat was exactly the same dismaying brown as the inside of the elevator) said, "Hello, Mrs. Miller."

Alexa smiled.

They talked about babies. Mr. Phillips, who had finished up inside, told them about the precosities of the two younger Phillipses: "I asked them what the dickens it was, a leaky sieve or what—"

It came to her, where she was supposed to be. Loretta had phoned last night when she was half asleep and she hadn't written it down. (Loretta's middle name was Dickens, and she claimed, in some complicated way, to be a descendant.) The appointment was for one o'clock and the Lowen School was on the other side of town. Panic whelmed up. It couldn't be done, she told herself; and the panic subsided.

"Do you know what it turned out to be?" Mr. Phillips insisted.

"No, what?"

"A planetarium."

She tried to think what this could possibly mean. "That's astonishing," she said and the woman who had known her name agreed.

"That's what I told my wife later—astonishing."

"A planetarium," Alexa said, as she retreated toward the mailboxes. "Well, well."

There was the winter number, one season overdue, of *Classics Journal;* a letter with a Burley, Idaho, postmark (from her sister Ruth); two letters for G., one from the Conservation Corporation that was probably an appeal for funds (as, with equal probability, Ruth's letter would be); and the crucial letter from Stuyvesant High School.

Tank had been accepted. He didn't have a scholarship but that, considering G.'s income, was only to be expected.

Her first reaction was sodden disappointment. She had wanted to be relieved of the decision and now it was squarely before her again. Then, when she realized she'd been hoping Stuyvesant would refuse him, she felt as sodden guilt.

She could hear the phone ringing from the elevator. She knew it would be Loretta Couplard wanting to know why she'd missed their appointment. She used the wrong key for the top lock. "My house is on fire," she thought, "and my children are burning." (And, as a kind of appendix to this thought: Have I ever seen a ladybug alive? Or only pictures of them on nursery-rhyme cassettes?)

It was a wrong number.

She settled down with the *Classics Journal*, which had gone, as everything did these days, from paper to flimsy. An article on the Sibyl in the *Satyricon;* a compendium of the references in Aristotle's *Poetics;* a new method of dating the letters of Cicero. Nothing she could use for therapy.

Then, with a mental squaring of her shoulders against her sister's devious demands, she began the letter:

March 29, 2025

Dear Alexa—
thank you and god-bless for the bundle of good things. they seem practically new so i guess i should thank Tancred too for his gentleness. thanks, Tank! Remus and the other kids certainly can use clothes, esp. now. it has been the worst winter ever for us— and thats going back 23 yrs. before i arrived— but we are well dug in & cozy as mice.

my news? well, since i last wrote you i have been getting into baskets! it certainly solves the problem of those long winter evenings. Harvey who is our big expert on just about everything—he's 84, would you believe that?—taught me and Budget, tho she has decided to return to dear old Sodom & Gonorreah (pun?) that was right at the low point of the Great Freeze. now with the sap running and birds singing— and its so beautiful, Alexa, i wish you could be here to share it—i get awfully restless sitting in front of my pile of withies. but i seem to be stuck with the job since its our biggest moneymaker now that the preserves are sold. (did you get the two jars i sent you at Christmas?)

i wish you'd write more often since you are so

good at it. i always am so happy to hear from you, Alexa, esp. whats been happening to that Roman alter-ego of yours. sometimes i want to return to the 3rd cent. or whenever and try and talk sense into the other "you." she/you seems so much more receptive and open, tho i suppose we all are inside our heads & the hard thing is to get those feelings working on the outside!

but don't let me preach at you. that has always been my worst fault—even here! again you and Tank are invited to come visiting for as long as you like. i'd invite Gene too if i thot there was any chance he'd come, but i know what his opinion is of the Village. . . .

i tried to read the book you sent with the bundle, by that Saint. i thot from the title it would be really trashy & exciting but 10 pages was as far as i could get. i gave it to elder Warren to read & he says to tell you its a great book but he couldn't disagree more. he would like to meet you & talk about the early Christian communities. i feel so commited now to our way of Life that i don't think i'll ever be getting back east. so unless you do visit the Village we may never see each other again. i appreciate your offering the flight fare for me and Remus to come out but the elders wont let me accept money for so light a purpose when we have to do without so many more important things. i love you—you must know that—& i always pray for you and for Tancred & for Gene too.

your sister,
Ruth

p.s. please, Alexa—not Stuyvesant! its hard to explain why i feel so strongly about this as i do without giving offense to G. but do I have to explain? give my nephew at least half a chance to live a human life!

Depression came down on her like August smog, thick and smarting. Ruth's utopian gush, silly as it could be at times, or sinister, always made Alexa see her own life as strenuous, futile, and unworthy. What had she to show for all her effort? She'd composed that inventory so often it was like filling out her weekly D-97 for the Washington

office. She had a husband, a son, a parakeet, a psycho-
therapist, sixty-four per cent equity in her pension fund,
and an exquisite sense of loss.

It wasn't a fair summation. She loved G. with a sad,
complicated, forty-four-year-old love, and Tancred un-
equivocally. She even loved Emily Dickinson to the
brink of sentimentality. It wasn't just and it wasn't reasonable that Ruth's letters should do this to her, but it
did her no good to argue against her mood.

Bernie's advice for coping with these minor disasters
was just to go on agonizing at full steam while maintaining oneself in a state of resolute inaction. Finally the
boredom became worse than the pain. Going off into
the past was escapism at best and could lead to a nasty
case of dichronatism. So she sat on the worn-out settee
hidden in the setback of the corridor and considered all
the ways in which her life was rotten through and through
until, at a quarter to four, Willa came for her pies.

Willa's husband, like Alexa's, was in thermal salvage,
which was still a rare enough specialization to have made
a loose kind of friendship inevitable between them, despite their natural New York-bred reluctance to get involved with anyone living in the same building. Thermal
salvage, on the miniature scale of oven-sharing, was
basically all that united Alexa and Willa too, but it didn't
serve them as well for conversational fodder as it did their
husbands. Willa, who claimed to have scored a prodigious
167 on the I.Q. part of her Regents, was a pure specimen
of the New French Woman celebrated in the movies of
twenty years ago, and indeed in all French movies. She
did nothing and cared for nothing and, with a precise
feeling for the mathematics involved, deployed the little
green pluses and pink minuses from Pfizer's labs to hold
her soul steady at zero. By never for a moment relaxing
at the effort, she had made herself as pretty as a Chevro-
let and mindless as a cauliflower. Five minutes talking to
her and Alexa had regained every shred of her usual
self-esteem.

Thereafter the afternoon rolled down the track to evening with a benign predictability, making brief stops at all
the local stations. The casserole came out looking as
formidable and joyful as the last still on the recipe cassette. Loretta finally did phone and they made a new

appointment for Thursday. Tancred came home an hour
late, having adventured into the park. She knew, he knew
she knew, but as part of his moral education Tank was
obliged to invent a pleasant, undetectable fiction (a game
of chess with Dicky Myers). At 5:50 she brought out the
rice pudding, which had gone all brown and peculiar.
Then, just before the news, the office called and took
Saturday away—a disappointment as usual as rain or
dimes lost into telephones.

G. arrived not more than half an hour late.

The casserole was a religious experience.

"Is it real?" he asked. "I can't tell."

"The meat isn't meat, but I used real pork fat."

"It's incredible."

"Yes."

"Is there any more?" he asked.

She doled out the last rosette (Tank got the sauce) and
watched, with an immemorial indulgence, husband and son
eat her tomorrow's lunch.

After dinner G. took to the tub and meditated. Once he
was deep into alpha rhythms Alexa came and stood beside
the toilet and looked at him. (He didn't like being
looked at. Once he'd almost beat up a boy in the park
who wouldn't stop staring.) The too hairy body, the
drooping, volute lobes and muscled neck, curve and coun-
tercurve, the thousand colors of the shadowed flesh called
from her the same mixture of admiration and perplexity
that Echo must have felt gazing at Narcissus. With each
year of their marriage he had become stranger and
stranger to her. At times—and these the times she loved
him best—he seemed scarcely human. Not that she blinded
herself to his flaws (he was—who isn't?—riddled);
rather that the core of him seemed never to have known
anguish, fear, doubt—even, in any important way, pain.
He possessed a serenity that the facts of his life did not
warrant, and which (here was the thorn on which she
could not resist rubbing her finger) excluded her. Yet
just when his self-sufficiency seemed most complete and
cruelest he would turn round and do something incon-
grously tender and vulnerable, until she'd wonder if it
were all just her own iciness and bitchery that kept
them, twenty-five days in a month, so far apart.

His concentration faltered (had she made a noise, leaning back against the sink?) and broke. He looked up at her smiling (and Echo replied): "What are you thinking, A.?"

"I was thinking—" she paused to think. "—how wonderful computers are."

"They're wonderful, all right. Any special reason?"

"Well, for my first marriage I relied on my own judgment. This time. . . ."

He laughed. "Actually, confess it, you just wanted me out of the bathtub so you could do the dishes."

"Actually, not." (Though she was aware, even as she said this, that the squeeze bottle of disinfectant was in her hand.)   7

"I'm done anyhow. No, don't bother with the syphon. Or the dishes. We've established a partnership—remember?"

That night as they lay next to each other in bed, sharing each other's warmth but not touching, she fell into a landscape, half nightmare and half purposed reverie. The villa had been stripped of its furnishings. The air was urgent with smoke and a continual cheng-cheng of finger cymbals. The mystae waited for her to lead them into the city. As they stumbled down Broadway, past heaps of junked-out cars, they chanted the praise of the god in thin, terrified voices—Alexa first, then the god-bearer and the cista-bearer, the neatherd and the guardian of the cave, and then the whole rout of Bacchae and mutes: "Woo-woo-woo, a-woo-woo-woo!" Her fawnskin kept slipping between her legs and tripping her. At 93rd Street, and again at 87th, unwanted children mouldered on compost heaps. It was one of the scandals of the present administration that these little corpses should be left to rot where anyone walking by could see them.

At last they came to the Met (so they couldn't have been going down Broadway, after all) and she mounted the crisp stone steps with dignity. A great crowd had gathered in anticipation—many of them the same Christians who had been clamoring for the destruction of the temple and its idols. Once inside, the noise and the stench disappeared, as though some obliging servant had whisked a rain-drenched cloak from her shoulders. She sat, in the semidarkness of the Great Hall, beside her old favorite, a late Roman candybox of a sarcophagus from Tarsus (the first gift the Museum had ever received). Stone garlands drooped from the walls of the tiny, doorless bungalow; just below the eaves winged children, Erotes, pantomimed a hunt. The back and lid were unfinished, the tablet for the inscription blank. (She had always filled it in with her own name and an epitaph borrowed from Synesius, who, praising the wife of Aurelian, had said: "The chief virtue of a woman is that neither her body nor her name should ever cross the threshold.")

The other priests had fled the city at the first rumor of the barbarians' approach, and only Alexa, with a tambourine and a few silk ribbons, now was left. Everything was collapsing—civilizations, cities, minds—while she was constrained to wait for the end inside this dreary tomb (for the Met is really more a charnelhouse than a temple), without friends, without faith, and pretend for the sake of those who waited outside, to perform whatever sacrifice their terror demanded.

2.

The teaching assistant, a brisk, muscular boy in tights and a cowboy hat, left Alexa alone in an office no larger than the second bedroom, so-called, of a MODICUM apartment. She suspected that Loretta was punishing her for her absence the day before yesterday, so she might as well settle down and watch the reels the assistant had left with her. The first was a pious, somber account of the genius and tribulations of Wilhelm Reich, Alexander Lowen, and Kate Wilkenson, foundress and still titular president of the Lowen School.

The second reel presented itself as being the work of the students themselves. Things wobbled, faces were cerise and magenta, the blurry children were always intensely aware of the camera. All this candid-seeming footage was cunningly edited to suggest that (at least here at the Lowen School): "Learning is a side-effect of joy." Unquote, Kate Wilkenson. The children danced, the children prattled, the children made (so gently, so unproblematically) love, of sorts. Even mathematics, if not an out-and-out ecstasy, became an entertainment. Here, for instance, sat a little fellow about Tank's age in front of a teaching machine. On the screen a frantic mickey-mouse, caught in the cleft of a steep, slippery parabola, was shrieking to be saved: "Help! Oh help me, I'm trapped!"

Doctor Smilax chuckled and the parabolas began filling with water, inexorably. It rose above Mickey's ankles, above his knees, above the two white buttons on his shorts.

Alexa felt an uncomfortable tickle of memory.

"Y equals x-squared *plus* 2, does it?" In his anger the evil scientist's flesh-shield flickered, revealing glimpses of the infamous skull beneath. "They, try *this* on for size, Earthling!" Using his fingerbone as chalk, he scribbled on the magic blackboard (it was actually a computer):

$$Y = x^2 - 2.$$

The parabola tightened. The water rose level with Mickey's chin, and when he opened his mouth a final wave diminished his would-have-been scream to a mere, silly gargle.

(It had been thirty years ago, or longer. The blackboard was wiped clean and she had punched the keys for a final equation: x^2, and then 8, and then the operant key for Subtract. She had actually clapped her hands with glee when the pathetic little mickeymouse had been crushed to death by the tightening of the parabola.)

As, in the movie, he was crushed to death now, as he had been crushed to death each day for decades all about the world. It was a fantastically successful textbook.

"There is a lesson in that," said Loretta Dickens Couplard, entering the room and filling it.

"But not about parabolas especially," Alexa had replied before she'd turned round.

They looked at each other.

The thought that came, unexpected and so dissembled, was: *How old she looks! how altered!* The twenty years that had merely nibbled at Alexa (twenty-four, in fact) had simply heaped themselves on Loretta Couplard like a blizzard. In '02 she had been a passably pretty girl. Now she was a fat old hen. Dissembling, Alexa stood up and bent forward to kiss the pink doughy cheek (they would not, so long as a kiss lasted, see each other's dismay), but the earphones reined her in inches short of her goal.

Loretta completed the gesture.

"Well then—" (after this memento mori) "—let's go into my shambles, shall we?"

Alexa, smiling, disconnected herself from the viewer.

"It's out the door and around the corner. The school is spread out over four buildings. Three of them official landmarks." She led the way, lumbering down the dark hall and chattering about architecture. When she opened the door to the street the wind reached into her dress and made a sail of it. There seemed to be enough orange Wooly © on her to rig up a fair-sized yawl.

East 77th was innocent of traffic except for a narrow, not very busy, bicycle path. Potted gingkos dotted the concrete and real grass pressed up voluptuously through the cracks. Rarely did the city afford the pleasure of ruins, and Alexa drank it in.

(Somewhere she had seen a wall, all built of massive blocks of stone. Birds rested in the cracks where mortar had been chipped away and looked down at her. It had been the underside of a bridge—a bridge that had lost its river.)

"Such weather," she said, lingering beside one of the benches.

"Yes, April." Loretta, who was still being blown apart, was reluctant to take the hint.

"It's the only time, except for maybe a week in October, that New York is even viable."

"Mm. Why don't we talk out here then? At least until the children claim it for their own." Then, once they'd plunked themselves down: "Sometimes, you know, I almost think I'd like the street rezoned again. Cars make such a soothing noise. Not to mention the graft I have to pay." She made a honking sound through her nose, expressive of cynicism.

"Graft?" Alexa asked, feeling it was expected of her.

"It comes under 'maintenance' in the budget."

They regarded the windy month of April. The young grass fluttered. Strands of red hair whipped Loretta's face. She clamped a hand upon her head.

"What do you think it *costs* to keep this place going for one school-year—what do you think?"

"I couldn't begin to . . . I've never. . . ."

"A million and a half. Just slightly under."

"It's hard to believe," she said. (Could she have cared less?)

"It would be a lot more if it weren't that half of us, including me, is paid directly from Albany." Loretta went on, with aggrieved relish, to render an accounting of the school's finances circumstantial enough to have satisfied the Angel of Judgment. Alexa could not have felt more embarrassed if Loretta had begun to relate the unseemliest details of her private life. Indeed, between old school chums a friendly titbit or two might have helped restore a lapsed intimacy. In the old days Alexa had even once been in the same room while Loretta was getting laid by the Geology lab assistant. Or was it vice versa? In any case there had been few secrets between them. But to bring up a subject like one's own private income so blatantly, and then to dwell upon it this way—it was shocking. Alexa was aghast.

Eventually a hint of purposefulness became apparent in the drift of Loretta's indiscretions. The school was kept alive by a grant from the Ballanchine Foundation. Beyond an annual lump sum of fifty thousand dollars, the Foundation awarded scholarships to thirty-two entering students. Each year the school had to round up a new herd of qualified candidates, for the grant was conditional upon maintaining a sixty/forty ratio between paying and scholarship students.

"So now you see," Loretta said, nervously dallying with her big zipper, "why your phone call was such a boon."

"No, I don't see, entirely." Was she angling, God forbid, for a donation? Alexa tried to think of anything she might have said on the phone that could have given Loretta so false an estimate of G.'s tax bracket. Their address, certainly, couldn't have led her to this mistake: West 87th was distinctly *modest*.

"You spoke of working for the Welfare Department," Loretta said, with a sense of having laid down all her cards.

The zipper, having reach aphelion, began to descend. Alexa stared at it with candid incomprehension.

"Oh, Alexa, don't you see? You can scout them up for us."

"But surely in all New York City you don't have any trouble finding thirty-two candidates? Why, you told me there was a waiting list!"

"Of those who can pay. The difficulty is getting scholarship students who can meet the physical requirements. There are enough *bright* kids in the slums, especially if you know what tests to use to find them, but by the time they're ten years old, eleven years old, they're all physical wrecks. It's the combination of a cheap synthetic diet and the lack of exercise." The zipper, rising, snagged in orange Wooly ©. "The grant is from the Ballanchine Foundation—oh dear, now see what I've done—so there has to be at least a pretense of these kids becoming dancers. Potentially."

The zipper wouldn't budge. The movement of her shoulders slowly spread apart the opened top of the dress, creating a vast décolletage.

"I'll certainly keep my eyes opened," Alexa promised.

Loretta made a final attempt. Somewhere something ripped. She rose from the bench and forced an operatic laugh. "Let's repair inside, shall we?"

On the way to the office Loretta asked all the questions she'd so far neglected—what sports Tancred played, what programs he watched, what subjects he was most apt at, and what his ambitions were, if any.

"Right now he's talking about whaling. In general we've tried not to coerce him."

"Is coming here his own idea then?"

"Oh, Tank doesn't even know we've applied. G. and I—that's Gene, my husband, we call each other by our initials—we thought it would be best if we let him finish out the semester in peace where he is."

"P.S. 166," Loretta said, just to prove that she had gone over the application.

"It's a good school for the early grades, but after that. . . ."

"Of course. Democracy can be carried too far."

"It can," Alexa conceded.

They had reached the shambles, which was neither an office nor a bedroom nor yet a restaurant altogether. Loretta rearranged the upper part of her person inside a

maroon sweater and tucked the lower, grosser half of
herself out of sight behind an oak desk. Alexa at once
felt herself more friendly disposed to her.

"I hope you don't think I'm being too pokey?"

"Not at all."

"And Mr. Miller? What does he do?"

"He's in heat-retrieval systems."

"Oh."

(G. would always add, at this point, "I fight entropy
for a living." Should she?)

"Well. Most of our parents, you know, come from the
humanities. Like *us*. If Tancred should come to the Lowen
School, it's not likely that he'll ever follow in his father's
technological footsteps. Does Mr. Miller realize that?"

"We've discussed it. It's funny—"in evidence she
laughed, once, meagerly, through her nose"—but it's actually G. who's been more in favor of Tank coming here.
Whereas my first thought was to enroll him at Stuyvesant."

"Did you apply there?"

"Yes. I'm still waiting to hear if he's been accepted."

"It would be cheaper, of course."

"We've tried not to let that be a consideration. G. went
to Stuyvesant, but he doesn't have good feelings about it.
And while I enjoyed my education well enough, I can't see
that it's enriched my life so awfully much more than
G.'s that I can feel justified in my uselessness."

"Are you useless?"

"Yes, relative to an engineer. The humanities! What
good has it done for either of us, practically? I'm a case-
worker and you're teaching kids the same things we
learned so that they can grow up to do what? At best,
they'll be caseworkers and teachers."

Loretta nodded her head consideringly. She seemed to
be trying to keep from smiling. "But your husband dis-
agrees?"

"Oh, he feels his life has been wasted too." This time
her laughter was genuine.

Loretta, after only a moment more of noncommital
silence, joined her.

Then they had coffee, from actual beans that Loretta
ground herself, and small hard cookies covered with pi-
gnoli. They were imported from South America.

3.

Towards the end of his campaign against the Marco-
manni, the Emperor Marcus Aurelius wrote: "Consider
the past: such great changes of political supremacies. One
may foresee as well the things which will be. For they
will certainly take the same form. Accordingly, to have
contemplated human life for forty years is the same as
to have contemplated it for ten thousand years. For what
more will you see than you have seen already?"

Dear Ruth—
Alexa wrote in ballpoint (it was after eleven, G. was
asleep) in the empty back pages of Tank's fifth grade
project about the moon. She remembered to stick in
the date: *April 12, 2025.* Now the page balanced. She
tried the sounds of various openings in her head but they
were all stiff with civility. Her usual *Introibo,* an apology
for being late to reply, was this once not so.

(What would Bernie have said? He'd have said, "Clear
the air—say what you're really *feeling!*")

First, to clear the air. . .
The pen moved slowly, forming large upright letters.

*. . . I must say that your p.s. about Tank pissed me
off more than somewhat. You and your tone of I Speak
for the Human Spirit! You always are so ready to trounce
on my values.*

It was peanut butter, the very thickest. But she slogged
on through it.

*As for Tank, his fate still hangs in the balance. Ideally
we'd like to send him somewhere (cheap) to be fed orts
and crumbs of every art, science, craft, and. . . .*

She waited for the last term of the series.

The new Monsanto commercial came roaring through the
wall: YOU LOOK SO PRETTY IN SHOES! YOU LOOK
SO NICE IN—

"Turn that down!" she called in to her son, and wrote:

*. . . fashion until he was old enough to decide for
himself what he "liked." But I might as well fill in his
Modicum application right now as doom him with that
kind of education. I'll say this much for the Lowen
School—it doesn't graduate a lot of useless Renaissance*

nincompoops! I know too many of that sort professionally, and the best sweep streets—illegally!

Maybe Stuyvesant is as bad as you say, a kind of institutional Moriah, an altar specially put up for the sacrifice of my only begotten. I sometimes think so. But I also believe—the other half of the time—that some such sacrifice is required. You don't like G., but it's G. and those like him who are holding our technological world together. If her son could be trained to be either an actor or a soldier, what choice do you think a Roman matron would have made? That's a bit overmuch but you know what I mean.

(Don't you?)

She realized that, probably, Ruth wouldn't know what she meant. And she wasn't entirely sure she meant it.

At the very beginning of the First World War, as the Germans advanced towards the Marne and the Austrians pressed northward into Poland, a thirty-four-year-old ex-highschool teacher living in a Munich rooming house had just completed the first draft of what was going to be the best-selling book of 1919 throughout Germany. In his introduction he wrote:

> "We are a civilized people: to us both the springtime pleasures of the 12th Century and the harvests of the 18th have been denied. We must deal with the cold facts of a winter existence, to which the parallel is to be found not in the Athens of Pericles but in the Rome of Augustus. Greatness in painting, in music, in architecture are no longer, for the West, possibilities. For a young man coming of age in late Roman times, a student abubble with all the helter-skelter enthusiasms of youth, it needn't have been too brutal a disappointment to learn that *some* of his hopes would, necessarily, come to nothing. And if the hopes that had been blasted were those he held most dear, well, any lad worth his salt will make do, undismayed, with what is possible, and necessary. Say that there is a bridge to be built at Alcantara: then he will build it—and with a Roman's pride. A lesson can be drawn from this that would be of benefit to coming generations, as showing them what can,

and therefore must, be, as well as what is excluded
from the spiritual possibilities of their own time. I
can only hope that men of the next generation may
be moved by this book to devote themselves to en-
gineering instead of poetry, to the sea instead of the
paintbrush, to politics instead of epistemology. Better
than this they could not do."

Dear Ruth,
she began again, on a fresh sheet.

*Each time I write you I'm convinced you don't under-
stand a word. (In fact, often as not, I don't even send
my finished letter.) It's not just that I think you're stupid,
though I suppose I do, but that you have so well trained
yourself in that difficult form of dishonesty that you call
"faith" that you can't any longer see the world the way
it is.*

*And yet . . . (with you there is always that redeeming
"and yet") . . . I do continue to invite your misunderstanding, just as I keep on inviting Merriam to the villa.
Merriam—have I introduced her yet?—is my latest transfigure of "you." A highly Christian, terribly sexy Jewess
who follows heresy the way other women follow the arena.
At her worst she can be as sententious as you at yours,
but there are other moments when I'm convinced she
really does experience . . . whatever it is . . . in a
different way than I do. Call it her spirituality, though
the word makes me squirm. We will be out in the
garden, watching hummingbirds or some such, and Merriam will sink into her own thoughts, and they seem to
glow inside her like the flame in an alabaster lamp.*

*Yet I wonder if this isn't, after all, an illusion. Every
lout learns at some point in his life to make his silences
seem weighty with unspoken meaning. A single word can
extinguish the flame in the lamp. It is, this spirituality of
yours and hers, so humorless! "Getting into baskets," indeed!*

*And yet . . . I would—and this is a confession—love to
pack a bag and fly out to Idaho and learn to sit still
and make baskets or any other dumb thing, so long as I
could throw off the weight of my life here. To learn to
breathe! Sometimes New York terrifies me and usually it*

*appalls me, and the moments of High Civilization that
should compensate for the danger and the pain of living
here are less and less frequent as I grow older. Yes, I
would love to surrender myself to your way of life (I
fancy it would be something like being raped by a huge,
mute, and ultimately gentle Nigger), though I know I
never will. It's important to me, therefore, that you are
out there in the wilderness, redeeming my urban sins. Like
a stylite.*

*Meanwhile I'll go on doing what I think is my duty.
(We are the daughters, after all, of an Admiral!) The
city is sinking, but then the city has always been sinking.
The miracle is that it works at all, that it doesn't just . . .*

The second page of the second letter was filled. Reading
it over she realized it could never be mailed to her sister.
Their relationship, already rickety, would never support
the weight of this much honesty. But she finished the
sentence anyhow:

. . . collapse.

A quarter of a millennium after the *Meditations* and
fifteen hundred years before *The Decline of the West,* Salvian, a priest of Marseilles, described the process whereby
the free citizens of Rome were gradually reduced to a
condition of serfdom. The upper classes had arranged the
tax laws to their own convenience and then administered
them crookedly to their further convenience. The entire
burden of supporting the army—Rome's army, of course,
was vast, a nation within a nation—fell on the shoulders
of the poor. The poor grew poorer. Finally, reduced to
utter destitution, some fled from their villages to live
among the barbarians, even though (as Salvian notes) they
did give off a dreadful odor. Others, living far from the
frontiers, became bagaudae, or homemade vandals. The
majority, however, rooted to the land by their property
and families, had to accept the terms of the rich *poten-
tiores,* to whom they made over their houses, their lands,
their possessions, and at last the freedom of their children.
The birth rate declined. All Italy became a wasteland.
Repeatedly the Emperors were obliged to invite the politer
barbarians across the borders to "colonize" the abandoned
farms.

The condition of the cities at this time was even less

agreeable than that of the countryside. Burned and pillaged by barbarians and then by the troops (themselves mostly recruits from lands bordering the Danube) that had been sent in to dispel these invaders, the cities existed, if at all, in ruins. "Though doubtless no one wished to die," Salvian writes, "still no one did anything to avoid death," and he welcomes the advent of the Goths into Gaul and Spain as being a release from the despotism of a totally corrupt government.

My dear Gargilius,
Alexa wrote.
It's one of those days and has been for weeks. Rain, mud, and rumors of Radiguesis north of the city, west of the city, east of the city, everywhere at once. The slaves fret and dither but so far only two have run off to enlist among our would-be conquerors. On the whole we've done better than our neighbors. Arcadius has nothing left now but that cook of his who has such a mistaken notion of garlic (the one person who should have joined the barbarians!) and the Egyptian girl Merriam brought with her. The poor thing speaks no known language and probably hasn't been told the world is coming to an end. As for the two we lost, Patrobas always was a troublemaker and so good riddance. I'm sorry to tell you the other one was Timarchus, whom you had had such hopes for. He went into one of his snits and shattered the left arm of the wrestler down by the pool. Then he had no choice but to leave. Or perhaps it was the other way round —he smashed up the statue as a gesture of farewell. Anyhow, Sylvan says it can be repaired, though the damage will always be visible.
My own confidence in the Army is undiminished, darling, but I think it wisest that I close the villa till the rumors have abated somewhat. I shall get Sylvan—whom else can I trust now?—to help me bury the plate and the bedposts and the three remaining jugs of Falernian somewhere quite secret (as we discussed the last time). The books, those that matter, I'll bring with me. I wish there were even a morsel of good news. Except for being lonely, I am in good health and good spirits. I do wish you were not so many miles. . .
She crossed out "miles" and wrote "stadia."

. . . stadia away.

For a moment in the mirror of art, for the blinking of an iris, Alexa witnessed her life the wrong way round. Instead of a modern housewife fantasying herself in classical poses, the past stiffened and became actual and she thought she could see clearly, across the span of years, the other Alexa, the sad contemporary self she usually managed to avoid, a shrill woman in a silly dress who had been equal to the small demands neither of her marriage nor of her career. A failure or (which was possibly worse) a mediocrity.

"And yet," she told herself.

And yet: didn't the world, to keep on going, need just such people as she was?

It had only been a moment. The question had restored a comfortable perspective, and she would end her epistle to Gargilius with some chilly, true-to-life endearment. She would write—

But her pen had disappeared. It was not on the desk, it was not on the rug, it was not in her pocket.

The upstairs noise had begun.

Two minutes to twelve. She might reasonably complain, but she didn't know who lived in the apartment above, or even for certain that that was where the sound came from. "Cheng-cheng," and then, after a pause, "Cheng-cheng."

"Alexa?" She could not place the voice (a woman's?) summoning her. There was no one in the room.

"Alexa."

Tancred stood in the doorway, looking a perfect cupid with an old silky shawl knotted at his hips, lemon on chocolate.

"You startled me."

Her left hand had lifted automatically to her lips, and there, lapsing back into existence, was the ballpoint.

"I couldn't sleep. What time is it?" He stepped toward the table soundlessly and stood with one hand resting on the arm of a chair, his shoulders level with hers, his eyes steady as a laser beam.

"Midnight."

"Could we play a game of cards?"

"And what about tomorrow?"

"Oh, I'll get up. I promise." G., when he begged a

favor, always smiled; Tancred, a better tactician, remained perfectly solemn.

"Well, get out the cards. One game and then we *both* have to get to bed."

While Tancred was out of the room, Alexa tore out her own pages from "What the Moon Means to Me." A face clipped from a news magazine came unstuck and fluttered to the rug. She stooped and got it.

"What were you writing?" Tancred asked, beginning, neatly, to shuffle.

"Nothing. A poem."

"I wrote a poem," he admitted, excusing hers.

She cut. He began to deal.

She studied the newsprint face. It seemed oddly devoid of experience despite its years, like a very young actor got up as a very old man. The eyes regarded the camera lens with the equanimity of a star.

Finally she had to ask: "Who is this?"

"That! You don't know who that is? Guess."

"Some singer?" (*Could* it be Don Hershey? Already?)

"It's the last astronaut. You know, the three who landed on the moon. The other two are both dead." Tank took the scrap of paper from her and returned it to its place in his project. "Now he is too, I guess. You start."

4.

From Roman times until the closing years of the 20th Century the Bay of Morbihan on the southern coast of Brittany had been the source of the world's most delectable seed oysters. Then in the late 80's the oystermen of Locmariaquere were alarmed to notice that their seedlings sickened when they were transplanted and that soon even those that remained in their native waters had become unpalatable. Researchers hired by the *departement* of Morbihan eventually tracked down the source of infection to wastes dumped into the estuary of the Loire, some sixty miles down the coast. (Ironically, the polluter was a subsidiary branch of the pharmaceutical concern that had supplied the investigators.) By the time this was discovered, sad to say, the Morbihan oyster was extinct. However, in death the species bequeathed mankind its final inestimable gift, a monomolecular pearl, Morbehanine.

As synthesized by Pfizer, Morbehanine quickly became the most popular drug in all countries where it was not prohibited, usually in some gentling combination with the traditional. Modified by narcotizing agents it was marketed as Oraline; with caffeine it became Koffee; with tranquilizers Fadeout. In its crude form it was used only by the half million or so members of the intellectual elite who practiced Historical Analysis.

Unmodified Morbihanine induces a state of intensely experienced "daydreaming" in which usual relationships of figure-to-field are reversed. During a common hallucenogenic high the self remains a constant while the environment, as in dreams, undergoes transformation. With Morbehanine the landscape that one inhabits, after the initial "fixing" period, is not much more malleable than our own everyday world, but one is aware of one's slightest action in this landscape as a free, spontaneous, willed choice. It was possible to dream responsibly.

What determines the outlines of the alternate world is the subject's sum knowledge of the period he chooses to fix during his first trips. Without continuous research one was apt to create a fantasy life as monotonous as the afternoon sex features. Most people, sensibly, preferred the mild, multidirectional zonk of Oraline, its euphoric illusion of freedom every which way.

For the few, however, the more strenuous pleasures of Pure Will were worth a greater effort. A century before the same people had covered themselves with useless degrees in the humanities, filling the graduate schools to overflowing. Now, with Morbihanine, there was a *use* for all the history history students are forever studying.

It had often been debated, among analysands, whether Historical Analysis was the best way to work out one's problems or the best way to escape them. The elements of psychotherapy and of vicarious entertainment were inextricably knotted. The past became a kind of vast moral gymnasium in which some preferred a hard workout in the weight room of the French Revolution or the Conquest of Peru while others jiggled about lickerishly on the trampoline of Casanova's Venice or Delmonico's New York.

Once a particular stretch of time had been fixed, usually with the help of an expert in that era, one was no more at liberty to depart from it than one could walk away from the month of June. Alexa, for instance, was confined to a period of less than eighty years, from her birth in 334 (which was also, not coincidentally, the address of one of the buildings on East 11th Street for which she was responsible at the MODICUM office) up to the lovely pink evening when the twice-widowed Alexa, lately returned from a lifetime in the provinces, was to die of a stroke just a providential few days before the Sack of Rome. If she tried, during contact, to broach either barrier, 334 or 410, she experienced nothing more than a mild pastoral flickering—leaves, clouds, a blurry water-glass, sounds of troubled breathing, a smell of melons rotting—like the test-patterns of some sempiternal teevee network.

On Friday morning, despite the weather, Alexa took the malls downtown and arrived at Bernie's office ten minutes early. A good-sized hole had been punched through the fiber panel of the outer door and the furniture inside was in a state of delirium. The couch had been sliced open, its innards garnishing the ruins.

"But," Bernie pointed out cheerfully, sweeping up the fluff and plaster dust, "they never got into the office, thank God. They might have done actual harm there."

"That's a rosy view."

"Well, the way I look at it, this is the best of all possible worlds." Without a doubt he was soothed by the consolations of chemistry, but amid these ruins, why not?

"Do you know who did it?" She picked a lump of plaster off the bench, dropped it into his basket.

"Oh, I think I do. A pair of girls that the Council saddled me with has been threatening to scrub the office for months. I hope it was them—then the Council can pick up the bill."

Like most analysts, Bernie Shaw did not make a living from his fees. Unlike most, he didn't teach either. Instead he received a comfortable retainer from the Hell's Kitchen Neighborhood Youth Council for occasional services as a

Reader and Advisor. Bernie had an uncle on the Council's advisory board.

"Which is just the same as Historical Analysis, really," he would explain at parties (and thanks to the same uncle he was invited to some very good parties), "except that it doesn't involve history or analysis."

When the basket was full, Bernie slipped on his professional manner, and they entered the inner, vandal-proofed office. His face gelled into a handsome, immotile mask. His voice thickened to a droning baritone. His hands froze into a single neat rock of thoughtfulness, which he planted in the middle of his desk.

They faced each other across this rock and began to discuss Alexa's other inner life—first money, then sex, then whatever odds and ends were left.

Moneywise she would soon have to decide whether to accept Arcadius's long-standing offer to buy her melon fields. His price was tempting, but it was hard to reconcile the sale of farmland—and her patrimony at that—with an affectation of republican virtue. On the other hand, the land in question could hardly be called ancestral, having been one of Popilius's last speculations before his death.

(Alexa's father, Popilius Flamininus—born 276 A.D., died 354 A.D.—lived most of his life as a relatively impoverished Senator of Rome. After years of vacillation he decided to follow the Empire eastward to its new capital. Accordingly, one fine day Alexa, aged ten, was bundled into an oxcart and told to wave good-bye to the pretty idiot daughter of the superintendent of their apartment house. The journey to Byzantium took them two hundred stadia to the north and no distance eastward at all, for Popilius Flamininus had discovered that his purple stripe, so useless to him in Rome, was a social and financial asset in the hillside towns of Cisalpine Gaul. By the time she'd married Gargilius, Alexa was considered, locally, a tolerable heiress.)

Bernie took up the matter of her legal position, but she could cite Domitian's revival of the Julian laws governing the property rights of married women. Legally the fields were hers to sell.

"So the question remains. Should I?"

The answer remained, adamantly, no. Not because it

was hers from her father (who would have probably advised her to take the money and run); her piety was on a grander scale—Rome! Liberty! Civilization! It was to that burning ship that duty bound her. Of course, *she* didn't know it was burning. One of the knottiest problems in analysis was to keep the historical Alexa innocent of the fact that she was fighting, for the short term anyhow, a losing battle. She might have her suspicions—who didn't, then?—but this was reason rather for resolution than for faintheartedness. A lost battle is not a lost cause. Take Thermopylae.

The contemporary transfigure of this temptation, whether she ought to keep her job with the MODICUM office, had the same hydraheaded way of surviving her most final decisions. She didn't, except now and then, enjoy her work. She often suspected that the great machineries of the welfare service might actually do more harm than good. Her salary was only large enough to cover the extra expenses the job involved her in. Duty in these circumstances was an article of faith as thorny as the resurrection of the body. Yet it was only this faith—and a vague conviction that a city *ought* to be lived in—that helped her resist G.'s gentle, persistent drift suburbsward.

They breezed through sex by mutual agreement, for in that respect the last three or four months had been unadventurously pleasant. When she indulged in daydreams just for fun they were likelier to be about barbecues than orgies. Alexa could compensate for her stints of dieting in the present with bouts of exquisite excess in the past, fantasies which she lifted whole from Petronius, Juvenal, or the younger Pliny—salads of lettuce, leeks, and fresh mint; the cheese of Trebula; trays of Picenumine olives, Spanish pickles, and sliced eggs; a roasted kid, the tenderest of his flock, with more of milk in him than blood; asparagus covered with the willful anachronism of a Hollandaise sauce; pears and figs from Chios, and the plums of Damascus. Besides, unnecessary talk about sex tended to make Bernie nervous.

With fifteen minutes still to go a puddle of silence formed between them. She searched through the week's memories for an anecdote to float across it. The letter she'd written last night to Merriam? No, Bernie would accuse her of literature.

The puddle spread.

"Monday night," she said. "On Monday night I dreamed a dream."

"Oh?"

"I think it was a dream. Maybe I tinkered with it a little before I was completely asleep."

"Ah."

"I was dancing out in the street with a lot of other women. In fact I was sort of leading them. Down Broadway, but I wore a palla."

"That's a dichronatism." Bernie's tone was severe.

"Yes, but as I say, I was dreaming. Then I was in the Metropolitan Museum. For a sacrifice."

"Animal? Human?"

"One or the other. I don't remember."

"Blood sacrifices were prohibited in 341."

"Yes, but in a crisis the authorities would look the other way. During the siege of Florence in 405, which was years after the destruction of the temples—"

"Oh very well." Bernie closed his eyes, conceding the point. "So, once again the barbarians are storming the gates." The barbarians were always storming Alexa's gates. Bernie's theory was that it was because her husband was fractionally a Negro. "Then what happened?"

"That's all I remember. Except one detail earlier in the dream. There were heaps of dead babies in the cess trenches in the middle of Broadway."

"Infanticide was a capital offense from the beginning of the third century," Bernie pointed out.

"Probably because it was becoming too common."

Bernie closed his eyes. Then, opening them: "Have *you* ever had an abortion?"

"Once, ages ago, in high school. I didn't feel much guilt though."

"What did you feel about the children in your dreams?"

"Anger, at the untidyness. Otherwise they were just a fact." She looked at her hands, which seemed too large, the knuckles especially. "Like a face in a news magazine." She looked at Bernie's hands folded on the desk. Another silence began to form, but gracefully, without embarrassment. She remembered the moment she'd found herself alone on the street; the sunlight, her pleasure. It seemed quite reasonable that people should expose their children to die. There was what Loretta had said yesterday—"I've stopped trying"—but it went beyond that. As though everyone had come to see that Rome, civilization, the whole burning issue wasn't worth the effort any longer, theirs or anyone's. Every infanticide was the kindness of a philosopher.

"Pish," Bernie said, when she'd said this four or five different ways. "No one sees his own culture declining till around the age of forty, and then everyone does."

"But things had been going downhill for two hundred years."

"Or three, or four."

"Farmlands had become deserts. It was *visible*. Look at the sculpture, the architecture."

"It's visible with hindsight. But *they* could be as blind as their comfort required. Trivial poetasters like Ausonius were declared the equals of Virgil, of Homer even, and the Christians, now that they were *official*, were positively giddy with optimism. They expected to see the city of God shoot up like an urbal renewal project."

"Then explain those dead children."

"Explain the living ones. Which reminds me. Last week you still hadn't made up your mind about Tancred."

"I sent off the letter this morning, with a check."

"To?"

"Stuyvesant."

The rock on the desk split open and became two hands. "Well—there you have it."

"What?"

"An interpretation for your dream. The blood sacrifice you were ready to make to save the city, the children on the scrapheap—your son."

She denied it.

5.

By three that afternoon the tops of buildings were invisible at street level. She had walked crosstown from the office in a lukewarm drizzle, then taken the subway down to East 14th. All the way, the argument with Bernie had continued inside her, like some battery-powered toy, a novelty doll with a loop of tape that croaks after each smack of the old smacker, "Oh, don't do that again! Oh, please don't, I can't stand it!"

Before she'd come out through the turnstile she could smell the grease from Big San Juan's, a dark ground of onion polka dotted with plantain. By the time she was up on the street, her mouth was watering. She would have bought a quarter bag but customers had gathered three deep around the counters (baseball season—already?) and she saw Lottie Hanson in the crowd in front of the screen. The plantains weren't worth the risk of a conversation. Lottie's blowzy sexiness always affected Alexa elegiacally, like a roomful of cut flowers.

Crossing Third Avenue between 11th and 12th, a sound dopplered at her, swelling in an instant from a hum to a roar. She whirled about, scanning the fog for whatever lunatic truck or. . . .

The sound as suddenly diminished. The street was empty. A block to the north the lights winked green. She got to the curb before the traffic—a bus and two shrill Yamahas—reached the second stripe of the ped crossing. Then, several beats after she'd figured it out, her idiot heart caught up with her panic.

A helicopter certainly, but flying lower than any she'd ever known.

Her knees took so to trembling that she had to lean against a hydrant. Long after the distant whirr had diffused into the general midday din the machineries of her glands kept her in a flutter.

Marylou Levin had taken her mother's place at the corner with the broom and the can. A homely, slow, earnest girl who'd grow up to be a day-care worker, unless, which would probably be more profitable both for Marylou and for society, she took over her mother's license as a sweep.

Alexa dropped a penny in the can. The girl looked up from her comic book and said thank you.

"I hoped I'd find your mother here, Marylou."

"She's home."

"I've got a declaration she had to fill out. I didn't get

it to her last time and now the office is starting to make a fuss."

"Well, she's sleeping." Marylou turned back to the comic book, a sad story about horses in a Dallas circus, then thought to add: "She relieves me at four."

It meant either waiting or walking up to the seventeenth floor. If the M–28 wasn't cleared through Blake's section by tomorrow Mrs. Levin might lose her apartment (Blake had been known to do worse) and it would be Alexa's fault.

Usually, except for the stink, she didn't mind the stairs, but all the walking today had taken it out of her. A weariness as of heavy shopping bags focused in the small of her back. On the ninth floor she stopped in at Mr. Anderson's to hear the poor tedious old man complain about the various ingratitudes of his adopted daughter. (Though "boarder" described that relationship more accurately.) Cats and kittens climbed over Alexa, rubbed against her, inveigled her.

On eleven her legs gave out again. She sat on the top step and listened to the commingled urgencies of a newscast one flight up and a song one flight down. Her ears filtered Latin words from the Spanish phrases.

Imagine, she thought, actually living here. Would one grow numb eventually? One would have to.

Lottie Hanson hove into sight at the landing below, clutching the rail and panting. Recognizing Alexa and conscious of having to look nice for her, she patted her damp, drizzly wig and smiled.

"Glory, isn't it"— she caught her breath, waved her hand in front of her face, decoratively—"exciting!"

Alexa asked what.

"The bombing."

"Bombing?"

"Oh, you haven't heard. They're bombing New York. They showed it on teevee, where it landed. These steps!" She collapsed beside Alexa with a great *huff*. The smell that had seemed so appetizing outside Big San Juan's had lost its savor. "But they couldn't show"—she waved her hand and it was still, Alexa had to admit, a lovely and a graceful hand—"the actual airplane itself. Because of the fog, you know."

"Who's bombing New York?"

"The radicals, I suppose. It's some kind of protest. Against something." Lottie Hanson watched her breasts lift and fall. The importance of the news she bore made her feel pleased with herself. She waited for the next question all aglow.

But Alexa had begun calculating with no more input than she had already. The notion had seemed, from Lottie's first words, inevitable. The city cried out to be bombed. The amazing thing was that no one had ever thought to do it before.

When she did at last ask Lottie a question, it came from an unexpected direction. "Are you afraid?"

"No, not a bit. It's funny, because usually, you know, I'm just a bundle of nerves. Are *you* afraid?"

"No. Just the opposite. I feel. . . ." She had to stop and think what it was that she did feel.

Children came storming down the stairs. With a gentle "Goddamn," Lottie squeezed up against the crusty wall. Alexa pressed up to the railing. The children ran down through the canyon they'd formed.

Lottie screamed at the last of them, "Amparo!"

The girl turned round at the landing and smiled. "Oh, hi, Mrs. Miller."

"Goddamn it, Amparo, don't you know they're bombing the city?"

"We're all going down to the street to watch."

Dazzling, Alexa thought. She'd always had a thing for pierced ears on children, had even been tempted to do Tank's for him when he was four, but G. had interposed.

"You get your ass back upstairs and stay there till they shoot that fucking airplane down!"

"The teevee said it doesn't make *any* difference *where* you are."

Lottie had gone all red. "I don't care about that. I say—"

But Amparo had already run off.

"One of these days I'm going to kill her."

Alexa laughed indulgently.

"I am, just wait and see."

"Not on stage, I hope."

"What?"

"Ne pueros coram," she explained, "populo Medea

trucidet. Don't let 'Medea kill her boys before the audience. It's Horace." She got up and bent round to see if she'd soiled her dress.

Lottie remained on the step, inert. An everyday depression began to blunt the exhilaration of the catastrophe, like fog spoiling an April day, today's fog, today's April day.

Smells filmed every surface like cheap skin cream. Alexa had to get out of the stairwell, but Lottie had somehow caught hold of her and she wriggled in the meshes of an indefinite guilt.

"I think I'll go up to the battlement now," she said, "to watch the seige."

"Well, don't wait for me."

"But later there's something I wanted to talk to you about."

"Right. Later."

When she was one landing up Lottie called after her—"Mrs. Miller?"

"Yes?"

"The first bomb got the museum."

"Oh. Which museum?"

"The Met."

"Really."

"I thought you'd want to know."

"Of course. Thank you."

Like a theater just before the movie starts, reduced by the darkness to a bare geometry, the fog had erased all details and distances. Uncertain sounds sifted through the grayness—engines, music, women's voices. She felt through her whole body the imminence of the collapse, and because now she *could* feel it, it was no longer debilitating. She ran along the gravel. The roof stretched on and on in front of her without perspective. At the ledge she swerved to the right. She ran on.

She heard, far off, the stolen plane. It neither approached her nor receded, as though it were executing an immense circle, searching for her.

She stood still and lifted her arms, inviting it to her, offering herself to these barbarians, fingers splayed, eyes pressed tightly closed. Commanding.

She saw, beneath her but unforeshortened, the bound

ox. She saw its heaving belly and desperate eyes. She felt, in her hand, the sharp obsidian.

She told herself that this was what she had to do. Not for her own sake, of course. Never for her own sake— for theirs.

Its blood drenched the gravel. It gushed and splattered. The hem of the palla was stained. She knelt in the blood and dipped her hands into the opened belly to raise the dripping entrails high above her head, tubes and wires in a slime of thick black oil. She wound herself in the soft coils and danced like some god-drenched girl at the festivals, laughing and pulling the torches from their sockets, smashing sacred articles, jeering at the generals.

No one approached her. No one asked what she had, read in the haruspices.

She climbed up into the jungle gym and stood peering into the featureless air, her legs braced against the thin pipes, raptured and strong with a dawning faith.

The airplane approached, audibly.

She wanted it to see her. She wanted the boys inside to know that she knew, that she agreed.

It appeared quite suddenly, and near, like Minerva sprung full-grown from the brow of Jupiter. It was shaped like a cross.

"Come then," she said with conscious dignity. "Lay waste."

But the plane—a Rolls Rapide—passed overhead and returned to the haze from which it had materialized.

She climbed down from the gym with a sense of loss: she had offered herself to History and History had refused. With a sense, equally, of what a fool she'd been.

She felt in her pockets for a pack of hankies but she'd run out at the office. She had her cry anyhow.

6.

Since the Army had begun celebrating its victory the city no longer seemed a sanctuary. Therefore early the next morning Merriam and Arcadius started back home on foot. During the darkest moments of the seige, with the generosity of despair, Arcadius had given the cook and the Theban girl their freedom, so that they were returning to the villa completely unattended.

Merriam was dreadfully hungover. The road was a slough, and when they came to the cut-off, Arcadius insisted on taking the even muddier path that went through Alexa's fields. But for all that, she felt happy as an apricot. The sun was shining and the fields steamed like some great kitchen full of soup kettles and sauceboats, as though the very earth was sending up its prayer of thanksgiving.

"Lord," she would murmur, "Lord." She felt like a new woman.

"Have you noticed," Arcadius pointed out, after they'd gone some distance, "that there is nowhere any sign of them?"

"Of the barbarians? Yes, I've been crossing my fingers."

"It's a miracle."

"Oh yes, it's God's work, beyond a doubt."

"Do you think she knew?"

"Who?" she asked, in not an encouraging tone. Talk always dissipated her good feelings.

"Alexa. Perhaps she's been sent a sign. Perhaps, after all, she danced in thanksgiving and not . . . the opposite."

Merriam pressed her lips together and made no reply. It was a blasphemous proposition. God did not give signs to the servants of the abominations he loathed and comminated! And yet. . . .

"In retrospect," Arcadius insisted, "there's really no other explanation."

(And yet, she *had* seemed altogether jubilant. Perhaps —she had heard this suggested by a priest in Alexandria— there are evil spirits whom God permits, to a limited degree and imperfectly, to see the shape of future things.)

She said, "I thought it was an obscene display."

Arcadius didn't contradict her.

Later, after they had circled round the base of the larger hill, the path sloped upward and grew dryer. The trees fell away on their left and permitted a view eastward across Alexa's melon fields. Hundreds of bodies were scattered over the trampled scenery. Merriam hid her eyes but it was not so easy to escape the scent of decay, which mingled, almost pleasantly, with the odor of smashed, fermenting melons.

"Oh dear," said Arcadius, realizing that their path would lead them straight through the midst of the carnage.

"Well, we'll have to do it—that's all," Merriam said, lifting her chin with a show of defiance. She took his hand and they walked through the field of defeated barbarians as quickly as they could.

Later, Lottie came up looking for her. "I was wondering if you were all right."

"Thank you. I just needed a breath of air."

"The plane crashed, you know."

"No, I hadn't heard any more than you told me."

"Yes—it crashed into a MODICUM project at the end of Christopher Street. One-seventy-six."

"Oh, that's awful."

"But the building was just going up. No one was killed but a couple of electricians."

"That's a miracle."

"I thought you might like to come down and watch the teevee with us. Mom is making Koffee."

"I'd appreciate that."

"Good." Lottie held open the door. The stairwell had achieved evening a couple hours in advance of the day.

On the way downstairs Alexa mentioned that she thought she could arrange for Amparo to get a scholarship at the Lowen School.

"Would that be good?" Lottie asked, and then, embarrassed by her question, "I mean—I've never heard of it till just now."

"Yes, I think it's pretty good. My son Tancred will be going there next year."

Lottie seemed unpersuaded.

Mrs. Hanson stood outside the door of the apartment gesturing frantically. "Hurry up, hurry up! They've found the boy's mother, and they're going to interview her."

"We can talk about it more later," Alexa said.

Inside, on the teevee, the boy's mother was explaining to the camera, to the millions of viewers, what she couldn't understand.

EMANCIPATION:

A Romance of the Times to Come

1.

Summer mornings the balcony would fill up with bona-fide sunshine and Boz would spread open the recliner and lie there languid as something tropical in their own little basin of private air and ultraviolet fifteen floors above entrance level. Just watching, half-awake, the vague geometries of jet trails that formed and disappeared, formed and disappeared in the pale cerulean haze. Sometimes you could hear the dinky preschoolers on the roof piping their nursery rhymes in thin, drugged voices.

> A Boeing buzzing from the west
> brings the boy that I love best.
> But a Boeing from the east. . . .

Just nonsense, but it taught directions, like north and south. Boz, who had no patience with Science, always confused north and south. One was uptown, one was downtown—why not just call them that? Of the two, uptown was preferable. Who wants to be MOD, after all? Though it was no disgrace: his own mother, for instance. Human dignity is more than a zipcode number, or so they say.

Tabbycat, who was just as fond of sunshine and out-of-doors as Boz, would stalk along the prestressed ledge as far as the rubber plant and then back to the geraniums, very sinister, just back and forth all morning long, and every so often Boz would reach up to stroke the soft sexy down of her throat and sometimes when he did that he would think of Milly. Boz liked the mornings best of all.

But in the afternoons the balcony fell into the shadow of the next building and though it remained almost as warm it didn't do anything for his tan, so in the afternoon Boz had to find something else to do.

Once he had studied cooking on television but it had nearly doubled the grocery bills, and Milly didn't seem to care whether Boz or Betty Crocker made her omelette fine herbes, and he had to admit himself that really there wasn't that much difference. Still, the spice shelf and the two copper-bottom pans he had given himself for Christmas made an unusual decorator contribution. The nice names spices have—rosemary, thyme, ginger, cinnamon —like fairies in a ballet, all gauze wings and toeshoes. He could see her now, his own little niecelette Amparo Martinez as Oregano Queen of the Willies. And he'd be Basil, a doomed lover. So much for the spice shelf.

Of course he could always read a book, he liked books. His favorite author was Norman Mailer and then Gene Stratton Porter. He'd read everything they'd ever written. But lately when he'd read for more than a few minutes he would develop really epic headaches and then be a complete tyrant to Milly when she came home from work. What she called work.

At four o'clock art movies on Channel 5. Sometimes he used the electromassage and sometimes just his hands to jerk off with. He'd read in the Sunday facs that if all the semen from all the Metropolitan Area viewers of Channel 5 were put all together in one single place it would fill a medium-sized swimming pool. Fantastic? Then imagine swimming in it!

Afterwards he would lay spread out on the sofa that looked like a giant Baggie, his own little contribution to the municipal swimming pool drooling down the clear plastic and he would think glumly: *There's something wrong. Something is missing.*

There was no romance in their marriage any more, that's what was wrong. It had been leaking out slowly, like air from a punctured Baggie chair, and one of these days she would mean it when she started talking about a

divorce, or he would kill her with his own bare hands or
with the electromassage, when she was ribbing him in bed,
or something dreadful would happen, he knew it.

Something really dreadful.

At dusk, in bed, her breasts hung above him, swaying.
Just the smell of her is enough, sometimes, to drive him
up the walls. He brought his thighs up against the sweaty
backside of her legs. Knees pressed against buttocks.
One breast, then the other, brushed his forehead; he
arched his neck to kiss one breast, then the other.

"Mm," she said. "Continue."

Obediently Boz slid his arms between her legs and pulled
her forward. As he wriggled down on the damp sheets
his own legs went over the edge of the mattress, and his
toes touched her Antron slip, a puddle of coolness on the
desert-beige rug.

The smell of her, the rotting sweetness, like a suet
pudding gone bad in a warm refrigerator, the warm
jungle of it turned him on more than anything else, and
way down there at the edge of the bed, a continent
away from these events, his prick swelled and arched.
Just wait your turn, he told it, and rubbed his stubbly
cheek against her thigh while she mumbled and cooed. If
only pricks were noses. Or if noses. . . .

The smell of her now with the damp furze of her veldt
pressed into his nostrils, grazing his lips, and then the first
taste of her, and then the second. But most of all the
smell—he floated on it into her ripest darknesses, the soft
and endless corridor of pure pollened cunt, Milly, or Africa,
or Tristan and Isolde on the tape recorder, rolling in
rosebushes.

His teeth scraped against hair, snagged, his tongue
pressed farther in and Milly tried to pull away just from
the pleasure of it, and she said, "Oh, Birdie! Don't!"

And he said, "Oh shit."

The erection receded quickly as the image sinks back
into the screen when the set is switched off. He slid out
from under her and stood in the puddle, looking at her
uplifted sweating ass.

She turned over and brushed the hair out of her eyes.
"Oh, Birdie, I didn't mean to. . . ."

"Like hell you didn't. Jack."

She sniffed amusement. "Well, now *you're* one up."

He flipped the limp organ at her self-deprecatingly. "Am I?"

"Honestly, Boz, the first time I really didn't mean it. It just slipped out."

"Indeed it did. But is that supposed to make me feel *better?*" He began dressing. His shoes were inside out.

"For heaven's sake, I haven't thought of Birdie Ludd for years. Literally. He's *dead* now, for all I know."

"Is that the new kick at your tutorials?"

"You're just being bitter."

"I'm just being bitter, yes."

"Well, fuck you! I'm going out." She began feeling around on the rug for her slip.

"Maybe you can get your father to warm up some of his stiffs for you. Maybe he's got Birdie there on ice."

"You can be so sarcastic sometimes. And you're standing on my slip. Thank you. Where are you going now?"

"I am going around the room divider to the other side of the room." Boz went around the room divider to the other side of the room. He sat down beside the dining ledge.

"What are you writing?" she asked, pulling the slip on.

"A poem. That's what *I* was thinking about at the time."

"Shit." She had started her blouse on the wrong button-hole.

"What?" He laid the pen down.

"Nothing. My buttons. Let me see your poem."

"Why are you so damn hung up on buttons? They're unfunctional." He handed her the poem!

> *Pricks are noses.*
> *Cunts are roses.*
> *Watch the pretty petals fall.*

"It's lovely," she said. "You should send it to *Time*."

"*Time* doesn't print poetry."

"Some place that does, then. It's pretty." Milly had three basic superlatives: funny, pretty, and nice. Was she relenting? Or laying a trap?

"Pretty things are a dime a dozen. Twelve for one dime."

"I'm only trying to be nice, shithead."

"Then learn how. Where are you going?"

"Out." She stopped at the door, frowning. "I do love you, you know."

"Sure. And I love you."

"Do you want to come along?"

"I'm tired. Give them my love."

She shrugged. She left. He went out on the veranda and watched her as she walked over the bridge across the electric moat and down 48th Street to the corner of 9th. She never looked up once.

And the hell of it was she *did* love him. And he loved her. So why did they always end up like this, with spitting and kicking and gnashing of teeth and the going of their own ways?

Questions, he hated questions. He went into the toilet and swallowed three Oralines, one just nicely too many, and then he sat back and watched the round things with colored edges slide along an endless neon corridor, zippety zippety zippety, spaceships and satellites. The corridor smelled half like a hospital and half like heaven, and Boz began to cry.

The Hansons, Boz and Milly, had been happily unhappily married for a year and a half. Boz was twenty-one and Milly was twenty-six. They had grown up in the same MODICUM building at opposite ends of a long, glazed, green-tile corridor, but because of the age difference they never really noticed each other until just three years ago. Once they did notice each other though, it was love at first sight, for they were, Boz as much as Milly, of the type that can be, even at a glance, ravishing: flesh molded with that ideal classic plumpness and tinged with those porcelain pink pastels we can admire in the divine Guido, which, at least, *they* admired; eyes hazel, flecked with gold; auburn hair that falls with a slight curl to the round shoulders; and the habit, acquired by each of them so young that it could almost be called natural, of striking poses eloquently superfluous, as when, sitting down to dinner, Boz would throw his head back suddenly, flip flop of auburn, his ripe lips slightly parted, like a saint (Guido again) in ecstasy—Theresa, Francis, Ganymede—or like, which was almost the same thing, a singer, singing

I am you
and you are me
and we are just two
sides
of the same coin.

Three years and Boz was still as hung up on Milly as he had been on the first morning (it was March but it had seemed more like April or May) they'd had sex, and if that wasn't love then Boz didn't know what love meant.

Of course it wasn't just sex, because sex didn't mean that much to Milly, as it was part of her regular work. They also had a very intense spiritual relationship. Boz was basically a spiritual type person. On the Skinner-Waxman C-P profile he had scored way at the top of the scale by thinking of one hundred and thirty-one different ways to use a brick in ten minutes. Milly, though not as creative as Boz according to the Skinner-Waxman, was every bit as smart in terms of IQ (Milly, 136; Boz, 134), and she also had leadership potential, while Boz was content to be a follower as long as things went more or less his own way. Brain surgery aside, they could not have been more compatible, and all of their friends agreed (or they had until very recently) that Boz and Milly, Milly and Boz, made a perfect couple.

So what was it then? Was it jealousy? Boz didn't think it was jealousy but you can never be sure. He might be jealous unconsciously. But you can't be jealous just because someone was having sex, if that was only a mechanical act and there was no love involved. That would be about as reasonable as getting uptight because Milly *talked* to someone else. Anyhow he had had sex with other people and it never bothered Milly. No, it wasn't sex, it was something psychological, which meant it could be almost anything at all. Every day Boz got more and more depressed trying to analyze it all out. Sometimes he thought of suicide. He bought a razor blade and hid it in *The Naked and the Dead*. He grew a moustache. He shaved off the moustache and had his hair cut short. He let his hair grow long again. It was September and then it was March. Milly said she really did want a divorce, it wasn't working out and she could not stand him nagging at her any more.

Him nagging at *her?*

"Yes, morning and night, nag, nag, nag."

"But you're never even home in the morning, and you're *usually* not home at night."

"There, you're doing it again! You're nagging now, And when you don't come right out and nag openly, you do it silently. You've been nagging me ever since dinner without saying a word."

"I've been reading a book." He wagged the book at her accusingly. "I wasn't even thinking about you. Unless I nag you just by *existing*." He had meant this to sound pathetic.

"You can, you do."

They were both too pooped and tired to make it a really fun argument, and so just to keep it interesting they had to keep raising the stakes. It ended with Milly screaming and Boz in tears and Boz packing his things into a cupboard which he took in a taxi to East 11th Street. His mother was delighted to see him. She had been fighting with Lottie and expected Boz to take her side. Boz was given his old bed in the living room and Amparo had to sleep with her mother. The air was full of smoke from Mrs. Hanson's cigarettes and Boz felt more and more sick. It was all he could do to keep from phoning Milly. Shrimp didn't come home and Lottie was zonked out as usual on Oraline. It was not a life for human beings.

2.

The Sacred Heart, gold beard, pink cheeks, blue blue eyes, gazed intently across twelve feet of living space and out the window unit at long recessions of yellow brick. Beside him a Conservation Corporation calendar blinked now BEFORE and then AFTER views of the Grand Canyon. Boz turned over so as not to have to look at Jesus, the Grand Canyon, Jesus. The tuckaway lurched to port side. Mrs. Hanson had been thinking of having someone in to fix the sofa (the missing leg led an independent existence in the cabinet below the sink) ever since the Welfare people had busted it on the day how many years ago that the Hansons had moved in to 334. She would discuss with her family, or with the nice Mrs. Miller from the MOD office, the obstacles in the way of this undertaking, which proved upon examination so ramiform and finally so formidable as very nearly to defeat her most energetic hopes. Nevertheless, *some* day.

Her nephew, Lottie's youngest, was watching the war on the teevee. It was unusual for Boz to sleep so late. U.S. gorillas were burning down a fishing village somewhere. The camera followed the path of the flames along the string of fishing boats, then held for a long time on the empty blue of the water. Then a slow zoom back that took in all the boats together. The horizon warped and flickered through a haze of flame. Gorgeous. Was it a rerun? Boz seemed to think he'd seen that last shot before.

"Hi there, Mickey."

"Hi, Uncle Boz. Grandma says you're getting divorced. Are you going to live with us again?"

"Your grandma needs a decongestant. I'm only here for a few days. On a visit."

The apple pie colophon, signaling the end of the war for that Wednesday morning, splattered and the decibels were boosted for the April Ford commercial, "Come and Get Me, Cop."

> *Come and get me, Cop,*
> *Cause I'm not gonna stop*
> *At your red light.*

It was a happy little song, but how could he feel happy when he knew that Milly was probably watching it too and enjoying it in a faculty lounge somewhere, never even giving a thought for Boz, or where he was, or how he felt. Milly studied all the commercials and could play them back to you verbatim, every tremor and inflection just so. And not a milligram of her own punch. Creative? As a parrot.

Now, what if he were to tell her *that?* What if he told her that she would never be anything more than a second-string Grade-Z hygiene demonstrator for the Board of Education. Cruel? Boz was supposed to be cruel?

He shook his head, flip-flop of auburn. "Baby, you don't know what cruel is."

Mickey switched off the teevee. "Oh, if you think this was something today you should have seen them yesterday. They were in this school. Parkistanis, I think. Yeah. You should have seen it. That *was* cruel. They wiped them out."

"Who did?"

"Company A." Mickey came to attention and saluted the air. Kids his age (six) always wanted to be gorillas or firemen. At ten it was pop singers. At fourteen, if they were bright (and somehow all the Hansons *were* bright, they wanted to write. Boz still had a whole scrapbook of the advertisements he'd written in high school. And then, at twenty . . . ?

Don't think about it.

"You didn't care?" Boz asked.

"Care?"

"About the kids in the school."

"They were insurgents," Mickey explained. "It was in Pakistan." Even Mars was more real than Pakistan and no one gets upset about schools burning on *Mars*.

A flop flop flop of slippers and Mrs. Hanson shambled in with a cup of Koffee. "Politics, you'd try and argue politics with a six-year-old! Here. Go ahead, drink it."

He sipped the sweet thickened Koffee and it was as though every stale essence in the building, garbage rotting in bins and grease turning yellow on kitchen walls, tobacco smoke and stale beer and Synthamon candies, everything ersatz, everything he'd thought he had escaped, had flooded back into the core of his body with just that one mouthful.

"He's become too good for us now, Mickey. Look at him."

"It's sweeter than I'm used to. Otherwise it's fine, Mom."

"It's no different than you used to have it. Three tablets. I'll drink this one and make you another. You came here to stay."

"No, I told you last night that—"

She waved a hand at him, shouted to her grandson: "Where you going?"

"Down to the street."

"Take the key and bring the mail up first, understand. If you don't. . . ."

He was gone. She collapsed in the green chair, on top

of a pile of clothes, talking to herself or to him, she wasn't particular about her audience. He heard not words but the reedy vibrato of her phlegm, saw the fingers stained with nicotine, the jiggle of sallow chin-flesh, the MOD teeth. My mother.

Boz turned his eyes to the scaly wall where roseate AFTER winked to a tawdry BEFORE and Jesus, squeezing a bleeding organ in his right hand, forgave the world for yellow bricks that stretched as far as the eye could see.

"The work she comes home with you wouldn't believe. I told Lottie, it's a crime, she should complain. How old is she? Twelve years old. If it had been Shrimp, if it had been you, I wouldn't say a word, but she has her mother's health, she's very delicate. And the exercises they make them do, it's not decent for a child. I'm not against sex, I always let you and Milly do whatever you wanted. I turned my head. But that sort of thing should be private between two people. The things you see, and I mean right out on the street. They don't even go into a doorway now. So I tried to make Lottie see reason, I was very calm, I didn't raise my voice. Lottie doesn't want it herself, you know, she's being pressured by the school. How often would she be able to see her? Weekends. And one month in the summer. It's all Shrimp's doing. I said to Shrimp, if you want to be a ballet dancer then *you* go ahead and be a ballet dancer but leave Amparo alone. The man came from the school, and he was very smooth and Lottie signed the papers. I could have cried. Of course it was all arranged. They waited till I was out of the house. She's your child, I told her, leave me out of it. If that's what you want for her, the kind of future you think she deserves. You should hear the stories she comes home with. Twelve years old! It's Shrimp, taking her to those movies, taking her to the park. Of course you can see all of that on television too, that Channel 5, I don't know why they. . . . But I suppose it's none of my business. No one cares what you think when you're old. Let her *go* to the Lowen School, it won't break my heart." She kneaded the left side of her dress illustratively: her heart.

"We could use the room here, though you won't hear me complaining about that. Mrs. Miller said we could apply for a larger apartment, there's five of us, and now six with you, but if I said yes and we moved and then Amparo goes off to this school, we'd just have to move back here, because the requirement *there* is for five people. Besides it would mean moving all the way to *Queens*. Now if Lottie were to have another, but of course her health isn't up to it, not to speak of the mental thing. And Shrimp? Well, I don't have to go into that. So I said no, let's stay put. Besides, if we did go and then had to come back here, we probably wouldn't have the luck to get the same apartment again. I don't deny that there are lots of things wrong with it, but still. Try and get water after four o'clock, like sucking a dry tit."

Hoarse laughter, another cigarette. Having broken the thread of thought, she found herself lost in the labyrinth: her eyes darted around the room, little cultured pearls that bounced off into every corner.

Boz had not listened to the monologue, but he was aware of the panic that welled up to fill the sudden wonderful silence. Living with Milly he'd forgotten this side of things, the causeless incurable terrors. Not just his mother's; everyone who lived below 34th.

Mrs. Hanson slurped her Koffee. The sound (her own sound, *she* made it) reassured her and she started talking again, making more of her own sounds. The panic ebbed. Boz closed his eyes.

"That Mrs. Miller means well of course but she doesn't understand my situation. What do you think she said I should do, what do you think? Visit that death-house on 12th Street! Said it would be an inspiration. Not to me, to *them*. Seeing someone at my age with my energy and the head of a family. My age! You'd think I was ready to turn to dust like one of those what-do-you-call-its. I was born in 1967, the year the first man landed on the moon. Nineteen. Sixty. Seven. I'm not even sixty, but suppose I were, is there a law against it? Listen, as long as I can make it up those stairs they don't have to worry about *me!* Those elevators are a crime. I can't even remember the last time. . . . No, wait a minute, I can. You were eight years old, and every time I took you inside you'd start to cry. You used to cry about everything though. It's my own fault, spoiling you, and your sisters went right along. That time I came home and you were in

Lottie's clothes, lipstick and everything, and to think she helped you. Well, I stopped that! If it had been Shrimp I could understand. Shrimp's that way herself. I always said to Mrs. Holt when she was alive, she had very old-fashioned ideas, Mrs. Holt, that as long as Shrimp had what she wanted it was no concern of hers or mine. And anyhow you'll have to admit that she *was* a homely girl, while Lottie, oh my, Lottie was so beautiful. Even in high school. She'd spend all her time in front of a mirror and you could hardly blame her. Like a movie star."

She lowered her voice, as though confiding a secret to the olive-drab film of dehydrated vegetable oil on her Koffee.

"And then to go and do that. I couldn't believe my eyes when I saw him. Is it prejudice to want something better for your children, then I'm prejudiced. A good-looking boy, I don't deny that, and even smart in his way I suppose. He wrote poems to her. In Spanish, so I wouldn't be able to understand them. I told her, it's your life, Lottie, go ahead and ruin it any way you like but don't tell me I'm *prejudiced*. You children never heard me use words like that and you never will. I may not have more than a high school education but I know the difference between . . . right and wrong. At the wedding she wore this blue dress and I never said a word about how short it was. So beautiful. It still makes me cry." She paused. Then, with great emphasis, as though this were the single unassailable conclusion that these many evidences remorselessly required of her: "He was *always* very polite."

Another longer pause.

"You're not listening to me, Boz."

"Yes, I am. You said he was always very polite."

"Who?"

Boz searched through his inner family album for the face of anyone who might have behaved politely to his mother.

"My brother-in-law?"

Mrs. Hanson nodded. "Exactly. Juano. And she also said why didn't I try religion." She shook her head in a pantomime of amazement that such things could be allowed.

"She? Who?"

The dry lips puckered with disappointment. The discontinuity had been intended, a trap, but Boz had slipped past. She *knew* he wasn't listening but she couldn't prove it.

"Mrs. Miller. She said it would be good for me. I told her one religious nut in the family is enough and besides I don't call that religion. I mean, I enjoy a stick of Oraline as much as anyone, but religion has to come from the heart." Again she rumpled the violet, orange, and heather-gold flames of her bodice. Down below there somewhere it filled up with blood and squirted it out into the arteries: her heart.

"Are *you* still that way?" she asked.

"Religious? No, I was off that before I got married. Milly's dead against it too. It's all chemistry."

"Try and tell that to your sister."

"Oh, but for Shrimp it's a meaningful experience. She understands about the chemistry. She just doesn't care, so long as it works."

Boz knew better than to take sides in any family quarrel. Once already in his life he had had to slip loose from those knots, and he knew their strength.

Mickey returned with the mail, laid it on the TV, and was out the door before his grandmother could invent new errands.

One envelope.

"Is it for me?" Mrs. Hanson asked. Boz didn't stir. She took a deep wheezing breath and pushed herself up out of the chair.

"It's for Lottie," she announced, opening the envelope. "It's from the Alexander Lowen School. Where Amparo wants to go."

"What's it say?"

"They'll take her. She has a scholarship for one year. Six thousand dollars."

"Jesus. That's great."

Mrs. Hanson sat down on the couch, across Boz's ankles, and cried. She cried for well over five minutes. Then the kitchen timer went off: *As the World Turns*. She hadn't missed an installment in years and neither had Boz. She stopped crying. They watched the program.

Sitting there pinned beneath his mother's weight, warmed by her flesh, Boz felt good. He could shrink down to the size of a postage stamp, a pearl, a pea, a

wee small thing, mindless and happy, nonexistent, utterly
lost in the mail.

3.

Shrimp was digging God, and God (she felt sure) was
digging Shrimp: her, here on the roof of 334; Him, out
there in the russet smogs of dusk, in the lovely poisons
of the Jersey air, everywhere. Or maybe it wasn't God
but something moving more or less in that direction.
Shrimp wasn't sure.

Boz, dangling his feet over the ledge, watched the
double moiré patterns of her skin and her shift. The
spiral patterns of the cloth moved widdershins, the flesh
patterns stenciled beneath ran deasil. The March wind
fluttered the material and Shrimp swayed and the spirals
spun, vortices of gold and green, lyric illusions.

Off somewhere on another roof an illegal dog yapped.
Yap, yap, yap; I love you, I love you, I love you.

Usually Boz tried to stay on the surface of something
nice like this, but tonight he was exiled to inside of himself, redefining his problem and coming to grips with it
realistically. Basically (he decided) the trouble lay in his
own character. He was weak. He had let Milly have her
own way in everything until she'd forgotten that Boz might
have his own legitimate demands. Even Boz had forgotten. It was a one-sided relationship. He felt he was
vanishing, melting into air, sucked down into the green-
gold whirlpool. He felt like shit. The pills had taken him
in exactly the wrong direction, and Shrimp, out there in
St. Theresa country, was no aid or comfort.

The russet dimmed to a dark mauve and then it was
night. God veiled His glory and Shrimp came down.
"Poor Boz." she said.

"Poor Boz," he agreed.

"On the other hand you've gotten away from this." Her
hand whisked away the East Village roofscape and every
ugliness. A second, more impatient whisk, as though she'd
found the whole mess glued to her hand. In fact, it had
become her hand, her arm, the whole stiff contraption of

flesh she had managed for three hours and fifteen minutes to escape.

"And poor Shrimp."

"Poor Shrimp too," he agreed.

"Because *I'm* stuck here."

"This morning who was telling me it isn't where you live, it's *how* you live?"

She shrugged a sharp-edged scapula. She hadn't been speaking of the building but of her own body, but it would have taken too much trouble to explain that to blossoming Narcissus. She was annoyed with Boz for dwelling on *his* miseries, *his* inner conflicts. She had her own dissatisfactions that she wanted to discuss, hundreds.

"Your problem is very simple, Boz. Once you face it. Your problem is that *basically* you're a Republican."

"Oh, come off it, Shrimp!"

"Honestly. When you and Milly started living together, Lottie and I couldn't believe it. It had always been clear as day to us."

"Just because I have a pretty face doesn't mean—"

"Oh, Boz, you're being dense. You know that has nothing to do with it one way or the other. And I'm not saying you should vote Republican because I do. But I *can* read the signs. If you'd look at yourself with a little psychoanalysis you'd be forced to see how much you've been *repressing*."

He flared up. It was one thing to be called a Republican but no one was going to call him repressed. "Well, shit on you, sister. If you want to know my party, I'll tell you. When I was thirteen I used to jerk off while I watched you undress, and believe me, it takes a pretty dedicated Democrat to do that."

"That's nasty," she said.

It was nasty, and as untrue as it was nasty. He'd fantasized often enough about Lottie, about Shrimp never. Her short thin brittle body appalled him. She was a gothic cathedral bristling with crockets and pinnacles, a forest of leafless trees; he wanted nice sunshiny cortiles and flowery glades. She was a Dürer engraving; he was a landscape by Domenichino. Screw Shrimp? He'd as soon turn Republican, even if she *was* his own sister.

"Not that I'm *against* Republicanism," he added diplomatically. "I'm no Puritan. I just don't enjoy having sex with other guys."

"You've never given it a chance." She spoke in an aggrieved tone.

"Sure I have. Plenty of times."

"Then why is your marriage breaking up?"

Tears started dripping. He cried all the time nowadays, like an air conditioner. Shrimp, skilled in compassion, wept right along with him, wrapping a length of wiry arm around his bare, exquisite shoulders.

Snuffling, he threw back his head. Flip-flop of auburn, big brave smile. "How about the party?"

"Not for me, not tonight. I'm feeling too religious and holy, sort of. Maybe later perhaps."

"Aw, Shrimp."

"Really." She wrapped herself in her arms, stuck out her chin, waited for him to plead.

The dog in the distance made new noises.

"One time, when I was a kid . . . right after we moved here, in fact . . ." Boz began dreamily.

But he could see she wasn't listening.

Dogs had just been made finally illegal and the dog owners were doing Anne-Frank numbers to protect their pups from the city Gestapo. They stopped walking them on the streets, so the roof of 334, which the Park Commission had declared to be a playground (they'd built a cyclone fence all round the edge to give it a playground atmosphere), got to be ankle-deep in dogshit. A war developed between the kids and dogs to see who the roof would belong to. The kids would hunt down off-leash dogs, usually at night, and throw them over the edge. German shepherds fought back the hardest. Boz had seen a shepherd take one of Milly's cousins down to the pavement with him.

All the things that happen and seem so important at the time, and yet you just forget them, one after another. He felt an elegant, controlled sadness, as though, were he to sit down now and work at it, he might write a fine, mature piece of philosophy.

"I'm going to sail away now. Okay?"

"Enjoy yourself," Shrimp said.

He touched her ear with his lips, but it wasn't, even in a brotherly sense, a kiss. A sign, rather, of the distance between them, like the signs on highways that tell you how far it is in miles to New York City.

The party was not by any means a form of insanity but Boz enjoyed himself in a quiet decorative way, sitting on a bench and looking at knees. Then Williken, the photographer from 334, came over and told Boz about Nuancism, Williken being a Nuancist from way back when, how it was overdue for a renaissance. He looked older than Boz remembered him, parched and fleshless and pathetically forty-three.

"Forty-three is the best age," Williken said again, having at last disposed of the history of art to his satisfaction.

"Better than twenty-one?" Which was Boz's age, of course.

Williken decided this was a joke and coughed. (Williken smoked tobacco.) Boz looked away and caught the fellow with the red beard eyeing him. A small gold earring twinkled in his left ear.

"*Twice* as good," Williken said, "and then a bit." Since this was a joke too, he coughed again.

He was (the red beard, the gold earring), next to Boz, the best-looking person there. Boz got up, with a pat to the old man's frayed and folded hands.

"And how old are you?" he asked the red beard, the gold earring.

"Six foot two. Yourself?"

"I'm versatile, pretty much. Where do you live?"

"The East Seventies. Yourself?"

"I've been evacuated." Boz struck a pose: Sebastian (Guido's) spreading himself open, flowerlike, to receive the arrows of men's admiration. Oh, Boz could charm the plaster off the walls! "Are you a friend of January's?"

"A friend of a friend, but that friend didn't show. Yourself?"

"The same thing, sort of."

Danny (his name was Danny) grabbed a handful of the auburn hair.

"I like your knees," Boz said.

"You don't think they're too bushy?"

"No, I like bushy knees."

When they left January was in the bathroom. They

shouted their goodbyes through the paper panel. All the way home—going down the stairs, in the street, in the subway, in the elevator of Danny's building—they kissed and touched and rubbed up against each other, but though this was exciting to Boz in a psychological way, it *didn't* give him a hard-on.

Nothing gave Boz a hard-on.

While Danny, behind the screen, stirred the instant milk over the hotcoil, Boz, alone in all that double bed, watched the hamsters in their cage. The hamsters were screwing in the jumpy, jittery way that hamsters have, and the lady hamsters said, "Shirk, shirk, shirk." All nature reproached Boz.

"Sweetener?" Danny asked, emerging with the cups.

"Thanks just the same. I shouldn't be wasting your time like this."

"Who's to say the time's been wasted? Maybe in another half-hour. . . ." The moustache detached itself from the beard: a smile.

Boz smoothed his pubic hairs sadly, ruefully, wobbled the oblivious soft cock. "No, it's out of commission tonight."

"Maybe a bit of roughing up! I know guys who—"

Boz shook his head. "It wouldn't help."

"Well, drink your Koffee. Sex isn't that important, believe me. There are other things."

The hamster said, "Shirk! Shirk, shirk."

"I suppose not."

"It isn't," Danny insisted. "Are you always impotent?" There, he had said the dreaded word.

"God, no!" (The horror of it!)

"So? One off-night is nothing to worry about. It happens to me all the time and *I* do it for a living. I'm a hygiene demonstrator."

"*You?*"

"Why not? A Democrat by day and a Republican in my spare time. By the way, how are you registered?"

Boz shrugged. "What difference does it make if you don't vote?"

"Stop feeling sorry for yourself."

"I'm a Democrat actually, but before I got married I was Independent. That's why, tonight, I never thought, when I came home with you, that—I mean, you're damned good-looking, Danny."

Danny blushed agreement. "Get *off* it. So tell me, what's wrong with your marriage?"

"You wouldn't want to hear about it," Boz said, and then he went through the whole story of Boz and Milly: of how they had had a beautiful relationship, of how that relationship had then soured, of how he didn't understand why.

"Have you seen a counselor?" Danny asked.

"What good would that do?"

Danny had manufactured a tear of real compassion and he lifted Boz's chin to make certain he would notice. "You should. Your marriage still means a *lot* to you and if something's gone wrong you should at least know what. I mean, it might just be something stupid, like getting your metabolic cycles synchronized."

"You're right, I guess."

Danny bent over and squeezed Boz's calf earnestly. "Of course I'm right. Tell you what, I know someone who's supposed to be terrific. On Park Avenue. I'll give you his number." He kissed Boz quickly on the nose, just in time for the tear of his empathy to plop on Boz's cheek.

Later, after one last determined effort, Danny, in nothing but his transparency, saw Boz down to the moat, which (also) was defunct.

When they had kissed good-bye and while they were still shaking hands, Boz asked, as though off-handedly, as though he had been thinking of anything else for the last half-hour: "By the way, you wouldn't have worked at Erasmus Hall, would you?"

"No. Why? Did you go there? I wouldn't have been teaching anywhere in your time."

"No. I have a friend who works there. At Washington Irving?"

"I'm out in Bedford-Stuyvesant, actually." The admission was not without its pennyworth of chagrin. "But what's his name? Maybe we met at a union meeting, or something like that."

"It's a she—Milly Hanson."

"Sorry, never heard of her. There are a lot of us, you

know. This is a big city." In every direction the pavement
and the walls agreed.

Their hands unclasped. Their smiles faded, and they became invisible to each other, like boats that draw apart,
moving across the water into heavy mists.

4.

227 Park Avenue, where McGonagall's office was, was
a dowdy sixtyish affair that had been a bit player back in
the glass-and-steel boom. But then came the ground-test
tremors of '96 and it had to be wrapped. Now it had the
look, outside, of Milly's last-year dirty-yellow Wooly ©
waistcoat. That, plus the fact that McGonagall was an
old-fashioned-type Republican (a style that still mostly
inspired distrust), made it hard for him to get even the
official Guild minimum for his services. Not that it made
much difference for them—after the first fifty dollars the
Board of Education would pay the rest under its sanity-
and health clause.

The waiting room was simply done up with paper mattresses and a couple authenticated Saroyans to cheer up
the noonday-white walls: an

> Alice

and:

> o r
> o r

Fashionwise, Milly was doing an imitation of maiden
modesty in her old PanAm uniform, a blue-gray gauzy
jerkin over crisp business-like pajamas. Boz, meanwhile,
was sporting creamy street shorts and a length of the same
blue-gray gauze knotted round his throat. When he moved
it fluttered after him like a shadow. Between them they
were altogether tout ensemble, a picture. They didn't talk.
They waited in the room designed for that purpose.

Half a damned hour.

The entrance to McGonagall's office was something from the annals of the Met. The door sublimed into flame and they passed through, a Pamina, a Tamino, accompanied appropriately by flute and drum, strings and horns. A fat man in a white shift welcomed them mutely into his bargain-rate temple of wisdom, clasping first Pamina's, then Tamino's hands in his. A sensitivist obviously.

He pressed his pink-frosted middle-aged face close to Boz's, as though he were reading its fine print. "You're Boz," he said reverently. Then with a glance in her direction: "And you're Milly."

"No," she said peevishly (it was that half-hour), "I'm Boz, and *she's* Milly."

"Sometimes," McGonagall said, letting go, "the best solution *is* divorce. I want you both to understand that if that should be my opinion in your case, I won't hesitate to say so. If you're annoyed that I kept you waiting so long, *tant pis,* since it was for a good reason. It rids us of our company manners from the start. And what is the first thing you say when you come in here? That your husband is a woman! How did it make you feel, Boz, to know that Milly would like to cut off your balls and wear them herself?"

Boz shrugged, long-suffering, ever-likeable. "I thought it was funny."

"Ha," laughed MaGonagall, "that's what you thought. But what did you *feel?* Did you want to strike her? Were you afraid? Or secretly pleased?"

"That's it in a nutshell."

McGonagall's living body sank into something pneumatic and blue and floated there like a giant white squid bobbing on the calm surface of a summer sea. "Well then, tell me about your sexlife, Mrs. Hanson."

"Our sexlife is pretty," Milly said.

"Adventurous," Boz continued.

"And quite frequent." She folded her pretty, faultless arms.

"When we're together," Boz added. A grace note of genuine self-pity decorated the flat irony of the statement. This soon he felt his insides squeezing some idle tears from the appropriate glands; while, in other glands, Milly had begun to churn up petty grievances into a lovely smooth yellow anger. In this, as in so many other ways, they achieved a kind of symmetry between them, they made a pair.

"Your jobs?"

"All that kind of thing is on our profiles," Milly said. "You've had a month to look at them. A half-hour, at the very least."

"But on your profile, Mrs. Hanson, there's no mention of this remarkable reluctance of yours, this grudging every word." He lifted two ambiguous fingers, scolding and blessing her in a single gesture. Then, to Boz: "What do *you* do, Boz?"

"Oh, I'm strictly a husband. Milly's the breadwinner."

They both looked at Milly.

"I demonstrate sex in the high schools," she said.

"Sometimes," McGonagall said, spilling sideways meditatively over his blue balloon (like all very clever fat men he knew how to pretend to be Buddha), "what are thought to be marital difficulties have their origin in *job* problems."

Milly smiled an assured porcelain smile. "The city tests us every semester on job satisfaction, Mr. McGonagall. Last time I came out a little high on the ambition scale, but not above the mean score for those who eventually have moved on into administrative work. Boz and I are here because we can't spend two hours together without starting to fight. I can't sleep in the same bed any more, and he gets heartburn when we eat together."

"Well, let's assume for now that you are adjusted to your job. How about you, Boz? Have you been happy being 'just a husband'?"

Boz fingered the gauze knotted round his throat. "Well, no . . . I guess I'm not completely *happy* or we wouldn't be here. I get—oh, I don't know—restless. Sometimes. But I know I wouldn't be any happier working at a job. Jobs are like going to church: it's nice once or twice a year to sing along and eat something and all that, but unless you really believe there's something holy going on, it gets to be a drag going in every single week."

"Have you ever had a real job?"

"A couple times. I hated it. I think most people must hate their jobs. I mean, why else do they *pay* people to work?"

"Yet something *is* wrong, Boz. Something is missing from your life that ought to be there."

"Something. I don't know what." He looked downhearted.

McGonagall reached out for his hand. Human contact was of fundamental importance in McGonagall's business. "Children?" he asked, turning to Milly, after this episode of warmth and feeling.

"We can't afford children."

"Would you want them, if you felt you could afford them?"

She pursed her lips. "Oh yes, very much."

"*Lots* of children?"

"Really!"

"There are people, you know, who do want lots of children, who'd have as many as they could if it weren't for the Regents system."

"My mother," Boz volunteered, "had four kids. They all came before the Genetic Testing Act, of course, except for me, and I was only allowed then because Jimmy, her oldest one, got killed in a riot, or a dance, or something, when he was fourteen."

"Do you have pets at home?" McGonagall's drift was clear.

"A cat," Boz said, "and a rubber plant."

"Who takes care of the cat mostly?"

"I do, but that's because I'm there through the day. Since I've been gone Milly's had to take care of Tabby. It must be lonely for her. For old Tabbycat."

"Kittens?"

Boz shook his head.

"No," Milly said. "I had her spayed."

Boz could almost hear McGonagall thinking: Oh ho! He knew how the session would continue from this point and that the heat was off him and on Milly. McGonagall might be right, or he might not, but he had an idea between his jaws and he wasn't letting loose: Milly needed to have a baby (a woman's fulfillment), and Boz, well, it looked like Boz was going to be a mother.

Sure enough, by the end of the session Milly was spread out on the pliant white floor, back uparched, screaming ("Yes, a baby! I want a baby! Yes, a baby! A baby!") and having hysterical simulated birth spasms. It was beautiful. Milly hadn't broken down, really broken all the way down, and cried in how long? Years. It was one hundred per cent beautiful.

Afterwards they decided to go down by the stairs, which were dusty and dark and tremendously erotic. They made it on the 28th floor landing and, their legs all atremble, again on the 12th. The juice shot out of him in dazzling gigantic hiccoughs, like milk spurting out of a full-to-the-top two-quart container, so much they neither could believe it: a heavenly breakfast, a miracle proving their existence, and a promise they were both determined to keep.

It wasn't all sweetness and roses, by any means. They had more paper work to do than from all the 1040 Forms they'd ever prepared. Plus visits to a pregnancy counselor; to the hospital to get the prescriptions they both had to start taking; then reserving a bottle at Mount Sinai for after Milly's fourth month (the city would pay for that, so she could stay on the job); and the final solemn moment at the Regents office when Milly drank the first bitter glass of the anticontraceptive agent. (She was sick the rest of the day, but did she complain? Yes.) For two weeks after that she couldn't drink anything that came out of the tap in the apartment, until, happy day, her morning test showed a positive reading.

They decided it would be a girl: Loretta, after Boz's sister. They redecided, later on: Aphra, Murray, Algebra, Sniffles (Boz's preferences), and Pamela, Grace, Lulu and Maureen (Milly's preferences).

Boz knitted a kind of blanket.

The days grew longer and the nights shorter. Then vice versa. Peanut (which was her name whenever they couldn't decide what her name really would be) was scheduled to be decanted the night before Xmas, 2025.

But the important thing, beyond the microchemistry of where babies come from, was the problem of psychological adjustment to parenthood, by no means a simple thing.

This is the way McGonagall put it to Boz and Milly during their last private counseling session:

"The way we work, the way we talk, the way we watch television or walk down the street, even the way we fuck, or maybe that especially—each of those is part of the problem of identity. We can't do any of those things *authentically* until we find out who we really are and *be* that person, inside and out, instead of the person other people want us to be. Usually those other people, if they want us to be something we aren't, are using us as a laboratory for working out their own identity problems.

"Now Boz, we've seen how you're expected, a hundred tiny times a day, to seem to be one kind of person in personal relationships and a completely different kind of person at other times. Or to use your own words—you're 'just a husband.' This particular way of sawing a person in two got started in the last century, with automation. First jobs became easier, and then scarcer—especially the kinds of jobs that came under the heading of a 'man's work.' In every field men were working side by side with women. For some men the only way to project a virile image was to wear levis on the weekends and to smoke the right brand of cigarette. Marlboros, usually." His lips tightened and his fingers flexed delicately, as again, in his mouth and in his lungs, desire contested with will in the endless, ancient battle: with just such a gesture would a stylite have spoken of the temptations of the flesh, rehearsing the old pleasures only to reject them.

"What this meant, in psychological terms, was that men no longer needed the same kind of uptight, aggressive character structure, any more than they needed the bulky, Greek-wrestler physiques that went along with that kind of character. Even as sexual plumage that kind of body became unfashionable. Girls began to prefer slender, short ectomorphs. The ideal couples were those, like the two of you as a matter of fact, who mirrored each other. It was a kind of movement inward from the poles of sexuality.

"Today, for the first time in human history, men are free to express the essentially *feminine* component in their personality. In fact, from the economic point of view, it's almost required of them. Of course, I'm not talking about homosexuality. A man can be *feminized* well beyond the point of transvestism without losing his preference for cunt, a preference which is an *inescapable* consequence of having a cock."

He paused to appreciate his own searing honestly—a

Republican speaking at a testimonial dinner for Adlai Stevenson!

"Well, this is pretty much what you must have heard all through high school, but it's one thing to understand something intellectually and quite another to feel it in your body. What most men felt *then*—the ones who allowed themselves to go along with the feminizing tendencies of the age—was simply a crushing, horrible, total guilt, a guilt that became, eventually, a much worse burden than the initial repression. And so the Sexual Revolution of the Sixties was followed by the dreary Counterrevolution of the Seventies and Eighties, when I grew up. Let me tell you, though I'm sure you've been told many times, that it was simply awful. *All* the men dressed in black or gray or possibly, the adventuresome ones, a muddy brown. They had short haircuts and walked—you can see it in the movies they made then—like early-model robots. They had made such an effort to deny what was happening that they'd become frozen from the waist down. It got so bad that at one point there were *four* teevee series about zombies.

"I wouldn't be going over this ancient history except that I don't think young people your age realize how lucky you are having missed that. Life still has problems—or I'd be out of work—but at least people today who want to solve them have a chance.

"To get back to the decision you're facing, Boz. It was in that same period, the early Eighties (in Japan, of course, since it would surely have been illegal in the States then), that the research was done that allowed feminization to be more than a mere cosmetic process. Even so, it was years before these techniques became at all widespread. Only in the last two decades, really. Before our time, every man had been obliged, for simple *biological* reasons, to deny his own deep-rooted maternal instincts. Motherhood is basically a psychosocial, and not a sexual, phenomenon. Every child, be he boy or girl, grows up by learning to emulate his mother. He (or she) plays with dolls and cooks mud pies—if he lives somewhere where mud is available. He rides the shopping cart through the supermarket, like a little kangaroo. And so on. It's only natural for men, when they grow up, to wish to be mothers themselves, if their social and economic circumstances allow it—that is to say, if they have the leisure, since the rest can now be taken care of.

"In short, Milly, Boz needs more than your love, or any woman's love, or any man's love, for that matter. Like you, he needs another *kind* of fulfillment. He needs, as you do, a child. He needs, even *more* than you do, the experience of motherhood."

5.

In November, at Mount Sinai, Boz had the operation —and Milly too, of course, since she had to be the donor. Already he'd undergone the series of implantations of plastic "dummies" to prepare the skin of his chest for the new glands that would be living there—and to prepare Boz himself spiritually for his new condition. Simultaneously a course of hormone treatments created a new chemical balance in his body so that the mammaries would be incorporated into its working order and yield from the first a nourishing milk.

Motherhood (as McGonagall had often explained) to be a truly meaningful and liberating experience had to be entered into wholeheartedly. It had to become part of the structure of nerve and tissue, not just a process or a habit or a social role.

Every hour of that first month was an identity crisis. A moment in front of a mirror could send Boz off into fits of painful laughter or precipitate him into hours of gloom. Twice, returning from her job, Milly was convinced that her husband had buckled under the strain, but each time her tenderness and patience through the night saw Boz over the hump. In the morning they would go to the hospital to see Peanut floating in her bottle of brown glass, pretty as a waterlily. She was completely formed now and a human being just like her mother and father. At those moments Boz couldn't understand what all his agonizing had been about. If anyone ought to have been upset, it should have been Milly, for there she stood, on the threshold of parenthood, slim-bellied, with tubes of liquid silicone for breasts, robbed by the hospital and her husband of the actual experience of maternity. Yet she seemed to possess only reverence for this new life they had created between them. It was as though Milly, rather than Boz, were Peanut's father, and birth were a mystery she might admire from a distance but never wholly, never intimately, share.

Then, precisely as scheduled, at seven o'clock of the evening of December 24, Peanut (who was stuck with this name now for good and forever, since they'd never been able to agree on any other) was released from the brown glass womb, tilted topsy-turvy, tapped on the back. With a fine, full-throated yell (which was to be played back for her every birthday till she was twenty-one years old, the year she rebelled and threw the tape in an incinerator), Peanut Hanson joined the human race.

The one thing he had not been expecting, the wonderful thing, was how busy he had to be. Till now his concern had always been to find ways to fill the vacant daylight hours, but in the first ecstasies of his new selflessness there wasn't time for half of all that needed doing. It was more than a matter of meeting Peanut's needs, though these were prodigious from the beginning and grew to heroic proportions. But with his daughter's birth he had been converted to an eclectic, new-fangled form of conservationism. He started doing real cooking again and this time without the grocery bills rocketing. He studied Yoga with a handsome young yogi on Channel 3. (There was no time, of course, under the new regime for the four o'clock art movies.) He cut back his Koffee intake to a single cup with Milly at breakfast.

What's more, he kept his zeal alive week after week after month after month. In a modest, modified form he never entirely abandoned the vision, if not always the reality, of a better richer fuller and more responsible life-pattern.

Peanut, meanwhile, grew. In two months she doubled her weight from six pounds two ounces to twelve pounds four ounces. She smiled at faces, and developed a repertoire of interesting sounds. She ate—first only a teaspoon or so—Banana-food and Pear-food and cereals. Before long she had dabbled in every flavor of vegetable Boz could find for her. It was only the beginning of what would be a long and varied career as a consumer.

One day early in May, after a chill, rainy spring, the temperature bounced up suddenly to 70°. A sea wind had rinsed the sky from its conventional dull gray to baby blue.

Boz decided that the time had come for Peanut's first voyage into the unknown. He unsealed the door to the balcony and wheeled the little crib outside.

Peanut woke. Her eyes were hazel with tiny flecks of gold. Her skin was as pink as a shrimp bisque. She rocked her crib into a good temper. Boz watched the little fingers playing scales on the city's springtime airs, and catching her gay spirits, he sang to her, a strange silly song he remembered his sister Lottie singing to Amparo, a song that Lottie had heard her mother sing to Boz:

> Pepsi Cola hits the spot.
> Two full glasses, thanks a lot.
> Lost my savior, lost my zest,
> Lost my lease, I'm going west.

A breeze ruffled Peanut's dark silky hair, touched Boz's heavier auburn curls. The sunlight and air were like the movies of a century ago, so impossibly *clean*. He just closed his eyes and practiced his breathing.

At two o'clock, punctual as the news, Peanut started crying. Boz lifted her from the crib and gave her his breast. Except when he left the apartment nowadays, Boz didn't bother with clothing. The little mouth closed round his nipple and the little hands gripped the soft flesh back from the tit. Boz felt a customary tingle of pleasure but this time it didn't fade away when Peanut settled into a steady rhythm of sucking and swallowing, sucking and swallowing. Instead it spread across the surface and down into the depths of his breast; it blossomed inward to his chest's core. Without stiffening, his cock was visited by tremors of delicate pleasure, and this pleasure traveled, in waves, into his loins and down through the muscles of his legs. For a while he thought he would have to stop the feeding, the sensation became so intense, so exquisite, so much.

He tried that night to explain it to Milly, but she displayed no more than a polite interest. She's been elected, a week before, to an important post in her union and her head was still filled with the grim, gray pleasure of ambition satisfied, of having squeezed a toe onto the very first rung of the ladder. He decided it would not be nice to carry on at greater length, so he saved it up for the next time Shrimp came by. Shrimp had had three children over the years (her Regents scores were so good that her pregnancies were subsidized by the National Genetics Council), but a sense of emotional self-defense had always kept Shrimp from relating too emphatically to the babies during her year-long stints of motherhood (after which they were sent to the Council's schools in Wyoming and Utah). She assured Boz that what he'd felt that afternoon on the balcony had been nothing extraordinary, it happened to *her* all the time, but Boz knew that it had been the very essence of unusualness. It was, in Lord Krishna's words, a peak experience, a glimpse behind the veil.

Finally, he realized, it was his own moment and could not be shared any more than it could be, injust the same way, repeated.

It never was repeated, that moment, even approximately. Eventually he was able to forget what it had been like and only remembered the remembering of it.

Some years later Boz and Milly were sitting out on their balcony at sunset.

Neither had changed radically since Peanut's birth. Boz was perhaps a bit heavier than Milly but it would have been hard to say whether this was from his having gained or Milly having lost. Milly was a supervisor now, and had a seat, besides, on three different committees.

Boz said, "Do you remember our special building?"

"What building is that?"

"The one over there. With the three windows." Boz pointed to the right where gigantic twin apartments framed a vista westward of rooftops, cornices, and watertanks. Some of the buildings probably dated back to the New York of Boss Tweed; none were new.

Milly shook her head. "There are lots of buildings."

"The one just in back of the right-hand corner of that big yellow-brick thing with the funny temple hiding its watertank. See it?"

"Mm. There?"

"Yes. You don't remember it?"

"Vaguely. No."

"We'd just moved in here and we couldn't really afford the place, so for the first year it was practically bare. I kept after you about our buying a houseplant, and you said we'd have to wait. Does it start to come back?"

"Mistily."

"Well, the two of us would come out here regularly and look out at the different buildings and try and figure out exactly which street each of them would be on and whether we knew any of them from sidewalk level."

"I remember now! That's the one that the windows were always closed. But that's all I remember about it."

"Well, we made up a story about it. We said that after maybe five years one of the windows would be opened just enough so we'd be able to see it from here, an inch or two. Then the next day it would be closed again."

"And then?" She was by now genuinely and pleasantly puzzled.

"And then, according to our story, we'd watch it very carefully every day to see if that window was ever opened again. That's how it became our houseplant. It was something we looked after the same way."

"*Did* you keep watching it, in fact?"

"Sort of. Not every day. Every now and then."

"Was that the whole story?"

"No. The end of the story was that one day, maybe another five years later, we'd be walking along an unfamiliar street and we'd recognize the building and go up and ring the bell and the super would answer it and we'd ask him why, five years before, that window had been open."

"And what would he say?" From her smile it was clear that she remembered, but she asked out of respect for the wholeness of the tale.

"That he hadn't thought anyone had ever noticed. And break into tears. Of gratitude."

"It's a pretty story. I should feel guilty for having forgotten it. Whatever made you think of it today?"

"That's the real end of the story. The window was open. The middle window."

"Really? It's closed now."

"But it *was* open this morning. Ask Peanut. I pointed it out to her so I'd have a witness."

"It's a happy ending, certainly." She touched the back of her hand to his cheek where he was experimenting with sideburns.

"I wonder why it was open, though. After all this time."

"Well, in five years we can go and ask."

He turned, smiling, to face her, and with the same gesture, touched *her* cheek, gently, and just for now they were happy. They were together again, on the balcony, on a summer evening, and they were happy.

Boz and Milly. Milly and Boz.

ANGOULEME

There were seven Alexandrians involved in the Battery plot—Jack, who was the youngest and from the Bronx, Celeste DiCecca, Sniffles and MaryJane, Tancred Miller, Amparo (of course), and *of course,* the leader and mastermind, Bill Harper, better known as Little Mister Kissy Lips. Who was passionately, hopelessly in love with Amparo. Who was nearly thirteen (she would be, fully, by September this year), and breasts just beginning. Very very beautiful skin, like lucite. Amparo Martinez.

Their first, nothing operation was in the East 60's, a broker or something like that. All they netted was cufflinks, a watch, a leather satchel that wasn't leather after all, some buttons, and the usual lot of useless credit cards. He stayed calm through the whole thing, even with Sniffles slicing off buttons, and *soothing.* None of them had the nerve to ask, though they all wondered, how often he'd been through this scene before. What they were about wasn't an innovation. It was partly that, the need to innovate, that led them to think up the plot. The only really memorable part of the holdup was the name laminated on the cards, which was, wierdly enough, Lowen, Richard W. An omen (the connection being that they were all at the Alexander Lowen School), but of what?

Little Mister Kissy Lips kept the cufflinks for himself, gave the buttons to Amparo (who gave them to her uncle), and donated the rest (the watch was a piece of crap) to the Conservation booth outside the Plaza right where he lived.

His father was a teevee executive. In, as he would quip, both senses. They had got married young, his mama and papa, and divorced soon after but not before he'd come to fill out their quota. Papa, the executive, remarried, a man this time and somewhat more happily. Anyhow it lasted long enough that the offspring, the leader and mastermind, had to learn to adjust to the situation, it being permanent. Mama simply went down to the Everglades and disappeared, sploosh.

In short, he was well to do. Which is how, more than by overwhelming talent, he got into the Lowen School in the first place. He had the right kind of body though, so with half a desire there was no reason in the city of New York he couldn't grow up to be a professional dancer, even a choreographer. He'd have the connections for it, as Papa was fond of pointing out.

For the time being, however, his bent was literary and religious rather than balletic. He loved, and what seventh grader doesn't, the abstracter foxtrots and more metaphysical twists of a Dostoevsky, a Gide, a Mailer. He longed for the experience of some vivider pain than the mere daily hollowness knotted into his tight young belly, and no weekly stomp-and-holler of group therapy with other jejune eleven-year-olds was going to get him his stripes in the major leagues of suffering, crime, and resurrection. Only a bonafide crime would do that, and of all the crimes available murder certainly carried the most prestige, as no less an authority than Loretta Couplard was ready to attest, Loretta Couplard being not only the director and co-owner of the Lowen School but the author, as well, of two nationally televised scripts, both about famous murders of the 20th Century. They'd even done a unit in social studies on the topic: A History of Crime in Urban America.

The first of Loretta's murders was a comedy involving Pauline Campbell, R.N., of Ann Arbor, Michigan, circa 1951, whose skull had been smashed by three drunken teenagers. They had meant to knock her unconscious so they could screw her, which was 1951 in a nutshell. The eighteen-year-olds, Bill Morey and Max Pell, got life;

Dave Royal (Loretta's hero) was a year younger and got off with twenty-two years.

Her second murder was tragic in tone and consequently inspired more respect, though not among the critics, unfortunately. Possibly because her heroine, also a Pauline (Pauline Wichura), though more interesting and complicated, had also been more famous in her own day and ever since. Which made the competition, one best-selling novel and a serious film biography, considerably stiffer. Miss Wichara had been a welfare worker in Atlanta, Georgia, very much into environment and the population problem, this being the immediate pre-Regents period when anyone and everyone was legitimately starting to fret. Pauline decided to do something, *viz.*, reduce the population herself and in the fairest way possible. So whenever any of the families she visited produced one child above the three she'd fixed, rather generously, as the upward limit, she found some unobtrusive way of thinning that family back to the preferred maximal size. Between 1989 and 1993 Pauline's journals (Random House, 1994) record twenty-six murders, plus an additional fourteen failed attempts. In addition she had the highest welfare department record in the U.S. for abortions and sterilizations among the families whom she advised.

"Which proves, I think," Little Mister Kissy Lips had explained one day after school to his friend Jack, "that a murder doesn't have to be of someone *famous* to be a form of idealism."

But of course idealism was only half the story: the other half was curiosity. And beyond idealism *and* curiosity there was probably even another half, the basic childhood need to grow up and kill someone.

They settled on the Battery because, one, none of them ever were there ordinarily; two, it was posh and at the same time relatively, three, uncrowded, at least once the night shift were snug in their towers tending their machines. The night shift seldom ate their lunches down in the park.

And, four, because it was beautiful, especially now at the beginning of summer. The dark water, chromed with oil, flopping against the buttressed shore; the silences blowing in off the Upper Bay, silences large enough some-

times that you could sort out the different noises of the
city behind them, the purr and quaver of the skyscrapers,
the ground-shivering *mysterioso* of the expressways, and
every now and then the strange sourceless screams that
are the melody of New York's theme song; the blue-pink of
sunsets in a visible sky; the people's faces, calmed by
the sea and their own nearness to death, lined up in
rhythmic rows on the green benches. Why even the statues
looked beautiful here, as though someone had believed
in them once, the way people must have believed in the
statues in the Cloisters, so long ago.

His favorite was the gigantic killer-eagle landing in
the middle of the monoliths in the memorial for the
soldiers, sailors, and airmen killed in World War II. The
largest eagle, probably, in all Manhattan. His talons ripped
apart what was *surely* the largest artichoke.

Amparo, who went along with some of Miss Couplard's
ideas, preferred the more humanistic qualities of the memorial (him on top and an angel gently probing an enormous book with her sword) for Verrazzano, who was not,
as it turned out, the contractor who put up the bridge
that had, so famously, collapsed. Instead, as the bronze
plate in back proclaimed:

IN APRIL 1524
THE FLORENTINE-BORN NAVIGATOR
VERRAZZANO
LED THE FRENCH CARAVEL LA DAUPHINE
TO THE DISCOVERY OF
THE HARBOR OF NEW YORK
AND NAMED THESE SHORES ANGOULEME
IN HONOR OF FRANCIS I KING OF FRANCE

"Angouleme" they all agreed, except Tancred, who
favored the more prevalent and briefer name, was much
classier. Tancred was ruled out of order and the decision
became unanimous.

It was there, by the statue, looking across the bay of
Angouleme to Jersey, that they took the oath that bound
them to perpetual secrecy. Whoever spoke of what they
were about to do, unless he were being tortured by
the Police, solemnly called upon his co-conspirators to
insure his silence by other means. Death. All revolutionary

organizations take similar precautions, as the history unit
on Modern Revolutions had made clear.

How he got the name: it had been Papa's theory that
what modern life cried out for was a sweetening of old-
fashioned sentimentality. Ergo, among all the other indignities this theory gave rise to, scenes like the following:
"Who's my Little Mister Kissy Lips!" Papa would bawl out,
sweetly, right in the middle of Rockefeller Center (or a
restaurant, or in front of the school), and he'd shout
right back, "I am!" At least until he knew better.

Mama had been, variously, "Rosebud," "Peg O' My
Heart," and (this only at the end) "The Snow Queen."
Mama, being adult, had been able to vanish with no other
trace than the postcard that still came every Xmas post-
marked from Key Largo, but Little Mister Kissy Lips was
stuck with the New Sentimentality willy-nilly. True, by
age seven he'd been able to insist on being called "Bill"
around the house (or, as Papa would have it, "Just Plain
Bill"). But that left the staff at the Plaza to contend with,
and Papa's assistants, schoolmates, anyone who'd ever
heard the name. Then a year ago, aged ten and able to
reason, he laid down the new law—that his name *was*
Little Mister Kissy Lips, the whole awful mouthful, each
and every time. His reasoning being that if anyone would
be getting his face rubbed in shit by this it would be Papa,
who deserved it. Papa didn't seem to get the point, or
else he got it and another point besides, you could never
be sure how stupid or how subtle he really was, which is
the worst kind of enemy.

Meanwhile at the nationwide level the New Sentimentality had been a rather overwhelming smash. "The Orphans," which Papa produced and sometimes was credited
with writing, pulled down the top Thursday evening ratings for two years. Now it was being overhauled for a
daytime slot. For one hour every day our lives were going
to be a lot sweeter, and chances were Papa would be a
millionaire or more as a result. On the sunny side this
meant that *he'd* be the son of a millionaire. Though he
generally had contempt for the way money corrupted
everything it touched, he had to admit that in certain
cases it didn't have to be a bad thing. It boiled down

to this (which he'd always known): that Papa was a necessary evil.

This was why every evening when Papa buzzed himself into the suite he'd shout out, "Where's my Little Mister Kissy Lips," and he'd reply, "Here, Papa!" The cherry on this sundae of love was a big wet kiss, and then one more for their new "Rosebud," Jimmy Ness. (Who drank, and was not in all likelihood going to last much longer.) They'd all three sit down to the nice *family* dinner Jimmyness had cooked, and Papa would tell them about the cheerful, positive things that had happened that day at CBS, and Little Mister Kissy Lips would tell all about the bright fine things that had happened to *him*. Jimmy would sulk. Then Papa and Jimmy would go somewhere or just disappear into the private Everglades of sex, and Little Mister Kissy Lips would buzz himself out into the corridor (Papa knew better than to be repressive about hours), and within half an hour he'd be at the Verrazzano statue with the six other Alexandrians, five if Celeste had a lesson, to plot the murder of the victim they'd all finally agreed on.

No one had been able to find out his name. They called him Alyona Ivanovna, after the old pawnbroker woman that Raskalnikov kills with an ax.

The spectrum of possible victims had never been wide. The common financial types of the area would be carrying credit cards like Lowen, Richard W., while the generality of pensioners filling the benches were even less tempting. As Miss Couplard had explained, our economy was being refeudalized and cash was going the way of the ostrich, the octopus, and the moccasin flower.

It was such extinctions as these, but especially seagulls, that were the worry of the first lady they'd considered, a Miss Kraus, unless the name at the bottom of her handlettered poster (STOP THE SLAUGHTER of The *Innocents!!* etc.) belonged to someone else. Why, if she were Miss Kraus, was she wearing what seemed to be the old-fashioned diamond ring and gold band of a Mrs.? But the more crucial problem, which they couldn't see how to solve was: was the diamond real?

Possibility Number Two was in the tradition of the original Orphans of the Storm, the Gish sisters. A lovely semiprofessional who whiled away the daylight pretending to be blind and serenading the benches. Her pathos was rich, if a bit worked-up; her repertoire was archaeological; and her gross was fair, especially when the rain added its own bit of too-much. However: Sniffles (who'd done this research) was certain she had a gun tucked away under the rags.

Three was the least poetic possibility, just the concessionaire in back of the giant eagle selling Fun and Synthamon. His appeal was commercial. But he had a licensed Weimaraner, and though Weimaraners can be dealt with, Amparo liked them.

"You're just a Romantic," Little Mister Kissy Lips said. "Give me one good reason."

"His eyes," she said. "They're amber. He'd haunt us."

They were snuggling together in one of the deep embrasures cut into the stone of Castle Clinton, her head wedged into his armpit, his fingers gliding across the lotion on her breasts (summer was just beginning). Silence, warm breezes, sunlight on water, it was all ineffable, as though only the sheerest of veils intruded between them and an understanding of something (all this) really meaningful. Because they thought it was their own innocence that was to blame, like a smog in their souls' atmosphere, they wanted more than ever to be rid of it at times, like this, when they approached so close.

"Why not the dirty old man, then?" she asked, meaning Alyona.

"Because he *is* a dirty old man."

"That's no reason. He must take in at least as much money as that singer."

"That's not what I mean." What he meant wasn't easy to define. It wasn't as though he'd be too easy to kill. If you'd seen him in the first minutes of a program, you'd know he was marked for destruction by the second commercial. He was the defiant homesteader, the crusty senior member of a research team who understood Algol and Fortran but couldn't read the secrets of his own heart. He was the Senator from South Carolina with his own peculiar brand of integrity but a racist nevertheless. Killing that sort was too much like one of Papa's scripts to be a satisfying gesture of rebellion.

But what he said, mistaking his own deeper meaning,

was: "It's because he deserves it, because we'd be doing society a favor. Don't ask me to give *reasons*."

"Well, I won't pretend I understand that, but do you know what I think, Little Mister Kissy Lips?" She pushed his hand away.

"You think I'm scared."

"Maybe you *should* be scared."

"Maybe you should shut up and leave this to me. I said we're going to do it. We'll do it."

"To him then?"

"Okay. But for gosh sakes, Amparo, we've got to think of something to call the bastard besides 'the dirty old man'!"

She rolled over out of his armpit and kissed him. They glittered all over with little beads of sweat. The summer began to shimmer with the excitement of first night. They had been waiting so long and now the curtain was rising.

M-Day was scheduled for the first weekend in July, a patriotic holiday. The computers would have time to tend to their own needs (which have been variously described as "confession," "dreaming," and "throwing up"), and the Battery would be as empty as it ever gets.

Meanwhile their problem was the same as any kids face anywhere during summer vacation, how to fill the time.

There were books, there were the Shakespeare puppets if you were willing to queue up for that long, there was always teevee, and when you couldn't stand sitting any longer there were the obstacle courses in Central Park, but the density there was at lemming level. The Battery, because it didn't try to meet anyone's needs, seldom got so overpopulated. If there had been more Alexandrians and all willing to fight for the space, they might have played ball. Well, another summer. . . .

What else? There were marches for the political, and religions at various energy levels for the apolitical. There would have been dancing, but the Lowen School had spoiled them for most amateur events around the city.

As for the supreme pastime of sex, for all of them except Little Mister Kissy Lips and Amparo (and even for them, when it came right down to orgasm) this was still something that happened on a screen, a wonderful hypothesis that lacked empirical proof.

One way or another it was all consumership, everything they might have done, and they were tired, who isn't, of being passive. They were twelve years old, or eleven, or ten, and they couldn't wait any longer. For what? they wanted to know.

So, except when they were just loafing around solo, all these putative resources, the books, the puppets, the sports, arts, politics, and religions, were in the same category of usefulness as merit badges or weekends in Calcutta, which is a name you can still find on a few old maps of India. Their lives were not enhanced, and their summer passed as summers have passed immemorially. They slumped and moped and lounged about and teased each other and complained. They acted out desultory, shy fantasies and had long pointless arguments about the more peripheral facts of existence—the habits of jungle animals or how bricks had been made or the history of World War II.

One day they added up all the names on the monoliths set up for the soldiers, sailors, and airmen. The final figure they got was 4,800.

"Wow," said Tancred.

"But that can't be *all* of them," MaryJane insisted, speaking for the rest. Even that "wow" had sounded half ironic.

"Why not?" asked Tancred, who could never resist disagreeing. "They came from every different state and every branch of the service. It has to be complete or the people who had relatives left off would have protested."

"But so *few*? It wouldn't be possible to have fought more than one battle at that rate."

"Maybe . . ." Sniffles began quietly. But he was seldom listened to.

"Wars were different then," Tancred explained with the authority of a prime-time news analyst. "In those days more people were killed by their own automobiles than in wars. It's a fact."

"Four thousand, eight *hundred?*"

". . . a lottery?"

Celeste waved away everything Sniffles had said or would ever say. "MaryJane is right, Tancred. It's simply a *ludicrous* number. Why, in that same war the Germans gassed seven *million* Jews."

"Six million Jews," Little Mister Kissy Lips corrected.
"But it's the same idea. Maybe the ones here got killed in
a particular campaign."

'Then it would say so." Tancred was adamant, and he
even got them to admit at last that 4,800 was an impres-
sive figure, especially with every name spelled out in
stone letters.

One other amazing statistic was commemorated in the
park: over a thirty-three-year period Castle Clinton had
processed 7.7 million immigrants into the United States.

Little Mister Kissy Lips sat down and figured out that
it would take 12,800 stone slabs the size of the ones
listing the soldiers, sailors, and airmen in order to write
out all the immigrants' names, with country of origin, and
an area of five square miles to set that many slabs up in,
or all of Manhattan from here to 28th Street. But would
it be worth the trouble, after all? Would it be that much
different from the way things were already?

Alyona Ivanovna:

An archipelago of irregular brown islands were mapped
on the tan sea of his bald head. The mainlands of his
hair were marble outcroppings, especially his beard, white
and crisp and coiling. The teeth were standard MODI-
CUM issue; clothes, as clean as any fabric that old can
be. Nor did he smell, particularly. And yet. . . .

Had he bathed every morning you'd still have looked
at him and thought he was filthy, the way floorboards in
old brownstones seem to need cleaning moments after
they've been scrubbed. The dirt had been bonded to the
wrinkled flesh and the wrinkled clothes, and nothing less
than surgery or burning, would get it out.

His habits were as orderly as a polka dot napkin. He
lived at a Chelsea dorm for the elderly, a discovery they
owed to a rainstorm that had forced him to take the
subway home one day instead of, as usual, walking. On
the hottest nights he might sleep over in the park, nest-
ing in one of the Castle windows. He bought his lunches
from a Water Street specialty shop, *Dumas Fils:* cheeses,
imported fruit, smoked fish, bottles of cream, food for
the gods. Otherwise he did without, though his dorm must
have supplied prosaic necessities like breakfast. It was a

strange way for a panhandler to spend his quarters, drugs being the norm.

His professional approach was out-and-out aggression. For instance, his hand in your face and, "How about it, Jack?" Or, confidingly, "I need sixty cents to get home." It was amazing how often he scored, but actually it wasn't amazing. He had charisma.

And someone who relies on charisma *wouldn't* have a gun.

Agewise he might have been sixty, seventy, seventy-five, a bit more even, or much less. It all depended on the kind of life he'd led, and where. He had an accent none of them could identify. It was not English, not French, not Spanish, and probably not Russian.

Aside from his burrow in the Castle wall there were two distinct places he preferred. One, the wide-open stretch of pavement along the water. This was where he worked, walking up past the Castle and down as far as the concession stand. The passage of one of the great Navy cruisers, the USS *Dana* or the USS *Melville*, would bring him, and the whole Battery, to a standstill, as though a whole parade were going by, white, soundless, slow as a dream. It was a part of history, and even the Alexandrians were impressed, though three of them had taken the cruise down to Andros Island and back. Sometimes, though, he'd stand by the guardrail for long stretches of time without any real reason, just looking at the Jersey sky and the Jersey shore. After a while he might start talking to himself, the barest whisper but very much in earnest to judge by the way his forehead wrinkled. They never once saw him sit on one of the benches.

The other place he liked was the aviary. On days when they'd been ignored he'd contribute peanuts or breadcrumbs to the cause of the birds' existence. There were pigeons, parrots, a family of robins, and a proletarian swarm of what the sign declared to be chickadees, though Celeste, who'd gone to the library to make sure, said they were nothing more than a rather swank breed of sparrow. Here too, naturally, the militant Miss Kraus stationed herself when she bore testimony. One of her peculiarities (and the reason, probably, she was never asked to move on) was that under no circumstances did she ever deign to argue. Even sympathizers pried no more out of her than a grim smile and a curt nod.

One Tuesday, a week before M-Day (it was the early A.M. and only three Alexandrians were on hand to witness this confrontation), Alyona so far put aside his own reticence as to try to start a conversation going with Miss Kraus.

He stood squarely in front of her and began by reading aloud, slowly, in that distressingly indefinite accent, from the text of STOP THE SLAUGHTER: "The Department of the Interior of the United States Government, under the secret direction of the Zionist Ford Foundation, is *systematically* poisoning the oceans of the World with so-called 'food farms'. Is this "peaceful application of Nuclear Power"? Unquote, the *New York Times,* August 2, 2024. Or a new Moondoggle!! *Nature World,* Jan. Can we afford to remain indifferent any longer. Every day 15,000 seagulls die as a direct result of Systematic Genocides while elected Officials falsify and distort the evidence. Learn the facts. Write to the Congressmen. *Make your voice heard!!*"

As Alyona had droned on, Miss Kraus turned a deeper and deeper red. Tightening her fingers about the turquoise broomhandle to which the placard was stapled, she began to jerk the poster up and down rapidly, as though this man with his foreign accent were some bird of prey who'd perched on it.

"Is that what you think?" he asked, having read all the way down to the signature despite her jiggling tactic. He touched his bushy white beard and wrinkled his face into a philosophical expression. "I'd *like* to know more about it, yes, I would. I'd be interested in hearing what *you* think."

Horror had frozen up every motion of her limbs. Her eyes blinked shut but she forced them open again.

"Maybe," he went on remorselessly, "we can discuss this whole thing. Some time when you feel more like talking. All right?"

She mustered her smile, and a minimal nod. He went away then. She was safe, temporarily, but even so she waited till he'd gone halfway to the other end of the sea-front promenade before she let the air collapse into her

lungs. After a single deep breath the muscles of her hands
thawed into trembling.

M-Day was an oil of summer, a catalog of everything
painters are happiest painting—clouds, flags, leaves, sexy
people, and in back of it all the flat empty baby-blue of
the sky. Little Mister Kissy Lips was the first one there,
and Tancred, in a kind of kimono (it hid the pilfered
Luger), was the last. Celeste never came. (She'd just
learned she'd been awarded the exchange scholarship to
Sofia.) They decided they could do without Celeste, but
the other nonappearance was more crucial. Their victim
had neglected to be on hand for M-Day. Sniffles, whose
voice was most like an adult's over the phone, was dele-
gated to go to the Citibank lobby and call the West 16th
Street dorm.

The nurse who answered was a temporary. Sniffles, always an inspired liar, insisted that his mother—"Mrs.
Anderson, of course she lives there, Mrs. Alma F. Anderson"—had to be called to the phone. This was 248 West
16th, wasn't it? Where *was* she if she wasn't there? The
nurse flustered, explained that the residents, all who were
fit, had been driven off to a July 4th picnic at Lake Hopatcong as guests of a giant Jersey retirement condominium.
If he called bright and early tomorrow they'd be back and
he could talk to his mother then.

So the initiation rites were postponed, it couldn't be
helped. Amparo passed around some pills she'd taken
from her mother's jar, a consolation prize. Jack left, apol-
ogizing that he was a borderline psychotic, which was the
last that anyone saw of Jack till September. The gang was
disintegrating, like a sugar cube soaking up saliva, then
crumbling into the tongue. But what the hell—the sea still
mirrored the same blue sky, the pigeons behind their
wicket were no less iridescent, and trees grew for all of
that.

They decided to be silly and made jokes about what the
M *really* stood for in M-Day. Sniffles started off with
"Miss Nomer, Miss Carriage, and Miss Steak." Tancred,
whose sense of humor did not exist or was very private,
couldn't do better than "Mnemone, mother of the Muses."
Little Mister Kissy Lips said, "Merciful Heavens!" Mary-
Jane maintained reasonably that M was for MaryJane.

But Amparo said it stood for "Aplomb" and carried the day.

Then, proving that when you're sailing the wind always blows from behind you, they found Terry Riley's day-long *Orfeo* at 99.5 on the FM dial. They'd studied *Orfeo* in mime class and by now it was part of their muscle and nerve. As Orpheus descended into a hell that mushroomed from the size of a pea to the size of a planet, the Alexandrians metamorphosed into as credible a tribe of souls in torment as any since the days of Jacopo Peri. Throughout the afternoon little audiences collected and dispersed to flood the sidewalk with libations of adult attention. Expressively they surpassed themselves, both one by one and all together, and though they couldn't have held out till the apotheosis (at 9.30) without a stiff psychochemical wind in their sails, what they had danced was authentic and very much their own. When they left the Battery that night they felt better than they'd felt all summer long. In a sense they had been exorcised.

But back at the Plaza Little Mister Kissy Lips couldn't sleep. No sooner was he through the locks than his guts knotted up into a Chinese puzzle. Only after he'd unlocked his window and crawled out onto the ledge did he get rid of the bad feelings. The city was real. His room was not. The stone ledge was real and his bare buttocks absorbed reality from it. He watched slow movements in enormous distances and pulled his thoughts together.

He knew without having to talk to the rest that the murder would never take place. The idea had never meant for them what it had meant for him. One pill and they were actors again, content to be images in a mirror.

Slowly, as he watched, the city turned itself off. Slowly the dawn divided the sky into an east and a west. Had a pedestrian been going past on 58th Street and had that pedestrian looked up, he would have seen the bare soles of a boy's feet swinging back and forth, angelically.

He would have to kill Alyona Ivanovna himself. Nothing else was possible.

Back in his bedroom, long ago, the phone was ringing its fuzzy nighttime ring. That would be Tancred (or Amparo?) trying to talk him out of it. He foresaw their arguments. Celeste and Jack couldn't be trusted now. Or, more

subtly: they'd all made themselves too visible with their
Orfeo. If there were even a small investigation, the
benches would remember them, remember how well they
had danced, and the police would know where to look.

But the real reason, which at least Amparo would have
been ashamed to mention now that the pill was wearing
off, was that they'd begun to feel sorry for their victim.
They'd got to know him too well over the last month and
their resolve had been eroded by compassion.

A light came on in Papa's window. Time to begin. He
stood up, golden in the sunbeams of another perfect day,
and walked back along the foot-wide ledge to his own
window. His legs tingled from having sat so long.

He waited till Papa was in the shower, then tippytoed to
the old secretaire in his bedroom (W. & J. Sloan, 1952).
Papa's keychain was coiled atop the walnut veneer. Inside
the secretaire's drawer was an antique Mexican cigar box,
and in the cigar box a velvet bag, and in the velvet bag
Papa's replica of a French dueling pistol, circa 1790.
These precautions were less for his son's sake than on account of Jimmy Ness, who every so often felt obliged to
show he was serious with his suicide threats.

He'd studied the booklet carefully when Papa had
bought the pistol and was able to execute the loading pro-
cedure quickly and without error, tamping the premeas-
ured twist of powder down into the barrel and then the
lead ball on top of it.

He cocked the hammer back a single click.

He locked the drawer. He replaced the keys, just so. He
buried, for now, the pistol in the stuffs and cushions of the
Turkish corner, tilted upright to keep the ball from rolling
out. Then with what remained of yesterday's ebullience he
bounced into the bathroom and kissed Papa's cheek, damp
with the morning's allotted two gallons and redolent of
4711.

They had a cheery breakfast together in the coffee
room, which was identical to the breakfast they would
have made for themselves except for the ritual of being
waited on by a waitress. Little Mister Kissy Lips gave an
enthusiastic account of the Alexandrians' performance of
Orfeo, and Papa made his best effort of seeming not to
condescend. When he'd been driven to the limit of this
pretense, Little Mister Kissy Lips touched him for a sec-

ond pill, and since it was better for a boy to get these things from his father than from a stranger on the street, he got it.

He reached the South Ferry stop at noon, bursting with a sense of his own imminent liberation. The weather was M-Day all over again, as though at midnight out on the ledge he'd forced time to go backwards to the point when things had started going wrong. He'd dressed in his most anonymous shorts and the pistol hung from his belt in a dun dittybag.

Alyona Ivanovna was sitting on one of the benches near the aviary, listening to Miss Kraus. Her ring hand gripped the poster firmly, while the right chopped at the air, eloquently awkward, like a mute's first words following a miraculous cure.

Little Mister Kissy Lips went down the path and squatted in the shadow of his memorial. It had lost its magic yesterday, when the statues had begun to look so silly to everyone. They still looked silly. Verrazzano was dressed like a Victorian industrialist taking a holiday in the Alps. The angel was wearing an angel's usual bronze nightgown.

His good feelings were leaving his head by little and little, like aeolian sandstone attrites by the centuries of wind. He thought of calling up Amparo, but any comfort she might bring to him would be a mirage so long as his purpose in coming here remained unfulfilled.

He looked at his wrist, then remembered he'd left his watch home. The gigantic advertising clock on the facade of the First National Citibank said it was fifteen after two. That wasn't possible.

Miss Kraus was *still* yammering away.

There was time to watch a cloud move across the sky from Jersey, over the Hudson, and past the sun. Unseen winds nibbled at its wispy edges. The cloud became his life, which would disappear without ever having turned into rain.

Later, and the old man was walking up the sea promenade toward the Castle. He stalked him, for miles. And then they were alone, together, at the far end of the park.

"Hello," he said, with the smile reserved for grown-ups of doubtful importance.

He looked directly at the dittybag, but Little Mister Kissy Lips didn't lose his composure. He would be wondering whether to ask for money, which would be kept, if he'd had any, in the bag. The pistol made a noticeable bulge but not the kind of bulge one would ordinarily associate with a pistol.

"Sorry," he said coolly. "I'm broke."

"Did I ask?"

"You were going to."

The old man made as if to return in the other direction, so he had to speak quickly, something that would hold him here.

"I saw you speaking with Miss Kraus."

He was held.

"Congratulations—you broke through the ice!"

The old man half-smiled, half-frowned. "You know her?"

"Mm. You could say that we're *aware* of her." The "we" had been a deliberate risk, an hors d'oeuvre. Touching a finger to each side of the strings by which the heavy bag hung from her belt, he urged on it a lazy pendular motion. "Do you mind if I ask you a question?"

There was nothing indulgent now in the man's face. "I probably do."

His smile had lost the hard edge of calculation. It was the same smile he'd have smiled for Papa, for Amparo, for Miss Couplard, for anyone he liked. "Where do you come from? I mean, what country?"

"That's none of your business, is it?"

"Well, I just wanted . . . to know."

The old man (he had ceased, somehow, to be Alyona Ivanovna) turned away and walked directly toward the squat stone cylinder of the old fortress.

He remembered how the placque at the entrance—the same that had cited the 7.7 million—had said that Jenny Lind had sung there and it had been a great success.

The old man unzipped his fly and, lifting out his cock, began pissing on the wall.

Little Mister Kissy Lips fumbled with the strings of the bag. It was remarkable how long the old man stood there pissing because despite every effort of the stupid knot to stay tied he had the pistol out before the final sprinkle had been shaken out.

He laid the fulminate cap on the exposed nipple, drew the hammer back two clicks, past the safety, and aimed.

The man made no haste zipping up. Only then did he glance in Little Mister Kissy Lips' direction. He saw the pistol aimed at him. They stood not twenty feet apart, so he must have seen it.

He said, "Ha!" And even this, rather than being addressed to the boy with the gun, was only a parenthesis from the faintly-aggrieved monologue he resumed each day at the edge of the water. He turned away and a moment later he was back on the job, hand out, asking some fellow for a quarter.

334

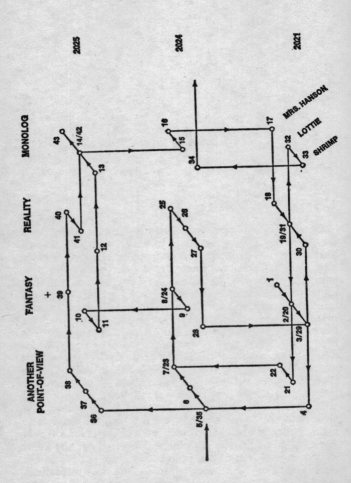

PART I: LIES

1. The Teevee (2021)

Mrs. Hanson liked to watch television best when there was someone else in the room to watch with her, though Shrimp, if the program was something she was serious about—and you never knew from one day to the next what that might be—, would get so annoyed with her mother's comments that Mrs. Hanson usually went off into the kitchen and let Shrimp have the teevee to herself, or else to her own bedroom if Boz hadn't taken it over for his erotic activities. For Boz was engaged to the girl at the other end of the corridor and since the poor boy had nowhere in the apartment that was privately his own except one drawer of the dresser they'd found in Miss Shore's room it seemed the least she could do to let him have the bedroom when she or Shrimp weren't using it.

With Boz when he wasn't taken up with *l'amour*, and with Lottie when she wasn't flying too high for the dots to make a picture, she liked to watch the soaps. *As the World Turns. Terminal Clinic. The Experience of Life.* She knew all the ins and outs of the various tragedies, but life in her own experience was much simpler: life was a pastime. Not a game, for that would have implied that some won and others lost, and she was seldom conscious of any sensations so vivid or threatening. It was like the afternoons of Monopoly with her brothers when she was a girl: long after her hotels, her houses, her deeds, and her cash were gone, they would let her keep moving her little lead battle-ship around the board, collecting her $200, falling on Chance and Community Chest, going to Jail and shaking her way out. She never won but she couldn't lose. She just went round and round. Life.

But better than watching with her own children she liked to watch along with Amparo and Mickey. With Mickey most of all, since Amparo was already beginning to feel superior to the programs Mrs. Hanson liked best—the early cartoons and the puppets at five-fifteen. She couldn't have said why. It wasn't just that she took a superior sort of pleasure in Mickey's reactions, since Mickey's reactions were seldom very visible. Already at age five he could be as interior as his mother. Hiding inside the bath-tub for hours at a time, then doing a complete U-turn and pissing his pants with excitement. No, she honestly enjoyed the shows for what they were—the hungry predators and their lucky prey, the good-natured dynamite, the bouncing rocks, the falling trees, the shrieks and pratfalls, the lovely obviousness of everything. She wasn't stupid but she did love to see someone tiptoeing along and then out of no-where: Slam! Bang! something immense would come crashing down on the Monopoly board, scattering the pieces beyond recovery. "Pow!" Mrs. Hanson would say and Mickey would shoot back, "Ding-Dong!" and collapse into giggles. For some reason "Ding-Dong!" was the fun-niest notion in the world.

"Pow!"

"Ding-Dong!"

And they'd break up.

2. A & P (2021)

It was the best time she could remember in how long, though it seemed a pity none of it was real—the rows and stacks and pyramids of cans, the lovely boxes of deter-gents and breakfast food—a whole aisle almost of each!

—the dairy shelf, and all the meat, in all its varieties. The meat was the hardest to believe. Candy, and more candy, and at the end of the candy a mountain of tobacco cigarettes. Bread. Some of the brands were still familiar, but she passed by these and put a loaf of Wonder Bread in the shopping cart. It was half full. Juan pushed the cart on ahead, moving to the half-heard melodies that hung like a mist in the museum's air. He rounded a corner toward the vegetables but Lottie stayed where she was, pretending to study the wrapper of a second loaf. She closed her eyes, trying to separate this moment from its place in the chain of all moments so that she'd always have it, like a pocketful of pebbles from a country road. She grappled details from their context—the nameless song, the spongy give of the bread (forgetting for the moment that it wasn't bread), the waxiness of the paper, the chiming of the registers at the check-out counters. There were voices and footsteps too, but there are always voices and footsteps, so she had no use for these. The real magic, which couldn't be laid hold of, was simply that Juan was happy and interested and willing to spend perhaps the whole day with her.

The trouble was that when you tried this hard to stop the flow it ran through your fingers and you were left squeezing air. She would get soggy and say the wrong thing. Juan would flare up and leave her, like the last time, staring at some insane cloverleaf miles from anywhere. So she put the so-called bread back and made herself available, as Shrimp was always saying she didn't, to the sunshine of here and now and to Juan, who was by the vegetables, playing with a carrot.

"I'd swear it's a carrot," he said.

"But it isn't, you know. If it were a carrot you could eat it, and it wouldn't be art."

(At the entrance, while they were waiting for a cart, a voice had told them what they were going to see and how to appreciate it. There were facts about the different companies who'd cooperated, facts about some of the more unusual products such as laundry starch, and what it would have cost the average person shopping for a week's groceries in terms of present-day money. Then the voice warned that it was all fake—the cans, the boxes, the bottles, the beautiful steaks, everything, no matter how realistic it might look, all just imitations. Finally, if you were still thinking of lifting something just for a souvenir, it explained the alarm system, which worked chemically.)

"Feel it," he said.

It felt exactly like a carrot, not that fresh, but edible.

"But it's plastic or something," she insisted, loyal to the Met's tape.

"It's a carrot, bet you a dollar. It feels like a carrot, it smells like a carrot——." He took it back, looked at it, bit into it. It crunched. "It *is* a carrot."

There was a general sense of letdown among the people who'd been watching, of reality having intruded where it didn't belong.

A guard came and told them they'd have to leave. They wouldn't even be allowed to take the items they'd already chosen through one of the check-out counters. Juan got obstreperous and demanded his money back.

"Where's the manager of this store?" he shouted. Juan, the born entertainer. "I want to talk to the manager." At last, to get rid of him, they refunded the price of both tickets.

Lottie had been wretched through the whole scene, but even at the bar under the airfield afterward she didn't bother to contradict his version. Juan was right, the guard was a son of a bitch, the museum deserved to be bombed.

He reached into his jacket pocket and took out the carrot. "Is it a carrot," he wanted to know, "or is it a carrot?"

Dutifully she set down her beer and took a bite. It tasted like plastic.

3. The White Uniform (2021)

Shrimp tried to focus on the music—music was the major source of meaning in her life—but she could only think of January. January's face and her thick hands, the pink palms roughened with calluses. January's neck, the tense muscles slowly melting beneath the pressure of Shrimp's fingers. Or, in the opposite direction: January's heavy thighs pressing against the tank of a bike, bare black flesh, bare black metal, its dizzying sound as it idled, waiting for the light, and then before it had gone quite to green its roar as it went tearing down the freeway on the way to. . . . What would be a suitable destination? Alabama? Spokane? South St. Paul?

Or this: January in a nurse's uniform—brisk, crinkly, blinding white. Shrimp would be *inside* the ambulance. The little white cap rubbing against the low ceiling. She would offer her the soft flesh of her inner arm. The dark fingers searching for a vein. A little daub of alcohol, a moment's chill, the hypodermic, and January smiling—"I know this hurts." Shrimp wanted to swoon at that point. Swoon.

She took out the plugs and let the music wind on, unheard, inside the little plastic case, for a car had left the street and pulled up to the little red charger. January lumbered out from the station, took the man's card, and stuck it in the credit slot, which replied, "Ding." She worked like a model in a shop window, never pausing, never lifting her eyes, off in her own universe, though Shrimp knew that she knew that she was here, on this bench, looking at her, longing for her, swooning.

Look at me! she thought at January fiercely. Make me exist!

But the steady flow of cars and trucks and buses and bikes between them dispersed the thought-message as though it were smoke. Perhaps some driver a dozen yards past the station would glance up with momentary panic, or a woman riding the 17 bus home from work would wonder what had reminded her of some boy she had thought she had loved twenty years before.

Three days.

And each day returning from this vigil, Shrimp would pass in front of a drab shop with a painted sign, Myers Uniforms & Badges. In the window a dusty mustached policeman from another town (the sprinkles on his jacket were wrong for New York) brandished, in a diffident way, a wooden billy club. Handcuffs and cannisters dangled from his black gunbelt. Touching the policeman, yet seeming not to notice, a fireman decked out in bright yellow rubber striped with black (another out-of-towner) smiled through the streaked glass at, in the opposite window, a tall black girl in a nurse's white uniform. Shrimp would walk past slowly and on as far as the traffic light then, like a boat when its engine conks out and it can no longer fight against the current, she would drift back to the window, the white uniform.

The third day she went inside. A bell clanked. The sales-clerk asked could he help her.

"I'd like—" she cleared her throat "—a uniform. For a nurse."

He lifted a slim yellow tape measure off a stack of vi-sored caps. "You'd be . . . a twelve?"

"It's not— Actually, it isn't for me. For a friend. I said that since I'd be passing by here. . . ."

"What hospital would she be with? Each hospital has its own little requirements, you know."

Shrimp looked up in his young-old face. A white shirt, the collar too tight. A black tie with a small, crisp knot. He seemed, in the same indefinite way as the mannikins in the windows, to be in uniform.

"Not a hospital. A clinic. A private clinic. She can wear . . . whatever she likes."

"Good, good. And what size is she, your friend?"

"A large size. Eighteen? And tall."

"Well, let me show you what we have." And he led Shrimp, enraptured, into the farther twilight of the shop.

4. January (2021)

She'd met Shrimp at one of the open sessions of The Asylum, where having come to recruit she'd found herself, in the most shameful way, recruited—to the point of tears and, beyond tears, of confessions. All of which January reported faithfully at the next meeting of the cell. There were four cell members besides herself, all in their twen-ties, all very serious, though none were intellectuals or even college dropouts: Jerry and Lee Lighthall, Ada Miller, and Graham X. Graham was the link upward to the organization but not otherwise "leader" since one thing they were against was pyramidal structures.

Lee, who was fat and black and liked to talk, said what they were all thinking, that having emotions and showing them was a completely healthy direction. "Unless you said something about us?"

"No. It was more just sexual things. Or personal."

"Then I don't see why you brought it up here."

"Maybe if you told us something more about it, Jan," Graham suggested, in Graham's gentle way.

"Well, what they do at The Asylum—"

"We've all been to The Asylum, honey."

"Stop being a fucking bully, Lee," his wife said.

"Lee's right, though—I'm taking up all our time. Anyhow I was there early, sort of sizing them up as they came in, and I could tell the minute this one arrived—her name is Shrimp Hanson—that she wasn't one of the regulars. I think she noticed me right away too. Anyhow we started off in the same group, breathing and holding hands and all that." Ordinarily January would have firmed up a narrative of this length with some obscenities, but any resemblance to bluster now would only have made her feel sillier than she did. "Then she started massaging my neck, I don't know, in a particular way. And I started crying. For no reason at all I started crying."

"Were you up on anything?" Ada asked.

January, who was stricter than any of them on that score (she didn't even drink Koffee), could legitimately bridle. "Yeah, on your vibrator!"

"Now, Jan," said Graham.

"But *she* was up," she went on, "very much up. Meanwhile the regulars were swarming around us like a pack of vampires. That's what most of them come there for, the sludge and the blood. So we went off into one of the booths. I thought we'd screw and that would be that, but instead we started talking. That is, I did—she listened." She could remember the knot of shame, like the pain of a too sudden swallow of water, as the words came out. "I talked about my parents, about sex, about being lonely. That kind of thing."

"That kind of thing," Lee echoed, supportively.

January braced herself and took a deep breath. "About my parents I explained about their being Republicans, which is all right of course, but I said that I could never relate sexual feelings with love because of their both being men. It doesn't sound like much now. And about being lonely I said—" she shrugged, but also she closed her eyes "—that I was lonely. That everyone was lonely. Then I started crying again."

"You covered a lot of ground."

She opened her eyes. No one seemed to be angry with her, though they might have taken the last thing she'd said as an accusation. "We were at it most of the fucking night."

"You still haven't told us anything about her." Ada observed.

"Her name is Shrimp Hanson. She said she's thirty, but I'd say thirty-four, or older even. Lives somewhere on East 11th, I've got it written down, with a mother and I can't remember how many more. A *family*." This was, at root, exactly what the organization was most against. Authoritarian political structures only exist because people are conditioned by authoritarian family structures. "And no job, just her allowance."

"White?" Jerry asked. Being the only nonblack in the group, it was diplomatic for her to be the one to ask.

"As fucking snow."

"Political?"

"Not a bit. But I think she could be guided to it. Or on second thought—"

"How do you *feel* about her now?" Graham asked.

He obviously thought she was in love. Was she? Possibly. But just as possibly not. Shrimp had reduced her to tears; she wanted to pay her back in kind. What were feelings anyhow? Words floating through your head, or hormones in some gland. "I don't know what I feel."

"What is it you want us to tell you then?" Lee asked. "Whether you should see her again? Or whether you're in love? Or if you should be? Lordie, girl!" This, with a heave of all that good-natured fat. "Go ahead. Have fun. Fuck yourself silly or cry your heart out, whatever you like. No reason not to. Just remember, if you do fall in love—keep it in a separate compartment."

They all agreed that that was the best advice, and from her own sense of being defluttered she knew it was what she'd wanted to be told. Now they were free to go on to basics—quotas and drops and the reasons why the Revolution, though so long delayed, was the next inevitable step. Then they left the benches and for an hour just enjoyed themselves. You would never have thought, to look at them, that they were any different from any other five people on the roller rink.

5. Richard M. Williken (2024)

They would sit together in the darkroom, officially the bedroom of his son, Richard M. Williken, Jr. Richard Jr. existed for the sake of various files in offices about the city, though upon need a boy answering to the name could be got on loan from his wife's cousin. Without their imaginary son the Willikens could never have held on to a two-bedroom apartment now that their real children had left home.

They might listen to whatever tapes were being copied, usually since they were his specialty to Alkan or Gottchalk or Boagni. The music was the ostensible reason, among other ostensible reasons such as friendship, that she hung around. He would smoke, or doodle, or watch the second hand simplify another day. His ostensible reason was that he was working, and in the sense that he was copying tapes and taking messages and sometimes renting out, for next to nothing an hour, his fictitious son's bed, he was working. But in the sense that counted he was not.

The phone would ring. Williken would pick it up and say, "One-five, five-six." Shrimp would wrap herself in her thin arms and watch him until by the lowering of his eyes she knew the call wasn't from Seattle.

When the lack of some kind of mutual acknowledgment became too raw they would have pleasant little debates about Art. Art: Shrimp loved the word (it was right up there with "epithesis," "mystic," and "Tiffany"), and poor Williken couldn't leave it alone. Despite that they tried never to descend to the level of honest complaint, their separate, secret unhappinesses would find ways to poke up their heads into the long silences or to become, with a bit of camouflage, the real subjects of the little debates, as when Williken, too worn out to be anything but serious, had announced: "Art? Art's just the opposite, trueheart. It's patchwork. It's bits and pieces. What you think is all flow and force—"

"And fun," she added.

"—are an illusion. But the artist can't share it. He knows better."

"The way prostitutes aren't supposed ever to have orgasms? I talked to a prostitute once, mentioning no names, who said she had orgasms all the time."

"It doesn't sound very professional. When an artist is being entertained, his work suffers."

"Yes, yes, that's certainly true," brushing the idea from her lap like crumbs, "for *you*. But I should think that for someone like—" she gestured toward the machinery, the four slowly revolving mandalas of "From Sea to Shining Sea" "—John Herbert MacDowell, for instance. For him it must be like being in love. Except that instead of loving one person, *his* love spreads out in every direction."

Williken made a face. "I'll agree that art is like love. But that doesn't contradict what I said before. It's all patchwork and patience, art and love both."

"And passion? Doesn't that come in at all?"

"Only for the very young." Charitably he left it for her to decide if that shoe fit.

This went on, off, and on for the better part of a month, and in all that time he indulged in only one conscious cruelty. For all his personal grubbiness—the clothes that looked like dirty bandages, the skimpy beard, the smells— Williken was a great fusspot, and it was his style of fuss (in housekeeping now as it had been in art) to efface the evidences of his own undesirable presence, to wipe away the fingerprints and baffle his pursuers. Thus each object that was allowed to be visible in the room came to possess a kind of heightened significance, like so many skulls in a monk's cell: the pink telephone, Richard Jr.'s sagging bed, the speakers, the long silvery swan-neck of the water faucet, the calendar with lovers tumbling in the heavy snows of "January 2024." His cruelty was simply not changing the month.

She never said, as she might have, "Willy, it's the tenth of *May*, for Christ's sake." Possibly she found some grueling satisfaction in whatever hurt his reminder caused her. Certainly she gnawed on it. He had no first-hand knowledge of such feelings. The whole drama of her abandonment seemed ludicrous to him. Anguish for anguish's sake.

It might have gone on like that till summer, but then one day the calendar was gone and one of his own photographs was in its place.

"Is it yours?" she asked.

His awkwardness was sincere. He nodded.

"I noticed it the minute I walked into the room."

A photograph of a glass half full of water resting on a

wet glass shelf. A second, empty glass outside the picture
cast a shadow across the white tiles of the wall.

Shrimp walked up close to it. "It's sad, isn't it?"

"I don't know," Williken said. He felt confused, insulted; anguished. "Usually I don't like having my own
things hanging about. They go dead on you. But I thought
—"

"I like it. I do."

6. Amparo (2024)

On her birthday, the 29th of May, she had realized that
she hated her mother. Her eleventh birthday. It was a horrible realization, but Geminis can't deceive themselves.
There was simply nothing about Mama you could admire
and so much to loathe. She bullied herself and Mickey
mercilessly, but what was worse were the times she'd mis-
calculate her stupid pills, slime off into a glorious depression and tell them sob-stories about her wasted life. It was,
certainly, a wasted life but Amparo couldn't see that she'd
ever made any effort not to waste it. She didn't know
what work was. Even around the house she let poor old
Grummy do everything. She just lay about, like some animal at the zoo, snuffling and scratching her smelly cunt.
Amparo hated her.

Shrimp, in the way she sometimes had of seeming tele-
pathic, said to her, before the dinner, that they had better
have a talk, and she concocted a thin lie to get her out of
the apartment. They went down to 15, where a Chinese
lady had opened a new shop, and Shrimp bought the
shampoo she was being so silly about.

Then to the roof for the inevitable lecture. The sunshine
had brought half the building up on top but they found a
spot almost their own. Shrimp slipped out of her blouse,
and Amparo couldn't help thinking what a difference there
was between her and her mother, even though Shrimp
was actually older. No sags, no wrinkles, and only a hint
of graininess. Whereas Lottie, with every initial advantage
on her side, had let herself become a monster of obesity.

Or at least ("monster" was perhaps an exaggeration) she was heading down the road lickety-split.

"Is that all?" Amparo asked, once Shrimp had produced her last pious excuse for Lottie's various awfulnesses. "Can we go downstairs now that I'm properly ashamed?"

"Unless you want to tell me your side of the story?"

"I didn't think I was supposed to have a side."

"That's true when you're ten years old. At eleven you're allowed to have your own point of view."

Amparo grinned a grin that said, Good old democratic Aunt Shrimp. Then she was serious. "Mama hates me, it's as simple as that." She gave examples.

Shrimp appeared unimpressed. "You'd rather bully her —is that your point?"

"No." But giggling. "But it would be a change."

"You do, you know. You bully her something dreadful. You're a worse tyrant than Madame Who's-It with the goiters."

Amparo's second grin was more tentative. "Me!"

"You. Even Mickey can see it, but he's afraid to say anything or you'll turn on him. We're all afraid."

"Don't be a silly. I don't know what you're talking about. Because I say sarcastic things now and then?"

"And then and then. You're as unpredictable as an airplane schedule. You wait till she's down, completely at the bottom, and then you go for juggler. What was it you said this morning?"

"I don't remember anything I said this morning."

"About the hippopotamus in the mud?"

"I said that to Grummy. *She* didn't hear. She was in bed, as usual."

"She heard."

"Then I'm sorry. What should I do, apologize?"

"You should stop making things worse for her."

Amparo shrugged. "She should stop making things worse for me. I hate to always *harp* about it, but I do want to go to the Lowen School. And why shouldn't I? It's not as though I were asking permission to go to Mexico and cut off my breasts."

"I agree. It's probably a good school. But you're *at* a good school."

"But I *want* to go to the Lowen School. It would be a *career*, but of course Mama wouldn't understand that."

"She doesn't want you living away from home. Is that so cruel?"

"Because if I left, then she'd only have Mickey to bully. Anyhow I'd be here officially, which is all she cares anyhow."

Shrimp was silent for a while, in what seemed a considering way. But what was there to consider? It was all so obvious. Amparo writhed.

At last Shrimp said, "Let's make a bargain. If you promise not to be Little Miss Bitch, I'll do what I can to talk her round to signing you up."

"Will you? Will you really?"

"Will *you*? That's what I'm asking."

"I'll grovel at her feet. Anything."

"If you don't, Amparo, if you go on the way you've been going, believe me, I'll tell her I think the Lowen School will destroy your character, what little there is."

"I promise. I promise to be as nice as—as what?"

"As a birthday cake?"

"As nice as a birthday cake, absolutely!"

They shook hands on it and put on their clothes and went downstairs where a real, rather sad, rather squalid birthday cake was waiting for her. Try as she might, poor old Grummy just couldn't cook. Juan had come by during the time they'd been on the roof, which was, more than any of her crumby presents, a nice surprise. The candles were lit, and everyone sang happy birthday: Juan, Grummy, Mama, Mickey, Shrimp.

> Happy birthday to you.
> Happy birthday to you.
> Happy birthday, dear Amparo.
> Happy birthday to you.

"Make a wish," Mickey said.

She made her wish, then with one decisive gust, blew out all twelve candles.

Shrimp winked at her. "Now don't tell anyone what it was or you won't get it."

She hadn't, in fact, been wishing for the Lowen School, since that was hers by right. What she'd wished instead was for Lottie to die.

Wishes never come true the way you think. A month

later her father was dead. Juan, who'd never been unhappy a day in his life, had committed suicide.

7. Len Rude (2024)

Weeks after the Anderson debacle, when he'd last been able to assure himself that there'd be no dire consequences, Mrs. Miller summoned him uptown for "a little talk." Though in the long-range view a nobody (her position scarcely brought her to middle management level), Mrs. Miller would soon be writing up his field summary, which made her, for now, a rather godlike nobody.

He panicked disgracefully. All morning he couldn't think of anything but what to wear, what to wear? He settled on a maroon Perry-Como-type sweater with a forest green scarf peeking out. Wholesome, not sexy, but not pointedly not-sexy.

He had a twenty-minute wait outside the lady's cubbyhole. Usually he excelled at waiting. Cafeterias, toilets, launderettes—his life was rich in opportunities to acquire that skill. But he was so certain he was about to be axed that by the end of the twenty minutes he was on the brink of acting out his favorite crisis fantasy: I will get up, I will walk out the door. Every door. With never a word of good-bye nor a look backward. And then? Ah, there was the rub. Once he was out the door, where could he go that his identity, the whole immense dossier of his life, wouldn't trail after him like a tin can tied to his tail? So he waited, and then the interview was over, and Mrs. Miller was shaking his hand and saying something bland and anecdotal about Brown, whose book had been decorating his lap. Then, thank you, and thank *you* for coming in. Goodbye, Mrs. Miller. Good-bye, Len.

What had been the point? She hadn't mentioned Anderson except to say in passing that of course the poor man ought to be in Bellevue and that a few like that are statistically inevitable for anyone. It was better than he'd expected and more than he deserved.

Instead of the axe there was only his new assignment: Hanson, Nora/ Apartment 1812/ 334 E. 11th St. Mrs.

Miller said she was a nice old lady—"if a little difficult at times." But all the cases he was put on this year were nice and old and difficult, since he was studying, in the catalogue's words, "Problems of Aging." The one odd thing about this Hanson was that she had a sizeable brood under her wings (though not as large as the printout had indicated; the son was married now) and would not seem to be dangerously lonely. However, according to Mrs. Miller, her son's marriage had "unsettled her" (Ominous word!) which was why she stood in need of *his* warmth and attention four hours a week. A stitch in time seemed to be what Mrs. Miller had in mind.

The more he thought about it the more this Hanson woman sounded like an impending disaster. Mrs. Miller had probably called him in to cover herself, so that if and when this one went in the same wrong direction Anderson had gone, it would be his fault, not the nice old difficult lady's, and not absolutely Alexa Miller's. She was probably doing her memorandum for the file right now, if she hadn't done it in advance.

All this for two miserable dollars an hour. Sweet fucking Jesus, if he'd know four years ago what he'd be getting into, he'd never have switched his major from English. Better to teach assholes to read the want ads than be an emotional nursemaid to senile psychotics.

That was the dark side. There was also a bright side. By the fall semester he'd have cleared up his field requirements. Then two years of smooth academic sailing, and then, O happy day, Leonard Rude would be a Doctor of Philosophy, which we all know is the next best condition to out-and-out freedom.

8. The Love Story (2024)

The MODICUM office had sent round an apologetic, shaggy boy with bad skin and a whining midwestern accent. She couldn't get him to explain why he'd been sent to visit her. He claimed it was a mystery just as much to him, some bureaucrat's brainstorm, there was never any sense to these projects but he hoped she'd go along with it for his sake. A job is a job is a job, and this job in addition was for his degree.

He was going to the university?

Yes, but not, he assured her at once, that he'd come here to *study* her. Students were assigned to these make-work projects because there wasn't enough real work to go around. That was the welfare state for you. He hoped they'd be friends.

Mrs. Hanson couldn't bring herself to feel unfriendly, but what she asked him quite bluntly were they supposed to do, *as* friends? Len—she kept forgetting his name and he kept reminding her it was Len—suggested that he read a book to her.

"Aloud?"

"Yes, why not? It's one I have to read this term anyhow. It's a super book."

"Oh, I'm sure it is," she said, alarmed again. "I'm sure I'd learn all kinds of things. But still." She turned her head sideways and read the golden title of a fat, black book he'd laid down on the kitchen table. Something OLOGY. "Even so."

Len laughed. "Fiddle-dee-dee, Mrs. Hanson, not that one! I can't read *that* one myself."

The book they were to read was a novel he'd been assigned in an English class. He took it out of his pocket. The cover showed a pregnant woman sitting naked on the lap of a man in a blue suit.

"What a strange cover," she said, by way of compliment.

Len took this for another sign of reluctance. He insisted that the story would seem quite commonplace once she accepted the author's basic premise. A love story. That's all. She was bound to like it. Everyone did. "It's a super book," he said again.

She could see he meant to read it, so she led him into the living room and settled herself in one corner of the sofa and Len in the other. She found the Oralines in her purse. As there were only three left, she didn't offer one to him. She began sucking complaisantly. Then, as a humorous afterthought she fit a premium button over the end of the stick. It said, I DON'T BELIEVE IT! But Len took no notice or else he didn't get the joke.

He started reading and right from page one it was sex.

That in itself wouldn't have upset her. She had always believed in sex and enjoyed it and though she did think that
having sex ought to be a private matter there was certainly no harm in a candid discussion. What was embar-
rassing was that the whole scene took place on a sofa that
was wobbling because one leg was missing. The sofa that
she and Len were sitting on also had a missing leg and
wobbled, and it seemed to Mrs. Hanson that some sort of
comparison couldn't be avoided.

The sofa scene dragged on and on. Then nothing at all
happened for a few pages, talk and descriptions. Why, she
kept wondering, would the government want to pay college students to come to people's homes and read pornog-
raphy to them? Wasn't the whole point of college to keep
as many young people as possible occupied and out of
jobs?

But perhaps this was an experiment. An experiment in
adult education! When she thought about it, no other explanation fit the facts half so well. Viewed in this light the
book suddenly became a challenge to her and she tried to
pay closer attention. Someone had died, and the woman
the story was about—her name was Linda—was going to
inherit a fortune. Mrs. Hanson had gone to school with
someone called Linda, a dull-witted Negro girl whose father owned two grocery stores. She'd disliked the name
ever since. Len stopped reading.

"Oh, go on," she said. "I'm enjoying it."

"So am I, Mrs. Hanson, but it's four o'clock."

She felt obliged to say something intelligent before he
went off, but at the same time she didn't want to show
that she'd guessed the purpose of the experiment. "It's a
very unusual plot."

Len bared small, stained teeth in a smile of agreement.
"I always say there's nothing that can beat a good love
story."

And before she could add her little joke ("Except perhaps a bit of smut"), Len had chimed in with: "I'll agree
with that, Mrs. Hanson. Friday, then, at two o'clock?" In
any case it was Shrimp's joke.

Mrs. Hanson felt she hadn't shown herself at all to advantage, but it was too late. Len was gathering himself together, his umbrella, his black book, talking steadily all

the while. He even remembered the wet plaid cap she'd hung up on the hook to dry. Then he was gone.

Her heart swelled up inside her chest, hammering as though it had slipped gears, ker-whop! ker-wham! She went back to the sofa. The cushions at the end where Len had sat were still pressed down. Suddenly she could see the room as he must have seen it: linoleum so filthy you couldn't see the patterns, windows caked, blinds broken, heaps of toys and piles of clothing and tangles of both everywhere. Then, as if to complete the devastation, Lottie came staggering out of her bedroom wrapped in a dirty sheet, and reeking.

"Is there any milk?"

"Is there any milk!"

"Oh Mom. What's wrong now?"

"Do you have to ask? Look at this place. It looks as if a bomb hit it."

Lottie smiled a faint, mussed smile. "I was asleep. *Did* a bomb hit it?"

Poor silly Lotto, who could ever stay angry with her? Mrs. Hanson laughed indulgently, then started to explain about Len and the experiment, but Lottie was off in her own little world again. What a life, Mrs. Hanson thought, and she went out to the kitchen to mix up a glass of milk.

9. The Air Conditioner (2024)

Lottie could hear things. If she were sitting near the closet that used to be the foyer she could understand whole conversations taking place out in the corridor. In her own bedroom anything else happening in the apartment was audible to her—the turbulence of voices on the teevee, or Mickey lecturing his doll in what he imagined was Spanish, or her mother's putterings and sputterings. Such noises had the advantage of being on a human scale. It was the noises that lay behind these that she dreaded, and they were always there, waiting for those first masking sounds to drop, ready for her.

One night in her fifth month with Amparo she'd gone out walking very late, through Washington Square and past the palisades of N.Y.U. and the junior deluxe co-ops on West Broadway. She stopped beside the window of her favorite shop where the crystals of a darkened chandelier caught glints from the headlights of passing cars. It was four-thirty, the stillest hour of the morning. A diesel roared past and turned west on Prince. A dead silence followed in its wake. It was then she heard that other sound, a sourceless far-off rumble, like the first faint premonition, as one glides down a quiet stream, of the cataract ahead. Since then the sound of those falls had always been with her, sometimes distinctly, sometimes only, like stars behind smog, as a dim presence, an article of faith.

Resistance of a kind was possible. The teevee was a good barrier, when she could concentrate and when the programs weren't themselves upsetting. Or talk, if she could think of something to say and find someone to listen to her. But she'd been submerged by too many of her mother's monologues not to be sensitive to signals of boredom, and Lottie could not, like her mother, keep going regardless. Books demanded too much and were no help. Once she'd enjoyed the stories, simple as tic-tac-toe, in the romance comics that Amparo brought home, but now Amparo had outgrown comic books and Lottie was embarrassed to be buying them for herself. In any case they cost too much for her to get addicted.

Mostly she had to get by with pills and mostly she could.

Then, in the August of the year Amparo was to start at the Lowen School, Mrs. Hanson traded off the second teevee, which hadn't worked for years, for a King Kool air conditioner of Ab Holt's that also hadn't worked for years except as a fan. Lottie had always complained about how stuffy her bedroom was. Sandwiched between the kitchen and the main bedroom, its only means of ventilation was an ineffective transom over the door to the living room. Shrimp, who was back home again, got her photographer friend from downstairs to take out the transom and install the air conditioner.

The fan made a gentle purring sound all through the night with every so often a tiny hiccoughing counterbeat, like an amplified heart murmur. Lottie could lie in bed for hours, long after the children were asleep in the bunks, just listening to the lovely syncopated hum. It was as calming as the sound of waves, and like the sound of waves it sometimes seemed to be murmuring words, or fragments of words, but however closely she strained to hear exactly what those words were, nothing ever clearly emerged. "Eleven, eleven, eleven," it would whisper to her, "thirty-six, three, eleven."

10. Lipstick (2026)

She assumed it was Amparo who was messing about in her makeup, had even gone so far as to mention the matter once at dinner, just her usual word to the wise. Amparo had sworn she hadn't so much as opened a drawer, but thereafter there were no more lipstick smudges on the mirror, no spilled powder, no problem. Then one Thursday coming back wasted and wornout from one of Brother Cary's periodic nonappearances, she found Mickey sitting at the dresser carefully laying on a foundation. His goggly dismay at her return was so ludicrous in the present blanked-out condition of his face that she simply burst out laughing. Mickey, without ever losing his look of comic horror, began laughing too.

"So—it was you all along, was it?"

He nodded and reached for the cold cream, but Lottie, misinterpreting, caught hold of his hand and gave it a squeeze. She tried to remember when she'd first noticed things out of place, but it was one of those trivial details, like when a particular song was popular, that wasn't arranged chronologically in her memory. Mickey was ten, almost eleven. He must have been doing this for months without her being aware.

"You said," in a self-justifying whine, "that you used to do the same thing with Uncle Boz. You'd dress up in each other's clothes and pretend. You said."

"When did I say that?"

"Not to me. You said it to him and I heard you."

She tried to think of the *right* thing to do.

"I've seen men wear makeup. Lots of times."

"Mickey, have I said anything against it?"

"No, but—"

"Sit down." She was brisk and businesslike, though looking at his face in the mirror she felt close to breaking up all over again. No doubt the people who worked in beauty shops had that problem all the time. She turned him round, with his back to the mirror, and wiped at his cheeks with a hankie.

"Now to start with, a person with your fair skin doesn't need a foundation at all, or next to none. It isn't the same, you know, as frosting a cake."

She continued a stream of knowledgeable patter as she made him up: how to shape the lips so there always seems to be a little smile lurking in the corners, how to blend in the shadows, the necessity, when drawing on the brows, of studying their effect in profile and three-quarter views. All the while, in contradiction to her own sensible advice, she was creating a doll mask of the broadest exaggerations. When she put on the last brushstroke she framed the result with pendant earrings and a stretch wig. The result was uncanny. Mickey demanded to be allowed to look in the mirror. How could she say no?

In the mirror her face above his and his face below hers melted together and became one face. It was not simply that she had drawn her own features on his blank slate, or that one was a parody of the other. There was a worse truth—that this was the whole portion Mickey stood to inherit, nothing but these marks of pain and terror and certain defeat. If she'd written the words on his forehead with the eyebrow pencil it couldn't have been any clearer. And on hers, and on hers. She lay down on the bed and let slow, depthless tears rise and fall. For a while Mickey stared at her, and then he went outside, down to the street.

11. Crossing Brooklyn Ferry (2026)

The whole family was there for the program—Shrimp and Lottie on the sofa with Mickey between them, Mrs. Hanson in the rocker, Milly, with little Peanut in her lap, in the flowered armchair, and Boz beside them being a nuisance on one of the chairs from the kitchen. Amparo, whose triumph this was to be, was everywhere at once, fretting and frothing.

The sponsors were Pfizer and the Conservation Corporation. Since neither had anything to sell what everybody wasn't buying already, the ads were slow and heavy, but no slower and heavier, as it turned out, than *Leaves of Grass*. Shrimp tried gamely for the first half hour to find aspects to admire—the costumes were ultra-authentic, the brass band went oomp-pa-pa very well, and there was a pretty sequence of some brawny blacks hammering a wooden house together. But then Don Hershey would reappear as Whitman, bellowing his dreadful poems, and she would just shrivel up. Shrimp had grown up idolizing Don Hershey, and to see him reduced to this! A dirty old man slobbering after teenagers. It wasn't fair.

"It makes a fella kinda glad he's a Democrat," Boz drawled, when the ads came on again, but Shrimp gave him a dirty look: no matter how dreadful it was they were obliged, for Amparo's sake, to praise it.

"I think it's wonderful," Shrimp said. "I think it's *very* artistic. The colors!" It was the utmost she could manage.

Milly, with what seemed honest curiosity, filled up the rest of station identification with classroom-type questions about Whitman, but Amparo brushed them aside. She no longer kept up a pretense that the show was about anyone but herself.

"I think I'm in the next part. Yes, I'm sure they said part two."

But the second half hour concerned the Civil War and Lincoln's assassination:

O powerful western fallen star!
O shades of night!—O moody, tearful night!
O great star disappear'd—O the black murk that hides the star!

For half an hour.

"You don't suppose they've cut out your scene, do you, Amparo?" Boz teased. They all came down on him together. Clearly it was what they'd all thought to themselves.

"It's possible," Amparo said dourly.

"Let's wait and see," Shrimp advised, as though they might have done anything else.

The Pfizer logo faded away, and there was Don Hershey again in his Santa Claus beard roaring off into a vast, new poem:

The impalpable sustenance of me from all things at all
    hours of the day,
The simple, compact, well-joined scheme, myself disin-
    tegrated, every one disintegrated yet part of the
    scheme,
The similitudes of the past and those of the future,
The glories strung like beads on my smallest sights and
    hearings, on the walk on the street and the passage
    over the river. . . .

And so on, endlessly, while the camera roved about the streets and over the water and looked at shoes—floods of shoes, centuries of shoes. Then, abrupt as flipping to another channel, it was 2026, and an ordinary crowd of people mulled about in the South Ferry waiting room.

Amparo rolled herself into a tight ball of attention. "This is it, coming up now."

Don Hershey rolled on, voice-over:

It avails not, time nor place—distance avails not,
I am with you, you men and women of a generation, or
    ever so many generations hence,
Just as you feel when you look on the river and sky, so I
    felt,
Just as any of you is one of a living crowd, I was one of a
    crowd,
Just as you are refreshed by the gladness of the river. . . .

The camera panned past conglomerations of smiling, gesturing, chattering people, filing into the boat, pausing now and then to pick out details—a hand picking nervously at a cuff, a yellow scarf lifting in a breeze and falling, a particular face.

Amparo's.

"There I am! There!" Amparo screamed.

The camera lingered. She stood at the railing, smiling

a dreamy smile that none of them watching could recognize. As Don Hershey lowered his volume and asked:

What is then between us?
What is the count of the scores or hundreds of years between us?

Amparo regarded, and the camera regarded, the moving surface of the water.

Shrimp's heart splattered like a bag of garbage dropped to the street from a high rooftop. Envy spilled out through her every vein. Amparo was so beautiful, so young and so damnably beautiful, she wanted to die.

PART II: TALK

12. The Bedroom (2026)

In crosssection the building was a swastika with the
arms revolving counterclockwise, the Aztec direction.
1812, the Hansons' apartment, was located halfway along
the inner forearm of the swastika's northwest limb, so that
its windows commanded an uninterrupted view of several
degrees southwestwards across the roofs of the lower
buildings as far as the windowless, megalithic masses of
the Copper Union complex. Above: blue sky and roving
clouds, jet trails and smoke wreathing up from the chim-
neys of 320 and 328. However one had to be right at the
window to enjoy this vista. From the bed Shrimp could
see only a uniformity of yellow brick and windows varie-
gated with different kinds of curtains, shades, and blinds.
May—and from two until almost six, when she needed
it most, there was direct, yellow sunlight. It was the only
advantage of living so near the top. On warm days the
window would be opened a crack and a breeze would
enter to ruffle the curtains. Lifting and falling, like the
shallow erratic breathing of an asthmatic, billowing, collapsing, the curtains became, as anything watched intently enough will, the story of her life. Did any of those

other curtains, shades, or blinds conceal a sadder story?
Ah, she doubted it.

But sad as it was, life was also irrepressably comic, and
the curtains caught that too. They were a mild, elaborate
joke between Mrs. Hanson and her daughter. The material
was a sheer spun chintz in sappy ice cream colors pat-
terned with sprigs and garlands of genetalia, his and hers,
raspberry, lemon, and peach. A present from January,
some ages ago. Loyally Shrimp had brought it home for
her mother to make her a pajama suit from, but Mrs. Hanson, without overtly disapproving, had never got round to
the job. Then, while Shrimp was in the hospital, Mrs. Hanson had made the material up into a pair of curtains and
hung them in their bedroom as homecoming surprise and
peace offering. Shrimp had to admit that the chintz had
met its just reward.

Shrimp seemed content to float through each day without goals or ideas, just watching the cunts and cocks
wafted by the breeze and whatever other infinitesimal
events the empty room presented her with. Teevee annoyed her, books bored her, and she had nothing to say to
visitors. Williken brought her a jigsaw puzzle, which she
worked on an upside-down dresser drawer, but once the
border was assembled she found that the drawer, though
it had been measured in advance, was an inch too short.
Surrendering with a sigh, she swept the pieces back in the
box. In every way her convelescence was inexplicable and
calm.

Then one day there was a tapping at the door. She said,
prophetically, "Come in." And January came in, wet with
rain and breathless from the stairs. It was a surprise.
January's address on the West Coast had been a well-
kept secret. Even so, it wasn't a large enough surprise.
But then what is?

"Jan!"

"Hi. I came yesterday too, but your mother said you
were asleep. I guess I should have waited, but I didn't
know whether—"

"Take off your coat. You're all wet."

January came far enough into the room to be able to
close the door, but she didn't approach the bed and she
didn't take off her coat.

"How did you happen to—"

"Your sister mentioned it to Jerry, and Jerry phoned me up. I couldn't come right away though, I didn't have the money. Your mother says you're all right now, basically."

"Oh, I'm fine. It wasn't the operation, you know. That was as routine as taking out a wisdom tooth. But impatient me couldn't stay in bed, and so—" She laughed (always bearing in mind that life is comic too) and made a feeble joke. "I can now, though. *Quite* patiently."

January crinkled her eyebrows. All yesterday, and all the way downtown today, all the way up the stairs, feelings of tenderness and concern had tumbled about in her like clothes in a dryer. But now, face to face with Shrimp and seeing her try the same old ploys, she could feel nothing but resentment and the beginnings of anger, as though only hours had intervened since that last awful meal two years before. A Betty Crocker sausage and potatoes.

"I'm glad you came," Shrimp said half-heartedly.

"Are you?"

"Yes."

The anger vanished and guilt came glinting up at the window of the dryer. "The operation, was it for— Was it because of what I said about having children?"

"I don't know, January. My reasons, when I look back, are still confused. Surely I must have been influenced by things you said. Morally I had no *right* to bear children."

"No, it was me who had no right. Dictating to you that way. Because of my principles! I see it now."

"Well." Shrimp took a sip from the water glass. It was a heavenly refreshment. "It goes deeper than politics. After all, I wasn't in any immediate *danger* of adding to the population, was I? *My* quota was filled. It was a ridiculous, melodramatic gesture, as Dr. Mesic was the first—"

January had shrugged off her raincoat and walked nearer the bed. She was wearing the nurse's uniform Shrimp had bought for her how many years ago. She bulged everywhere.

"Remember?" January said.

Shrimp nodded. She didn't have the heart to tell her that she didn't feel sexy. Or ashamed. Or anything. The horror show of Bellevue had taken it out of her—feeling, sex, and all.

January slipped her fingers under Shrimp's wrist to take her pulse. "It's slow," she observed.

Shrimp pulled her hand away. "I don't want to play games."

January began to cry.

13. Shrimp, in Bed (2026)

"You know?

"I 'd like to see it *working* again, the way it was meant to. That may sound like less than the *whole* revolution, but it's something that I can do, that I can try for. Right? Because a building is like. . . . It's a symbol of the life you lead inside it.

"One elevator, one elevator in working order and not even all day long necessarily. Maybe just an hour in the morning and an hour in the early evening, when there's power to spare. What a difference it would make for people like us here at the top. Think back to all the times you decided not to come up to see me because of these stairs. Or all the times I stayed in. That's no way to live. But it's the older people who suffer most. My mother, I'll bet she doesn't get down to the street once a week nowadays, and Lottie's almost as bad. It's me and Mickey who have to get the mail, the groceries, everything else, and that's not fair to us. Is it?

"What's more, do you know that there are *two* people working full time running errands for the people stranded in their apartments without anyone to help. I'm not exaggerating. They're called auxiliaries! Think what that must cost.

"Or if there's an emergency? They'll send the doctor into the building rather than carry someone down so many steps. If my hemorhaging had started when I was up here instead of at the Clinic, I might not be alive today. I was lucky, that's all. Think of that—I could be dead just because nobody in this building cares enough to make the fucking elevators *function!* So I figure, it's my responsibility now. Put up or shut up. Right?

"I've started a petition, and naturally everyone will sign

it. *That* doesn't take any effort. But what does is, I've started sounding out a couple of the people who might be helpful and they agree that the auxiliary system is a ridiculous waste, but they say that even so it would cost more to keep the elevator running. I told them that people would be willing to pay for *tickets,* it money's the only problem. And they'd say yes, no doubt, absolutely. And then—fuck off, Miss Hanson, and thank you for your concern.

"There was one, the worst of them so far, a toadstool at the MODICUM office called R.M. Blake, who just kept saying what a *wonderful* sense of responsibility I have. Just like that: What a wonderful sense of responsibility you have, Miss Hanson. What big guts you have, Miss Hanson. I wanted to say to him, Yeah, the better to crush you with, Grandma. The old whitened sepulcher.

"It's funny, isn't it, the way we've switched round? The way it's so symmetrical. It used to be I was religious and you were political, now it's just the reverse. It's like, did you see *The Orphans* the other night? It was sometime in the Nineteenth Century and there was this married couple, very cozy and very poor, except that each of them has *one thing* to be proud of. The man has a gold pocket watch, and the woman, poor darling, has her *hair.* So what happens? He pawns his watch to buy her a comb, and she sells her hair to get him a watch chain. A real ding-dong of a story.

"But if you think about it, that's what we've done. Isn't it? January?

"January, are you asleep?"

14. Lottie, at Bellevue (2026)

"They talk about the end of the world, the bombs and all, or if not the bombs then about the oceans dying, and the fish, but have you ever looked at the ocean? I used to worry, I did, but now I say to myself—so what. So what if the world ends? My sister though, she's just the other way—if there's an election she has to stay up and watch it. Or earthquakes. Anything. But what's the use?

"The end of the world. Let me tell you about the end of the world. It happened fifty years ago. Maybe a hundred. And since then it's been lovely. I mean it. Nobody tries to bother you. You can relax. You know what? I *like* the end of the world."

15. Lottie, at the White Rose Bar (2024)

"Of course there's that. When people want something so badly, say a person with cancer, or the problems I have with my back, then you tell yourself you've been cleared. And you haven't. But when it's the real thing you can tell. Something happens to their faces. The puzzlement is gone, the aggression. Not a relaxing away like sleep, but suddenly. There's someone else there, a spirit, touching them, soothing what's been hurting them so. It might be a tumor, it might be mental anguish. But the spirit is very definite, though the higher ones can be harder to understand sometimes. There aren't always words to explain what they experience on the higher planes. But those are the ones who can heal, not the lower spirits who've only left our plane a little while ago. They're not as strong. They can't help you as much because they're still confused themselves.

"What you should do is go there yourself. She doesn't mind if you're skeptical. Everybody is, at first, especially men. Even now for me, sometimes I think—she's cheating us, she's making it all up, in her own head. There are no spirits, you die, and that's it. My sister, who was the one who took me there in the first place—and she practically had to drag me—she can't believe in it anymore. But then she's never received any real benefit from it, whereas I— Thank you, I will.

"Okay. The first time was at a regular healing service I went to, about a year ago. This wasn't the woman I was talking about though. The Universal Friends—they were at the Americana. There was a talk first, about the Ka, then right at the start of the service I felt a spirit lay his hands on my head. Like this. Very hard. And cold, like a washcloth when you've got a fever. I concentrated on the pain in my back, which was bad then, I tried to feel if there were some difference. Because I knew I'd been healed in *some* way. It wasn't till after the meeting and out on Sixth Avenue that I realized what had happened. You know how you can look down a street late at night when things are quieter and see all the traffic lights changing together from red to green? Well, all my life I've been color-blind, but that night I could see the colors the way they really are. So bright, it was like—I can't describe it. I stayed up all that night, walking around, even though it was winter. And the sun, when it came up? I was on top of the bridge, and God! But then gradually during the next week it left me. It was too large a gift. I wasn't ready. But sometimes when I feel very clear, and not afraid, I think it's come back. Just for a moment. Then it's gone.

"The second time—thanks—the second time wasn't so simple. It was at a message service. About five weeks ago. Or a month? It seems longer, but—— Anyhow.

"The arrangement was, you could write down three questions and then the paper's folded up, but before Reverend Ribera had even picked up mine he was there and—I don't know how to describe it. He was shaking her about. Violently. Very violently. There was a kind of struggle whether he'd use her body and take control. Usually, you see, she likes to just talk *with* them, but Juan was so anxious and impatient, you see. You know what he was like when his mind was set on something. He kept calling my name in this terrible strangled voice. One minute I'd think, Yes, that's Juan, he's trying to reach me, and the next minute I'd think, No, it can't be, Juan is dead. All this time, you see, I'd been trying to reach him—and now he was there and I wouldn't accept it.

"Anyhow. At last he seemed to understand that he needed Reverend Ribera's cooperation and he quieted down. He told about the life on the other side and how he couldn't adjust to it. There were so many things he'd left unfinished here. At the last minute, he said, he'd wanted to change his mind but by then it was too late, he was out of control. I wanted so much to believe that was true and that he was really there, but I couldn't.

"Then just before he left Reverend Ribera's face changed, it became much younger, and she said some lines of poetry. In Spanish—everything had been in Spanish of course. I don't remember the exact words, but what it said, basically, was that he couldn't stand losing me. Even though this would be the last heartbreak that I'd ever cause him—*el ultimo dolor*. Even though this would be the last poem he'd write to me.

"You see, years ago Juan used to write poems to me. So when I went home that night I looked through the ones I'd saved, and it was there, the same poem. He'd written it to me years before, after we first broke up.

"So that's why when somebody says there's no scientific reason to believe in a life after this one, that's why I can't agree."

16. Mrs. Hanson, in Apartment 1812 (2024)

"April. April's the worst month for colds. You see the sunshine and you think it's short-sleeve weather already and by the time you're down on the street it's too late to change your mind. Speaking of short sleeves, you've studied psychology, I wonder what you'd say about this. Lottie's boy, you've seen him, Mickey, he's eight now—and he *will not* wear short sleeves. Even here in the house. He doesn't want you to see any *part* of his body. Wouldn't you have to call that morbid? I would. Or neurotic? For eight years old?

"There, drink that. I remembered this time and it's not so sweet.

"You wonder where children get their ideas. I suppose it was different for you—growing up without a family. Without a home. Such a regimented life. I don't think *any* child— But perhaps there are other factors. Advantages? Well, that's none of my beans-on-toast. But a dormitory, there'd be no privacy, and you, with all your studying! I wonder how you do it. And who looks after you if you're sick?

"Is it too hot? Your poor throat. Though it's little wonder that you're hoarse. That book, it just goes on and on and on. Don't misunderstand me, I'm enjoying it. Thoroughly. That part where she meets the French boy, or was he French, with the red hair, in Notre Dame Cathedral. That was very. . . . What would you call it? Romantic?

And then what happens when they're up on the tower, that was a real shockeroo. I'm surprised they haven't made a movie of it. Or have they? Of course *I'd* much rather be reading it, even if. . . . But it isn't fair to you. Your poor throat.

"I'm a Catholic too, did you know that? There's the Sacred Heart, right behind you. Of course, nowadays! But I *was* brought up Catholic. Then just before I was supposed to be confirmed there was that uprising about who owned the churches. There I was standing on Fifth Avenue in my first woolen suit, though as a matter of fact it was more of a jumper, and my father with one umbrella, and my mother with another umbrella, and there was this group of priests practically screaming at us not to go in, and the other priests trying to *drag* us over the bodies on the steps. That would have been nineteen-eighty. . . . One? Two? You can read about it now in history books, but there I was right in the middle of a regular battle, and all I could think of was—R.B. is going to break the umbrella. My father, R.B.

"Lord, whatever got me started on that track? Oh, the cathedral. When you were reading that part of the story I could imagine it so well. Where it said how the stone columns were like tree trunks, I remember thinking the same thing myself when I was in St. Patrick's.

"You know, I try and communicate these things to my daughters, but *they're* not interested. The past doesn't mean anything to them, you wouldn't catch one of *them* wanting to read a book like this. And my grandchildren are too young to talk with. My son, he'd listen, but he's never here now.

"When you're brought up in an orphanage—but do they call it an orphanage, if your parents are still alive?—do they bother with religion and all of that? Not the government, I suppose.

"I think everyone needs some kind of faith, whether they call it religion or spiritual light or what-have-you. But my Boz says it takes more strength to believe in nothing at all. That's more a man's idea. You'd like Boz. You're exactly the same age and you have the same interests and—

"I'll tell you what, Lenny, why don't you spend tonight here? You don't have any classes tomorrow, do you?

And why go out in this terrible weather? Shrimp will be gone, she always is, though that's just between you and me. I'll put clean sheets on her bed and you can have the bedroom all to yourself. Or if not tonight, some other time. It's a standing invitation. You'll like it, having some privacy for a change, and it's a wonderful chance for me, having someone I can talk to."

17. Mrs. Hanson, at the Nursing Home (2021)

"Is this me? It is. I don't believe it. And who is that with me? It isn't you, is it? Did you have a mustache then? Where are we that it's so green? It can't be Elizabeth. Is it the park? It says 'July the Fourth' on the back, but it doesn't say where.

"Are you comfortable now? Would you like to sit up more? I know how to. Like this. There, isn't that better?

"And look—this is that same picnic and there's *your* father! What a comical face. The colors are so funny on all of these.

"And Bobby here. Oh dear.

"Mother.

"And who is this? It says, 'I've got more where that came from!' but there's no name. Is it one of the Schearls? Or somebody that you worked with?

"Here he is again. I don't think I ever—

"Oh, that's the car we drove to Lake Hopatcong in, and George Washington was sick all over the back seat. Do you remember that? You were so angry.

"Here's the twins.

"The twins again.

"Here's Gary. No, it's Boz! Oh, no, yes, it's Gary. It doesn't look like Boz at all really, but Boz had a little plastic bucket just like that, with a red stripe.

"Mother. Isn't she pretty in this?

"And here you are together, look. You're both laughing. I wonder what about. Hm? That's a lovely picture. Isn't it? I'll tell you what, I'll leave it in here, on top of this letter from . . . ? Tony? Is it from Tony? Well, that's thoughtful. Oh, Lottie told me to be sure to remember to give you a kiss for her.

"I guess it's that time. Is it?

"It isn't three o'clock. I thought it was three o'clock. But it isn't. Would you like to look at some more of them? Or are you bored? I wouldn't blame you, having to sit there like that, unable to move a muscle, and listening to me go on. I *can* rattle. I certainly wouldn't blame you if you were bored.

PART III: MRS. HANSON

18. The New American Catholic Bible (2021)

Years before 334, when they'd been living in a single
dismal basement room on Mott Street, a salesman had
come round selling the New American Catholic Bible,
and not just the Bible but a whole course of instructions
that would bring her up to date on her own religion. By
the time he'd come back to repossess she'd filled in the
front pages with all the important dates of the family's
history:

Name	Relation	Born	Died
Nora Ann Hanson		Nov 15 1967	
Dwight Frederick Hanson	Husband	Jan 10 1965	Dec 20 1997
Robert Benjamin O'Meara	Father	Feb 2 1940	
Shirley Ann O'Meara	Mother	Aug 28 1943	July 5 1978
(born Schearl)			
Robert Benjamin O'Meara, Jr.	Brother	Oct 9 1962	July 5 1978
Gary William O'Meara	"	Sept 28 1963	
Barry Daniel O'Meara	"	Sept 28 1963	
Jimmy Tom Hanson	Son	Nov 1 1984	
Shirley Ann Hanson	Daughter	Feb 9 1986	
Loretta Hester Hanson	"	Dec 24 1989	

The salesman let her keep the Bible in exchange for the
original deposit and an additional five dollars but took
back the study plans and the looseleaf binder.

That was 1999. Whenever in later years the famly enlarged or contracted she would enroll the fact faithfully

in The New American Catholic Bible the very day it happened.

On June 30, 2001, Jimmy Tom was clubbed by the police during a riot protesting the ten o'clock curfew that the President had imposed during the Farm Crisis. He died the same night.

On April 11, 2003, six years after his father's death, Boz was born in Bellevue Hospital. Dwight had been a member of the Teamsters, the first union to get sperm preservation benefits as a standard feature of its group life policy.

On May 29, 2013, Amparo was born, at 334. Not until she'd mistakenly written down Amparo's last name as Hanson did she realize that as yet the Bible possessed no record of Amparo's father. By now, however, the official listing had acquired a kind of shadow of omitted relatives: her own stepmother Sue-Ellen, her endless in-laws, and Shrimp's two federal contract babies who had been called Tiger (after the cat he'd replaced) and Thumper (after Thumper in *Bambi*). Juan's case was more delicate than any of these, but finally she decided that even though Amparo's name was Martinez, Lottie was still legally a Hanson, and so Juan was doomed to join the other borderline cases in the margin. The mistake was corrected.

On July 6, 2016, Mickey was born, also at 334.

Then, on March 6, 2011, the nursing home in Elizabeth phoned Williken, who brought the message upstairs that R.B. O'Meara was dead. He had died peacefully and voluntarily at the age of eighty-one. Her father—dead!

As she filled in this new information it occurred to Mrs. Hanson that she hadn't looked at the religious part of the book since the company had stopped sending her lessons. She reached in at random and pulled out, from Proverbs: "Scorn for the scorners, yes; but for the wretched, grace."

Later she mentioned this message to Shrimp, who was up to her eyebrows in mysticism, hoping that her daughter would be able to make it mean more than it meant to her.

Shrimp read it aloud, then read it aloud a second time. In her opinion it meant nothing deeper than it said: "Scorn for the scorners, yes; but for the wretched, grace."

A promise that hadn't been and obviously wouldn't be kept. Mrs. Hanson felt betrayed and insulted.

19. A Desirable Job (2021)

Lottie had dropped out in tenth grade after her humanities teacher, old Mr. Sills, had made fun of her legs. Mrs. Hanson never lectured her about going back, certain that the combination of boredom and claustrophobia (these were the Mott Street days) would outweigh wounded pride by the next school year, if not before. But when fall came Lottie was unrelenting and her mother agreed to sign the permission forms to keep her home. She only had two years of high school herself and could still remember how she'd hated it, sitting there and listening to the jabber or staring at books. Besides it was nice having Lottie about to do all the little nuisance chores—washing, mending, keeping the cats off—that Mrs. Hanson resisted. With Boz, Lottie was better than a pound of pills, playing with him and talking with him hour after hour, year after year.

Then, at eighteen, Lottie was issued her own MODICUM card and an ultimatum: if she didn't have a full-time job by the end of six months, dependant benefits would stop and she'd have to move to one of the scrap heaps for hard-core unemployables like Roebling Plaza. Coincidentally the Hansons would lose their place on the waiting list for 334.

Lottie drifted into jobs and out of jobs with the same fierce indifference that had seen her through a lifetime at school relatively unscarred. She waited on counters. She sorted plastic beads for a manufacturer. She wrote down numbers that people phoned in from Chicago. She wrapped boxes. She washed and filled and capped gallon jugs in the basement of Bonwit's. Generally she managed to quit or be fired by May or June, so that she could have a couple months of what life was all about before it was time to die again into the death of a job.

Then one lovely rooftop, just after the Hansons had got into 334, she had met Juan Martinez, and the summertime became official and continuous. She was a mother! A wife! A mother again! Juan worked in the Bellevue morgue with Ab Holt, who lived at the other end of the corridor, which was how they'd happened to coincide on that July roof. He had worked at the morgue for years and it seemed that he would go on working there for more years, and so Lottie could relax into her wife-mother identity and let life be a swimming pool with her season ticket paid in full. She was happy, for a long while.

Not forever. She was a Capricorn, Juan was Sagittarius. From the beginning she'd known it would end, and how. Juan's pleasures became duties. His visits grew less frequent. The money, that had been so wonderfully steady for three years, for four, almost for five, came in spurts and then in trickles. The family had to make do with Mrs. Hanson's monthly checks, the supplemental allowance stamps for Amparo and Mickey, and Shrimp's various windfalls and makeshifts. It reached the point, just short of desperation, where the rent instead of being a nominal $37.50 became a crushing $37.50, and it was at that point that the possibility developed of Lottie getting an incredible job.

Cece Benn, in 1438, was the sweep for 11th Street for the block between First and Second Avenues, a concession good for twenty to thirty dollars a week in tips and scroungings plus a shower of goodies at Christmas. But the real beauty of the job was that since your earnings didn't have to be declared to the MODICUM office, you lost none of your regular benefits. Cece had swept 11th Street since before the turn of the century, but now she was edging up to retirement and had decided to opt for a home.

Lottie had often stopped at the corner in decent weather to chat with Cece, but she'd never supposed the old woman had regarded these attentions as a sign of real friendship. When Cece hinted to her that she was considering letting *her* inherit the license Lottie was flabbergasted with gratitude.

"If you want it, that is," Cece had added with a shy, small smile.

"If I want it! If I *want* it! Oh, Mrs. Benn!"

She went on wanting it for months, since Cece wasn't about to forfeit a consideration like Christmas. Lottie tried not to let her high hopes affect the way she acted toward Cece, but she found it impossible not to be more actively cordial, to the extent eventually of running errands for her up to 1438 and back down to the street. Seeing how Cece's apartment was done up, imagining what it must have cost, made her want that license more than ever. By December she was groveling.

Over the holidays, Lottie was down with flu and a cold. When she was better, there were new people in 1438, and

Mrs. Levin, from 1726, was out on the corner with the broom and the cup. Lottie found out later from her mother, who had heard it from Leda Holt, that Mrs. Levin had paid Cece six hundred dollars for her license.

She could never pass Mrs. Levin on the street without feeling half-sick with the sense of what she had lost. For thirty-three years she had kept herself above actually desiring a job. She had worked when she had had to work but she'd never let herself want to.

She had *wanted* Cece Benn's job. She still did. She always would. She felt ruined.

20. A & P, continued (2021)

After their beers under the airport, Juan took Lottie to Wollman Rink and they skated for an hour. Around and around, waltzes, tangoes, perfect delight. You could scarcely hear the music over the roar of the skates. Lottie left the rink with a skinned knee and feeling ten years younger.

"Isn't that better than a museum?"

"It was wonderful." She pulled him close to her and kissed the brown mole on his neck.

He said, "Hey."

And then: "I've got to go to the hospital now."

"Already?"

"What do you mean already? It's eleven o'clock. You want a ride downtown?"

Juan's motive in going somewhere was so he could drive there and then drive back. He was devoted to his car and Lottie pretended she was too. Instead of telling the simple truth that she wanted to go back to the museum by herself, she said, "I'd *love* to go for a ride, but not if it's only as far as the hospital. Then I'd have nowhere to go but home. No, I'll just plop down on a bench."

Juan went off, satisfied, and she deposited the butt of the souvenir carrot in a trash bin. Then through a side entrance behind the Egyptian temple (where she'd been led to worship the mummies and basalt gods in second, fourth, seventh, and ninth grades) into the museum.

A cast of thousands was enjoying the postcards, taking them out of the racks, looking at them, putting them back in the racks. Lottie joined. Faces, trees, people in costumes, the sea, Jesus and Mary, a glass bowl, a farm, stripes and dots, but nowhere a card showing the replica of the A & P. She had to ask, and a girl with braces on her teeth showed her where there were several hidden away. Lottie bought one that showed aisles disappearing at the horizon.

"Wait!" said the girl with braces, as she was walking away. She thought she'd had it then, but it had only been to give her the receipt for twenty-five cents.

Up in the park, in a baffle away from the field, she printed on the message side: "I Was here today + I Thout this woud bring back the Old Times for you." Only then did she consider who she'd send it to. Her grandfather was dead, and no one else she could think of was old enough to remember anything so far back. Finally she addressed it to her mother, adding to the message: "I never pass throuh Elizebeth without Thinking of you."

Then she emptied the other postcards out of her purse —a set of holes, a face, a bouquet, a saint, a fancy chest-of-drawers, an old dress, another face, people working out of doors, some squiggles, a stone coffin, a table covered with more faces. Eleven in all. Worth, she jotted the figures on the back of the card with the coffin—$2.75. A bit of shoplifting always cheered her up.

She decided that the bouquet, "Irises," was the nicest and addressed it to Juan:

> Juan Martinez
> Abingden Garage
> 312 Perry St.
> New York 10014.

21. Juan (2021)

It wasn't because he disliked Lottie and his offspring that he wasn't regular with his weekly dues. It was just that Princess Cass ate up his money before he could pay

it out, Princess Cass being his dream on wheels, a virginal
'15 replica of the last great muscle car, Chevy's '79 Vega
Fascination. About the neck of his little beauty he had
hung five years of sweat and tears: punched out power
with all suitable goodies; a '69 vintage Weber clutch
with Jag floorbox and Jag universals; leather insides; and
the shell and glory of her was seven swarthy perspec-
tivized overlays with a full five-inch apparent depth of
field. Just touching her was an act of love. And when it
moved? Brm brm? You came.

Princess Cass resided on the third floor of the Abingdon
Garage on Perry Street, and as the monthly rent plus
tax, plus tax, was more than he would have to pay at a
hotel, Juan lived there with, and in, the Princess. Besides
cars that were just parked or buried at the Abingdon, there
were three other members of the faith: a Jap ad man in a
newish Rolls Electric, 'Gramps' Gardiner in a self-assem-
bled Uglicar that wasn't much more, poor slut, than a
mobile bed; and, stranger than custom, a Hillman Minx
from way back and with zero modifications, a jewel be-
longing to Liz Kreiner, who had inherited it from her
father Max.

Juan loved Lottie. He did love Lottie, but what he felt
for Princess Cass went beyond love—it was loyalty. It went
beyond loyalty—it was symbiosis. ("Symbiosis" being what
it said in little gold letters on the fender of the Jap junior
executive's Rolls.) A car represented, in a way that Lottie
would never understand for all her crooning and her
protests, a way of life. Because if she had understood, she
wouldn't have addressed her dumb card in care of the
Abingdon. A blurry mess about some dumb flower that
was probably extinct! *He* didn't worry about an inspection,
but the Abingdon's owners had shit-fits when anyone used
the place as an address, and he didn't want to see the
Princess sleeping on the street.

If Princess Cass was his pride, she was secretly also
his shame. Since eighty per cent of his income was extra-
legal, he had to buy her basic necessities—gas, oil, and
glass fiber—on the black market, and there was never
enough, despite his economies in every other direction.
Five nights out of seven she had to stay indoors, and Juan
would usually stay there with her, puttering and polishing,
or reading poems, or sharpening his brains on Liz Kreiner's

chessboard, anything rather than have some smart-ass ask, "Hey, Romeo, where's the royal lady?"

The other two nights justified any suffering. The very best and happiest times were when he met someone who could appreciate largeness and they'd set off down the turnpike. All through the night, not stopping except to fill the tank, on and on and on and on. That was colossal but it wasn't something he could do all the time, or even with the same someone again. Inevitably they would want to know more and he couldn't bear to admit that this was it—the Princess, himself, and those lovely white flashes coming down the center of the road. All. Once they found out, the pity started flowing, and Juan had no defenses against pity.

Lottie had never pitied him, nor had she ever been jealous of Princess Cass, and that's why they could be, and had been, and would be, man and wife. Eight fucking years. Like Liz Kreiner's Hillman, she'd lost the flower of youth, but the guts were still sound. When he was with her and things went right, it was like butter on toast. A melting. The edges vanished. He forgot who he was or that there was anything in particular that had to be done. He was the rain and she was a lake, and slowly, softly, effortlessly, he fell.

Who could ask for more?

Lottie might have. Sometimes he wondered why she didn't. He knew the kids cost her more than he provided, yet the only demands she tried to make were on his time and presence. She wanted him living, at least part of the time, at 334, and not so far as he could tell for any other reason than because she wanted him near. She kept pointing out ways he'd save money and other kinds of advantages, like having all his clothes in one place instead of scattered over five boroughs.

He loved Lottie. He did love her, and needed her too, but it wasn't possible for them to live together. It was hard to explain why. He'd grown up in a family of seven, all living in one room. It turned people into beasts living that way. Human beings need privacy. But if Lottie didn't understand that, Juan didn't see what else he could say. Any person had to have some privacy, and Juan just needed more than most.

22. Leda Holt (2021)

While she was shuffling, Nora hatched the egg that she had so obviously been holding in reserve. "I saw that colored boy on the steps yesterday."

"Colored boy?" Wasn't that just like Nora, to find the worst possible way to put it? "When did you start keeping company with colored boys?"

Nora cut. "Milly's fellow."

Leda swam round in pillows and comforters, sheets and blankets, until she was sitting almost upright. "Oh yes," archly, *"that* colored fellow." She dealt the cards out carefully and placed the pack between them on the emptied-out cupboard that served as their table.

"I practically—" Nora arranged the cards in her hands "—had to split a gasket. Knowing that the two of them were in my room the whole while, and him wasting away for it." She plucked out two cards and put them in the crib, which was hers this time. "The droop!"

Leda was more careful. She had a 2, a pair of 3's, a 4, and a pair of 7's. If she kept the double run, she had to give Nora the 7's. But if she kept her two pairs and the starter didn't offer additional help. . . . She decided to risk it and put the 7's in the crib.

Nora cut again and Leda turned up the Queen of Spades for the starter. She dissembled her satisfaction with a shake of her head, and the opinion, "Sex!"

"Do you know, Leda?" Nora laid down a 7. "I can't even remember what that was all *about.*"

Leda played the 4. "I know what you mean. I wish Ab felt that way about it."

A 6. "Seventeen. You say that, but you're young, and you've got Ab."

If she played a 3, Nora could take it to 31 with a face card. She played the 2 instead. "Nineteen. I'm *not* young."

"And five makes twenty-four."

"And three. Twenty-seven?"

"No, *I* can't."

Leda laid down her last card. "And three is thirty." She advanced a hole.

"Five," and Nora took her hole. Then, at last, came the contradiction Leda was waiting for. "I'm fifty-four, and you're, what? Forty-five? It makes all the difference." She spread her cards beside the Queen. "And another crucial difference—Dwight has been dead for twenty years now. Not that I haven't had my opportunities now and then— Let's see, what have I got? Fifteen-two, fifteen-four, and a pair is six, and two runs is six, is twelve." She jumped the second matchstick forward. "But now and then is not the same thing as a habit."

"Are you bragging or complaining?" Leda spread her own cards.

"Bragging, absolutely."

"Fifteen-two, fifteen-four, and a pair is six, and two runs, it's just the same as yours, look—twelve."

"Sex makes people crazy. Like that poor fool on the steps. It's more trouble than it's worth. I'm well out of it."

Leda plugged her matchstick into a hole just four short of game. "That's what Carney said about Portugal, and you know what happened then."

"There's more important things," Nora maundered on, undeterred.

Here it comes, Leda thought, the theme song. "Oh, count your crib," she said.

"There's only the pair you gave me. Thanks." She went ahead two holes. "The family—that's the important thing. Keeping it together."

"True, true. Now get on with it, my dear."

But instead of taking the cards and shuffling, Nora picked up the cribbage board and studied it. "I thought you said you had twelve?"

"Did I make a mistake?" Sweetly.

"No, I don't think so." She moved Leda's matchstick back two holes. "You cheated."

23. Len Rude, continued (2024)

After his initial incredulity, when he realized she really did want him to move in, he thought: Arggh! But after all, why *not*? Being her lodger couldn't be much worse than living in the middle of a motherfucking marching

band the way he did now. He could trade in his meal
vouchers for food stamps. As Mrs. Hanson herself had
pointed out, it didn't have to be official, though if he
played his cards right he might be able to get Fulke to
give him a couple credits for it as an individual field
project. Fulke was always bitching at him for scanting
case work. He'd have to agree. It was only a matter, really,
of finding the right ribbon to tie around it. Not "Problems
of Aging" again, if he didn't want to be sucked down the
drainhole of a geriatrics specialty. "Family Structures in
a Modicum Environment." Too vast, but that was the
direction to aim in. Mention his institutional upbringing
and how this was an opportunity to understand family
dynamics from the inside. It was emotional blackmail,
but how could Fulke refuse?

It never occurred to him to wonder why Mrs. Hanson
had extended the invitation. He knew he was likeable and
was never surprised when people, accordingly, liked him.
Also, as Mrs. Miller had pointed out, the old lady was
upset about her son marrying and moving away. He would
replace the son she had lost. It was only natural.

24. The Love Story, continued (2024)

"Here's the key," and she handed Amparo the key.
"No need to bring it up here, but if there's a *personal*
letter inside—" (But mightn't he write to her on office
stationery?) "No, if there's anything at all, just wave your
arms like this—" Mrs. Hanson waved her arms vigorously
and the dewlaps went all quivery. "I'll be watching."

"What are you expecting, Grummy? It must be awfully
important."

Mrs. Hanson smiled her sweetest, most Grummy-like
smile. Love made her crafty. "Something from the MODI-
CUM office, dear. And you're right, it could be quite
important—for all of us."

Now run! she thought. *Run* down those stairs!

She took one of the chairs from the table in the kitchen
and set it by the living room window. She sat down. She

stood up. She pressed the palms of her hands against the sides of her neck as a reminder that she must *control* herself.

He'd promised to write whether he came that night or not, but she felt sure he'd forget his promise if he didn't intend to come. If a letter were there, it could mean only one thing.

Amparo *must* have reached the mailboxes by now. Unless she'd met a friend of hers as she went down. Unless she— Would it be there? Would it? Mrs. Hanson scanned the gray sky for an omen but the clouds were too low for planes to be visible. She pressed her forehead against the cool glass, willing Amparo to come round the corner of the building.

And she was there! Amparo's arms made a V, and then an X, a V, and an X. Mrs. Hanson signaled back. A deadly joy slithered across her skin and shivered through her bones. He *had* written! He *would* come!

She was out the door and at the head of the stairs before she recollected her purse. Two days ago, in anticipation, she'd taken out the credit card from where she kept it hidden in The New American Catholic Bible. She hadn't used it since she'd bought her father's wreath, when, two years ago? Nearer three. Two hundred and twenty-five dollars, and even so it was the smallest he got. What the twins must have paid for theirs! It had taken over a year to pay it back, and all the while the computer kept making the most awful threats. What if the card weren't valid now!

She had her purse and the list and the card were inside. A raincoat. Was there anything else? And the door, should she lock it? Lottie was inside asleep but Lottie could have slept through a gang bang. To be on the safe side she locked the door.

I mustn't run, she told herself at the third landing down, that was how old Mr. — I *mustn't* run, but it wasn't running that made her heart beat so—it was love! She was alive and miraculously she was in love again. Even more miraculously, somebody loved her. Loved *her!* Madness.

She had to stop on the ninth floor landing to catch her breath. A temp was sleeping in the corridor in a licensed

MODICUM bag. Usually she would only have been annoyed, but this morning the sight affected her with a delicious sense of compassion and community. Give me your tired, she thought with elation, your poor, your huddled masses yearning to breathe free, the wretched refuse of your teeming shore. How it all came pouring back! Details from a lifetime ago, memories of old faces and old feelings. And now, poetry!

By the time she was on one the backs of her legs were trembling so she could barely stand up straight. There was the mailbox, and there, slantwise inside it, was Len's letter. It had to be his. If it were anything else she would die.

The mailbox key was where Amparo always left it behind the scarecrow camera.

His letter said:

"Dear Mrs. Hanson—You can set an extra plate for dinner Thursday. I'm happy to say I can accept your kind invitation. Will bring my suitcase. Love, Len."

Love! There was no mistaking it, then: Love! She had sensed it from the first, but who would have believed—at her age, at fifty-seven! (True, with a bit of care her fifty-seven could look younger than someone like Leda Holt's forty-six. But even so.) Love!

Impossible.

Of course, and yet always when that thought had come to her there were those words beneath the title on the cover of the book, words that, as if by accident, his finger had pointed to as he read: "The Tale of an Impossible Love." Where there was love *nothing* was impossible.

She read the letter over and over. In its plainness it was more elegant than a poem: "I'm happy to say I can accept your kind invitation." Who would have suspected, reading that, the meaning which for *them* was so obvious?

And then, throwing caution to the winds: "Love, Len"!

Eleven o'clock, and everything still to be done—the groceries, wine, a new dress, and, if she dared— Did she? Was there anything she didn't dare now?

I'll go there first, she decided. When the girl showed her the chart with the various swatches she was no less decisive. She pointed to the brightest, carroty orange and said, "That."

25. The Dinner (2024)

Lottie opened the door, which hadn't been locked after all, and said, "Mom!"

She had figured out, coming up the stairs, just what tone to take and now she took it. "Do you like it?" She dropped the keys into her purse. Casualness itself.

"Your hair."

"Yes, I had it dyed. Do you *like* it?" She picked up her bags and came in. Her back and shoulders were one massive ache from hauling the bags up the stairs. Her scalp was still all pins and needles. Her feet hurt. Her eyes felt like the tops of lightbulbs covered with dust. But she *looked* good.

Lottie took the bags and she looked, but only looked, at the mercy of a chair. Sit down now and she'd never get up.

"It's so startling. I don't know. Turn around."

"You're supposed to say yes, stupid. Just 'Yes, Mom, it looks *fine*.' But she turned round obediently.

"I *do* like it," Lottie said, taking the recommended tone. "Yes, I do. The dress too is— Oh Mom, don't go in there yet."

She paused with her hand on the knob of the living room door, waiting to be told of whatever catastrophe she was about to confront.

"Shrimp's in your bedroom. She's feeling very, very bad. I gave her a bit of first aid. She's probably sleeping now."

"What's wrong with her?"

"They've busted up. Shrimp went and got herself another subsidy—"

"Oh Jesus."

"That's what I thought."

"A third time? I didn't think that was legal."

"Well, her scores, you know. And I suppose the first two must have their own scores by now. Anyhow. When she told January, there was a row. January tried to stab her —it's nothing bad, just a scratch on her shoulder."

"With a knife?"

Lottie snickered. "With a fork, actually. January has some kind of political idea that you shouldn't have babies for the government. Or maybe not at all, Shrimp wasn't too clear."

"But she hasn't come here to stay. Has she?"

"For a while."

"She can't. Oh, I know Shrimp. She'll go back. It's like all their other arguments. But you shouldn't have given her pills."

"She'll have to stay here, Mom. January's gone to Seattle, and she gave the room up to some friends. They wouldn't even let Shrimp in to pack. Her suitcase, her records, everything was sitting in the hall. I think that's what she was upset about more than anything else."

"And she's brought that all *here?*" A glance into the living room answered the question. Shrimp had emptied herself out everywhere in layers of shoes and underwear, keepsakes and dirty sheets.

"She was looking for a present she'd got me," Lottie explained. "That's why it's all out. Look, a Pepsi bottle, isn't it pretty?"

"Oh my God."

"She bought us all presents. She has money now, you know. A regular income."

"Then she doesn't have to stay here."

"Mom, be reasonable."

"She can't. I've rented the room. I told you I might. The man is coming tonight. That's what those groceries are for. I'm cooking a nice simple meal to start things off on the right foot."

"If it's a question of money, Shrimp can probably—"

"It's not a question of money. I've *told* him that the room is his, and he's coming tonight. My God, look at this mess! This morning it was as neat as a, as a—"

"Shrimp could sleep here on the couch," Lottie suggested, lifting off one of the cartons.

"And where will *I* sleep?"

"Well, where will *she* sleep?"

"Let her be a temp!"

"Mother!"

"Let her. I'm sure it wouldn't be anything new. All the nights she didn't come home, you don't suppose she was in somebody's *bed*, do you? Hallways and gutters, that's where she belongs. She's spent half her life there already, let her go there now."

"If Shrimp hears you say that—"

"I hope she does." Mrs. Hanson walked right up to the

door of the bedroom and shouted, "Hallways and gutters! Hallways and gutters!"

"Mom, there's no need to— I'll tell you what. Mickey can sleep in my bed tonight, he's always asking to, and Shrimp can have his bunk. Maybe in a day or two she'll be able to find a room at a hotel or somewhere. But don't make a scene now. She is very upset."

"*I'm* very upset!"

But she let herself be mollified on condition that Lottie cleared away Shrimp's debris.

Mrs. Hanson, meanwhile, started the dinner. The dessert first, since it would have to cool after it cooked. Cream-style Strawberry Granola. Len had mentioned liking Granola as a boy in Nebraska, before he'd been sent to a home. Once it was bubbling she added a packet of Juicy Fruit bits, then poured it into her two glass bowls. Lottie licked the pot.

Then they transported Shrimp from the front bedroom to Mickey's bunk. Shrimp wouldn't let loose of the pillow Mrs. Hanson had put out for Len, and rather than risk waking her she let her keep it. The fork had left four tiny punctures like squeezed pimples all in a row.

The stew, which came in a kit with instructions in three languages, would have taken no time at all, except that Mrs. Hanson intended to supplement it with meat. She'd bought eight cubes at Stuyvesant Town for $3.20, not a bargain but when was beef ever a bargain? The cubes came out of two Baggies dark red and slimey with blood, but after a fry in the pan they had a nice brown crust. Even so she decided not to add them to the stew till the last minute so as not to upset the flavor.

A fresh salad of carrots and parsnips, with a small onion added for zest—she'd been able to get these with her regular stamps—and she was done.

It was seven o'clock.

Lottie came into the kitchen and sniffed at the fried cubes of beef. "You're certainly going to a lot of trouble." Meaning expense.

"First impressions are important."

"How long is he going to stay here?"

"It probably depends. Oh, go ahead—eat one."

"There'll still be a lot left." Lottie chose the smallest cube and nibbled at it delicately. "Mm. Mmm!"

"Are you going to be late tonight?" Mrs. Hanson asked.

Lottie waved her hand about ("I can't talk now") and nodded.

"Till when do you think?"

She closed her eyes and swallowed. "Till morning sometime if Juan is there. Lee made a point of inviting him. Thanks. That was good."

Lottie set off. Amparo had been fed some snaps and sent up to the roof. Mickey, plugged into the teevee, was as good as invisible. In effect, till Len came, she was alone. The feelings of love that she had felt all day on the street and in stores returned, like some shy child who hides when there is company but torments you afterwards. The little rascal frolicked through the apartment, shrieking, sticking his tongue out, putting tacks on chairs, flashing images at her, like the glimpses you'd catch, switching past Channel 5 in the afternoon, of fingers sliding up a leg, of lips touching a nipple, of a cock stiffening. Oh, the anxiety! She delved into Lottie's makeup drawer, but there wasn't time for more than a dab of powder. She returned a moment later to put a drop of Molly Bloom beneath each earlobe. And lipstick? A hint. No, it looked macabre. She wiped it off.

It was eight o'clock.

He wasn't going to come.

He knocked.

She opened the door, and he stood before her, smiling with his eyes. His chest in its furry maroon rose and fell, rose and fell. She had forgotten, amid the abstractions of love, the reality of his flesh. Her erotic fancies of a moment before were all *images*, but the creature who came into the kitchen, hefting a black suitcase and a paper carrier full of books, existed solidly in three dimensions. She wanted to walk around him as though he were a statue in Washington Square.

He shook her hand and said hello. No more.

His reticence infected her. She couldn't meet his gaze. She tried to speak to him, as he spoke to her, in silences and trivialities. She led him to his room.

His hand stroked the bedspread and she wanted to surrender to him then and there, but his manner didn't allow it. He was afraid. Men were always afraid at the start.

"I'm *so* happy," she said. "To think you'll really be staying here."

"Yeah, so am I."

"You must let me go into the kitchen now. So that I can. . . . We're having stew, and a spring salad."

"That sounds terrific, Mrs. Hanson."

"I think you'll like it."

She put the fried cubes of meat into the simmering paste and turned up the heat. She took the salad and the wine out of the icebox. As she turned round he was in the doorway looking at her. She held up the wine bottle with a gesture of immemorial affirmation. The weariness was gone from her back and shoulders as though by the pressure of his gaze he'd smoothed the soreness from the muscles. What a gift it is to be in love.

"Haven't you done your hair differently?"

"I didn't think you'd noticed."

"Oh, I noticed the moment you came to the door."

She started laughing but stopped short. Her laughter, though its source lay deep in her happiness, had sounded harshly in her ears.

"I like it," he said.

"Thank you."

The red wine spurting from the Gallo tetrahedron seemed to issue from the same depths as her laughter.

"I really do," Len insisted.

"I think the stew must be ready. You sit."

She dished the stew out onto the plates at the burner so that he wouldn't see that she was giving him all of the real meat. But in the end she did take one of the cubes for herself.

They sat down. She lifted her glass. "What shall we drink to?"

"To?" Smiling uncertainly he picked up his own glass. Then, getting her drift: "To life?"

"Yes! Yes, to life!"

They toasted life, ate their stew and salad, drank the red wine. They spoke seldom but their eyes often met in complex and graceful dialogues. Any words either of them might have spoken at this point would have been in some way untrue; their eyes couldn't lie.

They'd finished the dinner and Mrs. Hanson had set out

the chilled pink Granola, when there was a thud and a loud cry from Lottie's room. Shrimp had awakened!

Len looked at Mrs. Hanson questioningly.

"I forgot to tell you, Lenny. My daughter came home. But it isn't anything for you to—"

It was too late. Shrimp had stumbled into the kitchen in one of Lottie's delapidated transparencies, unbuckled and candid as an ad for Pier 19. Not till she'd reached the refrigerator did she become aware of Len, and it took her another little while for her to remember to wrap her attractions in the yellow mists of the nightgown.

Mrs. Hanson made introductions. Len insisited that Shrimp join them at the table and took it on himself to spoon out some Granola into a third bowl.

"Why was I in Mickey's bed?" Shrimp asked.

There was no help for it. Briefly she explained Shrimp to Len, and Len to Shrimp. When Len expressed what polite interest the situation required, Shrimp started in on the sordid details, baring her shoulder to show the tine wounds.

Mrs. Hanson said, "Shrimp, please—"

Shrimp said, "I'm not ashamed, Mother, not any more." And went right on. Mrs. Hanson stared at the fork resting on her greasy dinner plate. She could have taken it and torn Shrimp to pieces.

When Shrimp led Len off into the living room, Mrs. Hanson got out of hearing any more by pleading the dishes.

Len had left three of the cubes of beef on the side of his plate untasted. The ounce of Granola he'd kept for himself was stirred about in the bowl. He'd hated the meal.

His wine glass was three-quarters full. She thought, should she pour it down the sink. She wanted to but it seemed such a waste. She drank it.

Len came back to the kitchen finally with the news that Shrimp had returned to bed. She couldn't bear to look at him. She just waited for the blade to drop, and it didn't take long.

"Mrs. Hanson," he said, "it should be obvious that I can't stay here now, not if it means putting your pregnant daughter out on the street."

"My daughter! Ha!"

"I'm disappointed and—"

"You're disappointed!"

"Of course I am."

"Oh, of course, of course!"

He turned away from her. She couldn't bear it. She would do anything to keep him. "Len!" she called after him.

He returned in no time with his suitcase and his bag of books, moving at the uncanny, hyped-up speed of the five-fifteen puppets.

"Len!" She stretched out a hand, to forgive him, to beg forgiveness.

The speed! The terrible speed of it!

She followed him out into the corridor, weeping, wretched, *afraid*. "Len," she pleaded, *"look* at me."

He strode ahead, heedless, but at the very first step of the stairs his bag swung into the railing and split open. Books spilled out onto the landing.

"I'll get you another bag," she said, calculating quickly and exactly what might hold him to the spot.

He hesitated.

"Len, please don't go." She grasped handfuls of the maroon sweater. "Len, I love you!"

"Sweet fucking Jesus, that's what I *thought!*"

He pulled away from her. She thought he was falling down the steps and screamed.

Then there were only the books at her feet. She recognized the fat black textbook and kicked it out through the gap in the rails. Then the rest, some down the steps, others into the abyss of the stairwell. Forever.

The next day when Lottie asked her what had become of the boarder, she said, "He was a vegetarian. He couldn't live anywhere where there was meat."

"He should have told you that before he came."

"Yes," Mrs. Hanson agreed bitterly. "That's what *I* thought."

PART IV: LOTTIE

26. Messages Are Received (2024)

Financially, being a widow was way ahead of being a wife. Lottie was able to phone Jerry Lighthall and tell her that she didn't need her job now, or anyone else's. She was free and then some. Besides the weekly, and now completely reliable, allotment Bellevue paid her a lump sum settlement of five thousand dollars. With Lottie's go-ahead the owner of the Abingdon sold what was left of Princess Cass through *Buy-Lines* for eight hundred and sixty dollars, off the top of which he skimmed no more than was reasonable. Even after paying out a small fortune for the memorial service that no one came to and and wiping up the family's various existing debts, Lottie had over four thousand dollars to do with as she pleased. Four thousand dollars. Her first reaction was fear. She put the money in a bank and tried to forget about it.

It was several weeks later before she found out, from her daughter, the probable explanation for Juan's killing himself. Amparo had heard it from Beth Holt who'd pieced it together from scattered remarks of her father's and what she already knew. Juan had been dealing with resurrectionists for years. Either Bellevue had just found out, which didn't seem likely, or the Administration had been pressured, for reasons unknown, to pounce on someone: Juan. He'd had time, apparently, to see it coming, and instead of concurring tamely in his sacrifice (it would have amounted to two or three years at most) he'd found this way to go out of the game with honor unblemished. Honor: for years he'd tried to explain to Lottie the intricacies of his private system of reckoning which squares were black and which white and how to move among them, but it had always made about as much sense to her as the engine under Princess Cass's hood, a man's world of mathematics—arbitrary, finicking, and lethal.

Emotionally it wasn't as bad as she'd expected. She cried a lot, but with a bounded grief. Some of Juan's own affectionate indifference seemed to have rubbed off without her ever realizing. In between the spells of mourning she experienced unaccountable elations. She went for long walks in unfamiliar neighborhoods. Twice she stopped in to visit places where she'd once worked, but she never managed to be more than a source of embarrassment. She increased her evenings with the Universal Friends to two nights a week at the same time that she began to explore in other directions as well.

One day, riding the crest of the highest wave yet, she wandered into Bonwit's for no other reason that it was right there on 14th and might be a bit cooler than the September concrete. Inside the sight of the racks and counters affected her like a lungful of ammyl nitrate on top of morbihanine. The colors, the immense space, the noise overwhelmed her—first with a kind of terror, then with a steadily mounting delight. She'd worked here most of a year without being impressed and the store hadn't noticeably changed. But now! It was like walking into a gigantic wedding cake in which all the desires of a lifetime had become incarnate, beckoning her to touch and taste and ravish. Her hand reached out to stroke the yielding fabrics—sleek blacks, scratchy russets, grays that caressed like a breeze from the river. She wanted all of it.

She began taking things from the racks and off the counters and putting them in her carryall. How strangely convenient that she should have that at hand today! She went to the second floor for shoes, yellow shoes, red shoes with thick straps, frail shoes of silver net, and to four for a hat. And dresses! Bonwit's was thronged with dresses of all descriptions, colors, and lengths, like a great host of disembodied spirits waiting to be called down to earth and named. She took dresses.

Descending a step or two from the heights, she realized that people were watching her. Indeed she was being followed about, and not only by the store detective. There was a ring of faces looking at her, as though from a great distance below, as though they yelled, "Jump! Jump! Why don't you jump!" She walked up to a cash cage in the middle of the floor and emptied her purse out into a hamper. A clerk took off the tags and fed them into a register. The sum mounted higher and higher, dazzling, until the clerk asked, with heavy sarcasm: "Will that be cash or charge?"

"I'll pay cash," she said and waved the brand-new checkbook at his scruffy little beard. When he asked for ID she rummaged among all the scraps and tatters at the bottom of her purse until she found, all munched up and bleached, her Bonwit's Employee Identification Card. Leaving the store she tipped her new hat, a big, good-natured, floppy thing dripping with all widths of (because she *was* a widow) black ribbon, and smiled a big smile for the benefit of Bonwit's detective, who had followed her every inch of the way from the cash cage.

At home she discovered that the dresses, blouses, and other bodywear were all lightyears too small for her. She gave Shrimp the one dress that still looked life-enhancing in the dark of common day, kept the hat for its sentimental value, and sent back all the rest the next day with Amparo, who already, at age eleven, had the knack of getting what she wanted from people in stores.

Since Lottie had signed the forms to let her transfer to the Lowen School, Amparo had been behaving tolerantly toward her mother. In any case she enjoyed the combat of a refund counter. She wasn't able to get cash, but she wangled what for her own purpose was better, a credit slip for any department in the store. She spent the rest of the day selecting a back-to-school wardrobe for herself in careful, mezzo-forte taste, hoping that after the explosion her mother, seeing the sense of sending her out into the world dressed in real clothes, would let her keep as much as half of what she'd pirated. Lottie's explosion was considerable, with screams and a whack or two of the belt, but by the time the late news was over it all seemed to be forgotten, as though Amparo had done nothing worse than to glance in the store's windows. The same night Lottie cleared out one whole drawer of the dresser for the new clothes. Jesus, Amparo thought, what a superannuated ass!

Not long after this adventure Lottie realized that she was no longer holding steady at 175, which was bad enough; she was gaining. She bought a coke machine and loved to lie in bed and let it fizzle the back of her throat, but noncaloric as this pleasure was, she went on gaining alarmingly. The explanation was physiological: she ate too much. Soon Shrimp would have to give up her polite fiction about her sister's Rubens-like figure and admit that she was just plain fat. Then Lottie would have to admit it too. You're fat, she'd tell herself, looking into the dark mirror of the living room window. Fat! But it didn't help, or it didn't help enough: she couldn't believe that she was the person she saw reflected there. She was Lottie Hanson, the five-dollar tomato; the fat woman was someone else.

Early one morning in the late fall, when the whole apartment smelled of rust (the steam had come on during the night), the explanation of what was going and had gone wrong presented itself to her in the plainest terms: "There's nothing left." She repeated the phrase to herself like a prayer and with each repetition the circumference of its meaning would expand. The terror of it slowly wound its way through the tangle of her feelings until it had merged with its opposite. "There's nothing left": it was cause to rejoice. What had she ever had that it wouldn't be a liberation to lose? Indeed, too much still clung to her. It would be long before she could say that there was *nothing* left, absolutely, blessedly nothing at all. Then, the way revelations do, the brilliance faded, leaving her with only the embers of the phrase. Her mind grew furry and she started developing a headache from the smell of the rust.

Other mornings there were other awakenings. Their common feature was that they all seemed to place her squarely on the brink of some momentous event, but facing in the wrong direction, like the tourists in the living room calendar's "Before" view of the Grand Canyon, smiling into the camera, oblivious of what lay behind them. The only thing she knew for sure was that something would be demanded of her, an action larger than any she'd ever been called on to perform, a kind of sacrifice. But what? but when?

Meanwhile her regular religious experience had enlarged to include the message services at the Albert Hotel. The medium, Reverend Inez Ribera from Houston, Texas, was the female side of the coin of Lottie's tenth grade nemesis, old Mr. Sills. She spoke, except when she was in trance, in the same flutey teacherish voice—broad r's, round vowels, whistling sibilants. Her less inspired messages were the same sour compound of veiled threat and headlong innuendo. However, while Sills had played favorites, Reverend Ribera's scorn withered impartially, which made her, if no more likeable, somewhat easier to take.

Besides, Lottie could understand the bitterness that drove her to lash out in all directions. Reverend Ribera was genuine. She achieved real contact only now and again, but when she did it was unmistakable. The spirits that laid hold on her were seldom gentle, and yet once they'd established their presence, the ridicule, the threats of aneurisms and financial ruin were replaced by mild, rambling descriptions of the other side. Instead of the usual abundance of counsels, the messages of these spirits were uncertain, tentative, even distressed and puzzled. They made little gestures of friendship and reconciliation, then skittered off, as though expecting to be refused. It was invariably during these visitations, when Reverend Ribera was so visibly not herself, that she would pronounce the secret word or mention the significant detail that proved her words weren't just the spiritual outpourings of some vague elsewhere but unique communications from real, known people. The first message from Juan, for instance, had been "his" beyond any doubt, for Lottie had been able to return home and find the same words in one of the letters he'd written to her twelve years before:

Ya no la quiero, es cierto, pero tal vez la quiero.
Es tan corto el amor, y es tan largo el olvido.

Porque en noches como esta la tuve entre mis brazos,
mi alma no se contenta con haberla perdido.

Annque este sea el ultimo dolor que ella me causa,
y estos sean los ultimos versos que yo le escribo.

The poem wasn't Juan's in the sense that he'd written it,
though Lottie had never let him know that she'd known
that. But even if the words came from someone else, the
feelings had been his, and were his now more certainly
than when he'd copied them into the letter. With all the
poems there are in Spanish, how could Rev. Ribera have
picked just that one? Unless Juan had been there that
night. Unless he'd wanted to find some way to touch her
so that she could believe that he *had*.

Later messages from Juan tended to be less other-
directed and more a kind of spiritual autobiography. He
described his progress from a plane of existence that was
predominantly dark brown to a higher plane that was
green, where he met his grandfather Rafael and a woman
in a bridal gown, barely more than a girl, whose name
came through as Rita or 'Nita. The ghostly bride seemed
determined to make contact with Lottie, for she returned
on several occasions, but Lottie was never able to see
what the connection was between herself and this Rita or
'Nita. As Juan advanced to higher planes, it became
harder to distinguish his tone from that of the other
spirits. He alternated between wistfulness and hectoring.
He wanted Lottie to lose weight. He wanted her to visit
the Lighthalls. Finally it became clear to Lottie that Reverend Ribera had lost contact with Juan and was now
only faking it. She stopped coming for the private meetings, and shortly thereafter Rafael and other distant relatives began to foresee all kinds of dangers in her path. A
person that she trusted was going to betray her. She would
lose large sums of money. There was, somewhere ahead,
a fire, possibly only a symbolic fire but possibly it was real.

About the money they had been well-informed. By the
first anniversary of Juan's death the four thousand dollars had been reduced to a little more than four hundred.

It was easier than it might have been to say good-bye

to Juan and the rest because she had begun to establish her own, more direct lines of communication with the other side. Off and on over the years Lottie had attended gospel meetings at the Day of Judgement Pentacostal Church, which met in a rented hall on Avenue A. She went there for the sake of the music and the excitement, not being deeply concerned about what seemed to draw in the majority of the others—the drama of sin and salvation. Lottie believed in sin in a general way, as a kind of condition or environment like clouds, but when she felt around inside herself for her own sins she drew a blank. The nearest she could approach to guilt was thinking about the ways she'd messed up Mickey's and Amparo's lives, and even this was a cause rather of discomfort than of out-and-out anguish.

Then one dreadful August night in '25 (an inversion layer had been stifling the city for days, the air was unbreathable) Lottie had stood up in the middle of the prayer asking for spiritual gifts and begun to prophecy in tongues. It lasted only a moment the first time and Lottie wondered if it might not be just a simple case of heat prostration, but the next time it was much clearer. It began with a sense of constriction, of being covered and enclosed, and then another kind of force struggled against this and emerged through it.

"Like a fire?" Brother Cary had asked her.

She remembered Juan's grandfather's warning about a fire that might be symbolic or might be real.

It was utterly dependable. She spoke in tongues whenever she came to the Day of Judgement Pentacostal Church and at no time else. When she felt the clouds gathering about her, she would stand, no matter what else might be happening, a sermon, a baptising, and the congregation would gather round her in a great circle, while Brother Cary held her and prayed for the fire to come down. When she felt it coming she would begin to tremble, but when it touched her she felt strong, and she spoke in a voice that was loud and clear with praise:

"Tralla goody ala troddy chaunt. Net nosse betnosse keyscope namallim. Zarbos ha zarbos myer, zarbos roldo teneview menevent. Daney, daney, daney sigs, daney sigs. Chonery ompolla rop!"

Or:

"Dabsa bobby nasa sana dubey. Lo fornival lo fier. Ompolla meny, leasiest mell. Woo—lubba dever ever onna. Woo—molit ule. Nok! Nok! Nok!"

PART V: SHRIMP

27. Having Babies (2024)

Shrimp's hangup was having babies—first the begetting, with the sperm; then the foetus growing inside her; finally the completed baby coming out. Since the Regents' System had gone into effect it was a fairly widespread syndrome, compulsory contraception having hit many of the old myths and icons with hurricane force, but with Shrimp it took a special form. She had enough psychoanalysis to understand her perversion but she went on having babies anyhow.

Shrimp had been thirteen years old and still a virgin, when her mother had gone to the hospital to be injected with a new son. The operation had had a doubly supernatural quality—the sperm had come from a man five years dead and the result was so clearly intended to be a replacement for the son Mrs. Hanson had lost in the riot: Boz was Jimmie Tom reborn. So when Shrimp had fantasies of the syringe going up into her own womb, it was a ghost that filled her, and its name was incest. The fact that it had to be a woman who did it for her to get excited probably made it even more multiple incest.

The first two, Tiger and Thumper, had not presented any problems on the rational level. She could tell herself that millions of women did it, that it was the only ethical way for homosexuals to procreate, that the children themselves were happier and better off growing up in the country or wherever with professional attention, and so on through a dozen other rationalizations, including the best of all, money. Subsidized motherhood certainly beat the pittance she could get killing herself for Con Ed or the even deadlier fates she'd met after she'd been fired from that. Logically what could be better than to be paid for what you craved?

Even so, through both pregnancies and the contractual months of motherhood she suffered attacks of unreasoning shame so intense that she often thought of donating. herself and the baby to the charity of the river. (If her hangup had been feet she'd have been ashamed to walk. You can't argue with Freud.)

The third was another story. January, though she was willing to go along with the thing on the fantasy level, was firmly opposed to the fantasy being acted out. But going in and filling out the forms, what was that but enjoying the fantasy at an institutional level? At her age and having had two already, it didn't seem likely that her application would be approved, and when it was, the temptation to go in for the interview was irresistible. It was all irresistible right up to the moment that she was spread out on the white platform, with her feet in the chrome stirrups. The motor purred, and her pelvis was tipped forward to receive the syringe, and it was as though the heavens opened and a hand came down to stroke the source of all pleasures at the very center of her brain. Mere sex offered nothing to compare.

Not till she was home from her weekend in the Caribbean of delight did she give any thought to what her vacation would cost. January had threatened to leave her when she'd heard about Tiger and Thumper, who were then ancient history. What would she do in this case? She *would* leave her.

She confessed one particularly fine Thursday in April after a late breakfast from Betty Crocker. Shrimp was into her fifth month and couldn't go on much longer calling her pregnancy menopause. "Why?" January asked, with what seemed a sincere unhappiness. "Why did you do it?"

Having prepared herself to cope with anger, Shrimp resented this detour into pathos. "Because. Oh, you know. I explained that."

"You couldn't stop yourself?"

"I couldn't. Like the other times—it was as though I were in a trance."

"But you're over it now?"

Shrimp nodded, amazed at how easily she was being let off the hook.

"Then get an abortion."

Shrimp pushed a crumb of potato around with the tip of her spoon, trying to decide whether there'd be any purpose in seeming to go along with the idea for a day or two.

January mistook her silence for yielding. "You know it's the only right thing to do. We discussed it and you agreed."

"I know. But the contracts are signed."

"You mean you won't. You *want* another fucking baby!"

January flipped. Before she knew what she was doing it was done, and they both stood staring at the four tiny hemispheres of blood that welled up, swelled, conjoined, and flowed down into the darkness of Shrimp's left armpit. The guilty fork was still in January's hand. Shrimp gave a belated scream and ran into the bathroom.

Safe inside she kept squeezing further droplets from the wound.

January banged and clattered.

"Jan?" addressing the crack of the bolted door.

"You better stay in there. The next time I'll use a knife."

"Jan, I know you're angry. You've got every right to be angry. I admit that I'm in the wrong. But wait, Jan. Wait till you see him before you say anything. The first six months are so wonderful. You'll see. I can even get an extension for the whole year if you want. We'll make a fine little family, just the—"

A chair smashed through the paper paneling of the door. Shrimp shut up. When she screwed up the courage to peek out through the torn door, not much later, the room was in a shambles but empty. January had taken one of the cupboards, but Shrimp was sure she'd be back if only to evict her. The room was January's, after all, not Shrimp's. But when she returned, late in the afternoon, from the therapy of a double feature (*The Black Rabbit* and *Billy McGlory* at the Underworld) the eviction had already been accomplished, but not by January, who had gone west, taking love from Shrimp's life, as she supposed, forever.

Her welcome back to 334 was not as cordial as she could have wished, but in a couple days Mrs. Hanson was brought round to seeing that Shrimp's loss was her own gain. The spirit of family happiness returned officially on the day Mrs. Hanson asked, "What are you going to call this one?"

"The baby, you mean?"

"Yeah, it. You'll have to name it something, won't you? How about Fudge? Or Puddle?" Mrs. Hanson, who'd given her own children unexceptional names, openly disapproved of Tiger's being called Tiger, and Thumper Thumper, even though the names, being unofficial, didn't stick once the babies were sent off.

"No, Fudge is only nice for a girl, and Puddle is vulgar. I'd rather it were something with more class."

"How about Flapdoodle then?"

"Flapdoodle!" Shrimp went along with the joke, grateful for any joke to go along with. "Flapdoodle! Wonderful! Flapdoodle it'll be. Flapdoodle Hanson."

28. 53 Movies (2024)

Flapdoodle Hanson was born on August 29, 2024, but as she had been a sickly vegetable and was not, as an animal, any healthier, Shrimp returned to 334 alone. She received her weekly check just the same, and the rest was a matter of indifference. The excitement had gone out of the notion of babies. She understood the traditional view that women bring forth children in sorrow.

On September 18 Williken jumped, or was pushed, out of the window of his apartment. His wife's theory was that he hadn't paid off the super for the privilege of operating his various small businesses in the darkroom, but what wife wants to believe her husband will kill himself without so much as a discussion of the theory? Juan's suicide, not much more than two months before, made Williken's seem justifiable by comparison.

She'd never given any thought to how much, since she'd come back to 334 in April, she'd come to depend on Williken to get through the evenings and the weeks. Lottie was off with her spirits or drinking herself blotto on the insurance money. Her mother's endless inanities got to be a Chinese water torture, and the teevee was no defense. Charlotte, Kiri, and the rest were past history— January had seen to that.

Just to escape the apartment she began seeing movies, mostly in the pocket theaters on 1st Avenue or around N.Y.U., since they showed double features. Sometimes she'd sit through the same double feature twice in a row, going in at four o'clock and coming out at ten or eleven. She found she was able to watch the movies totally, any movie, and that afterwards she remembered details, images, lines of dialogue, tunes, with weird fidelity. She'd be walking home through the crowds on Eighth Street and she'd have to stop because some face, or the gesture of a hand, or some luscious, long-ago landscape would have returned to her, wiping out all of her data. At the same time she felt completely cut off from everyone and passionately involved.

Not counting second helpings, she saw a total of fifty-three movies in the period from October 1st to November 16th. She saw: *A Girl of the Limberlost* and *Strangers on a Train*; Don Hershey as *Melmoth* and *Stanford White*; Penn's *Hellbottom*; *The Story of Vernon and Irene Castle*; *Escape from Cuernivaca* and *Singing in the Rain*; Franju's *Thomas l'Imposteur* and *Jude*; *Dumbo*; Jacquelynn Colton in *The Confessions of St. Augustine*; both parts of *Daniel Deronda*; *Candide*; *Snow White and Juliet*; Brando in *On the Waterfront* and *Down Here*; Robert Mitchum in *The Night of the Hunter*; Nicholas Ray's *King of Kings* and Mai Zetterling's *Behold the Man*; both versions of *The Ten Commandments*; Loren and Mastroianni in *Sunflower* and *Black Eyes and Lemonade*; Rainer Murray's *Owens and Darwin*; *The Zany World of Abbott and Costello*; *The Hills of Switzerland* and *The Sound of Music*; Garbo in *Camille* and *Anna Christie*; *Zarlah the Martian*; Emshwiller's *Walden* and *Image, Flesh, and Voice*; the remake of *Equinox*; *Casablanca* and *The Big Clock*; *The Temple* *of the Golden Pavilion; Star * Gut* and *Valentine Vox; The Best of Judy Canova; Pale Fire; Felix Culp; The Greek Berets* and *The Day of the Locust;* Sam Blazer's *Three Christs of Ypsilanti; On the Yard;* Wednesdays *Off;* both parts of *Stinky in the Land of Poop;* the complete ten-hour *Les Vampires; The Possibilities of Defeat;* and the shortened version of *Things in the World.* At that point Shrimp suddenly lost interest in seeing any more.

29. The White Uniform, continued (2021)

It was delivered by some derelict messenger. January didn't know what to make of the uniform, but the card that Shrimp had enclosed tickled her pink. She showed it to the people at work, to the Lighthalls, who always enjoyed a good joke, to her brother Ned, and all of them got a chuckle out of it. The outside showed a blithe, vulgar little sparrow. Written underneath in music was the melody he was chirping:

The lyrics of the song were on the inside: *Wanna fuck? Wanna fuck? I do! I do!*

At first January was embarrassed playing nurse. She was a largish girl, and the uniform, even though Shrimp had guessed her size correctly, didn't want to move the way her body moved. Putting it on, she would always feel, as she hadn't for a long time, ashamed of her real job.

As they got to know each other more deeply, January found ways of combining the abstract qualities of Shrimp's fantasies with the mechanics of ordinary sex. She would begin with a lengthy "examination." Shrimp would lie

in bed, limp, her eyes closed or lightly bandaged, while
January's fingers took her pulse, palpated her breasts,
spread her legs, explored her sex. Deeper and deeper the
fingers, and the "instruments" probed. January eventually
was able to find a medical supply store willing to sell her
an authentic pipette that could be attached to an ordinary
syringe. The pipette tickled morbidly. She would pretend
that Shrimp was too tight or too nervous and had to be
opened wider by one of the other instruments. Once the
scenario was perfected, it wasn't that much different
from any other kind of sex.

Shrimp, while all this was going on, would oscillate
between an excruciating pleasure and a no less excruciating guilt. The pleasure was simple and absolute, the guilt
was complex. For she loved January and she wanted to
perform with her all the acts that any ordinary pair of
women would have performed. And, regularly, they did:
cunilingus this way and that, dildoes here and there, lips,
fingers, tongues, every orifice and artifice. But she knew,
and January knew, that these were readings from some
textbook called *Health and Sex,* not the actual erotic lightning bolt of a fantasy that can connect the ankle bone
to the shin bone, the shin bone to the leg bone, the leg
bone to the thigh bone, the thigh bone to the pelvis, the
pelvis to the spine, and onward and upward to that source
of all desire and all thought, the head. Shrimp went
through the motions, but all the while her poor head sat
through yet another screening of those old classics,
*Ambulance Story, The White Uniform, The Lady and the
Needle,* and *Artsem Baby.* They weren't as exciting as
she remembered them but nothing else was playing, anywhere.

30. Beauty and the Beast (2021)

Shrimp thought of herself as basically an artist. Her
eyes saw colors the way a painter's eyes see colors. As
an observer of the human comedy she considered herself
to be on a par with Deb Potter or Oscar Stevenson. A
seemingly offhand remark overheard on the street could

trigger her imagination to produce the plot for a whole movie. She was sensitive, intelligent (her Regents scores proved that), and up-to-date. The only thing she was conscious of lacking was a direction, and what was that but a matter of pointing a finger?

Artistry ran in the Hanson family. Jimmie Tom had been well on the way to becoming a singer. Boz, though unfocused as Shrimp herself, was a verbal genius. Amparo, at age eight, was doing such incredibly detailed and psychological drawings at her school that she might grow up to be the real thing.

And not just her family. Many if not most of her closest friends were artists one way or another: Charlotte Blethen had published poems; Kiri Johns knew all the grand operas inside out; Mona Rosen and Patrick Shawn had both acted in plays. And others. But her proudest alliance was with Richard M. Williken, whose photographs had been seen all over the world.

Art was the air she breathed, the sidewalk she walked on to the secret garden of her soul, and living with January was like having a dog constantly shitting on that sidewalk. An innocent, adorable, cuddly puppy—you had to love the little fellow but oh my.

If January had simply been indifferent to art, Shrimp wouldn't have minded. In a way she'd have liked that. But alas, January had her own horrendous tastes in everything and she expected Shrimp to share them. She brought home library tapes the like of which Shrimp had never suspected: scraps of pop songs and snatches of symphonies were strung together with sound effects to tell such creaky tales as "Vermont Holiday" or "Cleopatra on the Nile."

January accepted Shrimp's snubs and snide remarks in the spirit of tolerance and good humor in which she thought they were intended. Shrimp joked because she was a Hanson and all the Hansons were sarcastic. She couldn't believe that anything she enjoyed so much herself could be abhorrent to another person. She could see that Shrimp's music was a better *kind* of music and she liked listening to it when it was on, but all of the time and nothing else? You'd go nuts.

Her eyes were like her ears. She would inflict well-meaning barbarities of jewelry and clothes on Shrimp, who wore them as tokens of her bondage and abasement. The walls of her room were one great mural of unspeakable, sickly-cute junk and sententious propaganda posters, like this jewel from the lips of a black Spartacus: "A Nation of Slaves is always prepared to applaud the clemency of their Master, who, in the abuse of Absolute Power, does not proceed to the last extremes of Injustice and Oppression." Bow-wow-wow. But what could Shrimp do? Walk in and rip them from the walls? January *valued* her crap.

What do you do when you love a slob? What she did—try and become a slob herself. Shrimp wallowed diligently, losing most of her old friends in the process. She more than made up for her losses by the friendships January brought with her as a dowry. Not that she ever came to like any of them, but gradually through their eyes she learned that her lover had virtues as well as charms, problems as well as virtues, a mind with its own thoughts, memories, projects, and a personal history as poignant as anything by Chopin or Liszt. In fact, she was a human being, and though it took a day of the very clearest air and brightest sunshine for this feature of January's landscape to be visible, it was such a fine and heartening sight that when it came it was worth every other inconvenience of being, and remaining, in love.

31. A Desirable Job, continued (2021)

After the sweeping license fell through, Lottie had one of her bad spells, sleeping up to fifteen hours a day, bullying Amparo, making fun of Mickey, living for days on pills and then demolishing the icebox on a binge. In general she fell apart. This time it was her sister who pulled her out. Living with January seemed to have made Shrimp one hundred per cent more human. Lottie even told her so.

"Suffering," Shrimp said, "that's what does it—I suffer a lot."

They talked, they played games, they went to whatever events Shrimp could get freebies for. Mostly, they talked; in Stuyvesant Square, on the roof, in Tompkins Square Park. They talked about growing old, about being in love, about not being in love, about life, about death. They agreed that it was terrible to grow old, though Shrimp thought they both had a long way to go before it got really terrible. They agreed that it was terrible to be in love but that it was more terrible not to be. They agreed that life was rotten. They didn't agree about death. Shrimp believed, though not always literally, in reincarnation and psychic phenomena. To Lottie death made no sense. It wasn't death she dreaded so much as the pain of dying.

"It helps to talk, doesn't it?" Shrimp said during one magnificent sunset up on the roof with rose-colored clouds zooming by.

"No," said Lottie, with a sour, here-I-am-again type smile to say to Shrimp that she was on her feet and not to worry, "it doesn't."

It was that evening that Shrimp mentioned the possibility of prostitution.

"Me? Don't be silly!"

"Why not? You used to."

"Ten years ago. More! And even *then* I never earned enough to make it worthwhile."

"You weren't trying."

"Shrimp, for God's sake, just look at me!"

"Many men are attracted to large, Rubens-type women. Anyhow I only mentioned it. And I was going to say that *if*—"

"If!" Lottie giggled.

"*If* you change your mind, January knows a couple who handle that sort of thing. It's safer than doing it as a free lance, so I'm told, and more businesslike too."

The couple that January knew were the Lighthalls, Jerry and Lee. Lee was fat and black and something of an Uncle Tom. Jerry was wraithlike and given to sudden meaningful silences. Lottie was never able to decide which of them was actually in charge. They worked from what Lottie believed for months was a bogus law office, until she found out that Jerry actually belonged to the New York State Bar. The clients arriving at the office behaved in a solemn deliberate way, as though they were after all here for a legal consultation rather than a good time. For the most part they were a sort of person Lottie had had no personal experience with—engineers, programmers, what Lee called "our technologically *ee*—leete clientele."

The Lighthalls specialized in golden showers, but by the time Lottie found this out, she had made up her mind to go through with it, come what may. The first time was awful. The man insisted that she watch his face the whole while he kept saying, "I'm pissing on you, Lottie. I'm pissing on you." As though otherwise she might not have known.

Jerry suggested that if she took a pink pill a couple hours beforehand and then sank back on a green at the start of a session it was possible to keep the experience at an impersonal level, as though it were taking place on teevee. Lottie tried it and the result for her was not so much to make it impersonal as to make it unreal. Instead of the scene becoming a teevee screen, she was pissed on *by* one.

The single largest advantage of the job was that her wages weren't official. The Lighthalls didn't believe in paying taxes and so they operated illegally, even though that meant charging much less than the licensed brothels, Lottie didn't lose any of her regular MODICUM benefits, and the necessity of spending what she made on the black market meant that she bought the fun things she wanted instead of the dull things she ought to have. Her wardrobe trebled. She ate at restaurants. Her room filled with knick-knacks and toys and the fruity reek of Faberge's Molly Bloom.

As the Lighthalls got to know and trust her, she began to be sent out to people's homes, often staying the night. Invariably this would mean something beyond golden showers. She could see that it was a job that she could grow to like. Not for the sex, the sex was nothing, but sometimes afterwards, especially on assignments away from Washington Street, the clients would warm up and talk about something besides their own unvarying predilections. This was the aspect of the job that appealed to Lottie—the human contact.

32. Lottie, in Stuyvesant Square (2021)

"Heaven. I'm *in* heaven.

"What I mean is, anyone if he just looked around and really understood what he saw. . . . But that's not what I'm supposed to say, is it? The object's to be able to say what you *want*. Instead, I guess what *I* was saying was that I'd better be happy with what I've got, cause I won't get any more. But then if I don't *ask* for more. . . . It's a vicious circle.

"Heaven. What is heaven? Heaven is a supermarket. Like that one they built outside the museum. Full of everything you could ever ask for. Full of fresh meat—I wouldn't live in any vegetarian heaven—full of cake mixes and cartons of cold milk and fizzies in cans. Oh, the works. And *lots* of disposable containers. And I would just go down the aisles with my big cart in a kind of trance, the way they say the housewives did then, without thinking what any of it was going to cost. Without thinking. Nineteen-fifty-three A.D.—you're right, that's heaven.

"No. No, I guess not. That's the trouble with heaven. You say something that sounds nice but then you think, would you really want it a second time? A third time? Like your highway, it would be great once. And then? What then?

"You see, it *has* to come from inside.

"So what *I* want, what I really do want. . . . I don't know how to say it. What I really want is to *really* want something. The way, you know, when a baby wants something? The way he reaches for it. I'd like to see something and reach for it like that. Not to be aware that I couldn't have it or that it wasn't my turn. Juan is that way sometimes with sex, once he lets loose. But of course heaven would have to be larger than that.

"I know! The movie we saw on teevee the other night when Mom wouldn't shut up, the Japanese movie, remember? Do you remember the fire festival, the song they sang? I forget the exact words, but the idea was that you should let life burn you up. That's what I want. I want life to burn me up.

"So that's what heaven is then. Heaven is the fire that does that, a huge roaring bonfire with lots of little Japanese women dancing around it and every so often they let out a great shout and one of them rushes into it. Whoof!"

33. Shrimp, in Stuyvesant Square (2021)

"One of the rules in the magazine was that you can't mention other people by name. Otherwise I could just say, 'Heaven would be if I were living with January' and then describe that. But if you're describing a *relationship*, you don't let yourself imagine all you could and so you learn nothing.

"So where does that leave me?

"Visualize, it said.

"Okay. Well, there's grass in heaven, because I can see myself standing in grass. But it isn't the country, not with cows and such. And it can't be a park, because the grass in parks is either sickly or you can't walk on it. It's beside a highway. A highway in Texas! Let's say in nineteen-fifty-three. It's a clear, clear day in nineteen-fifty-three, and I can see the highway stretching on and on past the horizon.

"Endlessly.

"Then what? Then I'll want to drive on the highway, I suppose. But not by myself, that would be anxiety-making. So I'll break the rule and let January drive. If we're on a motorcycle, it's scarcely a relationship, is it?

"Well, our motorcycle is going fast, it's going terribly fast, and there are cars and gigantic trucks going almost as fast as we are. Toward that horizon. We weave in and out, in and out. Faster we go, and faster and faster.

"Then what? I don't know. That's as far as I see.

"Now it's your turn."

34. Shrimp, at the Asylum (2024)

"What do I feel? Angry. Afraid. Sorry for myself. I don't know. I feel a bit of everything, but not— Oh, this is silly. I don't want to be wasting everyone's time with—

"Well, I'll try it. Just say the one thing over and over until— What happens?

"I love you. There, that wasn't so bad. I love you. I love you, January. I love you, January. January, I love you. January, I *love* you. If she were here it would be a lot easier, you know. Okay, okay. I love you. I love *you*. I love your big warm boobs. I'd like to squeeze them. And I love your . . . I love your juicy black cunt. How about that? I do. I love *all* of you. I wish we were together again. I wish I knew where you were so you'd know that. I don't want the baby, any babies. I want *you*. I want to be married. To you. For all time. I love you.

"Keep going?

"I love you. I love you. I love you very much. And that's a lie. I *hate* you. I can't stand you. You appall me, with your stupidity, with your vulgarity, with your third-hand ideas that you take off the party line like— You *bore* me. You bore me to tears. You're dumb nigger *scum*! Nigger bitch. Stupid! And I don't care if—

"No, I can't. It's not there. I'm just saying the words because I know you want to hear them. Love, hate, love, hate—words.

"It isn't that I'm resisting. But I don't *feel* what I'm saying, and that's the truth. Either way. The only thing I feel is tired. I wish I were home watching teevee instead of wasting everyone's time. For which I apologize.

"Somebody else say something and I'll shut up."

35. Richard M. Williken, continued (2024)

"Your problem," he told her, as they were rocking home in the RR after the big nonbreakthrough, "is that you're not willing to accept your own mediocrity."

"Oh shut up," she said. "I mean that sincerely."

"It's my own problem, just as much. Even more so, perhaps. Why do you think I've gone so long now without doing any work? It isn't that if I started in nothing would happen. But when I'm all done I look at what I'm left with and I say to myself, "No, not enough. In effect that's what you were saying tonight."

"I know you're trying to be nice, Willy, but it doesn't help. There's no comparison between your situation and mine."

"Sure there is. I can't believe in my pictures. You can't believe in your love affairs."

"A love affair isn't some goddamn work of art." The spirit of argument had caught hold of Shrimp. Williken could see her struggling out of her glooms as though they were no more than a wet swimsuit. Good old Shrimp!

"Isn't it?" he prompted.

She plunged after the bait without a thought. "You at least try to *do* something. There's an *attempt*. I've never gone that far. I suppose if I did I would be what you say—mediocre."

"You attempt too—ever so visibly."

"What?" she asked.

She wanted to be torn to pieces (no one at the Asylum had bothered even to scream at her), but Williken didn't rise above irony. "I try to *do* something; you try to *feel* something. You want an inner life, a spiritual life if you prefer. And you've got it. Only no matter what you do, no matter how you squirm to get away from the fact, it's mediocre. Not bad. Not *poor*."

"Blessed are the poor in spirit. Eh?"

"Exactly. But you don't believe that and neither do I. You know who we are? We're the scribes and Pharisees."

"Oh, that's good."

"You're a bit more cheerful now."

Shrimp pulled a long face. "I'm laughing on the outside."

"Things could be a lot worse."

"How?"

"You might be a loser. Like me."

"And I'm a winner instead? You can say that! After you saw me there tonight?"

"Wait," he promised her. "Just wait."

PART VI: 2026

36. Boz

"Bulgaria!" Milly exclaimed, and it took no special equipment to know that her next words were going to be: "*I've* been to Bulgaria."

"Why don't you get out your slides and show us," Boz said, clamping the lid gently on her ego. Then, though he knew, he asked, "Whose turn is it?"

January snapped to attention and shook the dice. "Seven!" She counted out seven spaces aloud, ending up on Go to Jail. "I hope I stay there," she said cheerfully. "If I land on Boardwalk again that's the end of the game for me." She said it so hopefully.

"I'm trying to remember," Milly said, elbow propped on the table, the dice held aloft, time and the game in suspense, "what it was like. All that comes back is that people told jokes there. You had to sit and listen for hours to jokes. About *breasts*." A look passed between them and another look passed between January and Shrimp.

Boz, though he'd have liked to retaliate with something gross, rose above it. He sat straighter in his chair, while in languid contrast his left hand dipped toward the dish of hot snaps. So much tastier cold.

Milly shook. Four: her cannon landed on the B & O.

She paid Shrimp $200, and shook again. Eleven: her token came down on one of her own properties.

The Monopoly set was an heirloom from the O'Meara side of the family. The houses and hotels were wood, the counters lead. Milly, as ever, had the cannon, Shrimp had the little racing car, Boz had the battleship, and January had the flatiron. Milly and Shrimp were winning. Boz and January were losing. C'est la vie.

"Bulgaria," Boz said, because it was such a fine thing to say, but also because his duty as a host required him to lead the conversation back to the interrupted guest. "But why?"

Shrimp, who was studying the backs of her property deeds to see how many more houses she could get by mortgaging the odds and ends, explained the exchange system between the two schools.

"Isn't this what she was being so giddy about last spring?" Milly asked. "I thought another girl got the scholarship then."

"Celeste diCecca. She was the one in the airplane crash."

"Oh!" Milly said, as the light dawned. "I didn't make the connection."

"You thought Shrimp just likes to keep up with the latest plane crashes?" Boz asked.

"I don't know what I thought, Trueheart. So now she's going after all. Talk about luck!"

Shrimp bought three more houses. Then the racing car sped past Park Place, Boardwalk, Go, and Income Tax, to land on Vermont Avenue. It was mortgaged to the bank.

"Talk about luck!" said January.

The talk about luck continued for several turns round the board—who had it and who lacked it and whether there was, outside of Monopoly, any such thing. Boz asked if any of them had ever known anyone who'd won on the numbers or in the lottery. January's brother had won five-hundred dollars three years before.

"But of course," January added conscientiously, "over the long run he's lost more than that."

"Certainly for the passengers an airplane crash is only luck," Milly insisted.

"Did you think about crashes a lot when you were a hostess?" January asked the question with the same leaden disinterest with which she played at the game.

While Milly told her story about the Great Air Disaster of 2021, Boz snuck around behind the screen to revise the orzata and add some ice. Tabbycat was watching tiny ball-players silently playing ball on the teevee, and Peanut was sleeping peacefully. When he returned with the tray the Air Disaster was concluded and Shrimp was spelling out her philosophy of life:

"It may look like luck on the surface but if you go deeper you'll see that people usually get what they've got coming. If it hadn't been this scholarship for Amparo, it would have been something else. She's worked for it."

"And Mickey?" January asked.

"Poor Mickey," Milly agreed.

"Mickey got exactly what he deserved."

For once Boz had to agree with his sister. "People, when they do things like that, are often *seeking* punishment."

January's orzata chose just that moment to spill itself. Milly got the board up in time and only one edge was wet. January had had so little money left in front of her that that was no loss either. Boz was more embarrassed than January, since his last words seemed to imply that she'd overturned her drink deliberately. God knew, she had every reason to want to. Nothing is quite so dull as two solid hours of losing.

Two turns later January's wish came true. She landed on Boardwalk and was out of the game. Boz, who was being ground into the dust more slowly but just as surely, insisted on conceding at the same time. He went with January out onto the veranda.

"You didn't have to give up just to keep me company, you know."

"Oh, they're happier in there without us. Now they can fight it out between themselves, fang and claw."

"Do you know, I've *never* won at Monopoly? Never once in my life!" She sighed. Then, so as not to seem an ungrateful guest. "You've got a lovely view."

They appreciated the night view in silence: lights that moved, cars and planes; lights that didn't move, stars, windows, streetlamps. Then, growing uneasy, Boz made his usual quip for a visitor on the veranda: "Yes—I've got the sun in the morning and the clouds in the afternoon."

Possibly January didn't get it. In any case she intended

to be serious. "Boz, maybe you could give me some advice."

"Me? Fiddle-dee-dee!" Boz loved to give advice. "What about?"

"What we're doing."

"I thought that was more in the nature of being already done."

"What?"

"I mean, from the way Shrimp talks, I thought it was a —" But he couldn't say "*fait accompli*," so he translated. "An accomplished fact."

"I suppose it is, as far as our being accepted. They've been very nice to us, the others there. It isn't us that I'm worried about so much as her mother."

"Mom? Oh, she'll get along."

"She seemed very upset last night."

"She gets upset but she recovers quickly, our Mom does. All the Hansons are great bouncers-back. As you must have noticed." That wasn't nice but it seemed to slip past January with most of his other meanings.

"She'll still have Lottie with her. And Mickey too, when he gets back."

"That's right." But his agreement had an edge of sarcasm. He'd begun to resent January's clumsy streaks of whitewash. "And anyhow, even if it is as bad as *she* seems to think, you can't let that stand in your way. If Mom didn't have *anyone* else, that shouldn't affect your decision."

"You don't think so?"

"If I thought so, then *I'd* have to move back there, wouldn't I? If it came to the point that she was going to lose the place. Oh, look who's here!"

It was Tabbycat. Boz picked her up and rubbed her in all her favorite places.

January persisted. "But you've got your own . . . family."

"No, I've got my own *life*. The same as you or Shrimp."

"So you *do* think we're doing the right thing?"

But he wasn't going to let her have it as easy as that. "Are you doing what you want to? Yes or no."

"Yes."

"Then it's the right thing." Which judgment pronounced, he turned his attention to Tabbycat. "What's going on in there, huh, little fella? Are those people still playing their long dull game? Huh? Who's going to win? Huh?"

January, who didn't know the cat had been watching television, answered the question straightforwardly. "I think Shrimp will."

"Oh?" *Why* had Shrimp ever. . . ? He had never understood.

"Yes. She always wins. It's incredible. The luck."

That was why.

37. Mickey

He was going to be a ballplayer. Ideally a catcher for the Mets, but lacking that he'd be content so long as he was in the major leagues. If his sister could become a ballerina, there was no reason he couldn't be an athlete. He had the same basic genetic equipment, quick reflexes, a good mind. He could do it. Dr. Sullivan *said* he could do it and Greg Lincoln the sports director said he had as good a chance as any other boy, possibly better. It meant endless practice, rigid discipline, an iron will, but with Dr. Sullivan helping him to weed out his bad mental habits there wasn't any reason he couldn't meet those demands.

But how could he explain that in half an hour in the visitors' room? To his mother, who didn't know Kike Chalmers from Opal Nash? His mother who was the source (he could understand that now) of most of his wrong ways of thinking. So he just told her.

"I don't want to go back to 334. Not this week, not next week, not. . . ." He pulled up just short of the word "never." "Not for a long time."

Emotions flickered across her face like strobes. Mickey looked away. She said, "Why, Mickey? What did I do?"

"Nothing. That's not it."

"Why then? A reason."

"You talk in your sleep. All night long you talk."

"That's not a reason. You can sleep in the living room, like Boz used to, if I keep you up."

"Then you're crazy. How's that? Is that a reason? You're crazy, all of you are."

That stopped her, but not for long. Then she was pecking away at him again. "Maybe everyone's crazy, a little. But *this* place, Mickey, you can't want to— I mean, look at it!"

"I like this place. The guys here, as far as they're concerned, I'm just like them. And that's what I want. I don't want to go back and live with you. *Ever.* If you make me go, I'll just do the same thing all over again. I swear I will. And this time I'll use enough fluid and *really* kill him too, not just pretend."

"Okay, Mickey, it's your life."

"Goddamn right." These words, and the tears on which they verged, were like a load of cement dumped into the raw foundation of his new life. By tomorrow morning all the wet slop of feeling would be solid as rock and in a year a skyscraper would stand where now there was nothing but a gaping hole.

38. Father Charmain

Reverend Cox had just taken down Bunyan's *Kerygma*, which was already a week overdue, and settled down for a nice warm dip into his plodding, solid, reassuring prose, when the bell went Ding-Dong, and before she could unfold her legs, again, Ding-Dong. Someone was upset.

A dumpy old woman with a frazzled face, curdled flesh, the left eyelid drooping, the right eye popping out. As soon as the door opened the mismatched eyes went through the familiar motions of surprise, distrust, withdrawal.

"Please come in." She gestured to the glow from the office at the end of the hall.

"I came to see Father Cox." She held up one of the form letters the office sent out: *If you should ever experience the need. . . .*

Charmain offered her hand. "I'm Charmain Cox."

The woman, remembering her manners, took the hand offered her. "I'm Nora Hanson. Are you. . . ?"

"His wife?" She smiled. "No, I'm afraid I'm the priest. Is that better or worse? But do come in out of this dreadful cold. If you think you'd be more comfortable talking with a man, I can phone up my colleague at St. Mark's, Reverend Gogardin. He's only around the corner." She steered her into the office and into the comfy confessional of the brown chair.

"It's been so long since I've been to church. It never occurred to me, from your letter. . . ."

"Yes, I suppose it's something of a fraud on my part, using only my initials." And she went through her disingenuous but useful patter song about the woman who had fainted, the man who'd snatched off her pectoral. Then she renewed her offer to phone St. Mark's, but by now Mrs. Hanson was resigned to a priest of the wrong sex.

Her story was a mosaic of little guilts and indignities, weaknesses and woes, but the picture that emerged was all too recognizably the disintegration of a family. Charmain began to assemble all the arguments why she wouldn't be able to take an active role in her struggle against the great octopus, Bureaucracy—chief among them that in the nine-to-five portion of her life she was a slave at one of the octopus's shrines (Department of Temporary Assistance). But then it developed that the Church, and even God, *were* involved in Mrs. Hanson's problems. The older daughter and her lover were leaving the sinking family to join the Sodality of St. Clare. In the quarrel that had tumbled the old lady out of her building and into this office the lover had used the poor dear's own Bible as ammunition. From Mrs. Hanson's extremely partisan account it took Charmain some time to locate the offending passage, but at last she tracked it down to St. Mark, third chapter, verses thirty-three to thirty-five:

And he answered them, saying, Who is my mother, or my brethren?

And he looked round about on them which sat about him, and said, Behold my mother and my brethren!

For whosoever shall do the will of God, the same is my brother, and my sister, and mother.

"Now I ask you!"

"Of course," Charmain explained, "Christ isn't saying there that one has a license to abuse or insult one's natural parents."

"Of course he isn't!"

"But has it occurred to you that this . . . is her name January?"

"Yes. It's a ridiculous name."

"Has it occurred to you that January and your daughter may be right?"

"How do you mean?"

"Let's put it this way. What *is* the will of God?"

Mrs. Hanson shrugged. "You've got me." Then, after the question had settled, "But if you think that *Shrimp* knows—ha!"

Deciding that St. Mark had done enough harm already, Charmain stumbled through her usual good counsels for disaster situations, but if she had been a shop clerk helping the woman to pick out a hat she couldn't have felt more futile or ridiculous. Everything Mrs. Hanson tried on made her look grotesque.

"In other words," Mrs. Hanson summed up, "you think I'm wrong."

"No. But on the other hand I'm not sure your daughter is. Have you tried, really, to see things from her side? To think why she wants to join a Sodality?"

"Yes. I have. She likes to shit on me and call it cake."

Charmain laughed without much zest. "Well, perhaps you're right. I hope we can talk again about this after we've both had a chance to think it over."

"You mean you want me to go."

"Yes, I guess that's what I mean. It's late, I have a job."

"Okay, I'm going. But I meant to ask: that book on the floor. . . ."

"*Kerygma?*"

"What does that mean?"

"It's Greek for message. It's supposed to be one of the things that the Church does, it brings a message."

"What message?"

"In a nutshell—Christ is risen. We are saved."

"Is that what *you* believe?"

"I don't know, Mrs. Hanson. But what I believe doesn't matter—I'm only the messenger."

"Shall I tell you something?"

"What?"

"I don't think you're much of a priest."

"Thank you, Mrs. Hanson. I know that."

39. The Five-Fifteen Puppets

Alone in the apartment, doors locked, mind bolted, Mrs. Hanson watched the teevee with a fierce, wandering attention. People knocked, she ignored them. Even Ab Holt, who should have known better than to be playing their game. "Just a discussion, Nora." Nora! He'd never called her Nora before. His big voice kept smashing through the door of the closet that had been a foyer. She couldn't believe that they would really use physical force to evict her. After fifteen years! There were hundreds of people in the building, she could name them, who didn't meet occupancy standards. Who took in any temp from the hallway and called them lodgers. "Mrs. Hanson, I'd like you to meet my new daughter." Oh yes! The corruption wasn't all at the top—it worked its way through the whole system. And when she'd asked, "Why me?" that slut had had the nerve to say, "Che sera sera, I'm afraid." If it had been that Mrs. Miller. There was someone who really did care, not a lot of fake sympathy and "Che sera sera." Maybe, if she phoned? But there wasn't a phone at Williken's now, and in any case she wasn't budging from where she was. They'd have to drag her. Would they dare go that far? The electricity would be shut off, that's always the first step. God knew what she'd do without the teevee. A blonde girl showed her how easy something was to do, just one, two, three. Then four, five, six, and it would be broken? *Terminal Clinic* came on. The new doctor was still in a feud with Nurse Loughtis. Hair like a witch, that one, and you couldn't believe a word she said. That mean look of hers, and then, "You can't fight City Hall, Doctor." Of course, that's what they wanted you to believe, that the individual person is helpless. She switched channels. Fucking on 5. Cooking on 4. She paused. Hands pushed and pulled at a great ball of dough. Food!

But the nice Spanish lady—though really you couldn't say she was Spanish, it was only her name—from the Tenants' Committee had promised her she wouldn't starve. As for water, she'd filled every container in the house days ago.

It was so *unfair*. Mrs. Manuel, if that was her name, had said she was being hung in a loophole. Somebody must have had their eye on the apartment for a long time, waiting for this opportunity. But try and find out from that asshole Blake who was moving in—oh no, that was "confidential." She'd known from one look at his beady eyes that he was getting *his* orange juice.

It was only a matter of holding out. In a few days Lottie would come home. She'd gone off before like this and she'd always come back. Her clothes were all here, except the one little suitcase, a detail she hadn't pointed out to Miss Slime. Lottie'd have her little breakdown or whatever and then come home and there'd be two of them and the department would *have* to grant a statutory six months' stay. Mrs. Manuel had emphasized that—six months. And Shrimp wouldn't last six months at that convent so-called. Religion was a hobby with her. In six months she'd have thrown it all up and started on something new, and then there'd be *three* of them and the department wouldn't have a leg to stand on.

The dates they gave you were just a bluff. She saw that now. It was already a week past the time they'd set. Let them knock on the door all they liked, though the idea of it drove her crazy. And Ab Holt, helping them. Damn!

"I *would* like a cigarette," she said calmly, as if it were something one always says to oneself at five o'clock when the news came on, and she walked into the bedroom and took the cigarettes and the matches from the top drawer. Everything was so neat. Clothes folded. She'd even fixed the broken blind, though now the slats were stuck. She sat on the edge of the bed and lit a cigarette. It took two matches, and then: Phew, the taste! Stale? But the smoke did something necessary to her head. She stopped worrying around in the same circle and thought about her secret weapon.

Her secret weapon was the furniture. Over the years she'd accumulated so much, mostly from other poeple's apartments when they'd died or moved out, and they couldn't evict her without clearing away every rag and stick of it. That was the law. And not just out into the corridor, oh no, they had to bring it down all the way to the street. So what were they going to do? Hire an army to take it down those stairs? Eighteen floors? No, so long as she insisted on her rights, she was as safe as if she were in a castle. And they'd just keep going on like they'd been going on, exerting psychological pressure so that she'd sign their fucking forms.

On the teevee a bunch of dancers had gotten up a party at the Greenwich Village office of Manufacturers Hanover Trust. The news was over and Mrs. Hanson returned to the living room, with her second awful cigarette, to the tune of "Getting to Know You." It seemed ironic.

At last the puppets came on. Her old friends. Her *only* friends. It was Flapdoodle's birthday. Bowser brought in a present in a gigantic box. "Is it for me?" Flapdoodle squeaked. "Open it," Bowser said, and you knew from the tone of his voice it was going to be something pretty bad. "For me, oh boy! It's something for me!" There was one box inside another box, and then a box inside that, and then still another box. Bowser got more and more impatient. "Go on, go on, open the next one." "Oh, I'm *bored*," said little Flapdoodle. "Let me show you how," said Bowser, and he did, and a gigantic wonderful hammer came out on a spring and knocked him on the head. Mrs. Hanson laughed herself into a fit, and sparks and ashes from the cigarette splashed all over her lap.

40. Hunt's Tomato Catsup

Before it was even daylight the super had let the two of them in through the closet with his key. Auxiliaries. Now they were packing, wrapping, wrecking the whole apartment. She told them politely to leave, she screamed at them to leave, they paid no attention.

On the way down to find the Tenants' Committee woman she met the super coming up. "What about my furniture?" she asked him.

"What *about* your furniture?"

"You can't evict me without my belongings. That's the law."

"Go talk to the office. I don't have anything to do with this."

"You let them in. They're there now, and you should see the mess they're making. You can't tell me that's legal—another person's belongings. Not just mine, a whole family's."

"So? So it's illegal—does that make you feel better?" He turned round and started down the stairs.

Remembering the chaos upstairs—clothes tumbled out of the closet, pictures off the walls, dishes stacked helter-skelter inside cheap carrier cartons—she decided it wasn't worth it. Mrs. Manuel, even if she could find her, wasn't going to stick her neck out on the Hansons' behalf. When she returned to 1812, the red-haired one was pissing in the kitchen sink.

"Oh, don't apologize!" she said, when he started in. "A job is a job is a job, isn't it? You've got to do what they tell you to."

She felt every minute as though she was going to start roaring or spinning in circles or just explode, but what stopped and held her was knowing that none of that would have had any effect. Television had supplied her with models for almost all the real-life situations she'd ever had to face—happiness, heartbreak, and points between—but this morning she was alone and scriptless, without even a notion of what was supposed to happen next. Of what to do. Cooperate with the damned steam-rollers? That's what the steamrollers seemed to expect, Miss Slime and the rest of them in their offices with their forms and their good manners. She'd be damned if she would.

She'd resist. Let the whole lot of them try to tell her it wouldn't do her any good, she'd go on resisting. With that decision she recognized that she had found her role and that it was after all a familiar role in a known story: she would go down fighting. Very often in such cases, if you held out long enough against even the most hopeless odds the tide would turn. She'd seen it happen time and again.

At ten o'clock Slime came round and made a checklist of the destruction the auxiliaries had accomplished. She

tried to make Mrs. Hanson sign a paper for certain of the
boxes and cupboards to be stored at the city's expense—
the rest presumably was garbage—at which point Mrs. Hanson pointed out that until she'd been evicted the apartment still belonged to her and so would Miss Slime please
leave and take her two sink-pissers with her.

Then she sat down beside the lifeless teevee (the electricity was off, finally) and had another cigarette. Hunt's
Tomato Catsup, the matchbook said. There was a recipe
inside for Waikiki Beans that she'd always intended to test
out but never got around to. Mix up Beef or Pork Chunkies, some crushed pineapple, a tablespoon of Wesson Oil,
and lots of catsup, heat, and serve on toast. She fell asleep
in the armchair planning an entire Hawaiian-style dinner
around the Waikiki Beans.

At four o'clock there was a banging and clattering at
the door of what was once again the foyer. The movers.
She had time to freshen herself before they found the
super to let them in. She watched grimly as they stripped
the kitchen of furniture, shelves, boxes. Even vacant, the
patterns of wear on the linoleum, of stains on the walls,
declared the room to be the Hansons' kitchen.

The contents of the kitchen had been stacked at the
top of the stairs. This was the part she'd been waiting for.
Now, she thought, break your backs!

There was a groan and shudder of far-off machineries.
The elevator was working. It was Shrimp's doing, her
ridiculous campaign, a final farewell slap in the face.
Mrs. Hanson's secret weapon had failed. In no time the
kitchen was loaded into the elevator and the movers
squeezed in and pressed the button. The outer and then
the inner doors closed. The disc of dim yellow light slipped
from sight. Mrs. Hanson approached the dirty window
and watched the steel cables shiver like the strings of
gigantic bows. After a long, long time the massive block
counterweight rose up out of the darkness.

The apartment or the furniture? It had to be one or
the other. She chose—they must have known she would
—the furniture. She returned one last time to 1812 and got
together her brown coat, her Wooly cap, her purse. In the
dusk, with no lights and the blinds off the windows, with
the walls bare and the floors cluttered with big sealed
boxes, there was no one to say good-bye to except the

rocker, the teevee, the sofa—and they'd be with her on the street soon enough.

She double-locked the door as she left. At the top of the stairs, hearing the elevator groaning upwards, she stopped. Why kill herself? She got in as the movers came out. "Any objections?" she asked. The doors closed and Mrs. Hanson was in free fall before they discovered they couldn't get in.

"I hope it crashes," she said aloud, a little afraid it might.

Slime was standing guard over the kitchen which was huddled together beyond the curb in a little island of light under a street lamp. It was almost night. A sharp wind with dry flakes of yesterday's snow swept down 11th Street from the west. With a scowl for Slime, Mrs. Hanson seated herself on one of the kitchen chairs. She just hoped that Slime would try and sit down too.

The second load arived—armchairs, the disassembled bunk, cupboards of clothes, the teevee. A second hypothetical room began to form beside the first. Mrs. Hanson moved to her regular armchair and tried, with her hands in the coat pockets, to warm her fingers in her crotch.

Now Miss Slime judged the time had come to really twist and squeeze. The forms came out of the briefcase. Mrs. Hanson got rid of her quite elegantly. She lit a cigarette. Slime backed off from the smoke as though she'd been offered a teaspoonful of cancer. Social workers!

All the bulkiest items came in the third load—the sofa, the rocker, the three beds, the dresser with the missing drawer. The movers told Slime that in one more trip they'd have it all down. When they'd gone back in, she started in again with her forms and her ballpoint.

"I can *understand* your anger, and I sympathize, Mrs. Hanson, believe me. But someone has to attend to these matters and see that things are handled as *fairly* as the situation permits. Now please *do* sign these forms so that when the van comes. . . ."

Mrs. Hanson got up, took the form, tore it in half, tore the halves in half, and handed the scraps back to Slime, who stopped talking. "Now, is there anything else?" she asked in the same tone of voice as Slime.

"I'm only trying to help, Mrs. Hanson."

"If you try to help for one more minute, so help *me*,

I'll spread you all over that sidewalk like so much . . .
like so much catsup!"

"Threats of violence don't solve problems, Mrs. Hanson."

Mrs. Hanson picked up the top half of the lamp pole
from the lap of the rocker and swung, aiming for the middle of her thick coat. There was a satisfying *Whap!* The
plastic shade that had always been such an eyesore
cracked off. Without another word Slime walked away in
the direction of First Avenue.

The last boxes were brought out from the lobby and
dumped beside the curb. The rooms were all scrambled
together now in one gigantic irrational jumble. Two colored brats from the building had begun bouncing on a
stack made from the bunk mattresses and the mattress
from Lottie's bed. Mrs. Hanson chased them off with the
lamp pole. They joined the small crowd that had gathered
on the sidewalk, just outside the imaginary walls of the
imaginary apartment. Silhouettes watched from the lower
windows.

She couldn't let them have it just like that. As though
she were dead and they could go through her pockets.
This furniture was her own private property and they just
stood about, waiting for Slime to come back with rein-
forcements and take her off. Like vultures, waiting.

Well, they could wait till they dropped—they weren't
going to get a thing!

She dug into her freezing purse for the cigarettes, the
matches. There were only three left. She'd have to be
careful. She found the drawers for the wooden dresser
that had come from Miss Shore's apartment when Miss
Shore had died. Her nicest piece of furniture. Oak. Before
replacing them she used the lamp pole to poke holes
through the pasteboard bottoms. Then she broke open the
sealed boxes looking for burnables. She encountered bathroom items, sheets and pillows, her flowers. She dumped
out the flowers, tore the broken box into strips. The strips
went into the bottom drawer of the dresser. She waited
until there was no wind at all. Even so it took all three
matches to get it started.

The crowd—still mostly of children—had grown, but
they kept well back from the walls. She scouted about for
the kindling. Pages of books, the remains of the calendar,

and Mickey's watercolors ("Promising" and "Shows independence") from the third grade were fed into the dresser. Before long she had a nice little furnace going inside. The problem now was how to get the rest of the furniture started. She couldn't keep pushing things into the drawers.

Using the lamp pole she was able to get the dresser over on its side. Sparks geysered up and were swept along by the wind. The crowd, which had been closing in more tightly around the bonfire, swayed back. Mrs. Hanson placed the kitchen chairs and table on the flames. They were the last large items she still had left from the Mott Street days. Seeing them go was painful.

Once the chairs had caught she used them as torches to start the rest of the furniture going. The cupboards, loosely packed and made of cheap materials, became fountains of fire. The crowd cheered as each one, after smoking blackly, would catch hold and shoot up. Ah! Is there anything like a good fire?

The sofa, armchairs, and mattresses were more obstinate. The fabric would char, the stuffing would stink and smoulder, but it wouldn't burn outright. Piece by piece (except for the sofa, which had always been beyond her), Mrs. Hanson dragged these items to the central pyre. The last mattress, however, only got as far as the teevee and her strength gave out.

A figure advanced toward her from the crowd, but if they wanted to stop her now it was too late. A fat woman with a small suitcase.

"Mom?" she said.

"Lottie!"

"Guess what? I've come home. What are you doing with—"

A clothes cupboard fell apart, scattering flames in modules scaled to the human form.

"I told them. I told them you'd be back!"

"Isn't this *our* furniture?"

"Stay here." Mrs. Hanson took the suitcase out of Lottie's hand, which was all cut and scratched, the poor darling, and set it down on the concrete. "Don't go anywhere, right? I'm getting someone but I'll be right back. We've lost a battle, but we'll win the war."

"Are you feeling all right, Mom?"

"I'm feeling fine. Just wait here, all right? And there's no need to worry. Not now. We've got six months for certain."

41. At the Falls

Incredible? Her mother running off through the flames like some opera star going out for a curtain call. Her suitcase had crushed the plastic flowers. She stooped and picked one up. An iris. She tossed it into the flames in approximately the direction her mother had disappeared in.

And hadn't it been a magnificent performance? Lottie had watched from the sidewalk, awestruck, as she'd set fire to . . . everything. The rocker was burning. The kid's bunk, in two pieces, was burning propped up against the embers of the kitchen table. Even the teevee, with Lottie's own mattress draped over it, though because of the mattress the teevee wasn't burning as well as it might. The entire Hanson apartment was on fire. The strength! Lottie thought. The strength that represents.

But why strength? Wasn't it as much a yielding? What Agnes Vargas had said years ago at Afra Imports: "The hard part isn't *doing* the job. The hard part is learning how." Such a commonplace thing to say, yet it had always stuck with her.

Had she learned how?

The beauty, that was what was so remarkable. Seeing the furniture standing about on the street, that had been beautiful enough. But when it burned!

The flowered armchair, which had only been smouldering till now, took hold all at once, and all its meaning was expressed in a tall column of orange flames. Glorious!

Could she?

At the very least she could try to approach it.

She fiddled open the locks of the suitcase. Already she'd lost so many of things she'd brought with her, all the little bones and bijoux from her past that hadn't for all her worrying at them yielded her one dribble of the feelings they were supposed to hold. Postcards she'd never sent. Baby clothes. The book of autographs (including three celebrities) she'd started keeping in eighth grade. But what junk she had left she'd gladly give.

At the top of the suitcase, a white dress. She threw it into the lap of the burning chair. As it touched the flames years of whiteness condensed into a moment's fierce flare.

Shoes, a sweater. They shriveled inside lurid haloes of green flame.

Prints. Stripes.

Most of these things didn't even fit her! She lost patience and dumped the rest in all in a heap, everything except the photographs and the bundle of letters. These she fed to the fire one by one. The pictures winked into flame like the popping of so many flashbulbs, leaving the world as they'd entered it. The letters, on lighter paper, went even more quickly: a single whoosh! and then they rose in the updraft, black weightless birds, poem after poem, lie upon lie—all of Juan's love.

Now she was free?

The clothes she wore were of no importance. As little time as a week ago she might have thought at this moment that she'd have to take her clothes off, too.

She herself was the clothing she must remove.

She went to where her own bed had been prepared atop the teevee. All else was in flames now, only the mattress still smoldered. She lay down. It was no more uncomfortable than entering a very hot bathtub, and as the water might have, the heat melted away the soreness and tension of the last sad days and weeks. This was so much more *simple*!

Relaxing, she became aware of the sound of the flames, a roaring all around her, as though she had finally come to the head of the falls she had been listening to so long. As her little boat had drifted towards this moment. But these waters were flames and fell upwards. With her head thrown back she could watch the sparks from the separate fires join, in the updraft, into a single ceaseless flow of light that mocked the static pallid squares of light gouged in the face of the brick. People stood within those squares of light, watching the fire, waiting, with Lottie, for the mattress to go.

The first flames curled around the edge, and through these flames she saw the ring of onlookers. Each face, in its separateness, in the avidity of its gaze, seemed to insist that Lottie's action was directed in some special way at him. There was no way to tell them that this was not for their sake but for the sake, purely, of the flames.

At the very moment that she knew she couldn't go on, that her strength *would* fail, their faces disappeared. She pushed herself up, the teevee collapsed, and she fell, in her little boat, through the white spray of her fear, towards the magnificence below.

But then, before she could see quite through the curtain of the spray, there was another face. A man. He aimed the nozzle of the firehose at her. A stream of white plastic foam shot out, blanketing Lottie and the bed, and all the while she was compelled to watch, in his eyes, on his lips, everywhere, an expression of insupportable loss.

42. Lottie, at Bellevue, continued

"And anyhow the world *doesn't* end. Even though it may try to, even though you wish to hell it would—it can't. There's always some poor jerk who thinks he needs something he hasn't got, and there goes five years, ten years, getting it. And then it'll be something else. It's another day and you're still waiting for the world to end.

"Oh, sometimes, you know, I have to laugh. When I think— Like the first time you're really in love and you say to yourself, Hey! I'm really in love! Now I know what it's about. And then he leaves you and you can't believe it. Or worse than that you gradually lose sight of it. Just gradually. You're in love, only it isn't as wonderful as it used to be. Maybe you're not even in love, maybe you just want to be. And maybe you don't even want to be. You stop bothering about songs on the radio and there's nothing you want to do but sleep. Do you know? But you can only sleep for so long and then it's tomorrow. The icebox is empty and you have to think who haven't you borrowed any money from and the room smells and you get up just in time to see the most terrific sunset. So it wasn't the end of the world after all, it's just another day.

"You know, when I came here, there was a part of me that was so happy. Like the first day of school, though maybe that was terrifying, I can't remember. Anyhow. I was so happy because I thought, here I am, this is the bottom. At last! The end of the world, right? And then, it was only the next day, I was up on the veranda and there it was again, this perfectly gorgeous sunset, with Brooklyn all big and mysterious, and the river. And then it was as though I could take a step back from myself, like when you're sitting across from someone in the subway and they don't know you're watching them, I could see myself like that. And I thought, Why you dope! You've only been here one day, and here you are enjoying a goddamned sunset.

"Of course it's also true, what we were saying before, about people. People are shits. In here just as much as out there. Their faces. And the way they grab things. It's like, I don't know if you've ever had children, but it's like that, eating at the same table with children. At first you can enjoy it. Like watching a mouse—nibble, nibble, nibble. But then there's another meal, and another, and if you don't see them other times there doesn't seem to be anything to them but an endless appetite. Well, and that's what I think can be so frightening, when you look at somebody and you can't see anything but their hungry face. Looking at you.

"Do you feel that way ever? When you feel something very strongly, you always suppose other people must have felt the same way, but do you know what? I'm thirty-eight years old, tomorrow I'll be thirty-nine, and I still wonder if that's so. Whether anyone ever feels the same way.

"Oh! Oh, the funniest thing, I have to tell you. This morning when I was on the can, Miss What's-It comes in, the nice one, and very matter-of-fact as though it were my office or something she asks did I want a chocolate birthday cake or a white birthday cake? For my birthday! A chocolate birthday cake or a white birthday cake? Because, you see, they had to order it today. God, I laughed. I thought I'd fall off the stool I laughed so hard. 'A chocolate birthday cake or a white birthday cake. Which will it be, Lottie?'

"Chocolate, I told her, and I was very serious about it too, believe me. It had to be chocolate. Nothing else would do."

43. Mrs. Hanson, in Room 7

"I've thought about it. For years. I don't talk about it because I don't think it's something you can discuss. Once. Once I met a lady in the park, that was a long time ago. We talked about it but I don't think that either of us. . . . Not then. Once you're serious, it isn't something you care to talk about.

"Here it's a different situation, I know. I don't mind discussing it with you. It's your job and you have to do it. But with my family, you see, that's a different matter. They'd try to argue against it but only because they felt they ought to. And I understand that. I was the same myself. I can remember visiting my father when he was in the hospital—that would be Twenty-twenty or twenty-one, in there, and talking away at him a mile a minute. Lord. But could I look him in the eye? Not for a moment! I kept showing him photographs, as though. . . . But even then I knew what he must have been thinking. What I didn't know was that it can all seem so possible.

"But I suppose you'll need better reasons than that for the form you're filling out. Well, just put down cancer. You must have a copy of my medical report. I've been cut open just once, to have my appendix taken out, and that was enough. The doctors explained to me what I can expect and that my chances are better than fifty-fifty and I believe them. It's not the risk I'm afraid of. That would be silly, wouldn't it?

"What I am afraid of is turning into some kind of old vegetable. There's so many like that where I am now. Some of them are just completely. . . . I stare at them sometimes. I know I shouldn't, but I can't help myself.

"And *they* don't realize. They don't have any idea. There's one of them who's gone like that just in the time I've been there. He used to spend every day off somewhere, independent wasn't the word for it, and then—a stroke. And now he can't control himself. They wheel him out on the porch with all the rest of us, and suddenly you hear him in his tin pot, tinkle tinkle tinkle. Oh, you have to laugh.

"Then you think, that could be me. I don't mean to say that *pissing* is so important. But the mental change! Old pisspot used -to be such a sharp bastard, crusty, full of fight. But now? I don't care if I wet my bed but I don't want my *brains* to go soft.

"The attendants are always joking about this one or that one. It's not malicious, really. Sometimes I have to laugh myself at what they say. And then I think. After my operation *I* might be the one they're making jokes about. And then it would be too late. You can see that in their eyes sometimes. The fact that they've let their chance slip by, and that they know it.

"After a certain point you ask yourself why. Why go on? Why bother? For what reason? I guess it's when you stop enjoying things. The day-to-day things. It's not as though there's all that much *to* enjoy. Not there. The food? Eating is a chore for me now, like putting on my shoes. I do it. That's all. Or the people? Well, I talk to them, they talk to me, but does anyone listen? You—do you listen? Huh? And when *you* talk, who listens to you? And how much are *they* paid?

"What was I talking about? Oh, friendship. Well, I've expressed my thoughts on that subject. So, what's left? What *is* left? Teevee. I used to watch teevee a lot. Maybe if I had my own set again, and my own private room, maybe I could gradually just forget about everything else. But sitting there in that room at Terminal Clinic—that's our name for it—with the others all sneezing and jabbering and I don't know what, I can't connect with the screen. I can't make it take me over.

"And that's it. That's my life, and I say, who needs it? Oh, I forgot to mention baths. Twice a week I get a nice warm bath for fifteen minutes and I love it. Also, when I sleep I enjoy that. I sleep about four hours a night. It's not enough.

"I've made sense, haven't I? I've been rational? Before I came here I made a list of the things I meant to say, and now I've said them. They're all good reasons, every one of them. I checked them in your little book. Have I left any out?

"Oh. Family relationships. Right. Well, I don't have any left that count. After a certain age that's true for everyone, and I've reached that age, I guess. It took a while, but I'm there.

"As I understand it, you've *got* to approve my application. If you don't, I'll appeal. As I have a right to. And eventually I'll win. I'm smart, you know. When I have to be, I am. My whole family was a smart family, with very high scores. I never did much with my intelligence, I have to confess, but I'll do this. I'll get what I want and what I have a right to. And sincerely, Miss Latham, I do want it. I want to die. The way some people want sex, that's how I want death. I dream about it. And I think about it. And it's what I want."

CRITIC'S CHOICE

For action-packed suspense thrillers.

CARTER'S CASTLE by Wilbur Wright	$3.95
DANGEROUS GAMES by Louis Schreiber	$3.95
THE ARAB by G. Lee Tippin	$3.50
THE CHINESE FIRE DRILL by Michael Wolfe	$2.95
THE MONEY BURN by Tony Foster	$3.95
THE CROWN OF INDIA by Samuel Fuller	$3.50
SHADOW CABINET by W. T. Tyler	$3.95
DOUBLE TAKE by Gregory Dowling	$2.95
STRYKER'S KINGDOM by W.A. Harbinson	$3.95
THE HAWTHORN CONSPIRACY by Stephen Hesla	$3.95
THE CORSICAN by Bill Ballinger	$3.95
AMBLER by Fred Halliday	$3.50
BLUE FLAME by Joseph Gilmore	$3.75
THE DEVIL'S VOYAGE by Jack Chalker	$3.75
THE STENDAL RAID by Al Dempsey	$3.95
SKYBLAZER by Peter Allen	$2.95
THE LAST PRESIDENT by Michael Kurland	$3.50